PLAY GROUPS & PROSECCO

JO MIDDLETON

EBURY
PRESS

First published by Ebury Press in 2019

1 3 5 7 9 10 8 6 4 2

Ebury Press, an imprint of Ebury Publishing
20 Vauxhall Bridge Road,
London SW1V 2SA

Ebury Press is part of the Penguin Random House group of companies
whose addresses can be found at global.penguinrandomhouse.com

Penguin
Random House
UK

www.penguin.co.uk

A CIP catalogue record for this book is available from the British Library

ISBN 9781529103366

Typeset in 11.75/15.5 pt Adobe Caslon Pro
by Integra Software Services Pvt. Ltd, Pondicherry

Printed and bound in Great Britain by Clays Ltd, Elcograf S.p.A.

Penguin Random House is committed to a sustainable future for
our business, our readers and our planet. This book is made
from Forest Stewardship Council® certified paper.

W

★★★★★

'As a mum of three I could totally relate to this on so
many levels. I loved everything about this book'
– Titian, Netgalley

★★★★★

'Very funny, it made me giggle – a lot. I LOVED this
book about everyday life with a young family'
– Noreen, Netgalley

★★★★★

'Hilarious – made me laugh out loud. Thoroughly
enjoyed it and would highly recommend'
– Dominique, Netgalley

★★★★★

'A light-hearted yet honest book about life as a single
mum. Lots of funny anecdotes that parents will
recognise!' – Claire, Netgalley

★★★★★

'With shades of Bridget Jones, Frankie stumbles
though life as a single mum. Very real characters and
brilliant, hilarious observations' – Ann, Netgalley

★★★★★

'A very funny and realistic look at motherhood'
– Katrina, Netgalley

★★★★★

'Hilarious, observant and completely relatable. A really
enjoyable read' – Emma, Netgalley

Jo Middleton has been blogging at Slummy Single Mummy since 2009. She has two daughters and lives in Somerset. You can find her on Twitter @mummybloggger, Instagram and Facebook @slummysinglemummy or at www.slummysinglemummy.com

Playgroups and Prosecco is her debut novel.

To Bee and Belle – a constant source of inspiration,
literary and otherwise

Monday 1 January 2018

There's nothing quite like the first page of a new diary to make you feel vaguely inadequate, is there?

I say nothing, but trying on clothes in front of a fourteen-year-old girl is definitely up there in the 'top ten ways to make yourself want to cry into the fridge', as I proved last night when I tried to get Flo to have a look at my outfit before I went over to Cassie's *it's super-casual, Frankie, darling, no need to bring anything as the wine cellar is well stocked* New Year's Eve party.

I'd been feeling understandably anxious since hearing the words wine cellar. Who has a wine cellar? Downton Abbey in 1912, maybe. No one in Dorset in 2018. I'd given myself a good talking to, though, and compiled a new Pinterest board full of inspirational quotes about not comparing yourself to others.

'What do you think?' I said, swooshing down the stairs and into the lounge, feeling pretty good in my wide-leg trousers and velvet wrap-around top, thigh chub hidden successfully, drawing attention to my relatively small waist, as advised by Lorraine Kelly.

Flo sighed, looked up from her phone – and raised her eyebrows.

'Yeah,' she said, lifting her voice at the end of the word just a little. Not enough to make it a question exactly, but enough to make me question *myself* and how I dare to ever go out in public. She looked back down, addressing the next sentence to the screen, as though I had really wasted enough of her time already. 'I mean it's fine – you just look a bit like a supply teacher.'

Hmm. Our regular supply teacher when I was at school was called Mrs Cartman and she had swollen feet that ballooned dangerously out of her orthopaedic shoes.

'In what way?' I asked.

'I don't know,' she said dismissively. 'You look fine.'

I couldn't think of anything in my wardrobe that looked *less* supply teachery, and I didn't want to risk going back upstairs and waking Jess, so I switched my heels for turquoise Converse and hoped the effect would be suitably sassy.

I said goodbye, muttering things about how grateful I was and how her sister was asleep already and shouldn't be any trouble. She told me she'd put the trainers she wanted into my ASOS shopping basket.

I wish I could say that Cassie's New Year's Eve party turned out to be a defining moment in my optimistic fantasy of reinvention, but I'm not sure it was. When I arrived, Cassie wafted towards me in a cloud of Chanel N°5 and gave me two fake kisses and a glass of prosecco, which I fingered nervously – I'm never sure whether you're meant to hold it by the glass or the stem. I stood for a while with a couple of women who were talking about children's tutors, but given that all of Flo's homework support comes from me, via *BBC Bitesize*, I didn't feel I had much to contribute. Fortunately, I spotted one of the mums from Busy Beavers, the playgroup I take Jess to on Thursday afternoons, loitering by the drinks table.

She doesn't know, but I once saw her crouched behind the sand table, eating loose Wotsits out her handbag, so I recognised a kindred spirit.

Possibly a little *too* kindred, on reflection. I don't think Cassie appreciated our Boasty Parent Scotch Bingo. If anything, though, it was the other guests who were to blame. If they hadn't kept mentioning their children's achievements, then we wouldn't have had to do so many shots. My new BFF (surely?) is called Sierra, which is the sort of exotic name I always wish my mum had given me, rather than Frances, which makes me sound like a nun and is why I've always made people call me Frankie.

I'm slightly annoyed with myself for not making more of an effort to mingle, as I wanted my first new diary entry to be full of wit and charm and anecdotes from meetings with interesting strangers. New year, new me and all that jazz. Also, I really do need to make some proper friends. We've been in Dorset over a year now and yet I'm still clinging desperately to the idea of London. I guess mid-divorce isn't necessarily the time for meeting new people and making a positive first impression.

I thought about looking back through past diaries for inspiration, but I only have one diary from my childhood. It's from 1990 and has a picture of Garfield on the front. He's holding a pen but there's a thought bubble above him that says, 'I'd rather be eating lasagne', which is basically me, right now. I wrote every entry in a different coloured ink, which I think shows a decent amount of dedication, but the entries stop on 13 January. Perhaps I ran out of pens.

Reading over the thirteen days I did manage, I don't feel like it was any great loss to literature. The highlight is probably 6 January. 'Went to Sainsbury's with Mummy, even though I wanted to stay at home, and she let me get *two* packets of Jaffa Cakes!!!!!' There's a little smiley face next to it. I do love Jaffa Cakes. On 8 January I 'went to Gran and Grandad's and had a mini milk. Grandad showed me how to do 3D lettering'.

It's pretty gripping stuff.

I was still feeling a little fragile by teatime and Flo had gone to her friend Sasha's house to watch videos on the internet of strangers take toys out of boxes, so Jess and I had Shreddies for tea and watched Flo's old *High School Musical* DVD. I feel it my duty to educate Jess in the classics.

(Question: how old *is* Zac Efron in the first *HSM*?)

Tuesday 2 January

Today I had a go at ironing.

Normally, I'm more of a careful drying-and-folding type of person, but I think I was trying to make up for the lingering shame of Boasty Parent Scotch Bingo. To give some ironing context: about six months ago I had to iron a dress for a hand-fasting ceremony – don't even ask – and when I got the iron out, Jess covered her ears and looked scared because she didn't know what it was. Is it OK to get to age three without ever having seen your mum iron?

I was putting out the recycling last night, though, and I could see down the steps and into the living room of the house that backs on to ours. They quite often have the lights on without closing the curtains – exhibitionists, my gran would have called them, although I'm not sure ironing in public is considered terribly saucy nowadays.

They clearly don't realise how often I sneak into the back garden after dark to escape the Disney Channel and scroll through Instagram. I know that @simple_dorset_life always makes me feel worse about my life, but I also can't stop looking. Every time I see a photo of some kind of organic avocado-based brunch she has rustled up between breastfeeds, I remember the time Jess threw a piece of avocado toast at that old woman in the café at the bottom of the hill and she sent me her dry-cleaning bill. The old woman, not Jess.

Anyway, the woman in the lights-on house was ironing. She was in a white robe with her hair pulled up in a messy ponytail and she was watching what looked like *EastEnders*. Her husband – I know they're married because I saw him in Tesco once, buying cat litter, and looked for a ring – was sitting on the sofa with their son, reading books. I watched them for quite a long time because it was such a nice, ordinary family scene. I mean, she *did* have her back to me, so I couldn't say for sure that she wasn't silently crying or anything, but it looked pleasant enough.

So, today I thought I would get myself a piece of that. I'm turning thirty-eight this year, after all, and ironing feels like something I should be getting into as a woman in my late thirties. Like gardening. Or not eating as many Jaffa Cakes.

I set up the ironing board and got some books out for Jess. I tried to get Flo to read to her, but she gave the ironing board a funny look and told me she had homework to do. I'm pretty sure this was a lie, but I smiled anyway, said something suitably encouraging, and set about my task. Ten minutes in I realised why I never watch *EastEnders* – it's bloody miserable.

I looked over to Jess to get her to change the channel but she wasn't sitting happily on the sofa, browsing through her wholesome book selection, as I had pictured her in my mind. I looked back just in time to see her running into the living room with something slopping about in a bowl. She tripped over the iron lead and what looked like milk with bits in sploshed into the basket of Flo's freshly pressed school uniform.

Jess immediately started to cry.

'Now my special relaxing drink is ruined!' she said, sobbing. 'I made it for you, Mummy,' she added, as she tried to pick bits of what looked like cheese out of the washing basket.

I checked. Zac Efron was eighteen when *High School Musical* came out. Not sure how I feel about myself.

Wednesday 3 January

Jaffa Cakes – 7. Times I was forced to watch a small child do a dance involving a dusty piece of ribbon found under the sofa – 4. Inappropriate thoughts about Zac Efron – undisclosed.

Back to school for Flo this morning, but in their infinite wisdom Jess's nursery decided that we definitely would not have seen enough of our preschool children over the last two weeks and that we would probably want an extra few days to enjoy some quality bonding time, so I'm off work for the rest of the week. Given that the whole point of nursery is to provide childcare for working parents, it's not exactly *helpful*.

I've always been dubious about the term 'quality time'. It implies the presence of craft materials or cookery books. Whose idea of a quality way to spend time involves glitter?

I decided we'd spend *our* quality time going to Tesco to buy fruit and vegetables as I've mainly eaten Toblerone since mid-December, but Jess fell asleep in the car on the way. Clearly, she doesn't want to bond any more than I do. She hardly naps at all since turning three so I made good use of the time by catching up on some personal admin: i.e., looking at Instagram. Apparently @simple_dorset_life was on the beach this morning, doing yoga and drinking a home-made kale smoothie.

'I love the feel of the winter wind's icy fingers on my face as I move into downward dog,' the caption read. *'It's so cold, but I feel totally alive! I got home to find the twins happily snoozing while Daddy was in the kitchen making a batch of organic buckwheat pancakes. #blessed.'*

I thought about *my* kitchen at home, which distinctly lacks a daddy *or* any buckwheat – what even *is* buckwheat? – and I wondered if @simple_dorset_life ever eats cereal with her hands from the box when Daddy isn't there. I do want to *be* her, but also I quite want to watch her try to get a bra wire out of a washing-machine drainage pipe and see how she yogas her way out of that one.

Jess stayed asleep for ages, but I found half a bottle of strawberry Ribena on the floor of the car so #blessed for me, too.

Ian came round for Jess after he'd picked Flo up from school. She showed him a picture she'd drawn of what looked like weird egg people but which was apparently me sitting on the toilet holding a cat while she mixed a cake in the sink.

I know that I'm really lucky that Ian has both the girls every Wednesday night as well as every other weekend and that Flo still seems happy to go, even though she's fourteen, but I worry that I don't make the most of it. I feel as if I should be doing something *worthwhile*, like writing a novel or taking a ceramics class or doing some exercises on a ball to improve my core strength. With this in mind, I'd planned to spend this evening making a New Year strategic plan for making my life more interesting. Turned out, though, that I was actually quite tired so I watched *Pointless* in the dark with a gin and tonic and then fell asleep on the sofa for two and a half hours instead. Excellent start.

Thought I might try jazzing things up with the occasional daily summary? If only to highlight the need for hobbies.

Thursday 4 January

Awkward pyjama-based encounters – 1. Rich tea fingers smuggled from the juice table to me by Jess at playgroup – 7.

I forgot to set my alarm so was woken at 8.45 a.m. by Ian bringing Jess home after dropping Flo off at school. Rather embarrassing opening the door in pyjamas, squinting against the sunlight, as I like Ian to think I spend my child-free Thursday mornings doing Pilates in the garden or drinking coffee and reading the papers on the terrace. I don't *have* a terrace, but you know what I mean.

It still feels weird, months down the line, seeing Ian in the context of the house but not having him live here. In a way, I'm glad that we only lived here for six months together before deciding, once and for all, to separate. I think it would have been much harder if we'd still been in the house in London, where we lived together for years. That place had so many happy memories in it that I'm not sure I could have lived there without him and not been reminded of him everywhere I looked.

Busy Beavers playgroup this afternoon. I'd been in two minds, but without nursery over Christmas,

Jess has definitely been on the twitchy side, plus I was hoping to see Sierra to consolidate the New Year's Eve party bonding. Post-Christmas playgroup atmosphere decidedly tense – other parents looking more frazzled than usual and three children had to be physically separated after an incident with the rich tea fingers.

Sierra seemed genuinely pleased to see me, which seems promising for the whole 'new BFF' thing. She told me she hasn't spoken to another grown-up in forty-eight hours, so it could just have been desperation. She introduced me to her son, Fox, who was wearing a Cinderella costume. 'He's refused to take it off since Tuesday,' she told me, 'even to go to bed.'

'Fox as in *a* fox?' I asked. Sierra looked confused. God, I'm such a moron sometimes. Still, she gave me her number and said that maybe we could meet up sometime. I gave her mine. I felt about eight years old. Medicinal glass of leftover Christmas prosecco* after tea for stress.

*By 'leftover' I mean bought in Tesco yesterday.

Friday 5 January

Mild panic attacks induced by thoughts about meaning of self – 1. Interesting tableaux created with tiny woodland creatures – 3.

Ian weekend. Praise the lord. At 4 p.m. closed the door to everybody, poured a glass of yesterday's prosecco (don't want to waste it), and settled down to make a sensible plan about goals.

I don't know where to start exactly, but I feel that at thirty-seven years old I should be *more*. I'm not sure more what. Just more together generally? Better at parenting? More Instagrammable? I don't know. I feel as though I should have a folder in the kitchen of tried-and-tested favourite family recipes that incorporate courgettes in ingenious ways. I feel that my underwear should match and that I should have a preferred skincare routine. I don't really understand what a skincare routine involves, but I want to be one of those women who says, 'Well, I always use blah de blah' and then other well-groomed women nod admiringly.

It's not even that I'm particularly unhappy. I have two lovely daughters, who really could be a lot worse. Jess is three, so mildly tedious, but also funny, and at least she isn't like the boy at playgroup who wees in the Lego box when he thinks no one is watching. Flo isn't especially communicative, but she's fourteen so I think she's *meant* to find me ridiculous. She seems to have plenty of friends and generally be quite normal. Between nursery four days a week and playgroup on Thursdays, Jess definitely has a better social life than me, though, so that's probably something to work on.

We live in a nice house in a nice town in a nice part of the country. It's all very *nice*. We have the beach and the girls are settled and I have a job. I mean sure, when I was a child I didn't think to myself, 'when I grow up what I absolutely definitely want to do is to

manage volunteers at a medium-sized fossil museum',
but it pays the bills and fits around the girls, so I can't
complain too much.

Obviously, there is the tiny matter of a husband.
I didn't exactly *plan* to be in my late thirties and
divorced with two children. When Ian and I moved
down to Barnmouth at the end of 2016 for our 'fresh
start', I think we both really knew that it wasn't going
to work, but I guess it would still have been nice to
have had that happily-ever-after with family walks
on the beach in the evenings rather than a quick,
amicable divorce.

I don't think it's that, though. I think it's more internal.
What is it? What's missing?

Close examination of life slightly overwhelming so had
another glass of prosecco and spent the evening sitting
on the floor in Jess's bedroom, arranging her Sylvanian
Families into funny scenes for when she gets home on
Sunday evening.

No message from Sierra.

Saturday 6 January

*Courgette cakes admired but not baked – 19. Jaffa cakes
– 8. (Bad.)*

I went online this evening to look up courgette cakes for
my imaginary folder of family recipes but got distracted
by a thread on Mumsnet. 'Am I being unreasonable,'

asked MilkThreeSugars, 'to be upset that DH doesn't want to wash baby clothes?'

What the actual? Who doesn't wash baby clothes? I was outraged on MilkThreeSugars' behalf. I'm not the most conscientious of parents, but at least I never made my babies just loll around all day in shit-stained Babygros. Christ.

But then I read more and it turns out she wanted to wash the baby's clothes *before he had even worn them*. As in when they were brand new and quite probably the cleanest they will ever be. Apparently, this is a 'thing' that parents do and she was very upset that her husband thought it was unnecessary. There was a flood of sympathy for her. 'What's the matter with him?' asked femidom13. 'Was he raised in a barn?'

Brushing over the name 'femidom13' because I just can't even *fathom* – had twelve people already claimed the name? – who *are* all these people washing brand-new clothes? Talk about making work for yourself.

Wondered for a while about all the things that other parents might be doing that no one has told me about. Honestly, I really do try to do my best for my kids, but someone needs to *tell* me if there are things like this that I'm meant to be doing.

Scrolled back through @simple_dorset_life's feed until I found a courgette cake – I knew she wouldn't let me down. *'My boys were worried at first that this cake might be naughty,'* she wrote, *'but when I told them about the courgettes they tucked right in!'*

Good grief.

Sunday 7 January

Number of times I've checked phone for a message from Sierra – too many. Hours of Netflix watched by Flo unregulated by me – all of them.

Here's a thing I don't understand about parenting: you spend days, weeks, longing for a bit of time on your own, counting the hours down until someone else can take over the responsibility. And then they're gone and you miss them and find yourself burying your face in their pillows to breathe in their smell. You know that thing when you look at your sleeping baby and are suddenly overwhelmed by love? It's like that, only you have to just stand in their rooms and *imagine* them asleep.

I watched all three of them out of my bedroom window this afternoon when Ian brought them home. Jess was on Ian's shoulders and she had her head thrown back, laughing. Flo was more animated than she ever seems to be with me and was walking hand in hand with Ian, their arms swinging between them. My breath caught in my chest and I ducked out of the way before they saw me behind the glass.

Flo let them in and I heard the noise of their laughter move into the kitchen as I came slowly down the stairs. I stopped in the doorway and Ian noticed me before the girls did and smiled at me over their heads. I smelt the smell of him, soaked up by our children, and for a second I longed to be able to love him in the way he once wanted me to. Or perhaps still does.

Jess turned and saw me and started to tell me about how she'd beaten everyone at bowling and the spell was broken.

'You did have the sides up *and* you used the ramp,' Flo pointed out, but as she said it she bent and prodded Jess's tummy fondly. 'Plus you ate all those chips, which definitely gave you extra powers.' I looked at them there in the kitchen, two sisters, and wondered how I had made such beautiful girls.

I offered Ian a cup of tea. He looked a bit sad and said no. He kissed the girls goodbye and I stood at the front door and watched him go.

'Can I watch Netflix?' shouted Flo from the lounge.

'As long as it's not vampires,' I shouted back, closing the door and going back into the kitchen to put the kettle on. Jess has been having vampire-related nightmares since she accidentally walked in on Flo watching a particularly gory scene involving a fight over an amulet.

I made a cup of tea and Jess went upstairs and put all of her Sylvanians in a carrier bag to 'take them on holidays' without so much as a mention of the attention to detail in my rustic farmers' market scene.

I thought quite a lot about Ian this evening. I know that the separation was the right thing to do, that we were always better as friends than as lovers, but sometimes I can't help but wonder if we did the right thing, especially when I see him with the girls and how happy they all are together. Am I chasing a dream of something that doesn't exist? Should I be settling for something simpler?

Not that it's my decision to make. Although it was me who said it out loud, Ian knew it wasn't working either and I don't think he would want to get back together, not really. For the girls, maybe, but that would hardly be fair.

The worst part of the break-up, of course, was telling my parents. They've always been amazingly supportive and I couldn't have asked for more from them, but when I married Ian you could tell that they were just so *relieved*. They'd felt responsible for me for a long time, especially after Cam left, and at last there was someone else that they felt they could trust to look after me.

They tried for years to have a baby and were in their early forties when I came along – that much-longed-for only child – so they were retired then by the time Flo was a toddler. They were a massive help when she was young and I was on my own with her, and I never felt as though I was imposing, exactly, but I knew, too, that they'd always had a dream of moving to France when they retired, and I couldn't help but feel as if they were putting their life on hold for me.

When Ian and I got married, they finally felt able to make that step, and so for a long time after we separated I didn't tell them – I didn't want them to feel as if they had to come back and take care of me again. It was difficult, but they seem OK with it now, especially knowing Ian is so close by. I know they'd be happier if we got back together. Hardly a reason, though, I guess.

Nothing from Sierra. I keep replaying the ridiculous Fox comment over and over in my head. Decided I was being ridiculous and messaged her instead.

Monday 8 January

Boring-looking work emails moved to 'TO ACTION' *folder, likely never to be seen again – 127. Baby beavers missing presumed dead – 1.*

Back to work today. Jess decided, just as we were leaving for nursery, that she wanted to take the carrier bag of Sylvanians with her. I said no. No way did I want them getting mixed up with the communal nursery toys – those critters are pricey.

Negotiations ensued.

By 'negotiations' I mean that Jess screamed and refused to let me put on her shoes until I agreed to her taking the beaver family in a leftover takeaway box. There were further discussions when we arrived at nursery and I suggested she leave them safely in the car for the day. Jess screeched. I was now late for work so I had to give in.

'I'll look after them, darling,' she assured me, sounding like a fifty-two-year-old ladies' golf club member. No idea where she picked up 'darling'.

Ten minutes late for work. Steve asked if I'd enjoyed my holiday and managed to say 'holiday' in a way that implied I'd been lying alone on a beach for two weeks being brought pina coladas by a stream of eligible bachelors.

As payback, I chose to forget to remind him that his meeting with the museum's board of trustees had been brought forward by half an hour. I loitered near his office to listen for the angry call from the chair ten minutes after the meeting start time.

Seven emails from Cecilia about the volunteer rota for the summer exhibition.

Drafted a reply: 'For Christ's sake, Cecilia, it's 4 January. We're a fossil museum. It's not exactly a fast-paced industry, the fossils aren't going anywhere. Do you not have any other hobbies?'

Indulged briefly in a fantasy where I actually sent the email and Cecilia resigned her position as volunteer summer exhibition co-ordinator and I never had to hear another story about her cocker spaniel's bowel condition.

One baby beaver was conspicuously missing from the takeaway box when I collected Jess from nursery. Her bag did contain a note, though, informing me that liqueur chocolates are not allowed in packed lunches and could I please refrain from sending Jess in with Grand Marnier in the future.

Must have got those muddled up with the Christmas Quality Street.

Tuesday 9 January

Fruitlessly battled with Flo to try to get her to wear a coat to school this morning, what with there being actual frost on the ground, but she assured me she wasn't cold. I could see her breath coming out in clouds as she spoke, so I wasn't convinced. She pushed her hands into her blazer pockets so I wouldn't see them turning blue and reminded me that *no one* wears coats and that, even if she did, what was she meant to do with it exactly, just carry it round with her all day?

I said yes and she looked at me pityingly, as if she understood *life* and I didn't. Sometimes I think she could be right.

I mentioned the baby beaver when I dropped off Jess at nursery and her key worker smiled over-enthusiastically and said they would 'hunt high and low!' Do nurseries train their staff to be so annoyingly jolly or do they purposely pick people who have it about them already?

No reply from Sierra. She clearly hates me.

Wednesday 10 January

*Minutes of life wasted in pursuit of the perfect body, as prescribed to me by society/*Heat *magazine – 8. Glasses of wine drunk and Jaffa Cakes eaten in a bid to prove to self that I am happy with body as is and don't need to be thin to be content – 3 + 9. (Point well made.)*

In the spirit of 2018 being the year I embrace change, get fit and thin and tanned etc., etc., I decided to use my child-free evening this week to have my first-ever sunbed. I'm thinking that if I have a 'just got back from a sexy winter sun holiday' tan then at least people might be distracted from the chub while I gather the motivation to join a gym.

I felt weirdly nervous parking the car and did a shifty look around me to make sure no one I knew was about before I opened the door. Inside, I was greeted by a woman whose face reminded me of a leather handbag I bought during my honeymoon with Ian in Mykonos. Her name badge said 'Sandra'.

Sandra helped me set up my 'membership', which made me feel a bit like perhaps I was as good as joining a gym after all, and I topped up my tan credit using my fingerprint. While Sandra was distracted by another customer, I accidentally used the touchscreen to buy three pairs of safety goggles.

Sandra then showed me into the tanning room and demonstrated how I should wipe down the bed with the provided spray before using it. Once inside, I was to pull the lid of the bed down over me. I made a joke about panini. She didn't laugh.

'Is there a start button or something?' I asked, feeling a bit stupid.

'No,' she said, 'it starts automatically, so you've got about ninety seconds now to get sorted.' I looked panicked. 'You'd best get going,' she added helpfully, and left the room.

I scrambled out of my clothes, in two minds as to whether or not I was meant to keep on my pants. I thought probably not, but then what if you actually *were* and I turned it into one of those 'accidentally naked in a sauna' moments? I'd locked the door, but you never knew in places like this.

I decided to risk it, took off my pants and lay down on the bed, wondering how many other bums had been in exactly the same spot. I pulled the sandwich toaster top down over me, ready to become Jennifer Aniston.

The safety goggles were like black swimming goggles, designed to be strung together and fixed around the back of your head. Sandra had made me nervous with her countdown, though, so I skipped fiddling about with the string and went for just balancing them on my eyes. This was fine until I turned my head to the side to check my positioning and the left goggle fell off on to the bed next to my head. I fumbled for it, trying at the same time to keep the right goggle in place, worried that at any moment the tanning would start and I would be immediately blinded.

I found it just as the bed lit up and a robot voice welcomed me to what turned out to be possibly the longest and hottest eight minutes of my life.

Sandra had shown me some buttons, but with my eyes closed behind the goggles (are you meant to do this? Not sure …) I couldn't figure out how to switch on the fans. I felt as if I might actually be being toasted, cheese-and-tuna panini-style. When I finally escaped I noticed a sign on the wall informing me (too late) – that the facial tanners are extremely powerful and can be turned down from the console. Fantastic.

I'd expected afterwards to feel kind of glowing and lustrous. Instead, I just felt sweaty. And I mean really sweaty. I stopped at little Tesco on the way home for a few essentials – bread, wine, Jaffa Cakes – and I could feel sweat pooling around my bum and rolling down the back of my thighs.

Spotted Flo's physics teacher so hid behind the coffee machine to avoid any kind of sweaty encounter. He had eight cans of cider and a meat feast pizza in his basket, so clearly enjoying the start of term.

Thursday 11 January

Busy Beavers this afternoon and Sierra brought me in a bag of mini chocolate-chip cookies to apologise for not being in touch. She told me that Fox had buried her phone in the garden and then watered it to see if it would grow into a phone tree. (It didn't).

Apparently, mini-cookie bags are ideal for stealth snacking as the smaller-than-normal cookie size means you can put a whole one in your mouth at once, thus minimising the risk that a small child will spot you daring to enjoy yourself.

I think she might be my soulmate.

Saturday 13 January

Changing room number tags accidentally shoplifted – 1. Strangers traumatised – at least 1. New ideas for ways to use bunting to bring a 'splash of colour' to a child's bedroom – more than necessary.

If anyone from Marks & Spencer ever reads this, I have a genius idea for you – paid childcare for changing rooms. I'm thinking something like one pound per three minutes? You'd hardly have them for any time at all, so you wouldn't even have to think up decent activities: you could literally just sit them in a corner with a mini fudge from the food hall or something. Seriously, wouldn't it be nice to *not* have to take a small child in with you while you try on swimming costumes? I can't say it was exactly a boost for my self-confidence to have Jess outright *laugh* when I took off my bra.

'Do a dance, Mummy!' she shrieked with glee. 'Make your boobies wobble!' I refused. She looked cross. 'Do a dance!' she shouted again, slightly less gleefully. I told her that I really didn't want to do a dance, I just wanted to try on some swimming costumes, but she didn't seem to be on board with that. She started slapping at my legs and crying, which I thought probably didn't sound great through the curtain.

I tried to ignore her and took the first costume off the hanger. I wrestled the Lycra over my thighs, the straps somehow becoming more twisted the more I tried to straighten them out. I looked in the mirror, my face red and shiny, thighs puckered, a stark V-shaped tan line on my increasingly wrinkly chest. I was *sure* I was younger and thinner last time I looked. When did my cleavage start to look like that of a sixty-four-year-old woman who likes to wear a lot of gold jewellery and lives for half the year in Spain?

I looked down for Jess, just in time to hear a startled gasp from the changing room next door and a 'Hello, lady!' from Jess. I yanked her back in, shouted apologies and kept my eyes fixed on her as I changed back into my clothes, nudging her into a corner with my feet whenever she tried to make a break for it.

Came out of the changing rooms and bumped into a pushchair containing a smiley toddler eating a carrot stick. It was being pushed by a serene-looking woman with the shiniest hair I have ever seen. I mumbled sorry and dragged Jess outside. I took her into the toyshop, thinking that might calm her down, but instead she had a tantrum because I wouldn't buy her a set of Sylvanian Family bunkbeds for her baby beavers. *Ten pounds* they wanted for them. Whoever invented Sylvanian Families must be chuckling to themselves as they recline on a lounger on the deck of their yacht.

Flo was in one of her lovely moods when we got home, where she decides Jess is her best friend ever, so I was able to recover quietly from the changing-room ordeal with a cup of tea and a scroll through Instagram. Way too many New Year-inspired smoothies for my liking, so I made myself feel bad by looking at kids' bedroom makeovers on Pinterest instead. Who are these parents with the time and inclination to build wigwams and hand-stitch bunting?

The girls disappeared upstairs again after tea and at about seven o'clock they came downstairs for the sofa cushions, saying they were having a sleepover in Flo's room and I mustn't come in. I happily agreed and moved to the beanbag. A small price to pay.

Poured a glass of wine and WhatsApped Sierra my tale of changing-room woe. She sympathised with a story about Fox involving a shoe fitting with a female shop assistant with an unfortunate amount of facial hair.

At about eight I heard Jess tiptoe downstairs and into the kitchen. She rummaged noisily in the snack cupboard and I used my phone as a sort of periscope to watch her run back up the stairs with two bags of Frazzles.

(Question: does anyone actually *like* bunting or are we all just too scared to be the first one to say we think it's shit?)

Sunday 14 January

I dreamed last night that I was at a soft play centre with the shiny-haired mum from M&S. She was stuck in the ball pit and I was just watching and laughing and holding a glass of prosecco in each hand.

To make up for yesterday I spent the afternoon with Jess, making our own versions of Sylvanian Family furniture. I made some bunk beds with two matchboxes, four cocktail sticks and some masking tape, which I was *very* pleased with. I also upcycled a Müller rice pot into a hot tub and made a mini firepit with an empty Petite Filous one and some twigs from the garden. I think I might have had more fun than Jess did. Bit worrying.

Monday 15 January

Jess's key worker, Millie, handed me one of the plastic changing-room tags from M&S when I got to nursery this afternoon. It had a number three on it. Apparently they'd had a 'what we did at the weekend' session and Jess had got it out of her backpack to illustrate her story about me 'taking my clothes off in the shops'.

I questioned Jess about it on the way home. She said she'd wanted to tell everyone about it because she thought it was funny that my bottom was so hairy but that the lady in the other changing room didn't have any hair at all.

'She looked just like my Tiny Tears dolly, Mummy,' she said.

Drove the rest of the way home in silence, wondering how I will ever look Millie in the eye again.

Tuesday 16 January

FaceTimed Mum and Dad this evening. Jess started to tell them about the woman in the changing room but I managed to change the subject by suggesting she show them her Sylvanians. Jess ran off to get her beavers and Mum started to ask me about Ian.

'Have you had any more thoughts about giving things another go?' she asked.

'Mum,' I said, 'it's been nine months now, and we're both much happier with how things are.'

'Are you, though?' she asked.

Jess ran back in then and snatched the laptop away so I was spared having to think about it.

Thursday 18 January

Norwegian cruise fantasies – 7. Potential Daddy Saddle-based nightmares – tbc. Jaffa Cakes – 4. (Pre-empting trauma of Daddy Saddle dreams.)

Cassie arrived at Busy Beavers today in a fur coat.

Aside from the whole animal cruelty thing, obviously, can you imagine anything less suitable to wear while carrying around a small child? If I wore a fur coat on a day out with Jess I'm pretty sure it would look like roadkill within about half an hour. When I got into work on Monday, Angela, who does fundraising and sits next to me, had to pick an actual piece of cheese out of my hair.

Sierra and I encouraged Jess and Fox towards the home corner so we could follow Cassie and the coat. We heard her tell Yvonne, who fawns around her like she's the bloody Queen or something, that her husband bought it for her as a surprise Christmas gift and that she felt awful about it. She didn't *look* like she felt awful.

'We'd promised we were only getting each other token gifts,' she told Yvonne, 'because of the Norwegian Fjord cruise, and then he goes and gets me this! I felt terrible as I only got him a Daddy Saddle!'

I was so busy thinking about the casualness of the cruise comment that for a second my brain didn't process

Daddy Saddle. Then I realised Sierra was choking on her rich tea finger. Cassie shot us a look as I escorted Sierra to the opposite side of the room, where she collapsed into mild hysterics.

She wanted to google Daddy Saddle there and then but I pointed out that if it was some kind of sex aid then I didn't want it showing up on the church hall Wi-Fi and God having another excuse to turn me away. Not that I believe in him, but you need to keep your options open.

Looked up Daddy Saddle when I got home. I think I'd have had more respect for Cassie if it *had* been a sex aid. Ian and I have both given plenty of horsey rides to the girls when they were small, letting them ride on our backs, but we never felt the need to use an *actual* saddle. I wonder if Cassie's husband is also made to wear a bit in his mouth?

Friday 19 January

Steve announced this morning that as I've been working at the museum for a year now, I'm due an appraisal and that he's putting it in the diary for 9 a.m. next Friday. I asked if perhaps we could make it 9.30, just to give me chance to arrive and get sorted but he said he was going to be very busy with other meetings and it had to be 9. I checked his diary while he was in the toilet and the only other thing in it on Friday was 'dental hygienist' at 3. He does it on purpose – jealousy, I think, because of my part-time hours. He likes testing me.

Maggie, my very favourite volunteer, came in to do her Friday afternoon exhibition tours and brought me a piece of home-made lemon drizzle cake. She told me not to mind Steve. She said she's pretty sure he lives at home with his mother as she saw them in Sainsbury's last week arguing over crunchy versus smooth peanut butter. She said Steve's mother won.

Sunday 21 January

Weekend too tedious to write about.

Monday 22 January

Message from Sierra at lunchtime.

'When do you work?' she said. I gave her the schedule: Monday 9–3, Tuesday until midday, Wednesday 9–6 because Ian picks up the girls and has them to stay and Friday 9–3.

'I have Thursdays off,' I told her, 'and Tuesday afternoons, and sometimes I work later on Fridays if it's an Ian weekend.'

'Blimey,' she replied, 'what a faff.' It really is. It's one of the main reasons I took the museum job when we moved down to Barnmouth, because the board of trustees agreed to be flexible around school hours so I can do nursery pick up three days a week.

Sierra said that Fox had insisted on wearing a leotard all weekend and did I want to go to toddler gymnastics with them tomorrow afternoon. I could feel my shoulders tense at the thought of an echoey hall full of toddlers almost literally bouncing off the walls but couldn't make an excuse about work as now she knew I was free – clever.

'I know it sounds shit,' she said, reading my mind, 'but if Fox attempts another cartwheel near the open kitchen shelving then I'm going to have a breakdown. It's only £2.50 a session and I will bring Jaffa Cakes.'

I dug out a pair of shorts and a T-shirt with a ballerina on the front for Jess – my best approximation at a gymnastics kit.

Tuesday 23 January

Toddler gymnastics class was forty-five minutes long and I think Jess attempted two forward rolls in that whole time. There were only nine of them in the class, but they had to line up and take turns to do a move, supervised by a member of staff. Jess was so excited that she couldn't quite manage to keep her place in the queue – she kept running over to tell me to watch her or running back in the line to talk to Fox.

The obsessive leotard-wearing had clearly paid off for Fox – he nailed the cartwheeling in about twenty minutes. Sierra was playing it cool with the whole 'Gawd, who are these parents forcing their kids into classes?' thing but I could tell she was enjoying it as she only ate one Jaffa Cake.

Wednesday 24 January

Money saved on Coke/popcorn combo – £8. Time that could have been spent not *in the cold if I had just stayed home in the first place – one hour.*

I decided to go to the cinema on my own this evening. I've never been by myself before, but it felt like the kind of thing that sassy, independent women approaching forty should be doing. Ian has the girls to stay every Wednesday night, plus Friday and Saturday night every other weekend – that's four nights every fortnight that I have to myself. I can't sit at home watching Netflix and eating crisps on *all* of them.

I didn't want to spend eight pounds on a handful of popcorn and can of Coke, so I thought I'd be clever and take in a cheeky gin and tonic from home. I didn't actually *have* any tonic though, so it ended up being a gin and Asda Double Strength Lemon Squash, which I'm sure is considered some kind of retro delicacy in London. A bit like those cereal cafés where you pay £8.95 for a bowl of Lucky Charms and get to pretend for twenty minutes that everything is OK and that you live at home with your mum and dad and not in a mouldy cupboard in Bethnal Green that's costing you two-thirds of your salary.

I searched the cupboards, trying to find something to put my vintage, hipster cocktail in, but could only find the old Peppa Pig flask that Jess insists on taking to Busy Beavers every week because she says the juice there 'tastes like rocks'.

When I got to the cinema, though, I couldn't go in. I couldn't face going up to the counter and asking for one ticket. How pathetic is that?

I should have gone to the big Odeon in Exeter where they have the self-service machines and no one need know you're on your own until the lights are down and it's too late. I sat for a little while on the bench opposite, drinking my gin and tonic and imagining how warm I would be in Cassie's fur coat, then I walked home again.

(Note to self: remember to rinse flask thoroughly.)

Thursday 25 January

Sympathy biscuits eaten in order to make new mum feel more comfortable around me – 4. Times I was grateful not to have twins – 5+.

There was a new mum at Busy Beavers today. She had twin boys with her, who looked about Jess's age. She was sitting in the sandpit corner and both boys were pawing at her, trying to get up on to her lap, while she half-heartedly waved a bucket and spade about a bit. She was smiling but seemed to be taking very deep breaths.

I was all for just watching from a distance and using the new mum's predicament as a way to feel better about my own life – which is surely the point of going to playgroup after all? – but Sierra is obviously a much nicer person that me and made us go over and say hello.

New mum – Louise – looked pathetically grateful, to the point where I thought she might be about to cry. Sierra got Fox over to lure Louise's boys away on the promise of having a go on the crane, and I went to get tea and biscuits. Louise asked for hot water and got out her own chamomile teabag. I didn't say anything but I felt like it was going to take something a bit stronger than a chamomile tea.

Louise chatted for a bit about the twins – Arthur and Edward – and their various food intolerances and how avoiding sugar is actually so easy for them as their favourite food is baby sweetcorn. While she was talking

I saw one of the boys snatch a chocolate Hobnob from a small girl doing a Postman Pat jigsaw.

Jess came over to get a drink, her fringe sweaty and pushed back off her head. I got out the Peppa Pig flask and held my breath in case she kicked up a fuss about the mild gin flavour. Despite a thorough scrub with very hot water, there was still a slight whiff of botanicals when she popped up the spout but I think I got away with it.

Sierra invited Louise to toddler gym with us on Tuesday. I was a bit sceptical. 'She seems a bit smug, don't you think?' I asked Sierra while Louise was in the toilet. 'All that baby sweetcorn talk?'

'Maybe,' said Sierra, 'but also she has her jumper on inside out and there were a lot of mascara-stained tissues in her bag.'

Friday 26 January

Appraisals attended – 0. Intricate plans hatched about leaving poisonous insects in Steve's office while he is out for lunch – 1. (But very solid.)

I remembered at 8.15 a.m. that I had my appraisal at 9 today, and before I could even say anything out loud Jess seemed to sense my need for speed and started eating her toast as slowly as possible. She was literally nibbling tiny corners like a goddamn mouse.

'Last night you told me not to rush my jelly,' she reminded me helpfully, 'because you said I would get tummy ache.' She smiled sweetly. I was sure she wasn't doing it on purpose, and yet…

'Yes, I did,' I said, 'but Mummy has something very important to do at work this morning, so we mustn't be late.'

'Don't worry, Mummy,' she said, 'I will eat this and then I just need to choose a pony to take to nursery.'

God, no!

'Perhaps you don't need to take one today?' I suggested, immediately regretting it. She looked horrified, as if the very notion would mean that she'd now have to give a *lot* more thought to the choosing process than she had originally planned.

Flo was ready to leave for school.

'Can I have that £20?' she asked me as she wrestled her shoes on, squashing down the backs in the process.

'God, Flo, can't you undo your laces?' I asked. 'Those shoes cost me £45 you know. And what £20?'

'You know, for the wood for DT, so I can make you a box. You said to remind you. You should be grateful I'm making you a hand-crafted gift, you know.'

'Did it occur to you to remind me perhaps more than thirty seconds before the time of actually needing it?' I asked, rummaging in my bag for my purse.

'I just remembered,' she said. 'You should have reminded me to remind you.'

'Well, I don't have cash,' I said. 'They can have a book token. Or my library card, although I owe £8.25 so they probably won't want that. Why on earth do you have to pay for your own wood, anyway? Isn't that up to school to provide? Like desks and teachers and stuff?'

'It's cuts, Mum,' she said, shoving her sandwich into her bag in a way that implied she probably wasn't going to be worrying about eating it. 'Everyone knows about the cuts.'

I sighed.

'Well, I'm sorry, but I don't have any cash on me, so you'll have to apologise and say you'll take it in next week.'

'Oh, brilliant,' she said. She practically threw her bag on to her back. 'Can't you bring it in later?'

'I'm sorry,' I said again. 'I'm working today. I can't just leave work and run errands for you.'

'No, right, of course, heaven forbid you want to do anything that might help me,' she shouted as she stormed off down the path. 'I'll just be humiliated in front of my friends, don't worry about me.'

I felt awful about her leaving like that because Ian was picking her up from school and I wouldn't see her again until Sunday afternoon. I knew I could have dealt with it better and that it wasn't her fault that I was rushed and stressed. I pressed my palms into my eyes for a few seconds, took a deep breath and turned back to Jess. 'Have you chosen a pony?' I asked brightly.

She hadn't chosen a pony, so by the time that was done and packed lunches were finished and we were in the car it was 8.45. Fifteen minutes to get to nursery, drop off Jess, get to work and be in my appraisal. Unlikely, but not impossible, not unless you turn out of your street and straight up behind the recycling truck, anyway.

It was 9.06 when I ran into Steve's office, chucking my stuff at my desk as I flew past. Steve was staring at his computer screen. 'Sorry, Frankie,' he said, not even looking up at me, 'I've had to reschedule as you were late. I have other things I need to do today and I didn't have the availability for it to overrun.'

What an utter bastard! I hope the dental hygienist slips and drills through his tongue, I thought. That happened to someone I know, once. They had to have eight stitches. Can you even imagine?

It was 9.12 when I got back to my desk and I realised I had Jess's lunch bag. Good luck, nursery, after she's had my iced coffee and Twix.

Saturday 27 January

Woke up at 6.30 a.m., wide awake, as though someone had thrown a bucket of cold water over me. I tried to go back to sleep but it was pointless. Why is it that when you have the kids you long for a lie-in, but when you're on a child-free weekend suddenly you're awake at the crack of bloody dawn?

Lay in bed in the dark and did a bit of Instagram stalking and discovered @simple_dorset_life had been busy in the kitchen yesterday, making raw brownies with coconut oil and Medjool dates.

'When those sugar cravings hit, these sweet and sticky raw brownies are just what you need!' the caption read. *Just one small square is enough to satisfy the sweetest tooth, so it's a good job they keep!'*

One small square seems doubtful, tbh.
(Question: what *is* a Medjool date?)

Sunday 28 January

Minibreaks taken – 0. Jars of ground coriander dusted
– 3. Shaped chicken pieces eaten – more than advisable.

I wish I had enough money to use my child-free weekends going on European city minibreaks or taking up exciting new hobbies like windsurfing. I went for a walk on the beach but it was decidedly bleak and also freezing cold, so I came home and spent three hours emptying out the kitchen cupboards, tutting at best before dates on mini jars of spices, and putting everything back in again. While I waited for the girls to come home I drew a little picture of a tree and wrote 'FLO' on the trunk. On each branch I drew a leaf and inside each leaf I wrote a something that I love about her. Then I folded it up and hid it under her pillow.

I'm waiting on payday so meals may get a little more creative over the next few days. Sunday dinner tonight was chicken fingers, potato waffles and cucumber for tea, followed by tinned mandarin segments and some rather frosty-looking toffee swirl ice cream. No one complained. In fact, Jess declared it 'scrumptious'. I should make less effort more often.

Also, chicken fingers are clearly just a ploy to try to make parents feel slightly less like they are giving their kids chicken nuggets, but why? Is it the word 'nugget'? Is it that a finger shape somehow seems more natural? Not sure how, as chickens don't have fingers, surely?

Wednesday 31 January

Payday, thank goodness. I was having one of those 'just been paid so feeling flush' moments this evening, so I signed Jess up for swimming lessons. There is something about her not being here in person that makes these ideas seem so much more manageable. She starts after half-term.

Thursday 1 February

Passive aggressive WhatsApp messages from Busy Beavers – 1. Hula Hoops picked up off the playgroup floor after Hula Hoop-gate – 23. Minutes of Peppa Pig *watched by Jess – more than recommended by Mumsnet.*

I almost *enjoyed* Busy Beavers today. I hung out in the home corner with Sierra and Louise and it felt like I was back in school and in a gang with the cool girls. Or midrange, at least. It would have been cooler if Louise hadn't kept harping on about the versatility of quinoa and jumping up in a panicky way every time one of her boys so much as wobbled a lip, but I think she has potential. I reckon we just need to get her drunk a couple of times, loosen her up. Probably during an evening rather than at playgroup.

Good vibes were slightly overshadowed by Jess throwing herself off the ride-on tractor and on to the floor in protest because I picked a Hula Hoop out of the packet and passed it to her, rather than offering her the packet for her to choose one herself. The hysteria worsened when she realised that in the meantime Fox had got *on* the ride-on tractor and was riding it away.

It was a messy five minutes.

I saw Cassie whisper something to Yvonne and nod over at us. Yvonne rolled her eyes in reply. Their children were sharing a Tupperware tub of raspberries and looking at a book about insects.

Stopped at Tesco on the way home for a payday shop. Jess wanted to sit inside the trolley with the shopping but a woman in a large hat overheard and told her that nice little girls sit properly in trolleys, so I was shamed into insisting on the seat. I waited until big-hat lady had moved out of the fruit and veg section and then let Jess watch *Peppa Pig* on my phone.

Flo was already home when we got back. I followed the trail of evidence – shoes left *next* to the shoe basket, (why?), blazer and bag hung on the bannisters and the orange juice left out on the side in the kitchen. I made her help me put the shopping away. You'd have thought I was asking her to hack through her own arm with a rusty axe.

I don't feel as though my expectations are high. I'm not looking for her to bound down the stairs as soon as she hears the door and usher me into the lounge while she puts the kettle on. Just some kind of sign of gratitude? Something small, once a week maybe, like putting her own crisp packets in the bin? Something that isn't 'these aren't the yogurts I like', or 'why didn't you get the smoothies I asked for?'

Message from Cassie via the Busy Beavers WhatsApp group: 'Would everyone mind having a look in their bags to see if they have a stray purple sippy cup? I'm sure no one has taken it home on purpose but we *would* be keen to have it returned – we do like to stay BPA-free with Aubyn as much as possible!'

Friday 2 February

New WhatsApp groups joined, signifying increasing popularity – 1. (Baby steps.) Resulting calculation of months since last sexual encounter – rather not think about it.

Sierra added me and Louise to a new WhatsApp group with her called WIB.

'I'm sick of the ridiculously patronising messages in the Busy Beavers group,' she said 'so this is an alternative where we can chat like normal people. And also bitch about the other mums and not be overheard, obviously.'

'What does the WIB stand for?' asked Louise.

'That's a Busy Beavers alternative, too,' explained Sierra. 'It stands for Woefully Inactive Beavers.'

I laughed and snorted wine out my nose. 'Woefully inactive' is definitely about right in the case of my beaver, to be fair.

'But the genius of WIB,' continued Sierra, 'is that if anyone sees it you can just make something up. Say it means Women in Business and it's the name of an empowering, female-led networking group that you've just set up. Something like that.'

Saturday 3 February

Number of times Jess yelled, 'Watch me, Mummy!' at the top of the slide at soft play – 273. Number of times I watched Jess go down the slide – zero.

It poured with rain all day. Wholesome family activities completed:

- Porridge cooked and eaten
- Small cakes baked. (Didn't have any icing sugar so let Jess decorate them with chocolate spread and peanut butter – actually quite impressed with this as a concept)
- Barbies bathed
- Necklace made from macaroni

At this point I felt sure it must be lunchtime, but it was somehow only 9.53 a.m. I spent some time wondering whether it's possible to actually *die* from boredom. What would that look like? I feel like it would be a sort of *shrivelling*, until you're left like an old raisin on the floor next to a pile of abandoned Duplo.

Jess was desperate to go to the park but I just couldn't face the arguments and the mess. Jess has this idea that going to the park in the rain is like going to the beach, and that you should be allowed to paddle in the puddles like you would in the sea.

We played animal snap twice but it was still only 10.13. I put my ear against the kitchen clock but it was definitely ticking. In an act of desperation I asked Jess if she fancied going to Micro Soft.

Micro Soft is our local soft play centre. The logo is four Lego bricks – red, green, blue and yellow – arranged in a square. Whoever set up Micro Soft clearly thinks they are very funny indeed, but I think they're an idiot and am looking forward to the day when actual Microsoft discovers them and bailiffs come in and try and seize the ball pit. I imagine two large men in black suits going back to the Microsoft offices with sacks full of plastic balls, looking pleased with themselves, and the boss just shaking his head and pointing at the door.

Micro Soft can go one of two ways for me. If I catch Jess in the right mood she will go off and make a friend and play happily for an hour while I drink coffee in peace and read the café's six-month old copies of *Grazia* magazine. Other times she'll decide she can't possibly enjoy herself unless I am next to her *at all times*. I've tried to discourage this since the time I got stuck in the foam rollers and had to be pulled to safety by a teenage staff member called Ellis.

Today was a relatively good day. Jess yelled, 'Watch me Mummy!' a *lot*, but she seemed happy enough with a cursory glance in her general direction and encouraging shouts of 'I'm watching!' and 'Great sliding!'

By the time we left I was up to date on everything I should have been wearing last autumn.

FaceTimed Mum and Dad after tea, Jess told them all about soft play and I casually dropped in having made new friends. Mum seemed so pleased for me – it was like being back at school when I joined the choir and got chosen to sing a solo at the Christmas concert. No matter how old I get my parents still seem able to make me feel about eight years old.

When Jess and I had done our bits, Flo took them off to her room. I love how close they are. They spent so much time together when she was young and I was never sure if they'd be able to maintain it once they moved away. Teenagers aren't exactly known for wanting to hang out with their grandparents, are they? Perhaps it's *because* they moved away, though – it means she enjoys the time they get to chat without having to actually go round for tea and be made to play card games and watch *Countdown*.

Monday 5 February

Arrived at work at five past nine to find that Steve had rescheduled my appraisal for 9.30 *today*. What a knob. I had to spend ten minutes making coffee, obviously, which left me just enough time to gather up a massive stack of random paperwork to carry under my arm for effect.

Steve glanced at my papers in a slightly intimidated way as I sat down in his office – probably a good job he didn't know that at least half of it was made up of blank paper I'd taken from the printer. At opportune moments throughout the meeting I licked my finger and looked over my imaginary glasses at him while I thumbed through my documents.

Most of the conversation reminded me of when Jess asks me some kind of nature question I don't know the answer to.

Me: 'So, Steve, are you happy with volunteer recruitment levels?'

Steve, in fake 'interested boss' voice: 'Are *you* happy with volunteer recruitment levels?'

Me: 'Were you pleased with the attendance at the January guest lecture and do you have any thoughts on future speakers?'

Steve: 'I'm interested in what you think about that one, Frankie.'

The main takeaway from the meeting was that Steve doesn't have a bloody clue what he's doing, which made me feel a bit better about my life in general, but a bit shit about work.

Tuesday 6 February

Cecilia came in to help me send out the members' magazines. Wooster, the cocker spaniel, wasn't with her today as he is trying out some new medication for his bowel issues and Cecilia says it's making him a little 'unpredictable'. I feel for Wooster, I really do – no one wants the indignity of shitting themselves if they can help it – but also I really wish Cecilia would just not tell me, especially when I'm trying to enjoy a chocolate Hobnob.

Toddler gym with Sierra and Louise after lunch. Arthur and Edward refused to join the queue for the springboard and spent the whole time draped across Louise's lap. She offered them carrot batons, apparently as an incentive, but to be honest they looked even *less* inclined after that. Caught them eyeing Jess's chocolate fingers enviously.

Exhausting evening trying to get Jess to go to sleep. She finally went quiet at about 9.45. Went up to bed about twenty minutes later to find her asleep in a ball on the landing. Her hands were covered with red felt-tip pen. I almost didn't want to move her, she looked so adorable, curled up like a little field mouse. I picked her up, carried her into her bedroom and tucked her into bed without her even stirring. Sat on the edge of the bed for a bit and watched her sleep.

Wednesday 7 February

Glasses of prosecco – 4. Cheese slices – 6. General feelings of inadequacy and frustration at life – multiple.

I was woken up at 7 a.m. by a knock on the door. Opened it to a man in shorts (shorts in February!) trying to deliver me a cat bed.

'I haven't ordered a cat bed,' I told him.

'Sign here, please,' he said, thrusting his electronic pen at me.

'I don't have a cat,' I explained.

'Then why did you order a cat bed?' he asked, looking confused.

Jess arrived on the scene and complicated matters further by inviting the delivery man to come in and look at her ponies. He declined. 'I'll just leave the cat bed here,' he said, placing it on the doorstep and turning to leave.

'I don't want a bloody cat bed!' I shouted.

'Returns information is inside!' he said and got in his van.

'Are we getting a cat?' asked Jess hopefully.

'Definitely not,' I said.

Flo came downstairs and looked at the parcel. 'What's that?' she asked.

'It's a bed for our new cat!' said Jess. 'I'm going to keep it in my room!'

'We're getting a cat?' asked Flo, looking even more confused than the delivery man.

'No!' I shouted again. 'It's just a cat bed!'

'Why did you order a cat bed if we're not getting a cat?' asked Flo. 'Was it meant to be a surprise?'

'No! We're not getting a cat. It's not my cat bed. Will everyone please be quiet and get dressed?'

I spent ten minutes trying unsuccessfully to wash the red pen off Jess's hands before nursery. I think it must have been Sharpie. Signed two letters presented to me by Flo without reading them. Sometimes I worry that she could take advantage of my slapdash approach to school correspondence – I could be agreeing to foreign exchange students or bank loans in my name or anything. (Not sure which would be worse – possibly the exchange students?)

Nightmare day at work. Angela revealed that she handed in her notice last week as she's got a new job managing the social media for a fancy arts centre. Apparently, she gets to choose her own hours and spend her time drifting about taking pictures of installations and posting them on Facebook.

Steve took me into his office to discuss potential changes in my role in light of Angela's departure. He thinks that given ever-increasing budget restrictions we should look at merging my role with the fundraising role – i.e., have me take on all of Angela's work.

'I don't have the scope to take on any extra though, Steve,' I said. 'I have to be able to work around my children. I have a routine set up with their dad and fixed nursery hours.'

'We wouldn't be looking at extra hours,' said Steve, trying to sound reassuring. 'We're thinking that with some streamlining of the roles that it's something you could do within your existing hours.'

Angela worked three days a week, so I can't help but feel like this isn't going to be great for me. I asked Steve what would happen if I didn't agree. He said that my contract includes a clause that allows the museum to make changes to my role when necessary, but that if I felt I didn't want to remain in the role, then that was up to me.

I told him I needed time to think about it as I really don't know what to do. I don't want to take on a load of extra work, especially not fundraising as I have barely any experience in it, but also how likely am I to find another job that's flexible enough to fit around the girls? As much as I complain about them, I do like having time with them during the week, especially as they're at Ian's every other weekend. Steve is a dick, sure, but the hours work for me, and they do say 'better the dick you know'. Sort of. Do I want to switch to another job where things might turn out to be even worse?

The kids were at Ian's so I stopped at Aldi on the way home and bought a packet of Edam slices and a £5.99 bottle of prosecco. Googled 'Netflix films to watch when you're sad' but got distracted by the fact that Google tries to finish the search with 'high' instead of 'sad', so I looked at those lists instead.

'It's been a tough day,' began one article, 'so what are you going to do with your evening now the kids are in bed? Nothing is better than zoning out with a good movie after a long day spent at work or chasing around after the children. If you're the type to get high to chill out at the end of the night, here are some great Netflix film choices to watch high.'

Seriously? Do parents do this?

'God, such a long PTA meeting tonight, I think I'm just going to stick a film on and get high now the kids are in bed.'

I like a gin and tonic as much as the next person, but waiting until you've read bedtime stories to get high? Blimey. The list that followed included *Finding Dory* and David Attenborough's *Planet Earth*, which wasn't what I was expecting, but clearly that's just because I'm out of touch with what other parents are doing with their evenings.

I decided to stick to my cheese and cheap prosecco, went back to the 'films to watch when sad' list and watched a 90s film about a lesbian cheerleader sent to straight camp. Went to bed with a new faith in the power of cheerleading to fight homophobia, intolerance etc.

Thursday 8 February

Exciting revelations from new friends – 1, but massive, *so probably counts as at least 3. Hangover Jaffa Cakes – 4.*

Got up feeling a little fragile (maybe the cheese didn't agree with me?) and went downstairs to make coffee. Tripped over the cat bed in the hallway.

I checked my phone and found an email from Amazon. 'Congratulations on your purchase,' it said. I opened it and discovered that at 11.34 last night I'd drunk ordered a pair of purple foil cheerleading pom-poms.

Ian arrived with Jess just as I'd finished getting dressed. He looked at the cat bed box and smiled. 'I hear you're getting a cat,' he said. I told him that we really weren't and moved the cat bed to the garage when he'd left.

Very exciting bonding moment at Busy Beavers in the afternoon. Louise arrived wearing sunglasses and the same man's hoodie that she came to gym class in on Tuesday. It looked like she might not have taken it off in between. She saw me and Sierra and came over.

'Are you OK?' I asked her.

'Not really,' she said, wiping her eyes behind the sunglasses with a crusty-looking sleeve. 'David has moved in with Sandra.'

I had no idea who David *or* Sandra were, but it felt quite exciting. Obviously you don't want your friends to be upset or anything, but still.

'Who's David?' asked Sierra.

'My husband,' said Louise.

Blimey.

'And who's Sandra?' I asked.

'She works in the bakery near his office,' said Louise.

'Christ,' said Sierra.

'He says she lets him eat chips and have sex with the light on,' added Louise in a small voice.

'At the same time?' asked Sierra.

I shot her a look. 'I don't think so,' said Louise, looking as though she might now be considering it.

Apparently David moved out last October, after telling Louise he felt like he just couldn't 'be himself' around her any more, and she's been on her own with the twins ever since. Then yesterday, at Monkey Music class, one of mums told Louise that she'd seen David and Sandra in IKEA at the weekend measuring up a pair of Björksnäs bedside tables.

'He wouldn't even look at a paint swatch with me,' sniffed Louise.

We all agreed that David is an utter bastard and that Sandra is welcome to him. I say 'all' – Louise didn't look 100 per cent convinced. Sierra offered to start going into the bakery regularly to complain about the number of chocolate chips in the muffins or to plant pubic hairs in the sausage rolls.

Friday 9 February

8 a.m.: made Flo delicious packed lunch – cheese and cucumber sandwiches, yogurt, apple and crisps.

4 p.m.: threw away cheese and cucumber sandwiches and yogurt. Returned slightly bruised apple to the fruit bowl, best side up. Cleared up crumbs from the toast Flo made as soon as she got in from school. Why is it a surprise to her that she comes home hungry?

5.58 p.m.: poured glass of wine, ready for 6 p.m. (Because standards.)

What is my life?

Saturday 10 February

Cleaned out my handbag. Found thirteen pens and an unidentified tooth. Cheerleader pom-poms arrived. Really couldn't visualise myself in a cheerleading outfit, even if it did help to combat race hate, etc, so hid them under the bed as a birthday present for Jess.

Monday 12 February

First day of half-term. I had a bit of a dilemma over what to do with work as Flo won't let me send her to holiday clubs any more, but I'm not entirely sure whether it's OK to leave her on her own all day? (Is there a *law*? It seems unclear.) In the end I'd decided not to risk it and booked the week off work and nursery. I feel exhausted at the thought of it.

I thought it might mean we got to all hang out together, but I couldn't get Flo out of bed until 3 p.m., so I may as well have taken Jess to nursery and gone to work.

Is this even normal? Who am I meant to ask?

Ate 921 calories of salted peanuts this evening. And I wonder why my size fourteen skinny jeans have started to make my legs look like a string of thick sausages.

Tuesday 13 February

I got cross with Ian tonight. I phoned him to chat about Flo as I was worried about her new habit of staying awake until the early hours and then just doing *nothing* when she's not at school. She hardly ever joins in with any of the things Jess and I are doing, and instead either just watches TV or is on her phone or, more usually, both. She does go round to Sasha's quite a bit, but I'm pretty sure that means she just does the same thing in a different location and with Sasha sitting there doing the same next to her.

I do try to jolly her along but she's almost as tall as me – I'm not sure how you're actually meant to make a fourteen-year-old *do* something they just don't want to do? How many times can you say 'How about going for a walk?' before they decide you're so annoying they want to run away and join a circus?

Ian was no use. He said she was fine when she was with him and that she was always up for going out as a family. That got my back up because 1) he only has them on Wednesday nights and every other weekend and it's easier to seem exciting when you're not the person nagging about homework every night and 2) he said 'as a family', meaning them and not me, and that made me feel left out and sulky, which I know is pathetic and I'm not proud.

It's difficult because I know he's an amazing dad, especially given Flo isn't even biologically his daughter, and I know he would probably have them more if I wanted him too, but no matter what happens, he is always going to be the fun option, isn't he? He's always going to be the parent who organises treats, not the one who has to try and make going to the dentist into an outing because it's free and fills up the time between school and tea.

I hung up just in time to catch Jess about to take a swig from my glass of rosé.

'But I want some juice!' she squawked.

'I'll get you some juice, but this is not juice for babies,' I told her, holding it above my head while she clawed at my legs.

'I'm not a baby!' she cried, looking very much like a baby in my opinion, although I sensibly didn't point this out to her. She lay on the floor for a bit, sobbing, looking at me every few seconds to check I was watching. I ignored her and googled some tips for the teenage sleep thing instead.

According to teen expert Dr Marjorie Monroe I need to keep my teen's sleep schedule the same on weekends and holidays. 'Establish a wake-up time on non-school days and enforce it,' advises Dr Marjorie. I laughed quite a bit at the thought of Dr Marjorie coming to our house to get Flo out of bed at 6.30 a.m. on a Sunday.

Sometimes Google *can* make you feel better.

Wednesday 14 February – Valentine's Day

Successful cocktail parties hosted – 1. Successful Tinder dates secured – 0, but surely now just a matter of time?

An excellent day today! As the girls were at Ian's I offered to host Valentine's Day for Lou and Sierra and make Bellinis. I messaged WIB with my idea when I woke up. Sierra sent back the cocktail glass emoji. Louise was less enthusiastic.

'What about the boys?' she wrote.

'Leave them with David and Sandra,' said Sierra. 'She can teach them how to make Eccles cakes or something.'

'But it's not his week?' said Louise.

'Fuck his week,' said Sierra. 'He ran off with the woman from the bakery. Make him swap weeks. Tell him you have an appointment with your therapist or something.'

I could see Louise typing, then stopping, then typing again.

'Fuck it,' she wrote eventually, 'you're right. Bloody Sandra. She can make them *all* chips.'

Jamie Oliver told me I needed to blend fresh white peaches for my Bellinis and mix them with sugar syrup before adding this to my prosecco but that seemed a bit labour intensive to me so I just cracked open a tin of Asda Basics peach slices in syrup. I added a bit of syrup to the bottom of each glass, topped up with prosecco and added a peach slice. Just call me Delia.

There was a small incident with the edge of the peach can, but the blood only got in my glass and the prosecco diluted it enough not to notice.

By the end of the second Bellini, Lou was getting a bit melancholy about the whole 'beauty-of-single-life thing' so I had the brilliant idea of setting Sierra and Louise up with Tinder profiles. According to the six-month-old *Grazia* I read at Micro Soft it isn't just twenty-somethings looking for one-night stands any more – people actually go on dates and have proper relationships. Although that was six months ago, so who knows. Louise was reluctant at first but after Bellini number three was slightly more open-minded. Sierra was unconvinced. She kept raging about the patriarchy and Facebook stealing her life, so I concentrated on Lou.

'I really don't think I'm ready for dating,' said Lou.

'You don't have to actually go on any dates,' I promised her. 'You're just having a look, seeing what's out there for when you *do* feel ready. It's a practice, that's all.'

'Aren't you going to do one?' asked Sierra.

I hadn't really thought about it, to be honest, although I guess I am now officially divorced. 'I'm not sure,' I said. 'It still hardly feels like any time at all since Ian left.'

'How long is it exactly?' said Lou.

'Well,' I said, thinking about it, 'we moved down here in 2016, in time for school in September. We had about six months then of trying to live the family-by-the-seaside dream, so I guess it's coming up to a year since we decided to call it quits for good?'

'Well, that's hardly *fresh*, is it?' said Sierra.

'I guess not,' I said, 'although he did stay living here for a while until we'd talked it all through properly and told the girls and he'd found somewhere decent to live.'

'If I'm doing a Tinder profile, then you definitely are too,' said Lou, knocking back her Bellini.

Turns out it is *very* easy to set up Tinder. No complicated questions about status or income or religious beliefs, just link it up and *boom*! It felt pretty exciting to be honest.

I drafted Lou a profile: 'Extremely bendy yoga enthusiast. Loves quinoa, walks on the beach and a well-chilled glass of prosecco. Hates cheating bastards who promise you the world and then run off with a woman called Sandra from the bakery.'

Lou said she'd probably work on it herself.

As we were having our first drunken bonding experience it felt like a good opportunity to tell them about the whole 'two kids, two dads' situation. I always feel like a bit of a traitor when I tell anyone that Ian isn't Flo's biological father, because I know in his eyes and in hers that he is her dad and that's it. Even though we didn't actually get together as a couple until she was seven, he's been in her life as my friend for, well, her whole life.

She certainly doesn't ever think of Cam as her dad. Not that I know of, anyway, although I wonder sometimes how much she thinks about it and doesn't tell me. It would be natural to be curious, I guess, even though he left when she was a baby. She was four years old the last time she saw him – not much older than Jess. I remember her hand, so small in mine, as we watched him get in his car and drive off.

I wanted to believe that he'd tried his best, that some people just can't cope with the responsibility of parenthood. I imagined him lying awake night after night, tormented by not being able to be the father and partner he so desperately wanted to be – but I think I was kidding myself. He never *looked* in torment. He looked tanned and carefree and like it hadn't even *occurred* to him that we might need him. He had this *spell* over me. It feels stupid saying it, but no matter how unreliable he was, how little he gave me, I always wanted him in my life.

At the time he didn't tell us that that final time he left would be for good. Part of me knew that it would be, and

I think part of Flo hoped it wouldn't. He broke both of our hearts. And then Ian fixed them.

We'd shared a house together, along with four other people, for our second and third years at uni in Bristol. He was the guy that all the girls wanted to be friends with. The guy who would make sure you got home safely at the end of the night, the guy whose shoulder you could cry on after you'd found out the boy you were seeing on the fine art course had cheated on you *again*. The guy that you could never imagine having sex with.

While Cam was in my life, Ian faded into the background a little bit. I think he could see what was happening and he didn't want to have to watch. He always answered the phone, though, when I called him, even if it was just to cry. When Cam finally left, Ian stayed back, but I couldn't have got through without him. Still, we were just friends, though.

No one was more surprised than him, or me, when we finally got together.

Ian had been working abroad for a while and had just moved back to London. Things with Cam were well and truly over, but I'd been so hurt by the whole experience and so focused on Flo that I was really only just coming out the other side. We met up for the first time in about a year, but it was as if it had only been a couple of days, as it so often is with the best type of friends.

Working abroad had caused a shift in him. He was confident and happy and suddenly I felt as though he might be just what I needed – something solid and secure, someone who I knew would never let me down. And he never has. Despite everything that has happened between us – growing apart, the separation – he's always been the good guy.

'Oh my God!' interrupted Lou. 'He sounds *amazing*! What does he do for work?'

'He *is* amazing!' I said. 'He's a management consultant. He started off working for other people and then he set up his own business with a friend. Mainly he sorts out failing businesses, fires people, that sort of thing. They do really well.'

'So why did you break up?' ask Sierra.

'I guess we just grew apart? He was always supportive and kind and lovely, but at some point he just went back to being that Ian from university no one could imagine sleeping with. I was restless and picking fights – I don't think I was much fun to live with – and he was growing his business and spending a lot of time working and travelling. And of course we were busy being parents – I think we both just lost that connection. Moving down here was a bit of a last-ditch attempt to see if we could rekindle things somewhere new, but it just made it really clear that we things were never going to be right, no matter where we lived.'

'That's so sad,' said Lou.

'It *is* sad,' I said, 'but separating was the right thing to do and we've tried to be as kind to each other as possible about it. It's all been pretty mature, really. I just miss being friends with him.'

Thursday 15 February

*Drafts of Tinder bio deleted – approx. 19. Jaffa Cakes
– 6. (Possibility of dating v. stressful.)*

Louise arrived at Busy Beavers wearing sunglasses today.

'God,' she said, coming to sit where Sierra and I had strategically positioned ourselves next to the biscuit table, 'what did you *do* to me last night? I feel awful!'

'Ah … yes,' I said, 'that might be my fault. I think when we ran out of the tinned peaches I started substituting with an old bottle of peach schnapps.'

Louise gagged a little bit.

'That might explain it. I had fun though, thank you. You were both right, I really needed that.'

We sat in silence for a little bit. That nice kind of silence that comes with having got over the initial hurdle of bonding with new friends over peach schnapps, and has become companionable and understanding.

'I'm still reeling for the whole "dark and handsome stranger in your past" story,' said Sierra. 'No offence, but when I first met you I had you down as more of the "long-term marriage with your childhood sweetheart" type. It's very glamorous of you.'

I laughed. 'There's nothing glamorous about wasting years of your life,' I said. 'Give me childhood sweetheart any day.'

'So has Cam not been in touch with Flo all this time?' asked Lou.

'No,' I said. 'No phone calls, no birthday cards – nothing. He hasn't ever given us any money, either. I did try to get him to pay something, but he wasn't often in steady work and then he moved abroad – he's not a man who likes to be pinned down.'

'That's so sad for Flo, though,' said Lou. 'How does she feel about him now?'

'I don't know if she even remembers him, really,' I said. 'She always calls Ian her dad. I was really worried actually about how our separation would affect her, given how Cam left, but she's been brilliant about it. She still goes with Jess to stay with him – I think it's really important to her to maintain that and to have him in her life.'

'Well, Cam sounds like a dick,' said Lou. 'Flo's lucky to have Ian in her life.'

'Talking of dicks,' said Sierra, 'did you finish your own Tinder profile after we left? Any hot dates lined up?'

'I haven't even got as far as washing the champagne flutes yet,' I said. 'Give me a chance.'

'Well, let's do it now,' said Louise.

So I explained how I wanted to write something that would make me seem interesting yet down to earth, intriguing yet honest. I wanted to imply that I was the kind of woman who has read a lot of classic literature and has possibly been to Asia, without actually committing myself to specifics.

'You should probably add a picture with some cleavage,' suggested Sierra. Louise looked horrified. 'Just to draw them in,' Sierra said. 'These are good boobs. No point wasting them.'

'I want people to like me for *me*,' I said, 'not the boobs.' I adjusted my bra a bit. They weren't actually looking bad today.

'I agree,' said Lou, 'it shouldn't be about how you look. It should be about your interests and experiences.'

'Yeah, but these are *men*,' said Sierra. 'They aren't scrolling through Tinder on the lookout for a woman with a keen interest in Thai food. Get the baps out, seal the deal.'

I looked from Sierra to Louise. Sometimes it really does feel like an unlikely friendship.

'What about the girls?' I asked.

'Flo is way too young for Tinder,' said Sierra.

'No! I mean do I mention them? I don't want to be all "Mum to two, love my kids, love my life" or anything, but I should at least acknowledge them, shouldn't I?'

'I don't know,' said Louise, looking over at Jess, who was crumbling a biscuit down the back of a small boy in a dinosaur T-shirt. 'They're lovely, of course ...' She winced a bit here, I'm sure. 'But maybe it's not something you need to say straight away?'

'Of course she has to say!' said Sierra. 'They're her flesh and blood, they *grew inside her*, that's pretty important, isn't it?'

'Perhaps I won't actually say "I grew two children *inside me*" in the bio,' I said, 'but I think Sierra is right: if it's going to put someone off, isn't it better that it puts them off right away rather than having them waste my time?'

We agreed that I'd mention them, but in a casual way, with the emphasis on other things.

'So what other things are you interested in?' asked Louise.

'Um…'

This was tricky. I couldn't exactly list prosecco and Jaffa Cakes as hobbies, could I? What *am* I interested in?

'I'm not sure,' I said, 'I don't have much time for other things, really.'

'Well, that's not exactly seductive, is it?' said Sierra. 'I feel you're going to need something a bit stronger than that. Unless you go with the boobs.'

'I like books?' I said, feeling a bit pathetic. 'But I haven't actually read a book for a while.'

'I can hear them swiping already!' said Sierra unhelpfully.

'All right, so not that,' I said. 'I like travelling?'

'Excellent!' said Louise. 'Travel always makes you sound cool. Where have you been? Do you have any pictures of you skiing or doing a skydive or anything exotic like that?'

'I went to Greece on my honeymoon?' I said hopefully. 'I've not really been anywhere much since. I like the *idea* of it, though.'

'Good God, woman,' said Sierra, 'you're not going to entice a man by talking about your honeymoon! Can't you just lie? Get some pictures off the internet of a woman snowboarding in goggles? No one will know.'

'I'm not sure that's the best foundation for an honest relationship,' I said. 'Look, leave it with me and I'll come up with something later and send it to you.'

'OK,' said Sierra, 'but given what you've just said you might want to seriously consider a cleavage shot. No offence.'

Is Sierra right? Am I boring? Quite possibly.

Friday 16 February

Tinder matches – 0. But still haven't written anything impressive in my bio. Glasses of wine needed to recover from soft play – 3 (reasonable).

Emergency end-of half-term trip to Micro Soft indoor play centre this afternoon. It was absolute carnage. All the parents were smiling to each other in tired, understanding ways. I gave half of my Twix to a woman who had fallen asleep holding a coffee and poured it on her skirt, and people were falling over themselves to share the Wi-Fi code. It was how I imagine it might have been living in London during the Blitz.

At one point Jess came out of the ball pit with another child's plaster stuck to the back of her skirt and eating a fizzy strawberry lace, which was suspicious as she had gone in with a mini box of raisins.

'Can I get a Slush Puppy?' she asked.

'No,' I said.

'OK!' she said, running off again. Sometimes I feel that she asks these things just to test me.

*

Ian picked the girls up for the weekend late afternoon. I had beans and cheese on toast for tea and did some Instagram stalking. @Simple_dorset_life seems to be doing much better with half-term than I am. She'd posted a picture of two small children standing at the shoreline and holding hands. They had their backs to the camera and were a long way away, so that they were just silhouettes against a sky that was turning pink around the edges.

'*My angels in the sunset,*' said the caption. '*My life until I met them was like a small boat, bobbing out at sea, carried wherever the wind took it. They are my rudder, my oars, my compass. Every day with them is a blessing. #windinmysails*'.

Swiped right *three times* on Tinder. No matches yet.

Going between Tinder and @simple_dorset_life's Instagram feed is like experiencing the very extremes of life in the space of two minutes.

Saturday 17 February

Second-hand leather sofas nearly purchased because of neat handwriting – 3. Rants about International Women's Day – 1 (out loud), 8 (in head).

I stopped for a look at the 'community wall' in Sainsbury's this afternoon. There is something very lovely about it. I imagine all the people writing out their little postcards, probably thinking for a good amount of time about exactly what to write and then using their best handwriting.

'Three-seater leather recliner, some minor wear and tear, £899 new. House move forces sale. Will take £200 ono. Buyer collects.'

There was a poster up for an International Women's Day event being held in the community hall, which seemed rather modern for them. Normally it's all Knit and Natter sessions and craft fairs full of bearded old men behind tables of badly carved wooden bowls. I do remember them once holding a meat bingo, but that must have been a bit too exotic because it never happened again.

The poster was printed on pink paper and had a clip-art flower border, which didn't feel like a promising start.

'Fun activities for women of all ages!' it promised. 'Come along and try your hand at watercolours, foot reading, and the intricate art of quilling!'

Quilling, so Google informs me, is 'an art form that involves the use of strips of paper that are rolled, shaped, and glued together to create decorative designs.'

I mean seriously, what the buggery? Where are the motivational women in business? Where are the discussions about women's representation in the media? Where is anything even vaguely aspirational or inspirational? Years of striving for equality of the sexes and we're meant to celebrate by looping a strip of paper into the shape of a flower? And foot reading? I don't even want to imagine the Knit and Natter group taking off their handmade woollen socks to compare fallen arches.

'Women of the world rejoice! Our day has come! I can see it in the curve of your big toe!'

Jesus.

No one was at home, of course, for me to complain to about it, so I had a smallish gin and watched reruns *of Sex and the City* to restore my sassiness levels. To be honest, I'm not sure that drinking cocktails in fetish bars in New York is really the way I want to go either, but between the two I felt as if I had achieved some balance in the day.

I WhatsApped a picture of the poster to WIB.

'Would you rather go to this or a New York fetish bar?' I asked.

'I'll fetch my whip,' replied Sierra.

(Question: what even *is* a meat bingo? Do people pull cuts of meat out of bucket and you win if they match the pork chop you were given on your way in?)

Sunday 18 February

Flo seemed a bit angsty when she got home this afternoon. I asked if she wanted to talk about anything but she said she had homework to do and went off upstairs looking a bit sorry for herself. It's back to school tomorrow and I think school is starting to ramp the pressure up a bit with GCSEs approaching. She'll be going into Year 10 in September and every parents' evening I go to is all about how vital it is that she do well at everything, and how important these exams are for her future.

It's tricky, because I don't want to undermine her teachers but, at the same time, I want her to know that, actually, GCSEs *aren't* really all that. I want her to feel that she has done her best, but as long as she gets what she needs to get to the next stage, does it really matter whether she gets a C or an A? Or a 7 or 8 or whatever it is they're changing into. The numbers make it all the more pointless as nobody will even know what they mean.

Seriously, how many job interviews do you go to as an adult where the interviewer says, 'Hmm … I'm not sure; we were really looking for someone with a better mark at GCSE geography …' *None*, that's how many.

I made sausages, mashed potato and baked beans for tea to cheer her up.

Monday 19 February – back to school

I went into Smiths at lunchtime and bought Flo some postcards in pastel colours for her revision notes. In my experience the amount of time spent browsing for stationery is directly proportional to exam success.

Jess had her first swimming lesson today.

I (foolishly) thought it might be a chance for me to have some peace and quiet for half an hour as the pool has a decent enough café, but as I wrestled Jess into her costume I noticed that all the other parents were heading poolside rather than in the direction of the coffee and flapjacks.

I wasn't sure quite what to do as I really didn't want to watch the class but also I didn't want to be *that* mum. Plus, what if you're legally obliged to be within sight or something? Flo learned to swim at school so I don't really know the rules. I imagined the headline in the *Dorset Echo* – 'local toddler drowns while mum eats all-butter flapjack' – and followed the other parents.

I know that I have lived a relatively privileged life, but the half an hour poolside was a new kind of hell. To be fair, I was traumatised to begin with as the last time I actually stood at the side of a pool was 'bikini-bottom gate'. I was very heavily pregnant with Jess and we'd gone on what was meant to be a relaxing CenterParcs holiday. It had actually been very relaxing up until that point, as Ian had basically done everything for me while I lounged about in the lodge with my feet up.

That morning, though, I'd decided it might be quite fun to go for a swim with Ian and Flo – the water does help you to feel like less of a heffalump. I'd come out of the changing rooms and on to the bit that slopes gently down to the water, which is meant to give you the impression that you're on a tropical beach. The noisy echoes of about a million small children shatter the illusion, but it's a nice thought. Flo was already in the pool and I was blowing up a giant rubber ring when I saw Ian come out and look around for me.

I waved.

He stopped and stared, his mouth open. He seemed to be pointing at my stomach. I looked down but literally all I could see was massive belly. I looked back and shrugged. He trotted over, in as much of a run as you're allowed to do in a CenterParcs swimming pool, still pointing.

It turns out I'd forgotten to put on the bikini bottoms.

I was hardly to blame was I? I was eight and a half months pregnant – my body, from what used to be my waist down, was a mystery at this point. Poolside at Jess's swimming lesson wasn't *that* uncomfortable, but it came close.

Imagine, for starters, being taken into a sauna fully dressed and the sweat immediately starting to collect under your boobs. Then take a group of excited three-year-olds and pass the sound through a machine that makes their voices bounce around as though they're in a vast underground cavern. Pipe this noise into the sauna.

Then try to pick out your own child in a pool full of similar-sized children, all splashing about wearing identical pink goggles and the same '*I'm really a mermaid*' swimming costumes. Shout at your child to watch the teacher, not you. Repeat every three minutes until you long for the sweet release of death.

Later, over tea – chicken nuggets, curly fries, tinned sweetcorn – I told Flo about the International Women's Day poster.

'So what are you going to do about it?' she asked.

'What do you mean, what am I going to do about it? What *can* I do?'

'I don't know,' she said, 'but you're always complaining about stuff like this and then just going about your life. No offence, Mum, but why not actually do something instead of just slagging it off?'

I quietly ate a chicken nugget.

'I'm not being funny,' said Flo. 'I just think you moan a bit sometimes about things you can actually change if you want to.'

Bloody kids, identifying your weaknesses and being brutally honest about them.

'Maybe I will, then,' I said, a tad sulkily.

'Yes! Do it, Mum!' said Flo.

'Yessss, Queeeeen!' said Jess through a mouthful of ketchup. Flo shot her a look. This is what happens when you turn a blind eye to your teenage daughter letting her little sister watch *RuPaul's Drag Race*.

Messaged WIB. 'Help!' I wrote. 'Have been bamboozled into putting on an inspirational event for International Women's Day. Any ideas?'

'Cake?' suggested Louise.

'Prosecco!' said Sierra.

I don't feel like we are exactly smashing stereotypes. I *do* like prosecco, though.

(Question: am I the only person on Tinder who automatically swipes left if someone has a lot of photos of them doing sports? It's not that I have anything against sports per se, it just feels like a lot of pressure and I can't help but feel I'd be a disappointment. I don't want a woodland hike sprung on me on a first date.)

Tuesday 20 February

Men on Tinder who look like they would rather be dead
– numerous. Cool ideas for IWD – 0. Jaffa Cakes – 7.

Angela suggested I host something for International Women's Day at the museum and ask the volunteers to get involved. I tried to picture Cecilia ushering visitors towards the tea table while Anne showed off her latest quilt. It's not that I don't think they are all extremely valuable and talented women in their own right, it's just not quite what I had in mind as an antidote to foot reading.

At that moment Cecilia knocked at the office door to tell us she wouldn't be able to come in and help with the guided tours at the weekend as she had an emergency chiropody appointment and Angela conceded the point.

I'm starting to get a little frustrated by Tinder. What is it with all the giant fish? Is it a code I don't understand?

Some of my favourite profile pictures so far:

- An out-of-focus bowl of linguine with mushrooms (?)
- A photo of a person in a hospital bed, covered in tubes. Not even a selfie as they are clearly unconscious, possibly in a coma
- A semi-shaved head, complete with foam
- A man holding a rifle (Because nothing says sexy like a lethal weapon)
- Selfie including a small open wound on one cheek. It doesn't feel like the wound is meant to be the focus, but there *is* an actual blood drip forming
- A man holding a meerkat next to his face. If you look closely the man has his tongue slightly out, almost touching the meerkat's nose

I screenshotted a few of my favourites to send to WIB. The group's favourite was definitely the open wound. 'Are you telling me you're not turned on by that?' asked Sierra. 'You must be dead inside.'

Louise is forty-five so she has her age bracket set higher than me. This means we have an extra pool of people to mock.

'I just can't get over how *old* everyone looks,' wrote Louise. 'It's not like I'm expecting Daniel Craig or anything, but it would be nice for someone just to look like they moisturised occasionally.'

She sent us a screenshot of a man called Ron, with his age blacked out. 'How old do you think this guy is?' she asked.

I looked at Ron. The picture was a close-up headshot which he had cleverly taken from below to emphasise his chins. He wasn't smiling, but not in a neutral, mysterious way – he genuinely looked *sad*. His skin was sallow. It sagged around his jaw but looked stretched taut over his cheekbones. The lines around his eyes were deep. More crow's thighs than crow's feet. He reminded me of the shots you see of prisoners on death row.

'Sixty-three?' I guessed.

'No way,' said Sierra. 'That guy has *seen* things. Sixty-seven, I reckon.'

Three dots appeared while Lou typed.

'He's forty-two,' she wrote.

Sierra sent back of row of six screamy faces.

'*I am going to be alone forever,*' wrote Lou. 'David is going to be shagging in the kitchen in the daytime while eating chips and I'm going to have to choose between dying alone or nursing Ron into old age.'

'Old*er* age,' wrote back Sierra.

Angela leaves work at the end of next week. I'm choosing not to think about it.

(Question: do crows *have* thighs?)

Wednesday 21 February

Minutes spent on perfect family fantasies – 30. Hula Hoops – 3 bags.

Back from work to an empty house and spent some time feeling lonely and imagining returning home in years to come to my own version of Ron, sitting on the sofa watching motor racing or something equally tedious, shouting into the kitchen to ask me what's for tea.

Ian sent me a video of Flo and Jess doing a hilarious dance routine that involved Flo standing like a scarecrow while Jess crawled backwards and forwards between her legs – I suspect Jess did the choreography. I wanted to talk to Ian about my imagined gloomy future with Ron, but the trouble with marrying the man who has been your best friend for nearly twenty years is that when you break up you can't turn to him for support. That person who has been your rock for all those years can't be your rock any more and it's pretty shit.

I poured a glass of wine, ate a bag of Hula Hoops and did some swiping on Tinder for non-Rons. Discounted eight men holding large fish, three taking topless selfies in a toilet mirror, and one whose profile picture was a pair of handcuffs on a table. So far I have four matches, but none of them have messaged me. Am I meant to wait or should I make the first move? What's the etiquette?

Pottered about in the girls' bedrooms for a bit, making the beds and arranging teddies. I didn't stay for too long in Flo's as, lately, I've started to feel like a bit of an intruder if I go in there without her. Not that I would poke around, just that it feels more like her own space, separate from me. I looked at the photos stuck on the wall above her desk – smiley selfies of her and Sasha on last year's school summer camp. Cast my eyes about a bit for empty vodka bottles but I don't think teenagers really *do* that nowadays. They're too busy Snapchatting.

Thursday 22 February

A new mum tried to make friends with me at Busy Beavers today but she was a bit on the glossy side for my liking. Ava, her two-year-old, had double fishtail plaits, which automatically put me on my guard. I once tried to do a fishtail plait for Jess after she'd watched a YouTube tutorial with Flo and decided she couldn't go on with life without one.

The video was called 'Easy, everyday fishtail braid' and was presented by a perky American woman – the kind of mum you just *know* would bake her own nut-free, gluten-free brownies for the summer fayre and judge you with her perfect white smile when you brought in a box of Asda mini flapjacks.

Suffice to say it was definitely *not* easy and if I had to do it every day I would have a serious drink problem.

As well as apparently being a pro-hairdresser, Riya, (even her name is glossy), is six months pregnant. 'It's so exhausting, isn't it?' she said, crouching seemingly effortlessly to offer Ava a cucumber stick, 'I can barely get to the gym any more!'

I don't feel like we are going to be *best* friends.

Genius idea from Flo for International Women's Day. Apparently there's a girl in her tutor group, Ellie, whose dad owns the bookshop on High Street. Ellie told Flo that they have a big room over the shop that her dad wants to use for events and meetings. Ellie is going to mention it to her dad and says I should go in and see him at the weekend.

A notification of a message on Tinder! It was from 'Ben, 39.' I opened it, eager to discover what witty opening lines Ben might have gone for.

'Hey,' it said.

FFS.

Saturday 24 February

IWD venue secured – 1. Awkward moments involving a copy of The Philosopher's Stone *– 1.*

Went in to see Ellie's dad in Chapter One today. I've not been in since we first moved to Barnmouth and it was a little more eccentric than I remembered it, to put it nicely. There were piles of crime novels propped up on the floor against the counter and the self-help section looked like it needed an intervention of its own.

Behind the counter a scruffy-looking man in his forties was peering over his glasses at a computer screen. His hair looked as if he had run his hands through it when he woke up and then forgotten about it.

'Are you Ellie's dad?' I asked. He jumped.

'Gosh! Sorry, yes, hello,' he said, knocking over a stack of *Harry Potters* on the counter as he reached over to shake my hand. 'I'm Dylan. You must be Flo's mum?'

'Frankie,' I said, picking a copy of *The Philosopher's Stone* up off the floor. 'Are you reorganising?' I asked, looking around at the chaos. 'It's a bit of a mess, isn't it?'

'Er, no,' he said. 'Well, not really. Since my wife died I've been struggling to keep on top of things as well as look after the kids, to be honest.'

Cheers, Flo, for the heads up on that one!

'Oh God,' I said, 'I'm so sorry, I didn't know. I didn't mean to be rude. Oh God. Shall I go?'

He laughed. 'Don't be silly,' he said, coming around from the behind the counter, 'it's OK, honestly. And you're right, it *is* a mess. I could do with taking on some more help, really, but I haven't quite got around to that, either.'

'Well, anyway, I *am* sorry,' I said. I was still holding the book and I went to pass it to him, but he must have thought I was going for some kind of sympathy hug, as he put his arm around me and trapped the book between us. He realised his mistake and backed off awkwardly. I did a sort of laugh/cough/hand gesture designed to say 'don't worry about it honestly'.

It was awful. I'd basically insulted his business, trivialised his dead wife and now I was embarrassing him in his own shop. Why am I such a goon? He said that he was about to close early as he had to pick up his kids from his parents – a likely story given hug-gate – but that Ellie had told him I was interested in using the upstairs room for International Women's Day and that he would absolutely love me to – and I could have it for free! Hooray!

I'm going to go back in next week and have a proper look at it. Now I just need to decide what to actually *do* in it.

Monday 26 February

Swimming lesson. Too dehydrated by poolside sauna experience to write.

Tuesday 27 February

Had a fundraising handover session with Angela this morning, going through all the different income streams for the museum and the fundraising applications she's currently working on. Some of the ongoing funding comes from the local and county council, some from gifts left in people's wills and some from entry donations and the gift shop. The rest has to be raised from grant-making trusts and organisations like the National Lottery. That's where I come in. I do really care about the museum and it does some interesting work, but it's just so much extra stuff to do on top of recruiting and managing the volunteers and managing the admin of the office. I'm just not sure how the trustees imagine I'm going to fit it all in.

I could see Steve smirking at me from his office, but I resisted the urge to get up and hit him with the Big Lottery Fund application, which I thought was very mature of me.

Absolute pain in the arse getting Jess to go to bed. It's almost as if she lies there, waiting to hear the fizz as I open the tonic water.

'Mummy!' she shouted downstairs as the ice clinked in my glass. 'I've got tummy ache!'

I didn't believe for a minute that she had a tummy ache, it's just what she says when she doesn't want to go to bed – a nice intangible ailment that I can't disprove. I'm always sympathetic when she really is ill, but night-time tummy ache is not one of those occasions.

'I expect you're just tired,' I shouted back up, 'a good sleep will help!'

In my experience most complaints can be fobbed off with 'I expect you're tired' or 'perhaps you're thirsty'. At the very least, making a child drink a glass of water buys you a good ten minutes. ('You have to sit nicely and wait for the water to work!')

'But I feel *sick*!' she shouted back. I went upstairs to tuck her in, moving about twenty-seven My Little Ponies from around her face. I'd feel sick if all of those crazy big horse eyes were staring at me as I slept. I'm sure when I was a child that My Little Ponies had normal-sized eyes.

I went to sit down and heard scampering feet on the stairs. A piece of toilet paper fluttered into the living room and Jess shouted, 'This is how I feel!' as she ran away again. I picked it up. It had a smudgy picture of a sad face on it, drawn in purple felt-tip pen.

I ignored it for a bit, scrolling through Instagram, trying to remember when I had started following all the people who post pictures of disgusting-looking plates of curry in semi-darkness. Realising she was not making progress, Jess moved on to gently groaning with pain, occasionally crying out, 'Ow!'

Under the guise of concerned parent, I went to investigate the source of her pain, and concluded that the only way to treat it was for her to take some medicine. I rummaged in the medicine box (old Roses tin) and found some kids' liquid fish oil – suitably disgusting – and expressed my regret that yes, she would have to drink a whole spoonful.

She had a sniff and decided that probably she felt a little bit better after all; if I would just pass her Rainbow Dash she would go to sleep now thank you.

Eight matches so far on Tinder, but no more messages. I don't get it – why are these men on a dating app if they don't actually want to go on a date? Perhaps it's me. Perhaps they match with me and then take a better look and change their minds.

Thursday 1 March

Number of World Book Day costumes created in a panic the night before – 0. Score! Celebratory glasses of wine at bedtime – 2.

The universe looked down on me today and decided that I needed a break. 'That Frankie does her best,' it said to herself, 'let's cut her some slack. Let's make World Book Day fall on a Thursday so she doesn't have to create a Gruffalo costume from scratch for Jess to wear to nursery.'

While I was waiting for Ian to drop off Jess I counted fourteen teenage girls walk past the house in school uniform and curly hair, carrying wands.

Had a slight panic at Busy Beavers as it's only one week to go until International Women's Day and I haven't exactly *planned* anything. Louise reluctantly volunteered the fact that she has quite a lot of photographs at home that she's taken over the years if we wanted to set up an exhibition. She's a dark horse, that one. I told her I was going over to the bookshop on Saturday and she said that David was having the boys so she would bring some photos and help me set up.

Another woman, who was sitting on the floor near us building a castle out of wooden blocks, chipped in and said that she co-owned a marketing company and would love to come and do a session on social media and branding for freelancers. Her friend turned out to be a local cheese producer and volunteered to speak about setting up and running a food-based business *and* provide cheese. Other mums started coming over and getting involved in the discussion and by the end of Busy Beavers I had a female blacksmith, an ex-Olympic sailor, a pension expert, and a performance poet. And cheese!

I almost don't care about the day itself; I felt empowered just being there and being part of *that*. All of these women, scrabbling about on the floor, picking up discarded raisins and settling squabbles over who gets to hold the maracas, and behind it there's this throb of creativity and dynamism. It was pretty ace.

Back at home I set about making some posters in Word. Flo looked over my shoulder and physically shuddered.

'Let me do it, Mum,' she said, taking the laptop. 'No offence, but that looks terrible.'

'I spent ages on that,' I protested.

'It's fine,' she said, 'you're old, you can't be expected to know about design.' I must have looked a bit sad because she laughed and got up to hug me. 'I'm really proud of you for doing this,' she said. 'It's going to be brilliant.'

I lay awake for quite a long time, thinking about work. All of the women at playgroup today were so inspiring, doing things they love without being afraid. Or maybe doing them *despite* being afraid. I want Flo and Jess to see me doing that too, to be proud of me every day.

Saturday 3 March

Moments where I thought I might have to burn down the bookshop and start again – 1 (significant). Moments when I gazed at my children with love and admiration – many (#blessed).

All three of us went around town this morning, giving out Flo's posters to the local shops. Grape and Grain, the independent wine shop, loved the idea so much they offered to give us half a dozen bottles of prosecco if we display their banner and give out a few leaflets, so now we have prosecco *and* cheese. Basically, my dream event.

Then we went down to Chapter One to tell Dylan the plan for the day and to have a look at the room. On reflection I should probably have done this *before* making all the other arrangements, because it wasn't quite what I had pictured. In my mind it was a light, airy space with high ceilings and tall windows looking out over the sea.

I imagined it full of vibrant women, chatting about their ambitions, sipping prosecco and nibbling a bit of Dorset Blue Vinny on an artisan cracker.

The reality was a stuffy, cobwebby room full of boxes and old display boards. There were windows, but it was hard to tell whether or not you could see the sea because so much junk was piled up in front of them.

Dylan stood behind us on the stairs. 'It might need a little bit of sprucing up,' he said sheepishly. Sprucing up? Fuck me. It needed something. Burning down, maybe? I felt my heart sink. How were we going to cover the walls with art when we couldn't even *see* the walls? How were we going to fit in a display about modern blacksmithery? More importantly, where were we going to have the prosecco?

'It's perfect!' said Flo, making me love her more than ever. 'We'll get this tidied up in no time, won't we, Jess?' Jess looked doubtful.

'There's a second room through here,' explained Dylan, manoeuvring himself around a rather intimidating life-size Noddy cut-out and opening a door, 'so all of this can go in here. I don't use it for anything else.'

I peered inside cautiously. It was just as untidy, but there was plenty of space. Perhaps we really could rescue things.

'Honestly, just do whatever you want up here,' he said. 'I'm not precious about any of it. I'll be downstairs if you need me.' He left, leaving the three of us looking at each other. Flo laughed.

'Your face!' she said. 'I thought you were going to cry!' I wasn't sure why that would have been funny. 'Mum, it's going to be fine. We'll just shove all the stuff in the other room and honestly, we can make it look amazing! Jess, you get anything small enough for you to carry and bring it in here – this is going to be fun!'

Three hours later and I couldn't believe what we had achieved between us. All of the boxes and rubbish had been moved out, revealing a beautiful wooden floor and the tall windows of my imagination. Jess had 'swept up', (pushed things around with the broom) – and Flo had found some folding tables and set them up around the edges of the room. The afternoon sun streamed in, making the dust in the air sparkle.

'Helloooo?' shouted a voice from the stairs, just as we were admiring our handiwork. 'Are you up there?'

'In here!' I called back and in came Lou carrying a stack of framed photos. 'What a gorgeous room,' she said, 'and a picture rail, too. Perfect. I've got loads more in the car if you want to give me a hand?'

She propped her armful of photos against the wall and we all went down to help unload.

An hour later and we were just finishing hanging the pictures when Dylan appeared. He was carrying a bottle of prosecco, a bottle of lemonade and a little stack of paper cups.

'I don't know if you drink normally,' he said (ha!), 'but I took the liberty of getting a little something by way of a thank you for tidying up.'

'Dylan,' said Lou, 'you're our hero! Come in and get that prosecco open.'

He set the paper cups out on one of the trestle tables and ceremonially popped the cork. Prosecco oozed into the cups. He poured lemonades for Flo and Jess and we all stood in a circle, cups raised.

'I would like to thank you,' I said to Dylan, 'for letting us invade your bookshop, even though I royally made a fool of myself when I first came to meet you.'

'You were right, though,' he said, 'the place *was* a shambles, *is* a shambles, apart from up here now. I needed someone to give me a bit of a kick up the backside. Caitlin would be so cross with me if she could see how I've let things go.'

His eyes shimmered and he looked off into the distance for a few seconds. I wondered if we were going to have a moment where I'd be forced to be all caring and sympathetic – sympathy doesn't come naturally to me – but he took a deep breath and turned his attention back to the circle.

'I'm so pleased you came in and I'm thrilled to be hosting your event next week. You guys have been just what I needed.' He looked down at Jess and she smiled up at him sweetly.

'Can we take some books home?' she asked.

'Jess!' I said.

'Well, you have too many, really,' Jess went on, 'especially in that room.' She pointed towards the door where we'd stacked Dylan's boxes, sloshing lemonade on the floor as she did.

'You can definitely take a book home,' said Dylan, 'as a thank you for all your hard work.' Jess beamed. 'Maybe finish your lemonade first, though?'

(Question: is blacksmithery a word? It sounds *weird*.)

Monday 5 March

Excuses made to self for not looking at fundraising spreadsheet – 8 (bad), Tinder messages sent – 8 (good).

First day at work without Angela. Opened the funding application spreadsheet. Closed it again. I don't need to be on top of it on the first day, surely? I need to ease myself in. Steve must have sensed my anxiety because he's put a meeting in the diary for next Monday for us to meet with the chair of trustees to get an update on all live and pending applications.

Swimming after work. I gave out leaflets for Thursday's event to all the mums and the pool agreed to put up a poster and leave a little pile of leaflets on the reception desk. Between shouts at Jess to pay attention, stalked @simple_dorset_life. She had been making falafel burgers. The picture looked amazing.

'*Why would anyone want fast food when you could have these beauties?*' read the caption. '*They're so simple to make too – just blend a can of chickpeas, an onion, garlic, coriander, cumin and a big spoonful of flour. Tiny hands can enjoy pressing the mixture into burger shapes – everyone finds food more delicious when they've had a hand in the preparation. #familylife #simplepleasures*'.

This is *such* a lie. I find food way more exciting if someone else has made it while I've been watching *Tipping Point* and drinking a glass of wine. Which never happens, obviously, apart from that time when I failed to notice the banging coming from the kitchen and Jess presented me with a 'sandwich' she had made using a saucepan, a bag of Quavers and an entire block of cheese.

After a glass of wine or two this evening I decided to take the bull by the horns (probably should be the giant fish by the fin on Tinder) and message some of my matches. Googled 'what to say in a first Tinder message' but most of them were for men, which backed up my theory that I really should be waiting for them to make the first move. Sod it, though: International Women's Day around the corner and all that.

Apparently I need to reference some detail in their profile, so it's clear I've actually read their bio and looked at their pictures and am not just sending out loads of copies of messages. Well sure, that would be fine if everyone wrote something vaguely interesting in their profiles, and not just stuff like, 'My friends would describe me as easy-going and a good listener.'

Well, of course they would, they're your friends, aren't they? They're not exactly going to say 'he's a total dick, I don't know why I even hang out with him'.

'Looking to find someone I can have a real connection with, someone to join me on the adventure of life.'

God. It's hard *not* to sound like a dick when referring to life as an adventure, isn't it? Still, I did my best and sent a personal, thoughtful but short message to each of my eight matches.

10.30 p.m.: no replies. Everyone hates me. Destined to die alone without even Ron for company.

Tuesday 6 March

We had a volunteers' meeting at work this morning. I gave everyone leaflets for Thursday and they all promised to spread the word. Ditto all the unsuspecting mums at gym class this afternoon.

I had a reply on Tinder! It was from 'Danny', if that *is* his real name. I've heard you can't be too careful. His profile read as follows:

Tall, glasses, books, coffee, vegetarian, able to count to twenty if I take my shoes off. Likes cats, libraries, eating two dinners, South Park, *reading, comedy.*

I let him off the *South Park* bit as he is a man. Eating two dinners I felt I could get on board with. Comedy – bit lame as a 'like'? I mean, who *doesn't* like comedy? Who would say, 'Oh yeah, I really hate being entertained with funny stories that make me laugh, it's my *worst thing*.' Still, compared to one guy I quickly swiped left for yesterday, his bio was basically Shakespeare.

'Love boobs and ass hourglass figure,' said Leroy, posing in the front seat of his car. 'Be warned, I've got a hang cock so preferably no virgin.'

Consider me warned, Leroy.

What really intrigues me about Leroy is whether or not he gets any women actually match with him? Am I just being old and naive? Are there hordes of women out there, swiping and swiping, fingers crossed for a penis the size of Leroy's?

(I just tried it and you *can* swipe and cross your fingers at the same time. Also, I'm assuming a 'hang cock' means 'well endowed'? Too scared to google it).

Perhaps there *are* women interested in Leroy getting his huge dick out for them in the back of his pimped Subaru, but I can't think of anything worse. Anyway, Danny didn't hint at penile dimensions on his profile, so I was forced to judge him based on character, interests, face, etc. You know, the old-fashioned way.

'So what would your two favourite dinners *be*?' I asked him. The two dinners thing had really stuck with me.

'Oh, that's easy,' he replied, 'Coco Pops and double bacon cheeseburgers. How about you?'

A man of sophisticated taste, clearly, but I was eating Aldi's own-brand onion rings and drinking wine out of a Cadbury Mini Eggs mug so I was hardly in a position to judge. Obviously, I didn't want to let on about the wine mug though at this delicate stage.

'I'm a bit of a sucker for a roast dinner,' I replied, implying down-to-earth and hearty, 'but I do like a good fish curry.' The fish curry was to hint at an experimental nature. Like I might spontaneously have a group of friends over for dinner and cook a big curry and serve fancy beer in bottles with wedges of lime. (Note: I have *never* done that, although I like the idea of it. If the house was tidier and I wasn't perpetually exhausted. Oh, and if I had a big group of friends.)

'Fish curry, eh?' said Danny, clearly impressed by my cosmopolitan tendencies. 'That's a very left-field choice!'

'I'm a very left-field woman,' I said, taking a swig of mug wine. This was my attempt at sounding seductive. Not sure how it came across.

We chatted for a bit and he seemed pretty normal, so you never know.

I have moved all fundraising emails to a folder marked 'fundraising', so excellent progress.

Wednesday 7 March

Bottles of prosecco set up at Chapter One ready for tomorrow – 8. Glasses of prosecco I wish I could drink to calm nerves – also 8.

I went around to Grape and Grain after work to pick up the prosecco. The woman there said she was going to come along in the afternoon too as she was really interested in finding out more about using social media to promote her business.

I took the prosecco over to the bookshop and Dylan helped me carry it upstairs and offered me a cup of tea. He looked as if he could do with someone to talk to, so I said yes. We sat in the two old armchairs he keeps in the A–L fiction section and he told me about his wife, Caitlin, and his daughters, Ellie, Sophie and Bonnie. Caitlin died a year ago and, although his parents moved down to Barnmouth to help with the practical side of things, he told me that he's found it hard to know what to do with the grief.

'My mum and dad have been amazing,' he said. 'They only retired a couple of years ago, but they've given up everything to move here and help with the girls. The trouble is that they think everything can be solved with a cup of tea, a casserole and a bit of hard work. They're a different generation, I guess, made of tougher stuff than me. My dad especially. I feel like I'm failing because I can't just oil the lawnmower or give the car a service and get over it.'

'You're definitely not failing,' I said. 'You've done an amazing job holding together a family and running your own business. I expect it's just that they don't know what to say. Maybe they even feel that they've failed *you* for not being able to make it all OK. Generally, that's how parents feel, isn't it?'

He looked thoughtful.

'I'd not thought about it like that,' he admitted, 'but you could be right. I know, if it was me and something like this happened to one of the girls, I'd just want to be able to take the pain away. But I don't suppose you can. Perhaps making a casserole is the next best thing?'

We sat for a bit and drank our tea and I stole glances around the bookshop. It *is* a mess, but it's quite a beautiful mess, full of promising-looking nooks and crannies. The floor is wooden boards and the bookcases are wooden too, stretching from floor to ceiling. There's a comforting smell – old books and warm dust. I noticed that, despite the chaos, I felt relaxed. My shoulders seem to drop a fraction each time I visit.

'You know, you could turn this place into something really special,' I said. 'I'm not one for "vibes" generally, but there is a lovely feeling in here. It's very welcoming.'

Dylan smiled. 'Caitlin always used to say that,' he said. 'Her mum and dad owned the shop from when she was really small – we inherited it – and she used to say she felt as though the books were alive, as if they were filling the shop with an energy. She'd tell people that if you could be still and quiet enough you wouldn't even need to worry about choosing a book, that a book would choose you. It sounds stupid, I know.'

'It doesn't sound stupid at all,' I said. 'It's lovely. And I think she was right. It's like the books are excited, just waiting for the right person to pick them up and read them.' We sat for a bit longer. 'How did she die?' I said quietly. 'If you don't mind me asking?'

'She was in a car accident,' he said, looking at his hands. 'A drunk driver ploughed into her when she was driving back from visiting a friend in hospital and she died before they could get her back there. The irony is not lost on me,' he added.

'Oh God, Dylan,' I said, 'I'm so sorry. That's awful.'

He stood up then. 'I'd better get home and make sure the girls are OK,' he said. 'My mum's there, with a casserole obviously, but I don't like not being around in the evenings.'

'Of course,' I said. 'Get back to your family. I'll see you bright and early for a day of female empowerment. And don't be so hard on yourself,' I added. 'You're doing your best. It's all we can do.'

*

Message from Danny when I got home asking, 'What are the three best animals?'

Not *my* favourite animals, the three *actual* best. OK, so he's a bit weird, but I quite like that. I said cats, seals and penguins, which he agreed were solid choices.

Thursday 8 March – International Women's Day

It's 10 p.m., the girls are in bed and I'm drinking a glass of leftover prosecco. I know it was a bit of a last-minute thing, and I was never expecting hundreds of people or anything, but I'm so chuffed with how everything went today.

The blacksmith from Busy Beavers had to pull out at the last minute because her daughter was throwing up and her husband was away on a business trip, but everyone else who had promised to be there was.

The ex-Olympic sailor was incredible. She spoke about balancing a sporting career with having a family and about how her husband had gone freelance so as to be able to take the lead with the children. She was so inspiring – it made me feel a bit ashamed about all the excuses I make for driving to Tesco Express when it's only a fifteen-minute walk away.

I embarrassed myself by volunteering to be a case study for the pension advisor, Ruth, and having to confess that in every job up until now I'd either not had the choice or had opted out of paying into a pension. I said I'd always thought it was something for old people, which was a nice springboard for Ruth to launch into a lecture about cumulative interest.

The social media talk went down really well. The woman doing the talk, Sam, was delighted because the owner of Grape and Grain now wants to employ her to manage their Instagram channel. I overheard Sam tell her that, ideally, she needed a professional photographer to take a bank of images for them, and perhaps have someone create some cocktail recipes, so I casually piped up that they should have a look at the photos we had on display as they were by a local professional. I'm sure Lou wouldn't mind me calling her that – I know she never would herself but her photos are *amazing*.

The cheese went down a storm, too. Who doesn't love a bit of free cheese?

My very favourite bit of the day, though, was when we were packing up. Everyone had left, Dylan was downstairs in the shop, and Jess was 'organising' leftover business cards in and out of my purse. Flo and I had one end each of a trestle table and she looked at me along the table's length.

'I'm really proud of you, Mum,' she said. 'You do a really good job of things, you know.'

I was so touched that I went to put my hands over my mouth, forgetting I was holding the end of the table, and dropped it on my feet.

(Note: corner Ruth at Busy Beavers and ask for some pension advice. Don't want to end up one of those old woman who can't afford to have the heating on and keeps empty food packets in the cupboard to fool visitors into thinking she can afford to eat.)

Friday 9 March

Emergency Jaffa Cakes eaten from office drawer when no one was looking – 3. Envelopes overestimated – 17. Number of times questioned self about talking to a man who would make me guess the number of envelopes in a tray – best not to think about it.

I was forced to take stock of the fundraising situation ahead of Monday's meeting. Angela had told me that we have five big funding applications 'in progress', which I had naively taken to mean that we were waiting on a decision or perhaps just needed to add in a few key bits of information before sending off.

Oh, how wrong I was!

It turns out that 'in progress' basically means that Angela had downloaded application forms from various websites, filled in name and address details, saved them in a folder marked 'in progress' and added them to the spreadsheet. She might as well have just emailed me a gif of Beyoncé tossing her head back and laughing at me.

Danny sent me a picture of a wire tray full of envelopes at lunchtime and asked me to guess how many there were. I was tempted to zoom in and try to actually count, because I *do* like to be right about things like this, but then I realised that would make me as odd as he clearly is, so I just guessed 127. There were apparently 110, which he told me made me the best guess all day.

How many other people is he making guess the number of envelopes in a tray? Also, secretly very pleased to have the best guess. We have agreed to meet in person – based on more chat, not just the envelope quiz.

Messaged WIB details of upcoming date. They were very excited, until I mentioned the envelope thing and the two dinners.

'He sounds like a nutter,' said Sierra.

'Also, Coco Pops are really high in sugar,' added Lou. 'He doesn't scream "mature man of the world" to me.'

I sent them a picture of my wine mug and the onion rings.

'But that's OK,' said Lou, 'because that's in secret on your own. You wouldn't say it to someone to seduce them, would you? If the Coco Pops are the thing you felt you could say out loud, then you have to wonder what he does in secret that he chooses *not* to mention.'

She may have a point, but also he is the only person to reply, so I need to start somewhere.

Monday 12 March

Minutes spent sweating poolside – big fat 0. Swimming cookies eaten after Jess had gone to bed – 2 (not bad).

Fundraising meeting didn't go too badly, all things considered. Basically, I completely passed the buck, explaining how I was misled into thinking that things were much further ahead than they actually were, and that I was going to need quite a bit more time for the research stage. The Chair was very understanding, which annoyed Steve no end. Just have to hope not to ever bump into Angela again.

I staged a personal intervention at swimming today. I told Jess that I wasn't going to be watching because the teacher had said that she needed to concentrate on her swimming, not on waving at me.

'But I really want you to watch,' she said, looking a bit sad.

'I really wish I could watch too, baby,' I said, lying, 'but I'm going to have to sit in the café instead. I will be there to meet you when you come out and the good thing is that I'll be able to buy you a snack!'

She thought it over.

'Can I have a cookie with chocolate in?' she asked.

'Definitely,' I said.

She looked pleased with this arrangement and scampered off towards the teacher. I turned to leave. 'Are you not watching?' asked one of the other mums.

'No, I'm going to the café,' I said. 'I'd really love to carry on watching every week but honestly, I just hate it.'

The absolute genius of the whole thing is that I'd seen her eyeing the giant, overpriced cookies last week – £1.29 each – so I'd bought a packet of *five* similar ones from Aldi for 89p and I had one in my bag ready. Not only had I saved 40p but I also had *four* cookies at home.

Every penny counts, especially with the cost of the swimming lessons.

Tuesday 13 March

I think I might quit toddler gymnastics. I enjoy hanging out with Sierra and Lou, but it seems a bit pointless paying £2.50 to do that when I could just invite them to my house and spend the £2.50 on a job lot of chocolate digestives. Also slightly jealous that Jess has a more active social life than I do.

I don't think Jess has learned anything at all – she's too busy chatting and jumping up and down and running over to check I'm watching. If anything, her basic coordination skills have got worse – last week she fell off the sofa and she hadn't even been *moving*, she'd just been sitting there watching the *Octonauts*. She told me she was busy with Captain Barnacle and 'forgot to stay sitting up'.

I FaceTimed Mum and Dad to tell them about International Women's Day. I hadn't spoken to them in a while, but talking to Dylan about Caitlin had made me think a bit. I've always just assumed they will always be there, but they aren't young any more. One day they *won't* be there, and I'm not sure how I will cope with that.

Mum told me about the new walking group they've joined. It's all expats living in the same area and they go out once a week with their dogs. Where they live in France has quite a strong English contingent. I sometimes wonder why they bothered moving all that way, really. Dad seemed distracted. I could see him nudging Mum and whispering behind his hand.

'Mum, Dad,' I said, 'you remember it's a video? I can see you whispering!' They laughed.

'I know,' said Mum, 'just ignore your dad, he wants me to ask you money questions.'

'What kind of money questions?'

'Nothing sinister,' said Mum, 'just to check you're managing really, and that you don't need any help.'

'I'm managing fine,' I reassured them. 'That's the benefit of swapping a house in London for one in Dorset, isn't it? The mortgage is really small – Ian's maintenance covers that – and he's in no hurry for us to think about selling while the girls are around.'

'But what about all those bills on your own?' said Dad. 'Are you sure we can't help you out?'

'It's all good, Dad,' I said. 'Ian and I split Jess's nursery costs that aren't covered by vouchers and my wages from the museum cover bills and food and stuff. We aren't going off on cruises every month or anything, but we manage. You mustn't worry about us.'

Mum laughed. 'Easier said than done as a mum!' she said.

I knew what she meant.

Wednesday 14 March

Chinese buffet dates secured – 1. (Excellent work.)

Feeling empowered by the success of International Women's Day, I have decided to take control of my menstrual cycle. I'm sick of having a day every month where I inexplicably want to stab everyone I see in the face with a fork, only to start my period the next day and go 'Ohhh! *That* was it, then.'

It's ridiculous for a grown-up woman to be taken by surprise every single month, like it hasn't happened hundreds of times already. On Louise's recommendation I have downloaded a period-tracking app that tells you every day how you may be feeling, based on your hormone levels. Obviously, I can't use it properly yet as I can't remember when my last period started to be able to set it up.

Message from Danny about our date venue. He suggested the all-you-can-eat Chinese buffet on King Street. It didn't scream romance to me, but I think we've established that he's not exactly run-of-the-mill.

'Be warned,' he said, 'I can eat a *lot*.'

Sexy times.

Saturday 17 March

Number of meals eaten just before meeting date for dinner – 0. As I am a normal person! *Thoughts about dying alone – many.*

Date Day!

Message from Danny at 9.45 a.m. 'Good morning,' he wrote, followed by a pineapple emoji. Brushed over that in my head. 'Do you still want to go out for food this evening?'

'Yes,' I replied. 'I'm excited to see how much you can eat. What time do you want to meet?'

'I finish work at 4.30, so any time after that?' A pause. 'Oh, hang on; I checked and the Chinese place doesn't open until 5.30.'

Christ, who goes out for dinner at 5.30?

'Are you planning an early start to fit in more spring rolls?' I asked. 'I have some things to do during the day, but I'll be done by about 6.30? How about we meet at the Boat and Anchor for a drink and go from there?'

'OK,' he replied, 'I'll see you at the Boat and Anchor at 6.30.'

Not exactly what I'd said, but still, it was a lie about having things to do (other than shave my legs, try on everything in my wardrobe etc.), so it didn't matter too much.

At 6.25 I was sitting in the car watching the door of the pub.

At 6.27 a young-looking man in shorts and a backpack arrived and stood outside. That made things a bit awkward for me as I'd assumed he'd go on in and I'd be able to get out of the car and adjust myself away from his gaze. From where he stood he'd be able to see me and know that I'd been sitting there watching. I'd have to get out immediately to make it look like I'd pulled up just before he arrived.

I pulled down the visor to check my lipstick quickly, grimaced a bit, and flipped it back up.

Can I say here, for the record, that I think that bit where you and a first date have seen each other, but you're not close enough to speak, is possibly one of the most awkward dating moments that exists? You're aware that you're watching each other, so you have to walk in a sassy yet casual way. Do you wave? Do you smile in acknowledgement? It's awful.

Fortunately, it's over quickly.

'Hello,' I said, when I was close enough for him to hear me. 'Have you been here long?' I asked, just to make the point that I hadn't been watching.

'Nope,' he said, 'I just arrived. Nice to meet you. Shall we get a drink, then?'

'I hope you're hungry,' I said, as we made our way to the bar. 'I feel you've made some pretty grand claims.'

'Oh no, don't worry,' he said, 'I'm not going to go mad. I've already eaten.'

Wait … what?

'You've already eaten?' I said, worried that I'd got the wrong end of the stick and perhaps we were just going to an all-you-can-eat Chinese buffet to check out the soft furnishings.

'Yeah, I had a McDonald's on the way,' he said, 'just to tide me over.'

'A McDonald's?' I said, baffled. 'What did you have?' As though *that* was really the question here.

'Just a double cheeseburger and fries,' he said.

Oh, right. Well, that's OK, then. *Just* a double cheeseburger and fries. That's fine.

By this point we were at the bar and doing the whole awkward ordering of drinks thing, so I didn't have time to think about the burger situation. We chatted for a bit about work, Barnmouth, films – all the dull things you talk about when you don't know someone but have to make sure there is never a silence.

When we arrived at the all-you-can-eat Chinese we were directed up to the tills where, apparently, you have to pay *before* you start eating. Not exactly romantic, but I guess at least it gets the whole 'who's going to pay for dinner' question out of the way. Over drinks he'd already said he preferred to watch illegally downloaded videos than spend money at the cinema – sexy – and that he didn't earn enough money to go out much, so I felt obliged to pay for myself.

Over satay chicken he told me all about his living situation. He'd moved to a new house a couple of years ago with his wife, who had since decided that being his wife wasn't really one of her long-term goals. They'd carried on living together while he saved a deposit for a place of his own, and in the meantime she'd moved in a new partner.

'Is this a prawn?' he asked, picking up a prawn.

'Yes,' I said, 'are you not a fan?'

'I'll give it a go,' he said, looking sceptical. He took a nibble. 'It's not too bad, but I don't think I'll have another one.'

Over crispy shredded beef he told me how, for most of his twenties, he'd mainly eaten cheese sandwiches as he was a bit fussy when it came to food. This put me off more than the whole 'living with ex-wife and new partner' situation, to be honest. I already have one child who won't eat vegetables and another who doesn't like different foods to touch on the plate, so I really didn't fancy having to prepare separate rounds of cheese sandwiches at every meal.

'I'm not that keen on this duck,' he said, poking about at a little mound of dry-looking shredded meat.

'I think you're meant to have it in a pancake with cucumber and sauce?' I said. 'I expect it would taste better then.'

'Oh, right,' he said. 'Like a crepe?'

'No, not really like a crepe.'

'Oh.'

I wonder what the thought process was for him when he signed up for Tinder? 'You know what, I'm living with my ex-wife still, I have no money and I don't know how to eat like a grown-up – this feels like I'm in the right place to start thinking about dating!'

Tuesday 20 March

Message from Danny tonight: 'Can you please name me the oldest cartoon you remember from your childhood?'

The 'most old'? I waited a while to reply because I was in the middle of an episode of *Millionaire Matchmaker* and I don't feel like Patti Stanger would be into replying straight away to WhatsApp messages from men who eat takeaway *on the way* to a dinner.

'*Pigeon Street*?' I wrote eventually. '*Thundercats*? *Fingermouse*?'

'*Pigeon Street* sounds fantastic' he replied. 'Also, I think it's pronounced *Dangermouse*.'

'There was also a creepy programme I watched called *Tottie*,' I said, 'which I googled recently and apparently it showed the first-ever murder on a kids' programme.'

'Hardcore,' he said. 'Like *The Wire* of its time.' Five minutes passed and he messaged again.

'I'm watching *Care Bears*,' he wrote. 'They are amazing.' A pause. 'They shoot love out of their chests.' Another pause. 'Ahead of their time.'

I pictured Patti the Millionaire Matchmaker's face and decided not to reply. I screenshotted the conversation to WIB though, obviously.

'WTF?' said Sierra. 'How old is he? Seven?'

'He's thirty,' I said, 'but he did get a bit squeamish over a prawn at the Chinese buffet. He mainly likes cheese sandwiches.'

'He sounds like he's perhaps not quite at the same life stage as you?' suggested Lou tactfully.

'Fox would get on well with him,' said Sierra. 'He loves all of the beige foods.'

What is it with kids and beige foods? Bread, cheese, pasta, potatoes – they can't get enough of them. You'd think that, instinctively, they'd be drawn to colourful things, wouldn't you? Primary colours and all that. Lego don't make all their bricks beige. But maybe that's because they know that kids would just eat them.

Thursday 22 March

Overheard Cassie and Yvonne at Busy Beavers talking about tutors. For a while I wondered if Cassie was thinking of learning a language, or perhaps Yvonne was retaking a maths GCSE (wouldn't surprise me), but it turns out they were talking about tutors for their three-year-old children.

Cassie said, 'You really cannot begin too early if you want give them the very best start. We're keen that Aubyn gets to grips with phonics as soon as possible.'

Just fuck off, Cassie. They're basically babies.

Friday 22 March

Stomped about all day feeling angry over nothing in particular.

Child-free weekend again as Jess wanted to be at home next weekend instead, so that the Easter bunny wouldn't get confused. She was *very* anxious about missing out on the Mini Eggs. She is her mother's daughter.

I thought about inviting Sierra or Lou over but the thought of having to speak to other people made me feel cross. Drank wine and re-watched *Legally Blonde* instead. Cried at Elle's graduation speech.

Saturday 24 March

*Profound pieces of advice received from hormone app – 0.
Wine – 3 (for menstrual cramps and general despair at
lack of purpose etc).*

Period started today, so the last couple of days make
sense now. Logged day one on the hormone app.

*'Today you may experience menstrual cramps and fatigue
that might leave you feeling like you want to curl up on the
sofa!'*

No shit, Sherlock. I hope it's more helpful than this,
generally.

Sunday 25 March

*Jaffa Cakes – 7 (as instructed by hormone app). Mild
feelings of jealousy – 0. (Lies.)*

According the hormone app, rising estrogen levels will
be improving my outlook slightly but I 'may still find
myself upset if someone eats the last cookie'. I finished
the Jaffa Cakes in my bedroom while Jess was watching
Flo play Sims … just in case.

Lou has got a photography job! The woman from
Grape and Grain who came to the IWD event got in
touch with her and asked if she'd be able to create some
product images that they can use on social media and in
their marketing. Lou is over the moon, obviously. I am
very pleased for her and not at all envious.

Monday 26 March

Bit of a shocker today. I had a WhatsApp message today from Cam, Flo's father, while the girls and I were watching an old *Death in Paradise* and eating pizza. I now know where the expression 'blood runs cold' comes from.

When I saw his name appear on my phone I felt the insides of my arms go icy and my heart started pounding so fiercely that I had to make my excuses and hide in the bathroom for a bit as I felt sure the girls would be able to hear it.

I put the lid down and sat on the toilet, staring at the phone cradled in my lap. I didn't know what to do. Should I read it? Should I delete it without even looking? It's ten years since we last heard from him. I decided that I couldn't not read it.

'Hey Franny,' it said, 'how's things? I'm back in the UK and wondered if you fancied catching up? I've missed you. And Flo, of course. Call me. X'

I thought I might cry, but I didn't; I just took very quick, shallow breaths. I felt numb. My eyes moved from side to side but my head was still. I didn't know how to move my hands.

There was a knock on the door.

'Mummy!' It was Jess. 'I need a wee! When are you coming out?'

'I'm coming out now, darling!' I said, standing up. I put my phone in the bathroom cabinet, behind the countless half-empty bottles of Calpol. I didn't want it near me.

I went back downstairs and tried to do normal things, in a normal way, until bedtime.

At 2 a.m. I got my phone back out of the bathroom cabinet and the read the message again. And again. And again, until I knew it by heart.

I was mad, now.

How dare he? How dare he be so fucking casual about everything? Like we only saw him a few weeks ago. Like he didn't leave me a broken mess on the floor of my life, Flo without a father, me without even a sense of who I was any more. And the 'And Flo, of course'. Always an afterthought. Always someone to think about if it was convenient to him.

According to the hormone app my 'thoughts are turning to secret crushes. Rising estrogen making you more likely to focus on that special someone's strengths than their weaknesses.'

Not the time, estrogen, not the time.

Wednesday 28 March

Energy surges noted – 0. Episodes of Friends *watched – 5. Chocolate digestives – 3.*

Hormone app says I should be noticing a 'significant surge in physical and mental energy today'. I'm beginning to be suspicious of its accuracy.

Horribly long day at work, taking calls from volunteers, promoting a sponsored skydive and ordering toilet paper at the same time as trying to fill out grant application forms.

'What is the need you have identified; how did you identify it and how will your idea meet it?'

I have a 250-word limit for that question. Stared at it for a while, but realised I didn't know the answers to any of it. Reluctantly knocked on Steve's door.

'Could I have a word?' I asked him.

'Of course,' he said, 'my door is always open!' Not true, as I had to open it after I knocked on it, but I let it go.

'I'm working on some of these funding applications that Angela identified, but I'm not entirely clear on what it is we need the money for?'

'To run the museum!' said Steve, doing a weird flourish with his hands, like Willy Wonka or something.

'Yes, but what, specifically?' I said. 'What needs have we identified and how does what we do meet them?'

He looked kind of blank. 'Isn't that your job?' he asked. *Is* it my job? I don't *think* so.

'I thought perhaps there might be a little bit more strategic guidance?' I asked, not sure if Steve would even know what that meant. 'You know, some key objectives, market research?'

'I trust you to take care of that,' said Steve, and he started shuffling papers about. Excellent. So Steve has no idea about anything. Super.

Maggie came in with the collection boxes from Sainsbury's and a slice of double chocolate brownie. I told her about the fundraising issues. She said it sounded like it might be the time for me to find something new. I asked if she was trying to get rid of me.

'As long as you're local I can always bring cake,' she said.

No more messages from Cam and I haven't replied. Spent all evening watching reruns of *Friends* and eating chocolate digestives.

Thursday 29 March – last day of term

Last day of term today and the much anticipated Busy Beavers Easter bonnet parade. This has always been a nerve-wracking time of the year for me, ever since my first brush with bonneting back in 2009 when I made the infamous 'bonnet of death' for Flo's reception class Easter party.

It wasn't long after the last time we saw Cam and, looking back, I wasn't perhaps the most together I have ever been. I wanted to do well with the Easter bonnet, with that desperate sort of panic that comes from feeling like you just need this one thing to go well, to make everything else OK.

I bought an old straw hat in a charity shop and lengths of yellow satin ribbon and the night before the party I'd made a huge, ornate ribbon bow and decorated the brim of the hat with some fluffy chicks that I'd saved from the top of some Easter cakes we'd had the week before.

When I'd finished, I stood back to admire it, but it had felt as though something was missing. I hit on the genius idea of making some hard-boiled eggs and gluing three of them in a cluster, surrounded by twigs. I boiled the eggs and put them in the box to cool overnight before gluing them on in the morning.

Flo looked adorable. There were sighs of admiration from other parents as she took her turn on the stage in the school hall. She looked so proud – and for a second it felt like perhaps everything really was going to be OK, after all.

Then she spotted me in the audience and did a little skip of excitement. One of the eggs wobbled and came away from its gluey fixing. It fell to the floor in front of Flo and smashed open, white and yolk oozing out on to the stage. One of the other children screamed.

'Flo killed a chick!' yelled a boy who I think was called Kai.

'The Easter bunny is dead!' shouted someone else.

Flo started to cry, of course, looking between me and the egg, betrayal in her eyes. Apparently, I'd got a bit muddled and glued the uncooked eggs to the hat, leaving the hard-boiled ones in the box. I do feel the teacher overreacted a little bit, asking me to take Flo home. Once I'd taken the other two eggs off the hat and disposed of them safely there wasn't anything to worry about. On the plus side, though, we got to have egg mayonnaise sandwiches for lunch.

My point being that you can understand why I was nervous about making Jess a bonnet.

Inevitably, I'd left it until the last minute and when the doorbell rang to signify Jess's return, the extent of 'plan bonnet' was a vague idea involving egg boxes and mini eggs.

I opened the door.

'Look what I made, Mummy!' squealed an excited Jess, bouncing up and down on the spot. 'It's an Easter bonnet!'

She carefully tipped her head back to peer out at me from beneath what was undoubtedly a bonnet triumph. There were crepe paper daffodils, chicks made of woollen pom-poms and even some real foliage.

'Oh my goodness,' I exclaimed, 'that's incredible! What a great job you've done, Jess!'

'Daddy helped a little bit,' she said, 'but I did most of it all by myself!'

'What can I say,' said Ian, shrugging. 'She's a pom-pom whizz.'

I didn't know what to say. 'Ian, it's amazing! Thank you so much.'

'You don't mind, then?' he asked. 'I was a bit worried in case you'd already made something, but Jess didn't seem to think you had.' There was a hint of a smile.

'Oh well,' I said, 'I was working on something, obviously, but this is *way* better. I can shelve what I've done for next year. Or, you know, just put the egg boxes back in the recycling.'

No more messages from Cam. I'm trying really hard to concentrate on other things – thinking about him gives me this horrible sense of being out of control, a kind of body-wide panic.

Friday 30 March – Good Friday

Body parts accidentally eaten – 1. Number of times Jess made me watch her do a 'show' – 7. (7 too many.)

Part of a tooth fell off today. I am thirty-seven years old and I am *literally crumbling*. Parts of me are just falling away like some sort of neglected country house where you aren't allowed to touch the walls and old trees are propped up with steel rods.

What's worse is that I didn't even notice right away. I had been eating nachos and for a while afterwards I thought I just had a bit of salsa stuck between my teeth because it felt a bit weird. And then I realised the tooth felt weird because it wasn't there any more. I must have actually eaten it, thinking it was a bit of tortilla chip, so I don't even have it for the dentist to glue back on. (Can they even do that?) I will have to say I swallowed it, thinking it was a snack.

How embarrassing.

It was the side of a tooth around a root canal filling, so it doesn't actually hurt – I'm guessing the tooth is just dead? It's very sharp, though and obviously I have to poke at it with my tongue every twenty-seven seconds or so, so that's not at all annoying. I phoned the dentist but then remembered it's a bank holiday. This could really cramp my style when it comes to Mini Eggs.

According to the hormone app it's a 'great day to try out a new software program', which seems a very oddly specific suggestion.

Saturday 31 March

*Number of times tooth gap poked with tongue –
43,291. Medicinal gins swilled around my mouth – 3
(and swallowed so as not to waste it).*

Bit down on the side of my tongue with my snaggle tooth while carefully eating a hot cross bun and scared Jess a bit by issuing forth a rather elaborate scream.

'The tooth!' I yelped.

'God, Mum,' said Flo, 'how much longer are you going to go on about that tooth? You know that we can see when you're poking it? It's gross.'

'Half of my tooth fell off Flo,' I said indignantly, 'and I *ate* it. Have a little sympathy.'

'You said yourself it doesn't even hurt,' she said. She made a face and put on an annoying voice that I can only assume was meant to be me: 'If you keep poking it you're only going to make it worse.'

As my own flesh and blood clearly have no interest in my health and well-being, I turned to the Internet for support. 'Part of tooth fallen off on bank holiday weekend,' I typed into Google. I added the bank holiday weekend bit for drama. Suggestions ranged from gargling frequently with salt water (yuk) to plugging the gap with bubblegum (questionable) with lots of talk of crowns and bridges and other expensive-sounding procedures. Perhaps I could fashion something out of Mini Egg shell?

I'm sure @simple_dorset_life has perfect teeth, brushed twice daily with some sort of organic, hemp-infused toothpaste. She has been doing yoga again on Instagram. Her latest picture is a close-up of her feet – her hands are flat on the floor between them. I was inspired to see if I could do the same, but I couldn't even bend enough to touch my toes. I'm pretty sure I *used* to be able to touch my toes. When does your body just seize up?

The caption read, '*Sometimes you just need to pause, clear your mind, open your heart and breathe deep. Family life can be hectic, but nothing centres me like taking half an hour out of my day to connect with my body and my soul through yoga. I'm so much more tolerant with my children when I'm balanced inside and out. #thatyogalife #blissful #thepowerofthebreath*'.

Having had a go at touching my toes certainly didn't make me more patient with Jess at bedtime. Perhaps I'm missing something.

Sunday 1 April – Easter Sunday

Injuries sustained in semi-darkness due to own stupidity – 3. Easter eggs accidentally eaten on good side of mouth during hiding process – 8 (had bought extra especially).

Woke up at about 3 a.m. in a cold sweat because I'd forgotten to hide the Easter eggs before I went to bed last night. I got out of bed and put on yesterday's dress, which was, helpfully, in a heap on the floor where I'd stepped out of it. It took me a little while to remember where I'd put the eggs, what with it being the middle of the night and me having had all those medicinal gins while I watched reruns of *Queer Eye*.

I poked at the tooth a bit with my tongue to bring me back to reality. The hole was still there.

Having located the eggs I fumbled my way around the lounge and hallway in the dark, trying to feel for suitable hiding places. I cursed myself for not being one of those grown-ups who keeps a torch in the cupboard under the stairs like my gran and grandad used to. I didn't want to switch on any lights for fear of waking up Jess and shattering the whole Easter Bunny illusion for good.

She's only three but she already has her suspicions about Father Christmas. During December last year Flo kept picking things up every time we went into Claire's and saying, 'Can I have this in my stocking, Mum?'

I had to keep saying ridiculous things in a loud voice like, 'I'm sure Father Christmas would be happy to get that for you, why don't I pop it in the basket now and then I can send him a special message to let him know that an elf can come and collect it from me?' Even I thought it sounded lame.

As I hid the last egg and smacked my toe into the kitchen door frame I remembered about the whole phone-with-a-torch thing.

Monday 2 April

Times listened to last two bars of Thomas the Tank Engine *theme tune – 52. Number of times I wanted to smash* the Thomas the Tank Engine *machine with a bat – 52.*

We've turned into Easter savages. It rained all morning so we ate chocolate buttons for breakfast and stayed in our pyjamas to watch *Lilo & Stitch*. By 2 p.m. Jess was starting to get a little bit 'bouncy', as nursery would say if they were being kind, so I took her to Micro Soft to sweat out the sugar.

I spent quite a lot of time watching a man in his forties who was there with a boy who looked about a year old. He could barely walk, (the child not the man), so his dad had to follow him around, shoving him up the foam steps one by one. Dad was nicely dressed and had a pretty sharp haircut. He looked as though he could be thinking of things he'd rather be doing, like balancing his investment portfolio, training for a marathon or stabbing himself in the leg with a sharpened stick.

The indignity of the whole situation kept me watching. This man, who in his professional life is probably successfully and well respected, is crawling on his hands and knees through a ball pit, occasionally having to pick off things that have stuck to him along the way. The child would probably be just as happy at home, sitting in a cardboard box with some plastic cups but he's forced to go down a slide again and again, unable to say, 'Would you mind *not* pushing me through those rollers, please?'

There is a ride-on Thomas the Tank engine machine in one corner of Micro Soft and due to the number of parents at their wits' end after the chocolate fiasco of Easter weekend I'd been forced to sit near it. These things really piss me off because you've just paid a ridiculous amount to come into the building and have a disgusting cup of coffee and now you have to fend off requests for fifty-pence pieces every five minutes.

Also, Thomas's front lights flash continuously and every few minutes he plays the closing bars from the title music. Just those last few notes – 'Dum, dum, da da dum, DUM!' The kids are drawn to him like flies to a cowpat.

The music bit drives me mad. So mad that I decided to time it. It was ninety seconds. Every goddamn ninety seconds. The only respite came when the well-groomed dad paid for his son to have a ride (sucker) and we got the full song.

I messaged WIB.

'I'm at Micro Soft if anyone fancies it.'

There was a conspicuous silence, even though I could see after five minutes that both of them had read it.

Eventually Sierra replied. 'I would, only I've got my parents over for a late Easter lunch.' I know for a fact that Sierra's parents are dead.

'Really?' I said. 'Did it take them long to get there, what with the bank holiday traffic and having to travel from *beyond the grave*?'

'OK, OK,' she replied, 'they're not really here.'

'I figured,' I said, 'unless you've dug them up, which would be a bit extreme just to get out of soft play.'

'I just hate it there,' she wrote. 'No offence.'

'I can't go because of the germs,' wrote Louise. 'I read on Mumsnet that there are more bacteria on a single ball in one of those ball pits than on all the toilet seats in any public toilets combined.'

That felt like a bit of a made-up fact to me.

To pass the time I let myself be lulled into conversation with a man on Tinder called Stuart, who described himself as an 'aspiring fiction writer'. It sounded a bit like he might work in IT and spend his evenings writing and illustrating his own comics (with felt-tip pens), but he wrote in nice long sentences and didn't say tedious things like 'what are you up to today?' so I gave him the benefit of the doubt.

I was just on the brink of thinking I could consider him for a date when he casually asked me to name my favourite sexual position. He volunteered the information that his is reverse cowgirl.

Unmatch.

I messaged another guy, who said he was a teacher, asking him to tell me a fun fact about himself that not many people knew, which I thought was relatively interesting as an opener.

He replied with, 'I have a massive cock.'

A *teacher*? This man is basically responsible for the future of the human species. Perhaps not single-handedly, but it's still worrying. I sent a screenshot to WIB.

'Perhaps he meant to write "I *am* a massive cock"?' suggested Sierra.

Business idea: workshops for men to teach them how to interact with women on dating sites like *normal human beings*.

Tuesday 3 April

Given how much of half-term Flo spent asleep and how much I love my job (ha!) I decided not to bother taking time off work for the Easter holidays. I don't have enough annual leave as it is so I might as well make the most of nursery being open all year round. I have no idea what I'm going to do when Jess goes to school next year – fork out hundreds of pounds to have her go to holiday clubs, I guess, to learn basic tennis skills or whatever it is they do there.

I bribed Flo to hoover the whole house this evening on the promise of a packet of Bounty ice creams next time I go shopping. She wasn't impressed with the equipment provided.

'Why do we have this shitty vacuum,' she said, wrestling it up the stairs. 'What is even the point of a vacuum cleaner if it's so crap you have to actually pick stuff up off the floor with your hands and *put it in* the vacuum?'

I said that if she wanted to forgo the Bounty ice creams that I'd happily put the money towards a new vacuum cleaner.

She declined.

Phoned the dentist. They can fit me in tomorrow morning at 9.05 a.m. Steve is off this week (Maggie told me she thinks he and his mother have gone on a cruise) so I'm hoping I might be able to sneak into work late without anyone noticing. Cleaned teeth thoroughly in case of errant Mini Eggs being stuck in the hole.

Faith in hormone app restored as today it genuinely said that this week is a good time to schedule a dental appointment! Apparently, my currently high estrogen levels act to blunt pain, so fingers crossed.

No more messages from Cam. Maybe I should have replied? What if he was genuine about wanting to see us? What if for the last ten years he's been on the run or under witness protection or something?

Wednesday 4 April

Imagined encounters with customs where I have to explain why I'm smuggling something illegal into the country – 4. Polystyrene tiles on the dentist's ceiling – 42.

I read back what I wrote about Cam last night when I woke up and immediately hated myself. This what he DOES to me. He makes me question myself. I know he hasn't been living under witness protection, of course he hasn't, but there always seems to be that little part of me that wants to believe that he wants me, that he could be the man I want him to be, the father I want him to be, given enough time. And then when he isn't he somehow makes me feel like it's my fault, like I've expected too much or pushed him away.

So why do I keep thinking about him?

It makes me feel so weak and pathetic. I don't want to be in that place again, but I'm scared. I deleted the message *and* his phone number while I was thinking straight (bold move – very impressed with self) – and went to the dentist instead.

I always feel guilty when I go to the dentist even though I brush my teeth twice a day and floss when I remember (but really, who flosses every day?), and don't use them to open beer bottles or anything. It's a bit like when you see a police car or go through airport customs. You know you've not done anything wrong but what if you actually *did* pack an ornamental doll in national costume stuffed full of cocaine and you've just forgotten about it?

I did my usual apologising for the state of my teeth, most of which have had fillings since my early twenties, and the dentist was very kind and said things about genetics and 'otherwise good oral hygiene'. I didn't tell her about my Jaffa Cake habit.

She said that the centre part of the filling that was left was also wobbly, so she was going to take that out too to make sure I didn't swallow it. I hadn't even mentioned that I ate the first broken bit, mistaking it for a nacho, so perhaps I just *looked* like the sort of person who'd swallow bits of themselves by accident.

I counted the ceiling tiles over and over again while she packed in some temporary filling and arranged a second appointment with the dental nurse.

'Shall I say thirty minutes?' the nurse asked her.

The dentist made a face. 'Best say forty,' she said.

Super.

Parted with fifty-odd quid that I really cannot spare and made an appointment to go back again on 19 April. I will have to take Jess with me, but it was either that or wait until mid-May. As the dentist had laughed and said, 'I'm not sure how long that will last!' when she finished the temporary filling, I figured it was probably worth going sooner than later.

Thursday 5 April

Encounters involving whipped cream and a postman –
1. (1 too many.) Glasses of wine – 3, but with friends,
so counts for less than if drunk alone.

Made myself get up as soon as I woke up this morning because I didn't want to lie in bed thinking about Cam. I went downstairs to make a cup of tea and look in the fridge.

I ate some ham from the packet and a finger full of hummus and threw away a couple of limp carrots. The postman walked up the path with a letter to sign for just as I was squirting cream into my mouth from the can. It was a bit awkward as we made eye contact through the kitchen window, mid-squirt.

I decided not to draw attention to it.

'Can you just sign here?' he said, handing me the parcel and proffering his electronic box. I signed, trying to look casual.

'Thanks,' he said. He smiled and looked a bit uncomfortable, as though he wanted to say something.

'Um ...' He pointed at my face. 'You have a bit of cream, just there.'

Good God.

No Busy Beavers today as it's the school holidays. I've never quite understood why playgroups shut at the very time that you need adult company the most. Even if I'm working, there is something about *knowing* that it's the school holidays that makes you feel the urge to drink at lunchtime.

Instead, I invited Lou and Sierra and various children (theirs, not randoms from the street), to come to our house for the afternoon, which Flo was *very* excited about.

'They're not allowed in my room,' she said, gathering up a selection of lip balms and headphones from around the lounge, 'and don't give them my Oreos.'

'They're not actually *your* Oreos,' I pointed out, 'I think you'll find that *I* bought them.'

'But I *asked* for them,' said Flo. 'And what's the point of you asking if there is anything I'd like if you're just going to give them all to a load of kids?'

'I haven't given anyone anything!' I said, feeling the need to defend myself.

'I'm taking them to my room, just in case,' she said, snatching the Oreos from the cupboard and stomping off upstairs.

I was glad she'd made herself scarce, to be honest, as I wanted to talk to Sierra and Lou about Cam. I wasn't able to show them the message, obviously, but I knew it from memory. They were both appalled.

'It's so *casual*,' said Sierra, 'as if you were only just chatting last week and he happens to be in town and he's not the father of your firstborn child. What a dick.'

'What should I do, though?' I asked.

'You shouldn't do anything,' said Sierra. 'The guy is clearly a narcissist; he's not interested in Flo, he's barely interested in you – it sounds like he's just testing you, seeing if he can still pull your strings.'

'I'm worried, though, in case he can,' I admitted.

'Has he sent anything else?' asked Lou.

'No, just that one,' I said.

'Well, there you go, then,' said Sierra. 'He's not exactly desperate to see you both, is he? I'd ignore him. You don't need him coming in and messing things up for you.'

They were right, of course.

And yet...

Although I knew, deep down, that he was no good, there was still that part of me that wanted him to message me again, a slither of me that craved the excitement. Plus, he *is* Flo's father. He may not have exactly earned the title, but that blood link must mean something, surely?

At five o'clock I made a big vat of pasta for the kids and glasses of wine for the grown-ups, because everyone knows that if you have guests, then wine o'clock comes forward from six to five. It's just the rules.

Message on Tinder this evening from a cabinetmaker called Robbie. I hadn't been sure about him to start with as there was a picture of him snowboarding, and you know how I feel about winter sports, but also there was one where he had a small black-and-white kitten on one shoulder. Plus, he used the wine glass emoji in his profile.

We got chatting about cats and the seaside and our favourite *Friends* episodes and then after about half an hour he asked me out. Clearly I am irresistible.

'I know it's probably a bit forward,' he said, 'but I've had a few experiences of chatting to people for ages and then when we've met in person they've just not been the same. I think it's difficult to know if you like someone unless you actually see each other, isn't it?'

I agreed.

'I'm away next week for work,' he said, 'but how about after that? Maybe we could get a drink or dinner or something?'

'That's sounds good to me,' I said.

'Cool,' he wrote. 'I'll message you when I'm back and we can set it up.'

Would he, though? It seemed unlikely.

Saturday 7 April

Rained all day.

Sunday 8 April

Jaffa Cakes – 3. (Excellent given the circumstances.)
Pebbles admired – 27,139. (Possible exaggeration.)
Money swindled from me by toddler – £2.43.

*

Cannot even talk about today. Two rainy weekends in a row – how did I cope when Ian and I actually lived together and I had to see my children *all the time*? It's not even like I do anything especially exciting when they aren't here – fold washing, do food shopping, piss about on the internet, drink wine, etc. – but apparently I need that time to function as a regular, sympathetic single parent because today I had no patience at all.

I blame 'shops'.

'Shops' has to be one of my least favourite games of all time. There is only so long I can pretend to get excited about buying pebbles and individual pieces of toilet paper – about ninety seconds, normally – but today even less. It is just so mind-numbingly tedious. People are quick to tell you all about the sleepless nights but why will no one say out loud how *boring* parenting can be?

I wish I was more like @simple_dorset_life. She was pressing spring flowers today in a home-made press.

'*I love seeing the connection that my boys have with nature,*' she wrote under the photo, '*and I do everything I can to encourage it, even if sometimes it does mean stopping a dozen times on the way to preschool to look at leaves! When I see the way they look up at their daddy, their eyes full of curiosity, gazing down into their chubby hands at the latest creepy-crawly they've discovered, my heart just bursts for my perfect little family.*'

Kill me now!

Admired Jess's insistence that I had to use real money in her shop. Must remember to get it out of her piggy bank before she learns to properly count.

Hormone app suggests beating constipation caused by high progesterone with dried plums or a slice of rye bread. Had glass of wine and a digestive. Basically the same.

Monday 9 April

Almost a relief to go to work after the weekend, which says a lot.

Things I like about work:

- Being able to drink a cup of coffee while it's hot
- Browsing the internet (at lunchtime, *obviously*), without someone throwing themselves into my lap and asking if they can watch *Octonauts*
- Doing a poo without anyone watching. I once had a friend who told me she couldn't poo *anywhere* but at home and definitely not at work. I try to *always* poo at work. Not only is it away from children, but it's a legitimate way to take a ten-minute break. No one wants to question your bowel movements in an office do they?
- I can't think of any more.

I really need to get a new job if the only things I get satisfaction from could similarly be achieved by going to Starbucks for an hour.

No more messages from Cam. I wish I could stop thinking about him. It's not even in a romantic way, it's just this obsessive thought pattern repeating and repeating itself.

According to Google it's because I've never had closure – that last time he left I didn't know it was the last time, and so part of me hasn't been able to finish things emotionally. It makes sense. But then he's never likely to give me that chance, so perhaps I just need to make my own ending? Put myself vaguely in control for once?

Hormone app says that a dip in estrogen is likely to be chipping away at my confidence in my 'appearance and brain skills' – which sounds about right.

Thursday 12 April

Estimated number of chicken nuggets cooked in lifetime so far – 7,280. Fantasies involving a personal chef – many.

In all the parenting books and articles I have ever read (not that many, to be honest) they talk a lot about sleep routines and tummy time and birth plans but not once have I seen anyone tackle what is possibly one of the most difficult things about parenting.

'What's for tea?' asks Flo at about four o'clock.

Every frickin' day. Every day for at least ten years someone has asked me that question and every time they ask it I want to bang my head against a wall and shout '*I don't know! I don't want to decide any more!*'

Whatever you make won't be right, anyway, so why do we even bother? Why has someone not yet invented a chocolate button-shaped meal replacement that we can give to children three times a day that contains all the vitamins and minerals they need and never gets rejected because it's 'the wrong shape' or 'has sauce on it' or is 'touching the peas'.

'How about *you* decide for a change?' I want to say. 'How about you think about it and then go to Sainsbury's to buy it and then have to go to Tesco because Sainsbury's don't have the *one thing* that's key to the meal, and then get home and realise you've forgotten a tin of tomatoes, so you have to make something different that no one likes?'

'Chicken-and-sweetcorn nuggets, mashed potato and carrots,' I say instead. Flo made a face like she was being sick.

'What's the matter with that?' I ask.

'Chicken-and-sweetcorn nuggets sound *grim.*'

'They do not sound grim! Six of them equals one of your five a day, so the packet says.'

'Can't I have normal chicken nuggets and eat an apple later?'

'No. Anyway, you like chicken nuggets and you like sweetcorn.'

'Yeah, but not together. That's like saying I like ice cream and I like mayonnaise, so I'd like mayonnaise flavour ice cream.'

'It's really not the same,' I say, but she's already lost interest and put her headphones back in.

(Question: I wonder how many hours/days of my life have been taken up by trying to think up things that counts as one of a child's five a day?)

Friday 13 April

Awful day at work. Steve must have been reading some sort of motivational book on his cruise (he is telling everyone he has been on a 'retreat' but Maggie says she overheard his mother in the butcher's talking about how much he'd enjoyed the P&O all-you-can-eat buffet), because he keeps swaggering around the office and saying things like 'someday is not a day of the week' and 'don't count the days, make the days count'.

What I *really* wanted to count was the number of times I could hit him with the stapler before he begged for mercy.

I spent five hours this afternoon trying to put together a convincing argument for why the Wolfson Foundation should give us money, but when I asked Steve if he had any evidence to support our 'excellent interpretation of designated collections of national significance' he just said 'never allow a person to tell you no who doesn't have the power to say yes', which was unhelpful to say the least.

Girls at Ian's tonight. I toyed with the idea of doing something wholesome like a Zumba class but I was too exhausted, so instead I lay on the sofa watching Netflix. Also, I have never done a Zumba class before and it sounds horrific.

I checked my status with the hormone app. Apparently I am likely to have 'limited pep' today and I should eat delicious foods including asparagus, cucumber and watermelon. I didn't have any of these things so I went for Wispa Bites. I ate half the bag and then had to throw the rest of the bag to the other side of the room, banking on my limited pep to stop me retrieving them and eating any more.

(Question: surely I am not the only person to do this with snacks?)

Saturday 14 April

I went into Chapter One today to see if they had any books about fundraising. Dylan was behind the counter, the piles of crime novels on the floor were gone and there was music playing quietly in the background.

He smiled when I came in. 'Hello, stranger,' he said. 'How're things in the world of female empowerment?'

'Not great, to be honest,' I said, 'that's why I'm here. I'm hoping to inspire myself. It looks great in here, though! Have you been tidying up?'

'I've started,' he said. 'I've got plenty to do yet, but at least it feel less like a Channel 5 documentary on hoarding when you first walk in. Why do you need inspiring?'

I told him all about work and my new responsibilities and the fact that I am struggling to find time to really *care* about fossil workshops.

'Sounds pretty harsh to expect you do take on all that extra work,' he said. 'Have you talked to your boss about it?'

'I would,' I said, 'except my boss is a moron. I don't think he really knows what he's doing, plus he begrudges me having a family and getting the board to agree to me working non-standard hours. He pretty much said I can either do the fundraising or leave. It's my *choice*, of course. Lucky me!'

'He sounds like a dick,' said Dylan.

'He is a dick,' I agreed, feeling better about it already. 'Anyway, my work life is boring – how's things here? Have you been putting that new upstairs room to good use?'

'Not yet,' admitted Dylan, 'but if you have any ideas then let me know. For now I wouldn't be looking to charge anyone – it would just be nice to get some more people coming through the shop.'

'Don't you need to make some money, though?' I asked, my usual tactless self.

'Well, ideally,' he said, 'long-term, but it's not critical. Caitlin was pretty savvy about finances and very protective of the shop because it belonged to her parents, so she was well insured. No amount of money can compensate, of course, but it's taken the pressure off turning a massive profit in the short-term at least. I don't think I could have dealt with money worries on top of everything else.'

I said I'd keep my ear to the ground for him. It would be a shame if it just got filled back up with junk because the shop is so lovely and Dylan is such a sweetheart.

Had a flick through *The Zen of Fundraising* but couldn't bring myself to buy anything. It felt like that would be admitting that this was what I was planned to do with my life for long enough to warrant buying a book about it.

I nearly bought a book about parenting teenage girls through the 'seven transitions into adulthood' but I've probably missed at least three of them already and I don't especially want to be made aware of things I've already messed up and can't do anything about. Instead, I used the book token I've had in my purse since Christmas to buy Flo the latest instalment in the vampire series she's reading. I wrapped it up and put it under her pillow for when she got home with a little note saying 'Don't tell Jess.' I know that it's not easy being a teenager and having a loud, three-year-old sister.

Sunday 15 April

Dates secured – 1 (goddess). Jaffa Cakes – 4 (celebrating).

I had a message from Robbie, the guy who was going away for a week! I'd fully expected not to hear from him ever again, although obviously I'd looked through his pictures and reread our messages at least once a day.

'I'm back!' he said. 'I bet you thought I was giving you the brush-off didn't you?' he asked with a winky face.

'Of course not,' I said, lying. 'I'm a catch, you'd be a fool to not take me out.' He sent a smiley face back.

'So how are you fixed for this week?' he asked. 'If you're that much of a catch then I'd better not mess about, had I? I don't want you getting snapped up by anyone else!'

I looked down at my red wine-stained pyjama bottoms and thought it unlikely that there was going to be a great deal of snapping going on any time soon, but I didn't say this obviously.

'How about Wednesday?' I said.

'Wednesday's good,' he said. 'Do you like Thai food? There's a lovely place near the beach, down at the far end of the promenade?'

Ha! And Lou said men weren't looking for a woman who liked Thai food!

'I love it,' I said. 'Shall I meet you there about eight?'

'Perfect! I'm really looking forward to meeting you!'

And there I was, date number two in the bag and at a restaurant with an actual menu and everything. How sophisticated!

Monday 16 April – back to school

Cecilia came in today. She doesn't normally come in on a Monday but apparently her sister had called off their usual bridge match and she thought she might be 'helpful'. She asked if I would like her to go around the museum and wipe down all the laminated information sheets.

I thought 'like' was a really strong word for it: 'couldn't care less' might be more accurate. I thought about asking her if she'd pop to Tesco Express for me instead and choose something for tea but that felt like it might be taking liberties, so I just gave her a J-cloth from the kitchen and let her get on with it.

The highlight of the day for Jess came when we were peeling potatoes and found one that looks a bit like a bum. She wouldn't let me cook it and obviously, then, she couldn't possibly eat the mash as that was me having cruelly crushed to death all of Bum's friends. She made a bed for it next to hers using a baby wipe she fished out of the bathroom bin, so that was nice.

Lay awake for quite a long time worrying about tomorrow's date. What should I wear? Should I *shave* anything? (Like legs – not head.) How much make-up says, 'I take care of myself but am not high maintenance'?

Wednesday 18 April

Today I kissed a boy!

OK, not an actual boy, a real grown-up man, but you know what I mean. I don't think the date with Robbie could have gone any better if it had been created for one of those scenes in a film where a date goes *really* well and the heroine swings around a lamp post on her way home. We ate green curry and drank wine and talked about books and laughed and had that eye contact that goes on just a little bit too long.

It's been so long since I had that that I'd forgotten about it, and how giddy it makes you feel. It's amazing, isn't it, how much that extra second can say, without either of you having to say anything at all?

After dinner we walked along the seafront. It was dark, but the promenade was lit with strings of lights and you could hear the sea lapping at the sand. I love the noise of the sea when it's dark and everything else is silent – it's very different to how it sounds in the daytime, for some reason. It has a much more magical air about it.

We were about halfway along the front when he stopped and took both my hands, turning me to face him.

'I really want to kiss you right now,' he said. So masterful! I had clearly got the make-up balance right. I leant in towards him and went up on my tiptoes (he was as tall as his profile claimed) and we kissed and I lifted my right foot off the floor in one of those little kicks, even though no one was watching, just to reinforce that fact that I was *kissing a boy*. (Sometimes I worry that I overthink things.)

Now I am lying in bed, wide awake with a big smile on my face like I'm about thirteen years old and I've just been passed a note in chemistry from a boy I like.

Thursday 19 April

Wine – 3 glasses (medicinal due to new filling and not at all to do with Robbie). Jaffa Cakes – 0 (dentist guilt).

I had a message from Robbie this morning when I woke up.

'Just wanted to say how lovely it was to meet you last night,' he wrote, 'I had a great time.'

'Me too,' I wrote back, smiling to myself and doing a little toe wriggle under the duvet. 'That was definitely the best date I've had in a long time!'

He sent back a smiley face.

'Just to let you know, though,' he wrote, 'next time we go out I will expect sex.'

Err…?

Perhaps it was a typo? I gave him a minute to correct himself. Maybe he'd meant to write 'the chance to hang out with you for a bit longer' or even 'split the bill'?

'Um … what?' I replied.

'I had a great time,' he said, 'it's just that sex is very important to me in a relationship.'

'Well, sure,' I said, 'nobody's asking you to commit to celibacy, but we have only met once!'

'I understand if you're just not a very sexual person,' he wrote, 'but it would be best for me to know if that's the case.'

Seriously? We had such a good time! We kissed! I did the little 'lifting one foot off the floor' thing, for Christ's sake. What's the matter with me? What's the matter with men? I'm not sure that online dating is for me if it's going to be so fucking brutal. I don't swear much, but this warrants it, surely? Properly brutal.

Stared at the ceiling for a bit, trying not to cry for the state of mankind/my destiny to die alone. Should I have stuck with Ian? Am I being unreasonable to want a partner who I find sexually desirable and who is, at the same time, a decent human being?

Passed around Robbie conversation at Busy Beavers for Sierra and Lou to read in stunned silence. Sierra shook her head. 'What an absolute bellend,' she said. 'At least you know now what a complete bastard he is.'

Lou was about to comment when a small girl with pigtails threw up near her feet.

Friday 20 April

Bum the Potato has been going to nursery with Jess every day this week. He is starting to look a little sorry for himself.

Sunday 22 April

Period started but I'd forgotten the check the app for the last week so it caught me by surprise and I didn't have any tampons. Gawd.

Maybe I need an app to remind me to check the app?

Monday 23 April

I snuck in and removed the sprouting Bum from Jess's room while she was asleep.

Tuesday 24 April

Mr Kipling Angel Slices accidentally shoplifted – one pack of 5. Portions of fruit consumed by self and children – one of 5.

Operation Bum removal was a *big mistake*. Of course she spotted him missing as soon as she woke up and demanded to know what I had done with him. I feigned innocence.

'Perhaps Bum was getting lonely without any potato friends nearby,' I offered hopefully, 'and has gone off to explore the world?' She looked highly doubtful and marched off into the kitchen where she discovered him in the bin.

'Maybe he wanted somewhere dark and cosy to sleep?' I suggested.

It all backfired on me horribly when we went to Sainsbury's later that afternoon. We were in the fruit and veg section and I suggested we put Bum in my handbag so that nobody thought that we were trying to steal him. Jess did not like the idea at all and starting writhing around in the trolley seat and shouting.

'Leave my Bum alone!' she yelled, much to my horror. 'You're always trying to touch it and it doesn't like it!' I tried to shush her with a Mr Kipling Angel Slice.

'I know it was you who came into my room in the night and tried to get my Bum!'

Out of the corner of my eye I could see an elderly woman having a word with a member of staff and looking over at me. Jess wouldn't shut up about Bum so, in the end, I had to abandon the trolley and take her home.

Wholesome vegetables a little light on the ground at teatime as a result, but I found a tin of peach slices at the back of the cupboard. Pretty sure that's the same.

Wednesday 25 April

Crappy day at work today. Steve says he wants at least three funding applications finalised within the next week and that 'the fate of the museum is in my hands.'

I don't know how much longer I'm going to be able to do it. I went out at lunchtime and sat in the museum garden and tried not to cry. How did I end up going from studying Emily Brontë and Mary Shelley to writing fundraising begging letters? Steve is unbearable – how his mother lives with him I don't know. But if I quit, then what am I meant to do instead? We barely have enough money now, and that's with my salary and Ian's maintenance, there's no way I'd be able to survive without working. I lay down on the bench and watched the clouds for a bit, hoping for inspiration. None came, but a seagull pooped on my *actual face* so that was a nice bit of symbolism at least.

Spent the evening googling 'ways to make money from home'. Looked at completing surveys, but you seem to average out at about forty pence an hour. Considered working on a phone sex line under the alias 'Jolene', but I don't think I would know what to say. Googled 'what do people say on a sex chat line' and discovered that 'sex with mother-in-law' quite often makes it into the top ten.

Really not sure I'm up for that.

Perhaps I could become an Instagram Influencer? I'm normally more of a lurker, but have fourteen followers already and have posted two photos – one of a particularly tasty sandwich and one of my feet on a colourful tiled floor, which I know for a fact is exactly the sort of thing that *all* the cool kids do. I mean sure, I'd probably need to up my photography game a little bit and come up with more 'inspirational' captions, but how hard can it really be?

Thursday 26 April

Inspirational Pinterest boards it would be possible to create from Sierra's kitchen alone – at least 17. Incredible secret lives uncovered – 1. (Massive.)

Revelation today.

After last week's Busy Beavers vomiting incident and a stream of follow-up passive-aggressive WhatsApp messages about 'taking care to check for food intolerances before committing to a social group', we skived off this afternoon and went to Sierra's house instead. It was Lou's suggestion – she thought we should take turns, but she couldn't volunteer her house as she was having her house cleansed by a spiritual healer. (A genuine thing, apparently.)

There was an awkward WhatsApp silence from Sierra and I wondered if it was because her house was a bit of a shithole and she was embarrassed about it. 'My house is currently 34 per cent empty wine bottles, Jaffa Cake boxes and Sylvanian families,' I told her, 'in case that makes you feel any better.'

'It's not that,' she said, and there was a few minutes of typing/not typing, which is *very* unlike Sierra. Of all the women I know, she is the least likely to think about what she says before saying it.

'OK,' she wrote in the end, 'come over about two?' She gave us her address.

Her house is *amazing*. I mean, like 'Interior Goals' Pinterest board amazing. It was beautiful, but relaxed and homely. Sort of the opposite to how I imagine Lou's house, which would be all sterilised white surfaces and wall-mounted hand sanitiser.

'Fuck me,' I said as she showed us into her kitchen. There were plants hanging from the ceilings in macramé hangers and copper pots strung up over the central island. 'Seriously, Sierra,' I said, 'what *is* this? Is this your actual house? I was imagining you and Fox sharing a pull-out bed in some kind of dingy but sassy-looking bedsit.'

'Well, thanks!' said Sierra. 'Nice to know you have such a high opinion of me. And yes, it *is* my actual house.'

'Did your husband die and leave you a fortune or something?' asked Lou, tactless for once.

'No, said Sierra, looking shifty, 'he's not dead.'

'Well, you did OK in the divorce, then!' I said.

'Actually, I'm not divorced either,' she said.

So it turns out that Sierra is married to this hugely successful businessman, Clyde, who works overseas a lot but is otherwise very much her husband. All this time I imagined she was a single parent, struggling to make ends meet, knocking back the pinot to while away the lonely nights, and there she was, happily married and living in a Pinterest mansion.

The scandal.

On reflection, I guess I never really *asked*, I just kind of assumed it. She went to that New Year's Eve party on her own, after all, and then there's the whole 'Woefully Inactive Beavers' WhatsApp group. I guess you just never know.

Tonight @simple_dorset_life had a picture on her feed that reminded me of the view through the honeysuckle pergola in Sierra's garden.

The caption said: '*We're always being told to stop and smell the roses, but today I stopped instead to smell the honeysuckle. Life is yours to live as you choose. #followyourownpath #livewithpurpose #beaflamingoinaflockofpigeons*'.

Saturday 28 April

Woke up in the night and lay awake, worrying about work, children, Cam, state of thighs, not having a businessman husband called Clyde etc., etc. Ate a Creme Egg. Hid wrapper under bed. (From whom?) Went back to sleep.

Tuesday 1 May

Pasta shells eaten by Jess at teatime – 7. Sniggers to self about use of the phrase 'bona fide' – too many for a grown-up woman.

Still reeling from Sierra's secret-husband shocker. Messaged WIB when I was meant to working on the lottery application. Only recently discovered that you can get WhatsApp on the desktop – who knew? Now I can message people while looking like I am working diligently on my case for support for guided fossil tours on the beach for over-fifties who have recently suffered the death of a pet. Steve has decided we need a niche.

'Sierra,' I wrote, 'I still can't believe that you have a bona fide husband. I'm suspicious now of exactly how woefully inactive your beaver really is – are you even allowed to be in this group?'

'I can assure you that although the husband might be bona fide, I don't get to see much of the bona part of it,' she wrote. 'He's hardly ever here, honestly. I may as well be a single parent. Only without all the responsibility, shortage of cash and all that.'

There was a pause while she typed something else.

'God, I'm sorry guys,' she wrote, 'I feel ridiculous now. And of course it's not the same at all.'

'It's fine,' I said. 'If anything it's worse because you don't get every other weekend to lie in the dark, drinking wine and watching Netflix. I feel sorry for you, if anything, having to maintain that dream house and entertain a husband. It sounds like a *chore*.'

'I can't believe I didn't just tell you straight away,' she said. 'What a fraud. Do you hate me?'

'We don't hate you,' reassured Lou, 'it was just a bit of a surprise, that's all.'

'It was just that he didn't come up, initially,' wrote Sierra, 'and then by the time I thought to say anything you'd already sort of assumed, and I just really wanted to be in the gang. That's pathetic, isn't it?'

'Of course not,' I said, 'because we *are* amazing. Who wouldn't want to be friends with us?'

'Just let me know if you need any more input for the Pets and Pebbles group,' said Steve from behind me, making me jump. God knows how long he'd been standing there.

Also, I *must* think of a different name for the tours. If we have to go with Steve's suggestions of 'Pets and Pebbles' I really don't think I'll be able to face the funding panel.

Flo had words with me this evening. 'I know you mean well, Mum,' she said, 'but do you think you could stop writing those notes for me?'

'What notes?' I said, trying to look innocent.

'The ones you do on my bananas with Sharpies,' she said. 'I get some funny looks sometimes when

151

I get my lunch out and my banana says things like '#followyourownpath' – I'm not sure people at school get that you're being ironic.'

I laughed. 'OK,' I said, 'if you're sure? Because they are pretty motivational, you know.'

'Yesterday's was "Dance Like No One's Watching", Mum,' she said. 'It was really cringy.'

'That's the point!' I said. 'Cringy motivational fruit quotes.' She raised her eyebrows and gave me a look. 'OK, fine, I'll stop writing on your bananas.'

'Or any other fruit,' she said.

'Or any other fruit,' I said.

Killjoy.

Wednesday 2 May

I saw Cam today! Actual Cam, in the flesh.

He didn't see me. I was walking home from work and saw him sitting outside a bar with a blonde woman in dungarees and a ponytail. She looked about twenty-five. They were laughing and she was twirling her ponytail around her fingers.

My eyes felt hot and prickly and my vision started to swim. People were walking past and looking at me so I took a deep breath, trying to compose myself. He had his back to me so I wondered if perhaps I'd made a mistake. What would he be doing here? But then he turned his head to talk to a waiter and I had to duck behind a post box because it was him. Just there. In public for anyone to see.

I saw Barnmouth's 'eccentric' coming towards me – an elderly man who wears cowboy boots and says 'howdy' to everyone he passes on the street. I didn't want to get into a conversation with him about cattle – it has happened before – so I started walking, head down, forcing myself not to look back. I kept walking until I could turn into our street and forced another breath hard out of my mouth, as though I was blowing out candles on a birthday cake, only with less of a celebratory feel.

I could see our house through the tears that were spilling over, silently. I concentrated on one step in front of another. In control, in control, I said to myself, in time with my feet. I opened the door. Slow breaths.

I closed the door behind me and hung up my coat and suddenly I wasn't in control. My chest was tight. I was breathing faster and harder but couldn't seem to take in enough oxygen. I crouched down, my back against the wall.

Sobs that made my stomach knot. 'Stop it,' I said out loud. 'It's OK, you're all right.'

I slid further down the wall, until I was on the cold, tiled floor, gulping for air. I clenched my hands and then stretched out my fingers. Clench again. Stretch.

I focused on breathing slowly, letting out a quiet 'shhhh' on every out breath until the buzzing in my hands and arms subsided. I rested my forehead on my knees, making my jeans soggy.

'Calm. Be calm.'

I sat for a while. So he was here. Really here. What should I do? Should I tell Flo? I took more deep breaths.

When I started to feel calmer, I messaged WIB.

'I just saw Cam,' I wrote.

Sierra replied almost immediately. 'What? I thought you weren't even going to reply to him?'

'He didn't see me,' I said, 'I just saw him. He was sitting outside a bar in town with some young girl. She was very pretty.'

'What the *fuck*?' said Sierra, summing up my thoughts. 'What's he doing here? Did you get any more messages from him? Is he stalking you?'

'If he's stalking me, then he's doing it via the medium of flirting with young blonde women and paying me no attention,' I wrote, 'which suggests he's not very good at it.'

'Or *very* good at it,' wrote Sierra.

Lou joined the conversation. 'That's awful, Frankie!' she wrote. 'Are you OK? That must have been a bit of a shock.'

'Just a bit,' I said. 'I'm OK now I've stopped crying into my own knees. I lost it for a bit, though. This is what's so scary about him – he has this *power* over me, I can't explain it. I feel so stupid.'

'You are absolutely not stupid,' said Lou, 'you're human that's all. You just saw the father of your firstborn child, out of the blue, after he abandoned you ten years ago. It's hardly stupid to be upset by that.'

'Shall I come round?' said Sierra. 'Clyde is here, so I can be there in ten minutes.'

'Yes please,' I said. 'Unless it's your one opportunity this month to put the woefully inactive beaver to use?'

'I'll be there in ten minutes,' she wrote.

I'm regretting deleting Cam's number now. It's not that I especially want to speak to him, but seeing him like that put me on such a back foot, I feel like I have no control over the situation any more – I have to just wait and see what happens next.

Also I'm terrified.

Has he been here all along, ever since he sent that first message? Is he still here? Has he been near Flo's school? Does he know where we live? I don't want to feel nervous every time the doorbell rings or anxious walking around my own town.

I really wanted to call Ian. He is the person I talk to about things that upset me like this. I wonder if it is ever really possible to go back to being friends with someone after a relationship?

Thursday 3 May

Reservations about being too old to go 'up in da club' –
many. Glasses of wine – 2. (Warming up for night out.
Akin to marathon training.)

Emergency Cam conference at Busy Beavers this afternoon. It's impressive, really, how much a small group of women with too much time on their hands can read into a ponytail twiddle and choice of skinny dungarees.

'He's in Barnmouth for you,' said Sierra, 'He must be, surely? It would be a bit of a coincidence if you received a message from him after ten years and then a few weeks later he just happened to meet someone – basically a child – who happened to live here.'

'I think we need a night out,' said Lou.

'Well, maybe,' I said, 'but we have bigger issues right now.'

'That's exactly my point,' said Lou. 'He's come back into your life, waved this dungaree-clad Topshop model in your face; unintentionally, maybe, but still … and now it's all you can think about. You don't *want* it to be though, do you?'

'Well, no,' I said.

'Exactly. So we need to go out and drink too much and strut about like we could shop in Topshop if we *chose* to, and just forget about him for a night.'

She was right, of course. We were wasting far too much time on a man who really did not deserve it.

'It's my birthday on the twelfth,' I said. 'Ian's got the kids…'

'Oh my God, Frankie!' said Sierra. 'We definitely need to go out then! You kept that a bit quiet.'

Saturday twelfth is now officially WIB on tour night.

(I really could shop in Topshop if I wanted to. Handbags and jewellery, definitely.)

Monday 7 May – bank holiday

Bottles of wine belonging to 'Mr J Sampson' currently hidden in my stair cupboard under the guide of 'waiting for me to call and get it sorted' – 12.

Whose idea were bank holidays? What are they even *for*? People who work in banks don't need more rest than normal people do they? Bank holidays, like a lot of things – weekends generally, pubs, restaurants, sense of self – change a *lot* when you have children.

When I was in my early twenties, bank holidays just meant you got to go out on Sunday nights without the worry of being sick in your handbag on the tube on the way to work the next day. Bank holidays were like finding a ten-pound note on the floor, with no one else around who could have dropped it. They were like a case of wine left at your house by mistake by one of those mail order wine companies, without a signature, so really, what can you do but take it quickly inside?

(Definitely haven't done that.)

Bank holidays when you have children are more like when you go to take a sip of wine and realise the glass is empty or finish a big load of washing up and then find four coffee mugs, two cereal bowls and a week-old lasagne dish in your bedroom.

(Honestly, who on earth would take half a leftover lasagne to bed with them? Outrageous.)

It's like a normal weekend, full of uneaten Marmite sandwiches and too much unchaperoned Netflix and then *boom*, you have to do one of the days *all over again*, only things aren't properly open, and all the things that *are* open are full of equally despondent-looking parents and their hyperactive children.

It's just a joy.

Wednesday 9 May

Lou has been banging on for ages about her Mooncup, which is apparently an environmentally friendly tampon alternative that she says can reduce cramps, so I went out from work to Boots at lunchtime to have a look. I can see the logic from the whole waste angle, but also I'm sick of starting my period every month, having forgotten to buy tampons and having to wrap a streamer of toilet paper around my pants while I go to Tesco Express. Also, Flo started her periods last year and I want to be able to offer her alternatives to pads at some stage.

The Mooncup comes in two sizes, which was a bit disconcerting. Obviously I couldn't buy the 'young and child-free with your whole life ahead of you' size, so I had to go for the very kindly named 'size A' for women who are over thirty or who have had a vaginal birth. Basically, a sort of sink plunger.

I had a go with it when I got home but couldn't quite get the art of 'pre-insertion folding' and it kept springing back into shape at all the wrong moments.

Thursday 10 May

Jess woke me up two in the morning by getting into bed with me. Her eyes were wide and she was all warm and fuzzy from sleep.

'I had a bad dream,' she said, nuzzling into my armpit. Rather her than me.

'I'm sorry to hear that, sweetie,' I said, stroking her back. 'What was your dream about?'

'It was about a robot,' she said, 'but it was a mean robot, and he kept trying to punch you. But he was made of cake and there was cream all over you.'

'You had a dream about a mean cake robot? That doesn't sound fun.' But she was asleep again already. I drew my legs up and made a nest around her.

Plans were made for Saturday night at Busy Beavers. As in we *made* the plans at Busy Beavers, we aren't having our night out there, that would be a bit desperate. I'm going to make some dinner at my house so we can preload on prosecco.

Then we'll go to a few bars, 'hit up a club', (pretty sure that's the expression), clear the dance floor with our cool moves, and then I'll quite probably meet the man of my dreams. Bob's your uncle.

It's a foolproof plan.

Saturday 12 May – my birthday

Pre-taxi glasses of prosecco – 5. (Too many on reflection.) Dubious dance moves performed with age-inappropriate men – probably best we don't think about it.

Ian had offered to swap weekends so that the girls could be home on my birthday, but, quite honestly, it was kind of nice waking up on my own. I lay in bed reading and drinking tea for a little while, ate smoked salmon bagels in the bath, and generally swanned about feeling very decadent and old, but in a nice way.

At six o'clock Sierra and Lou arrived on a cloud of expensive-smelling perfume looking properly tarted-up. I'd made a big bolognese for dinner (pasta to line stomachs), Sierra had brought two bottles of prosecco and Lou had a fruit salad.

'It's not a family reunion BBQ,' said Sierra, pouring her a drink. 'Why the chuff have you brought a fruit salad?'

'There is actually some research that shows that fructose speeds up metabolism of alcohol,' said Lou, 'thus reducing the impact of a hangover. Also, last weekend I bought two different types of melon because the boys said it was their very favourite food of all time and now they're denying all knowledge of ever having been able to so much as *look* at a melon without crying. So just eat the melon and be grateful.'

Melon was actually pretty tasty with prosecco. Probably a very classy cocktail, in fact. Although probably normally made with melon purée rather than just putting a lump of melon in your mouth and then taking a big gulp of your drink.

Sunday 13 May

Juice. Gah! Please send juice. And bacon sandwiches. Help.

I'm definitely never drinking prosecco again.

Rolled out of bed at three in the afternoon and crawled to the bathroom. Climbed into the bath and ran the shower over me while I had a little lie down.

I don't think I even drunk *that* much. I swear when I was twenty-two I used to be able to drink twice as much and then be in the pub at ten the next morning, eating poached eggs and drinking bloody Marys. Oh God! Shouldn't have thought about poached eggs. *Bleurgh.*

Aside from physically feeling like death in a pair of stained pyjamas, Lou was right: the night out did really help. I think I've been sitting on all these feelings about Cam for so long that I'd lost perspective. The only people I've ever properly talked to about him are people who know him or knew us together. Telling the stories all over again to Sierra and Lou, and seeing their reaction, made me think about a lot of things in a new way. Stuff that seemed romantic or tragic at the time just sounded shitty. Perhaps I really just have grown up in the last ten years? It doesn't often feel like it, but I guess it's inevitable.

Managed to be dressed and sitting on the sofa when Ian brought the girls home. We used the voucher that I had stuck to the fridge to get 2-for-1 takeaway pizza and the three of us sat on the sofa together and watched *Lilo*

& Stitch. Jess fell asleep with her head on my lap, leaving greasy cheese stains on my jeans with her sweaty hands. Flo stroked her hair.

'She's cute when she's asleep, isn't she?' said Flo.

'So are you,' I said. 'Sometimes I watch you before I go to bed and you do that cute little snuffly snore you used to do when you're small.'

'You watch me sleep?' she said. 'That's so creepy.' But she looked pleased.

Monday 14 May

Looked at the Mooncup for a bit. Jess came into the bathroom and looked confused.

'What's that, Mummy?' she asked.

'It's a Mooncup,' I said, not sure where else I could go with it right now.

'A moo cup?' she said. Not looking any less confused to be honest. 'A cup for cows?'

'No, it's for people,' I said.

'A cup for people? Like a tiny wine glass?'

I said yes just because I couldn't face explaining. That will definitely come back to bite me.

Tuesday 15 May

Renewed Mooncup efforts tonight after doing some video-based research into folding methods. Managed to get it in and it felt OK. Sat down. It did *not* feel OK. The video did say 'some women may find they need to trim the stem' but at no point did it say 'the stem will feel like someone is operating you on a stick like some kind of grotesque, olden-days puppet.'

Wrestled it out again. Trimmed stem. Much better.

Friday 18 May

Peppermint creams to get over trauma of having to explain Mooncup to nursery staff – 5. Number of times

*I went up and down the stairs to Jess at bedtime because
she 'felt sick' – 3,247,813 (felt like).*

Millie asked if she could have a quick word when I arrived
to pick up Jess at lunchtime. Jess was busy finishing a
painting so Millie took me into the office.

'I'm sure it's nothing to worry about,' she said, looking
like it was something to worry about, 'only we overheard
Jess saying something rather odd to Tabitha in the home
corner and we thought it was worth flagging.'

I hoped it wasn't more *RuPaul's Drag Race* references.
She's started saying 'not today, Satan' when I tell her it's
bedtime.

'They were making a pretend dinner together,'
explained Millie, 'and Tabitha was setting the table. Jess
told her to pick small glasses for the wine and said, "My
Mummy has a special glass for small wine and she puts
it in her bottom." Obviously, we were a little concerned.'

I considered pretending to faint just to give me a
minute to get over the embarrassment but then had a
flashback to the performance of *Snow White* I starred
in, aged nine. That bloody thing still haunts me. The
audience openly laughed when I took a bite of the
poisoned apple and swooned, knocking over a dwarf in
the process. The dwarf fell into Scott Thompson, who
was dressed as a tree, and Mr Lewis had to come on
stage and stand him up again.

Instead, I was forced to tell her about my misjudged
explanation of the Mooncup, which I don't think went
very far to reassure her, if I'm honest. I looked at my watch,

remembered I don't *wear* a watch, mumbled something about an optician's appointment, and retrieved Jess as quickly as possible, my face burning.

Put the TV on for Jess when we got home and went and hid in the bathroom to get over the nursery shame. Ate quite a few of the peppermint creams I have hidden in an empty box of haemorrhoid cream for emergencies.

Saturday 19 May

Royal wedding day!

If ever there was an excuse to pop open the prosecco at eleven in the morning, then a royal wedding is it. Jess put on the crown she'd made at nursery as soon as she got up and even Flo seemed quite interested. I don't think it hurts that the royal bride is also a Hollywood actress.

We all went over to Sierra's house, as it basically *looks* like a wedding venue already, in time for all the preliminaries and to eat smoked salmon and mini cucumber sandwiches ahead of having to concentrate on important things like what the guests are wearing and trying to lip read what Harry and William are saying to each other as they wait for Meghan.

The smaller children got bored after about ten minutes – Jess seemed surprised that the whole thing wasn't animated. I think she was expecting a Disney wedding, so finding out that it was real people and not a musical was something of a disappointment for her.

I enjoyed myself very much, though. Very lovely drinking prosecco, celebrating monarchy, eating crisps, etc., with friends.

Sunday 20 May

Period started today. I was ready for it, though, Mooncup poised for deployment. I almost chickened out because of feeling a teeny bit queasy after wedding celebrations, but I thought about what Meghan would want me to do and I feel like she'd be rooting for the Mooncup.

Slight issue later in the day with the emptying side of things, which didn't go quite as smoothly as putting it in. I managed to get hold of the end of it OK, with a small amount of birthing-style bearing down, but I think it's best not to talk out loud about what happened next. Eventually managed to get myself and the Mooncup cleaned up. I think I'll try emptying it in the shower tomorrow.

Monday 21 May

*Actual animals harmed in the emptying of the Mooncup
– 0 (despite appearances). Peppermint creams offered as
bribes – 3.*

The shower is definitely more suited to Mooncup
manoeuvres although I recommend emptying it quite
near the bottom of the shower to avoid *splatter* from any
sort of height. Horrifying how water *spreads* things…

Flo found all of the peppermint cream wrappers in the
bathroom bin and questioned me about them while Jess
was outside building a nest for snails out of soggy leaves
and an empty packet of Quavers. I felt like a fifteen-
year-old year caught with an empty bottle of Lambrini
under the bed.

I couldn't think of a legitimate reason why the
bathroom bin would be full of peppermint cream
wrappers other than the truth, so I went with that.
Flo seemed almost impressed with my cunning and
promised not to tell Jess as long as she could share them.
Made a mental note to get some Poundland sweets for
the haemorrhoid box and to empty the Canesten out
of its packet to make room for the Bendicks. No point
wasting the good chocolates on a child, just because I've
been caught out.

WhatsApp from Busy Beavers about a parents' social on
Wednesday evening at The Boat and Anchor. Messaged
WIB to see if either of them fancied it, but both said they

were at home with the kids. I don't like Cassie or Yvonne much, obviously, but if I'm really going to become a part of Barnmouth and make more friends then maybe I need to stop being a baby and go to things like this?

I will think about it.

Tuesday 22 May

Instagram post from @simple_dorset_life of an old wooden signpost that says 'to the sea'. Behind it you can see an overgrown pathway leading down towards the beach.

'*Sometimes you have to walk a difficult path to find the beauty at the end of a journey,*' said the caption. '*The walk isn't always easy, but the feel of the warm sand between your toes could be all the reward you need. #takeupthechallenge #blessed #lifeisajourney*'.

I took this as a sign that I should man up and go on the playgroup social tomorrow.

Wednesday 23 May

Playgroup committee roles accidentally volunteered for – 1. Glasses of prosecco drunk in the process – 3 (very necessary).

I've been duped!

I was extremely brave and went to the playgroup 'social', after a large glass of wine at home for courage, and what was my reward?

A playgroup committee meeting!

I blame @simple_dorset_life for this, with her stupid paths and signposts and warm sand.

It started out so innocently – 'Thanks so much for coming, Frankie! Here, have a glass of prosecco, Frankie!' – that I was almost relaxed when Cassie stood up and did a little chink on her glass with a perfectly manicured fingernail.

'Thanks so much, everyone, for coming,' said Cassie, managing to look humble and superior at the same time. 'I know it's not easy getting away from the little ones at bedtime!'

Who actually says 'little ones' in normal speech? I thought it was just used in marketing materials by organic, reusable nappy companies and other people who generally want to patronise you. Oh hang on, I see now.

'It really is lovely to see so many new faces on the playgroup committee, though.'

What? Playgroup committee?

I was there for the prosecco, no way did I sign up for a committee. I pride myself on having managed fourteen years of parenting without ever *once* having got myself roped into the PTA. I've never manned a tombola or had to co-ordinate a bake sale. How had I ended up at a playgroup committee meeting?

'I know that our little ones enjoy being busy little beavers every Thursday,' she went on, 'but it takes busy grown-up beavers behind the scenes to make it happen!'

Sweet Jesus. I looked around the table at the other mums. A couple of them were looking as confused as me, but no one was brave enough to protest. The ex-Olympic sailor (Jen), made a move, almost as if to interrupt, but then thought better of it and poured another glass of prosecco instead.

'So the first thing we need to sort out,' Cassie continued, 'is committee roles.'

OK, so this was the key stage. All I had to do was *not* put my hand up for anything and I could leave without a particular responsibility, making it easier to step down (via email) after the meeting.

'I guess the chair is the *most* important role,' said Cassie, doing her best to look coy. 'Does anyone fancy putting themselves forward for this?' She moved her eyes around the table, as if challenging anyone to speak up.

'Oh, *you* should *definitely* do it,' said Yvonne, practically drooling into her Scampi Fries. 'You've done such an amazing job so far.'

'Well,' said Cassie, giggling coquettishly, 'that's ever so sweet of you, Yvonne. I do try my best! It isn't easy when you're dealing with *two* children with dairy intolerances! I wouldn't want to monopolise the job, though, if anyone else wanted to have a go.' The table was silent. The rest of the pub fell briefly silent too, as though everyone was being careful not to accidentally volunteer.

'Well, if you're all sure,' said Cassie, 'then I'm flattered that you all have such confidence in me! Now, how about squash and biscuits co-ordinator?'

In a manner similar to a horror film I once saw where the main character had their fingernails ripped out one by one, Cassie assigned six more roles. I sat on my hands, lips pressed together (between sips of prosecco, obviously).

'So that just leaves the important role of Busy Beavers treasurer!' said Cassie. She looked at me. With horror, I realised that there were only seven of us around the table. By saying nothing I appeared to have inadvertently landed myself with the most hideous role of all. How had I let this happen? Why hadn't I put my hand up when Christmas Party Liaison Officer had come up? That's a cushy job – once a year, with plenty of time in between to think up an excuse to get out of it. Riya looked pretty smug right about now, clutching the list Cassie had made of potential Santas.

'Oh, I don't know, Cassie,' I said, looking around the rest of the group desperately. 'My mental arithmetic is terrible, plus I have Flo starting her GCSEs, I'm really not sure I—'

'Oh, Frankie,' said Cassie, cutting me off before I had time to wriggle my way out of it, 'you're such a sweetie, playing down your talents like that! Don't worry, though, we have every faith in you! Plus, of course, I will be just at the other end of the phone should you have any questions at all. Shall we move on to the next item? It's plans for a summer cake sale to raise funds for a new glockenspiel.'

And so there I was, Treasurer of the Busy Beavers Playgroup. FML, as Flo would say.

Very little sympathy from WIB. 'This is what happens when you fraternise with the enemy,' said Sierra.

Friday 25 May

Message from Cassie today. She wants to arrange a meeting so that we can chat over the responsibilities of the Busy Beaver treasurer and she can hand over all the records for me to keep and store. I absolutely must think up a reason to get out of this. Firstly, I really do not want to do it. I cannot imagine how stressful it would be to worry that every time my phone beeped that it was a message from Cassie, questioning our spend on squash or asking for profit and loss on the sponsored toddle.

Secondly, I can't be storing financial records. I throw away most of my bank statements because I don't want to look at them and I don't even *shred* them – I just tear them in half and put them at opposite ends of the recycling bin. I can't be trusted to keep someone else's financial information secure. I drafted a reply to her.

Hi, Cassie, I would love to meet up but I've been thinking a lot about the role and I just don't think I'm at a point right now where I can take on any new responsibilities. Flo has GCSEs next year and Jess has so many commitments at the moment. I'm afraid I'm going to have to resign my post.

Lame. I'll never get away with that one. It needs to be something more conclusive.

Saturday 26 May

Another message from Cassie. 'I saw that you read my last message,' she wrote, 'so I just wanted to check that you're OK as I didn't hear back?'

Oh God. This is why I can't be the treasurer. There will be *no escape*. I drafted a new reply.

Dear Cassie, it is with deep regret that I have to bow out of my new job as treasurer for Busy Beavers playgroup. I would have loved to have had the chance to get to know you and the other mums better through this vital role, but unfortunately my doctor has just diagnosed an RSI in both wrists and has said that it would be very dangerous for me to do any additional work that might aggravate it, e.g., filing, using a calculator, etc.

Sunday 26 May

Hey Cassie, how's things? Sorry it has taken me so long to reply, it's because I met a charming circus performer called Antoine and he insisted I learn the trapeze so that I could accompany him around the world on his upcoming tour! How exciting! I am sure you will understand that this means I can no longer take on the role as treasurer.

God damn it.

Monday 27 May

Hi Cassie, apologies for my untimely response to your messages. I've had something I wanted to tell you, but I didn't know how to say it. I'm sorry, but I cannot take on the role of treasurer. I long for an excuse to be close to you but it wouldn't be fair on you or your husband. You see, Cassie, I have developed feelings for you, and I can deny them no longer. I think it started when I saw you in that fur coat back in January. I haven't been able to get the image out of my head. I feel it best that I resign from the committee for fear of falling deeper in love with you than I already am. Kind regards.

What is the matter with me? Why can't I just tell her I don't want to do it? I'm pathetic.

Messaged WIB instead for moral support.

'Perhaps you'll just have to do it?' said Lou. '*Be* the treasurer?' God, that woman is so unhelpful sometimes.

'Bollocks to that,' said Sierra, 'you just need a bit of Dutch courage, that's all. Have a couple of glasses of wine and *then* message her. Just be straightforward about it, tell her you don't have the time to do it properly and you wanted to let her know now, before you wasted her time with a handover. It won't be as bad as you think.'

Seemed like a pretty good idea to me, so I opened a bottle of Pinot and waited for the courage to build.

Tuesday 29 May

Woke up this morning to a message from Cassie.

'I have to admit I was shocked to receive your message last night,' she wrote, 'but I agree that perhaps in light of your feelings it would be better for you not to be part of the committee.'

Hooray!

'It worked!' I wrote to WIB. 'You are talking to the *ex*-treasurer of Busy Beavers!'

'Fantastic!' replied Sierra, 'I knew you could do it!'

'What did you tell her?' asked Lou.

I looked back at what I'd written. *Shit.* I'd sent the declaration of love message. Still, better than being on the playgroup committee.

Wednesday 30 May

I had a second message from Cam tonight.

After the shock of seeing him outside that bar I felt better prepared this time. Although I'd deleted his number so it didn't say 'Cam' I could see that the message began 'Hey, Franny', and no one else ever calls me that. I poured a glass of wine (and by poured a glass I mean 'necked some straight from the bottle standing at the fridge') and took some calming breaths before I read it.

'Hey, Franny,' it said. *'I was disappointed that you didn't reply to my last message, but not surprised – I totally deserve*

to be blanked. I've been thinking a lot about you over the last month and don't blame you at all for not wanting to speak to me. I came down to Barnmouth a couple of weeks ago so that if you did get in touch I'd be here for you. I'm staying in a cheap Airbnb and am basically holed up there, just working and thinking about you and Flo – it's a bit of a lonely life! I'm doing some travel writing work, which I can do anywhere, so I'm going to hang around a bit longer just in case. I've missed you, Franny. X'

I read it twice and wasn't in a heap on the floor, so excellent progress. I think it helped that he went a little bit *too* far in the 'woe is me stakes'. He hadn't looked massively lonely when I'd seen him outside the pub and I wasn't entirely convinced he was staying here just for me – it didn't sound like him.

I messaged WIB.

'I've had a second Cam contact,' I told them. 'I think I'm going to reply this time.'

'Noooo!' said Sierra. 'Seriously?'

'Are you sure that's a good idea?' asked Lou. 'What did he say?'

'Don't worry, guys,' I wrote. 'I've been thinking about it a lot over the last few weeks and I think maybe I need to do *something*. If I keep ignoring him he's always going to be hanging over me. I think I need to see him and put it to bed.'

'As long as he doesn't end up putting *you* to bed,' said Sierra.

'We're here if you need us,' said Lou, 'or if you want us to come with you?'

'Thank you,' I said, 'but let's see how I get on. I need to think, too, about what I say to Flo. He is her father, after all, in blood at least; she probably has the right to know if he's around.'

'I guess so,' said Sierra, 'although it's tempting just not to tell her, isn't it?'

Sierra had a point, it *was* tempting, but is that really my decision to make? Flo will be fifteen soon, and although I know she thinks of Ian as her dad, she deserves the right to make that call for herself. Can you imagine if I didn't say anything and then she found out? I'd always be the bad guy, then. How would she trust me again?

I also need to tell Ian, which should be fun.

'Have you spoken to your mum and dad about it?' asked Lou.

'God, no,' I said, 'they would be so worried about Flo. If he sticks around and she wants to see him regularly, then I guess I'll have to, but until there is something more concrete to tell them then there's no point; they'd only worry, and there would be nothing they could do.'

'I guess so,' said Lou, 'although I'm sure they'd want to support you.'

'I know they would,' I said, 'and I will tell them if it comes to it. Just not for now.'

I drafted a reply to Cam instead.

'Hi, Cam,' I wrote. 'It's been a while, hasn't it?' (Talk about stating the bloody obvious – ten years is definitely a while.) 'I'm glad you got in touch, though – it's time we talked about what happened and drew a line under the past. Meet up for a coffee this week? Frankie.'

I deliberately didn't use Franny as I didn't want him thinking we had any kind of special relationship left at all. He doesn't get to have a name for me any more.

I sent it to WIB for approval.

'*Love* it,' said Sierra. 'It's straightforward and assertive and you're totally in charge.'

'It's perfect,' agreed Lou. 'I'm so proud of you.'

'If I can resign from Cassie's playgroup committee, then I can pretty much do anything, right?' I said.

I downed the last of the wine and sent it.

I watched one grey tick become two. Five minutes. A beep.

'Franny,' said his reply, 'I'm so pleased to hear from you! I'd love to meet up – I'm so glad you want to see me! I can be free tomorrow?'

I would have Jess, obviously, as it was a Thursday, but I didn't want to put it off any longer than I had to. I quickly formulated a plan.

'Ladies,' I wrote to WIB, 'I need your help. Cam has replied and he wants to meet tomorrow. I've asked nursery to take Jess for the morning, but would one or both of you be free to "accidentally" happen to be in the same café as us? Just to keep an eye? I'm feeling strong about it, but it would make me feel so much better knowing you guys were nearby.'

'Oh my God, I thought you'd never ask!' said Sierra. 'Where are you going to meet him?'

'I was thinking up at the café by the bike hire place,' I said. 'It's a bit out of the way, I know, but I don't want to run the risk of Cassie coming in and introducing herself or anything awful like that. I'm going to suggest eleven o'clock, so perhaps you could be there about 10.45, get a prime position?'

'Oooh, yes!' said Lou. 'Count me in. Shall we wear dark glasses? Do you want us to plant a mic?'

Now, of course, I'm absolutely shitting myself.

Thursday 31 May

Number of times I found myself thinking about glitter slime while Cam was harping on about his 'writing' – 9. Slices of chocolate cake paid for – 2, apparently. Sense of closure and new-found strength of character brought about by facing demons – 1. Hooray!

I arrived at the café at about ten to eleven. I wanted to be there first to settle myself and make sure I was sitting somewhere where I could see Sierra and Lou for moral support, but not so close that Fox, Arthur or Edward would spot me and run over to say hello. Lou gave me a wink as I walked past and I ordered a flat white and took it over to a table in the corner where I could see the door.

I opened the internet on my phone and watched a YouTube video of someone making rainbow glitter slime that was there from the last time the girls used it. I can see what Flo likes about the whole slime thing, to be honest – you really get sucked in. In fact, I didn't notice Cam arrive until he was standing next to the table.

'Hi, Franny,' he said, smiling.

He'd caught me off guard. 'Just catching up on some work,' I said, muting the chirpy American teenager in the slime video and putting my phone face down on the table with my purse.

'You look amazing,' he said.

I did not look amazing. In fact, I had deliberately *not* made an effort so that if he paid me a compliment I would know he was lying. One point to me. He stood there, clearly waiting for me to get up and kiss him. I stayed sitting down. 2–0.

He caught the eye of the waitress and, as he sat down, ordered a coffee and two pieces of chocolate orange cake – the one I'd been eyeing up when I got my coffee. Damn it. 2–1.

I took a minute to look at him, testing myself. He looked mostly the same, but something was missing. When I used to look at him, back when we first met, I swear I could almost see him *glowing*. He definitely wasn't glowing today. He was starting to show his age and he needed a shave. His hair was messy, but rather than looking cool with it, he just looked, well, messy. 3–1.

We talked a bit about work and family. I asked him about his travel writing job, and it turned out he was writing the copy for the website of a friend of a friend.

'What's the site about?' I asked. 'Is it the chance for you to share all those amazing travel experiences?'

'Well, yeah, sort of,' he said, looking cagey.

'Sort of?'

'It's more of a camping site,' he said. 'Product descriptions for tents and camping stoves. But the guy who runs it has definitely said that he wants to start creating more aspirational content, once the basics are done.'

'Well, that's great,' I said, 'and it's brilliant that you can work remotely.'

He is writing descriptions of camping stoves! Ha!

'I hear you got married,' he said. 'How long did you stick it out with Mr Nice?'

I bristled. Ian and I might not have worked as husband and wife but he *was* nice. More of a man than Cam would ever be – a man who had taken Cam's daughter on as his own because Cam hadn't faced up to his own responsibilities.

I changed the subject.

'What about Florence?' I asked him. Using her full name somehow kept a distance between them.

'I want to see her, of course,' he said. Of course. Only he hadn't mentioned her until I did. 'How is she?'

'She's really good,' I said. 'School's going well.' I couldn't bring myself to share anything personal. It didn't feel like he deserved any details.

'Maybe I could meet up with her?' he asked. 'No pressure, just somewhere like this. You could come too, if you wanted to.'

How generous.

'I'm going to need to talk to her,' I said, 'then perhaps we can organise something.'

It was all getting a bit overwhelming, so I made my excuses and went to the bathroom for a quick bathroom-mirror pep talk.

When I came back, he'd paid the bill. He never used to do that. Perhaps there is a little bit of him that's changed after all? I guess it would be difficult to get ten years older and not mature even a tiny bit. We said our goodbyes outside the café. He went to put his arms around me but I kept my hands in my pockets and he was forced to abandon the hug and make do with a forced smile from me.

After I was sure he'd gone, I went back into the café. Sierra and Lou were waiting expectantly.

'Well?' said Lou. 'How did it go? How are you feeling?'

'I think I feel OK,' I said. 'He was his usual charming self, but somehow it felt different. Less charming ... He did pay for everything, though, so perhaps he's not all bad.'

Sierra raised her eyebrows.

'You reckon?'

'What do you mean?' I asked.

'How much money was in your purse when you came out?' she asked.

'I don't know, exactly,' I said. 'A twenty-pound note and some change.'

'Have a look now,' said Lou.

I looked. There were no notes.

'He took it out of your purse when you went to the bathroom,' said Sierra. 'Sorry. Looks like he really is trying to have his cake and eat it. Or have someone else pay for it, at least.'

You'd think I would be mad, but honestly? I was pleased. If there had been any doubt at all left in my mind, then that just stamped all over it. I felt like I'd just put on a pair of prescription glasses after years of denial. Everything came into focus and for the first time I felt I was seeing the whole situation clearly.

'I'm such an idiot,' I said.

'You're definitely not an idiot,' said Lou.

'But all this time? All those years I wasted, thinking he was the one who could make me happy, thinking that if I could just be understanding and supportive and forgiving that he could be the person I wanted him to be,' I said. 'That's pretty stupid.'

'It's not stupid,' said Lou. 'You felt those things because you are a good person. You are kind and sympathetic and generous of spirit. There is no shame in wanting to see the best in people. And you know, now, which is the important thing. You were amazing and strong and now he doesn't have to have that power over you any more.'

He doesn't.

And that's a pretty nice feeling. But he's still Flo's dad.

Friday 1 June

Glasses of wine required to block out the image of Steve as Hannibal Lecter – 4. Stress Jaffa Cakes – 8. (Seriously, if I don't do something about the work situation soon then I am going to be the size of a house.)

Steve told me today that he has recommended to the board that we increase my hours to cover the extra fundraising responsibilities. I told him I didn't want extra hours – I wanted the hours I had already to fit in with school and nursery and Ian.

'But I thought you said it was too much work within the time?' said Steve.

'It *is*,' I said, 'but I don't want more hours to do it in; I never wanted the fundraising work in the first place.'

Steve accused me of being 'deliberately obstructive'. He said he is doing his best to offer solutions and I'm blocking him.

'I'm trying to help you, Frankie,' he said. 'Let me help you.' He leered at me like a serial killer in a really bad horror movie. It would be funny if it wasn't my life.

Saturday 2 June

Slices of toast, butter and Marmite throughout the day to keep mild hangover at bay – 6.

Since Thursday, I've been thinking a lot about Cam and the next steps.

I need to talk to Ian, and *we* need to talk to Flo. It's not going to be fun, but in a strange way I'm almost excited to tell Ian about it. Perhaps excited is the wrong word, but I want to be able to tell him what happened and how sorry I am for not seeing it all before. I want him to know that I *know*, and to be proud of me. Does that sound a bit pathetic?

I don't want Cam to be in charge of me any more, or to always feel like I'm waiting on his next move, so I decided to message him.

'Cam,' I wrote, 'thanks for taking the time to meet yesterday. I need to take some time to think about the next steps and to talk to Flo about things. I'll be in touch when we are ready to move forward.'

I was tempted to add something about the £20, but I think for now I feel better just having that knowledge to myself. I know what he's like, anyway: he'd just deny it, say I must have been mistaken about having it in the first place, and then I'd have to say that I had people watching, and he'd turn that into something, and before I knew it I'd be the one defending myself, even though he'd stolen actual cash from my purse.

Seriously, how am I only just seeing all this?

Sunday 3 June

I invited Ian in for a cup of tea when he dropped the girls off.

'Oh, don't worry, I'm OK,' he said.

I gave him a look that said 'you're staying for a cup of tea', and put the kettle on.

'Oh, go on then,' he said. 'Maybe a quick one.'

'Do you and Jess want to play some *Sims*?' I asked Flo, with a look that said 'take Jess to play *Sims* and I'll make it worth your while.'

It was like a Derren Brown stage show in that kitchen. My eyebrows were all over the place.

Flo took Jess upstairs and I took Ian and our tea out into the back garden. We sat down on my peeling old garden chairs and he leaned forward in his, resting his arms on his knees and holding his tea in both hands.

'I need to tell you something,' I said. I was looking at the arm of my chair and picking at the flaky paint.

'I figured that,' he said. 'Is everything OK with the girls?'

'Yes, they're fine,' I said. I wasn't sure how to start so I just went for it. 'I saw Cam last week.'

Ian let out a deep breath and sat back in his chair, as though the force of his exhalation had pushed him back against his seat. I looked up briefly. His face was stony. I couldn't tell what he was thinking, although I knew what he was thinking.

'The first thing I want to say is how sorry I am,' I said. 'I'm sorry for always bringing my problems to you, and for never appreciating what a dick he was and how supportive you were.' And then I told him everything that had happened, not stopping to let him speak or even to look at him until it was all done.

'He took *money from your purse?*' said Ian finally.

'Yes,' I said, 'although there were already no feelings there. That was just a nail in the coffin.'

'What do you mean "no feelings"?' he said, leaning forwards. 'We have been married in between, you know. Are you saying there were feelings there when we were together?'

'Not romantic feelings,' I reassured him.

This was difficult. I wanted to be as honest as I could, but it felt difficult to describe the power that I'd felt Cam had over me.

'I guess I was scared that I was going to feel angry, or out of control, that he might be able to manipulate me,' I said. 'It's not that I thought I'd fall madly in love with him or anything, but the way he left – well, it's always felt as though I wasn't allowed to decide how things ended. It's always felt a bit like something unfinished, but when I saw him I realised I'd been wrong the whole time – it *was* finished. I didn't feel anything at all. I want to say pity but honestly, not even that. Just … nothing.'

I waited then for a few minutes while Ian stared at the ground between his feet.

'It's a lot to take in,' he said calmly. His reasonableness is one of the things that has always made him such a great friend – he never flies off the handle, he takes his time to consider things.

'Of course,' I said.

Another few minutes of silence.

'So what happens next?' Ian asked eventually, looking back up at me. 'Have you spoken to Flo?'

'No, of course not,' I said. 'You're her dad, Ian. I don't care what Cam says or does: in my heart – and in hers – you're her dad, and whatever we do next we do together.'

It all got a bit messy then. I started to cry and when I looked at Ian he was crying too. I tried to hug him but I ended up spilling tea in his lap and then we both laughed and I knew everything was going to be OK, no matter what happened.

We decided we wanted to do something as soon as we could, so Ian is going to come over tomorrow night once Jess is asleep and I'm going to prep Flo.

Monday 4 June

Bad start to the day when I was woken up by the sound of the binmen and realised I'd forgotten to take out the bins. I ran downstairs and out into the street in my pyjamas but they were already turning back out on to the main road. Waved awkwardly to my neighbour across the road who was getting in his car (fully clothed).

At 8.30 p.m., when Jess had finally given up complaining about tummy ache, I messaged Ian. I'd already had a word with Flo earlier in the evening to let her know Ian was coming over. I had tried to be all casual and reassuring about it but it was a bit tricky without being able to tell her what it was about and she was very quiet over tea.

I *really* wanted a glass of wine while I waited for Ian but I also wanted to seem super calm and in control for Flo, so I resisted the call of the Chardonnay from the fridge door.

When Ian arrived, he looked fidgety. He kissed me on the cheek and whispered, 'I'm terrified' in my ear. I gave him a smile which I hoped said, 'It's going to be OK. You're a brilliant dad and Flo and I love you very much' but that's a lot to convey in a split second, so who knows?

Flo was in the lounge watching TV, so we went through. Flo was sitting under a blanket with it pulled right up under her chin.

'Hey, Dad,' she said as Ian came in.

'Hey, sweetheart,' he said, 'what are you watching?'

'Just *Friends*,' she said, switching it off. 'So … what's going on?'

'Well,' I said, leaning forward and looking right at her, 'first of all I want you to know that we both love you.'

Ian laughed, which broke the tension. 'Frankie!' he said. 'You're making it sound as though one of us is dying! Flo, please don't worry – your mother is doing her "concerned parent" bit, not deliberately trying to scare you.'

I frowned at him, but Flo was laughing, so I stopped. Perhaps I *had* been a bit full on.

'Sorry,' I said, 'I'm just not very good at this sort of thing.'

Fortunately, Ian is, so he took the lead. We told her about her father getting in touch and how I had met with him and how, if she wanted to, she could see him, and we could be there or not be there, whatever made her feel most comfortable.

We'd agreed to keep it very straightforward, but no pressure. We didn't tell her about the stealing – we knew that wouldn't help matters. We just wanted to give her the basic facts and to be as supportive as possible. Ian was amazing. It was hard enough for me as her mum, but there's Ian, not even her biological father, having to offer to be there when she meets this other man. I can't even imagine how that must feel. None of that was on his face, though; only concern for Flo.

She was quiet for quite a long time after we'd finished our bit.

'Has he had any other children?' she asked. I hadn't been expecting that to be her first question.

'I don't think so,' I said. 'He didn't say that he had, but I didn't actually think to ask. I can find out for sure, though?'

'OK,' said Flo.

She was quiet again.

'I don't really know,' she said eventually. 'Honestly, I'm not that fussed – he's the one who left and we've always done perfectly fine without him.'

'That's true,' I said. She didn't look convinced though.

'But then maybe it would be good to get some closure?' she said. 'I might regret it if I didn't meet him.' She's so bloody mature sometimes, for a fourteen-year-old, she makes me so proud. 'So maybe I *should* meet him, just to see. If you didn't mind, Dad?' She looked at Ian.

'Of course I don't mind,' he said. 'I think you're right.'

'But it wouldn't be because I want him to be my dad,' she said, 'it's just to see.'

'It's OK, Flo,' said Ian, getting up and giving her a hug, 'don't think you'd get rid of me that easily. You're going to be my girl, no matter what.'

I had a little cough at this point to sort my face out.

We agreed that I'd message Cam and we would arrange to see him. I fetched the Chardonnay and two glasses and a packet of Quavers for Flo and we all watched *Friends* until bedtime.

Tuesday 5 June

Messaged Cam. No reply.

Wednesday 6 June

*Desk items considered briefly as weapons but deemed
unsuitable – 6. Jaffa Cakes eaten directly from desk
drawer – 5. (Totally understandable in the context.)*

I had a letter back about one of my fundraising
applications at work today. I'd only sent it off a couple of
weeks ago and I wasn't sure if the quick response was a
good or a bad thing. Turns out it was bad.

'*Many thanks for your application blah blah. We regret
to inform you that your application has not been successful
blah blah. At the current time our available funds are very
limited and we didn't feel that your project showed enough
measurable benefit for our target groups etc.*'

I took it in to show Steve. He read the whole thing,
painfully slowly, with his lips pursed, shaking his head at
intervals.

'It's pretty disappointing, Frankie,' he said, handing
the letter back. He carefully laced his fingers together
and made a point with his index fingers, like I do when
I'm playing 'Here's the church, here's the steeple' with
Jess. He rested his index fingers on his mouth and looked
at me over the top of them. 'It's a shame that you weren't
able to make the project fit the funding well enough.'

I scanned his desk for something to hit him with.

'I think the whole thing about fundraising,' I said, 'is that the project has to be created with the need in mind *and then* you find the right funding for it. You can't *make* something fit. This project you wanted to do and the funder you wanted me to apply to just didn't match.'

I've tried to tell him this several times over the last few months, but he was insistent that we go with the list that Angela had identified.

'Isn't it the job of the fundraiser though to work their magic and create that connection?'

Book? Only paperback, probably wouldn't hurt him enough. Hole punch? That might do it. My hand twitched.

'As I keep saying, Steve, I'm not a fundraiser, and I'm definitely not a magician. I have an English literature degree and I work here purely out of convenience. I try to make the best of it because it fits around my family. I tolerate *you* at best, Steve, although I have to admit it's difficult working with someone who clearly doesn't have a clue what they're doing.'

Steve looked appalled.

I raised my eyebrows, gave him a stare, then I turned around and left his office, slamming the door behind me. I sat down at my desk. I wanted to high five someone but there was no one there so I had to make do with messaging WIB and telling them all about it.

'Bloody hell,' said Sierra, 'I'm impressed! Could you come round and sort Fox out this afternoon, maybe?

He's just told me I'm a big fat poo that should be shut in a box.'

Thursday 7 June

Reply from Cam. We arranged to meet him tomorrow afternoon. Ian is going to come over and stay with Jess. Flo seems OK about it, but she can be pretty hard to read sometimes. She says she doesn't remember him, so I suppose it's difficult to have very much of an emotional connection with someone who is basically a stranger.

Friday 8 June

Flo was quiet in the car on the way to meet Cam, but not sobbing or chewing her knuckles or anything. I asked if there was anything she wanted to know beforehand, or anything she wanted me to ask or not ask. She told me I really needed to chill out. She was probably right.

We'd arranged to meet back at the bike café at four o'clock. We were about ten minutes early, so I got us both tea and cake and we talked a bit about school, Flo looking up at the door every time someone came in.

At 4.15 there was still no sign of Cam and no messages. Flo was starting to look a bit dejected. I felt responsible for him, for her – for everybody, really. You'd think after ten years that he would make the effort to show up on time, wouldn't you? We waited another fifteen minutes, but still nothing. I decided to call him. He answered after three rings.

'Hey, Franny!' he said. 'How's things?'

'How's things?' I said, trying to be calm. 'We've been waiting for you for half an hour at the bike café!'

'Oh shit, sorry!' he said. 'Was that today? I thought it was tomorrow. God, I'm so sorry, Franny.'

'We can hang on if you want to come now?' I suggested. I thought I could hear laughter in the background.

'Err …' he said, 'now isn't really a good time, to be honest. It's the camping site – we've had a bit of an issue and I need to get it sorted ASAP.'

'Right,' I said, sarcastically, 'busy time of the year for tents, I guess.'

'Exactly,' he said, totally missing the sarcasm, 'I'm so glad you understand, Franny. How about next week instead? Wednesday, maybe?'

'Sure,' I said, just wanting him gone now, 'Wednesday.' I hung up the phone.

'He's not coming, is he?' asked Flo.

'I'm so sorry, darling,' I said, 'he got the days confused and he has this big thing at work…'

'I heard, Mum,' she said, 'and it's OK, it's not your fault. Let's not go home yet, though – it's nice here just us.'

So we stayed and ate more cake and Flo told me about Sasha's brother setting off the fire alarms at school. It was nice, just us.

Monday 11 June

Minutes spent worrying about whether or not I'm a good parent because I don't like reading books that rhyme – 38. Glasses of wine to numb the guilt – 2.

Jess asked me this evening if I still like her.

'Of course I like you!' I said, scooping her up and kissing her squidgy cheeks. 'I love you, too! Why would you ask that?'

'Because you are always looking at your phone and you don't watch properly when I do dances or shows with the ponies and you haven't read me any *Famous Five* for ages.'

I felt *awful*.

I've been so preoccupied over the last few weeks with Cam and Flo and work that I probably have been neglecting her. When a three-year-old spells it out to you, though, it does not make you feel good about yourself.

I made a big fuss of bedtime and got Flo to come into Jess's room to listen to some *Famous Five* with us. I moved Jess on to my own favourite children's books as soon as I could because as much as it *looks* like a blissful bonding moment on TV shows, reading about Poppy and Sam's adventures on the farm again and again, every night for six months, makes me want to put the book down and throw myself under the nearest bit of farm machinery while Rusty and the children watch my blood and bones get spewed out on to the 'field of ripe corn'.

I used to feel terrible about it, because I love books and I want my children to love books and every other parent I speak to talks about story time like it's the best thing to happen to them since they were single and child-free and had that one night of passion with the Swedish Pilates instructor from the gym, when their bodies were still tight and bendy, but I just found it so tedious.

Famous Five, though – you know where you are with a romp about smugglers in secret passages. Also, I tell myself that Jess is really just listening to the soothing sound of my voice and not noticing the gender stereotypes and casual racism.

Tuesday 12 June

Men on Tinder discounted based purely on inability to use capital letters properly in their bio – 13. Further men discounted for including the line 'does anyone even read this? Lol' in their bio – 6.

Work is decidedly tense since my 'chat' with Steve last week. He looks almost scared of me, but also sort of shifty, as if he might be plotting some horrible revenge. I'm talking to him with the edge in my voice that I use when Flo has done something to annoy me and hasn't yet apologised.

Cecilia noticed the atmosphere when she came in today for a meeting about the summer exhibition. It starts at the end of July and, with all of the fundraising applications I've been working on, plans are not as far along as they should be.

Cecilia took me aside after the meeting to ask if everything was OK. Her eyes were twinkling and she could barely contain herself. 'If I didn't know better I'd say you'd had a passionate affair gone wrong!' she said quietly in the kitchen. 'It was *electric* in there!'

I laughed – a lot.

I'm taking Flo for a second attempt at seeing Cam after school tomorrow so I told Steve I had to leave early tomorrow for a hospital appointment. He asked what it was about. I told him I was having a cervical examination because I'd been experienced some irregular bleeding. He didn't ask any more. I expect I will get a sad face on my performance sticker chart.

I'm really nervous about tomorrow. I tried to talk to Flo about it but she just said she was fine. She was watching a YouTube make-up tutorial and barely looked up. Parenting teens is so difficult because you really have no idea whether they are actually tormented and just putting on a brave face or if, genuinely, the make-up tutorial is just *that* good. I have watched some and they can be pretty hypnotic, to be honest.

I had a little play with Tinder to distract me – I've neglected it lately. I had matched with a man called Mike. I read his profile and then messaged WIB.

'What does it mean if someone is interested in "exploring a more dynamic idea of a relationship"?' I asked.

Sierra replied. 'It means they want the option to shag about and you have to be OK with it.'

Unmatched with Mike.

Wednesday 13 June

Left work at three to pick up Flo, wishing I actually was going to an invasive cervical exam.

Cam was already at the café, which was an improvement on last time at least. I feel like this is the point where I should fill in lots of detail about what an emotional experience it was, but honestly? It really wasn't. Cam was fine – friendly and chatty – although he talked more about himself than anything else. Flo seemed OK with it, bored if anything.

After about forty-five minutes he looked at his watch and made excuses about a work meeting. They hugged awkwardly, like work colleagues who weren't sure of one another.

'So?' I said to Flo as soon as he had gone.

'It was fine, I guess,' said Flo.

'Just fine?'

'Well, no offence, Mum, as I know you must have liked him once,' she said, 'but he's a bit of a dick, isn't he? All that talk about his creative spirit when his job is just writing about tents?'

I laughed. 'He's certainly always had a bit of a way with words,' I agreed. 'Do you think you'll want to see him again?'

'I don't mind keeping in touch,' she said, 'but I can't ever see any kind of deep and meaningful father/daughter situation going on. Ian's my dad, isn't he? Really.'

'Yes,' I said, giving her a big hug, 'he really is.'

We were in the car on the way home when Ian called. Flo answered my phone for me.

'Hey, Dad,' I heard her say. Then a pause while Ian talked. 'Yeah, yeah, I'm fine.' Another pause, and then she laughed. 'I know,' she said, 'I love you too.'

More silence at Flo's end and then she turned to me, twisting the phone away from her mouth. 'Mum,' she said, 'Jess is hungry and Dad is ordering pizza – do we want some?'

'Well, dur,' I said. 'I think we deserve a pizza, don't you?'

She turned back to the phone.

'Mum says yes,' she said. 'See you soon!'

Slightly regretted the seven slices of ham and pineapple when I was lying in bed later on my back and my stomach *still* looked about four months pregnant, but totally worth it.

Friday 15 June

Email from Steve at work today copying in the chair of trustees. He had the cheek to question my ability to do my job in light of fundraising results to date and 'certain inappropriate remarks' made recently. He wants me to attend an 'emergency' meeting with a representative from the trustees to discuss how we move forward.

That man has got a bloody nerve. *My* ability to do my job? He is an absolute joke. I didn't even *want* to take on the fundraising role in the first place, told them I didn't have the right experience. It might have worked if I had the backing of someone who wasn't a complete and utter moron, but when your boss's idea of support is to tag you in a motivational quote on Twitter then you seriously have to question whether they are really cut out for management.

What was absolutely the shittiest part of it, though, was that he must have sent it *just* as he was leaving for the weekend, so by the time I had read it he had already gone and I'll be forced to stew over it all weekend.

So pissed off. What a coward.

Very tempted to go home and drink the entire bottle of wine that's in the fridge but I didn't want Steve to win. He wanted to ruin my weekend and, damn it, I wasn't going to let him.

I ate four Jaffa Cakes instead, slowly. (Basically mindfulness.)

I messaged Dylan to see if he was going to be in the shop tomorrow – I've been wanting for ages to get rid of some of Jess's baby toys and I thought I could help him create a bit of a friendlier children's corner, plus I'd feel better having something to do rather than just sitting at home eating biscuits and worrying about work and Cam.

'I'll be here!' he replied. 'Funnily enough, I don't have loads of staff chomping at the bit to work Saturdays in June. Not ones I could leave in charge, anyway. Tom is keen, bless him, but last week I overheard him tell a customer that Emily Dickinson has a new book of poems out soon.'

'Perfect,' I replied. 'I'm child-free and would otherwise be doing exciting jobs like picking bits of Lego out of the vacuum cleaner or taking things out of their packets in the fridge so that Flo doesn't get on my back about best before dates.'

'Well, that *does* sound like a treat,' said Dylan, 'I wouldn't want to impose…'

'It's a sacrifice I'm prepared to make.'

Saturday 16 June

Book covers stroked fondly – many. Actual rooms I can call entirely my own – none. (Bit disappointing.)

I had an ace day today, mooching about the bookshop and complaining to Dylan about Steve. Bless him, he's very patient. He's on his own with three daughters so I guess he's used to women/girls offloading their problems on to him.

He made me a coffee in a Penguin Books mug (*A Room of One's Own* – that would be nice) and gave me free rein in the children's corner. I rearranged some of the shelves to make a bit more space and filled a box with Jess's old toys. I'd brought a rainbow rug that Flo used to have in her bedroom, plus a couple of cushions, to make a little reading corner.

'Dylan,' I said, coming back through to the front of the shop, 'when I was clearing up upstairs I noticed a small armchair in that second room. Would you be up for us bringing it down?'

'Do you need a sit down already?' he said, winking.

'Har har,' I said. 'No, I was thinking of parents coming in with children. It would be nice for them to have somewhere to sit while the children looked at the books – it might encourage them to stay a bit longer. I was also wondering about moving a selection of the current adult fiction choices into the kids' section and having a special "quick picks for grown-ups" shelf? That way you're not stuck there with nothing but *The Gruffalo* – you can choose something for yourself at the same time.'

'That's a genius idea!' said Dylan. 'I love it. And yes, let's go and get the chair now.' He headed towards the stairs and then looked back. 'You'd better not be about to present me with a bill for bookshop consultancy services, mind,' he said.

'I definitely am,' I said. 'I take payment in prosecco or Jaffa Cakes.'

I haven't heard anything from Cam since Wednesday. I'd (foolishly) thought he might be in touch to see how Flo was after their meeting, or to ask if she wanted to see him again, but nothing. If I don't hear anything over the next few days then I will call him. I kind of want to leave it, though, and see how long it takes him, see how much of a careless shit he really is.

Sunday 17 June

Snails removed from Jess's bedroom, collected under the guise of 'snail sanctuary' – 4. Glamorous parties cancelled to accommodate Ian's plans – ha!

Ian was looking decidedly sheepish when he dropped the girls off this evening. 'I've got a favour to ask,' he said, 'and you might be mad.'

'What is it?' I asked, suspiciously.

'Josh and I have got a potential new client based in New York. They're a massive company and this could be a really big deal for us.'

'Yeah, yeah, I know you're important,' I said sarcastically, rolling my eyes. 'So how does it impact me?'

'It involves going there in person,' he said, 'in a couple of weeks. It would be over the weekend, though, when it would be my turn to have the girls.' The calendar was right there on the wall next to my head. Ian looked at it at the same time as I did and we could both see it was empty for two weekends' time. 'Normally we'll be able to be more flexible with them, or Josh can meet them, but we both need to be there for the pitch.'

He looked back at me hopefully. 'I could have them next weekend instead?' he suggested.

'That's fine,' I said, looking at the calendar. 'Obviously, I'll have to get out of all of the parties and whatnot that

I've been invited to, but it shouldn't be a problem.' I smiled at him and he made a move as if to kiss me and then checked himself. 'And well done,' I said, 'on the new client. I'm sure you'll nail it.'

'Thanks,' he said, awkward now. 'I hope so.'

'There's one more thing,' he added. 'Jess has been invited to a birthday party on the Saturday – here's the invite.'

He handed me a garish-looking invitation. A sprinkle of glitter fluttered on to the floor.

'It's Macy from nursery,' he said. 'Her mum gave me this on Wednesday. She's the one who always dresses entirely in pink,' he added. 'Macy, not the mum.'

'I know the one,' I said. 'Jess says she always goes straight for the dressing-up box and never lets anyone else have a go on the tiara.' I stuck the invite on the fridge with a magnet in the shape of an Irish leprechaun that Ian brought Jess back from his last trip to Dublin.

'Thanks, Frankie,' he said, 'I appreciate it. In fact, I got you these as a pre-emptive thank you.' He produced a double pack of Jaffa Cakes from behind his back. I laughed.

'If this is the deal then we may have to swap more often,' I said.

'Actually,' he said, 'there was something else I wanted to talk to you about too, only perhaps just the two of us?' I must have looked a bit worried as he quickly reassured me. 'It's nothing bad,' he said, 'and I'm not going to ask you to give things a second try or anything ...' Cue awkward laugh. 'I just thought it might be something to talk about when I have your full attention.'

Intriguing.

We agreed to go out for a drink on Tuesday night – Flo can stay home with Jess for an hour, I'm sure it won't kill her. (Although Jess might.) What does he want to talk to me about though?

Monday 18 June

Didn't sleep well last night – I kept having weird dreams about Ian where he did things like announce he was emigrating and then turn up to pick up the girls to take them with him. In one dream he arrived at the house wearing my wedding dress and announced he was having a sex-change operation.

'Ian wants to *meet*,' I messaged to WIB. 'What do you think it's about?'

'How do you mean *meet*?' asked Lou. 'Like a date?'

'God, no, not a date,' I replied. 'He reassured me quickly on that one. A bit too quickly, if anything.'

'Do you think he's met someone else?' asked Sierra, never one to beat around the bush. 'Perhaps he wants to tell you he's getting married again?'

Nooooo. He wouldn't, would he? I mean he *could* obviously, I'm not saying that. It would hardly be very fair of me to divorce him and then tell him that he now had to live and die alone, but still … That would be *weird*.

'How would you feel about that?' asked Lou

'I don't know,' I said. 'I shouldn't really feel anything, should I? I didn't want to be married to him, so I can hardly refuse to let him marry anyone else.'

'No,' said Sierra, 'but that doesn't mean you're not allowed to *feel* anything about it. He's still the father of your children. Well, child at least. But children, too. You know what I mean.'

'Plus he was your best friend for all that time,' said Lou, 'and if he marries someone else then that probably draws a line on you ever being able to get that back, doesn't it?'

Oh God. Does it? I know things are still strange between us at the moment, but I guess a part of me had always assumed that one day we'd get back on track and he would go back to being just Ian, not ex-husband Ian. I don't want someone else to replace me. How selfish is that? Very.

'Maybe he's been offered a new job?' said Lou. 'What exactly is it he does again?'

'He's a management consultant,' I said. 'He co-owns the business with a friend and they've done it for years. It would be pretty big news if he was leaving.'

'Well, he *did* want to talk to you alone,' said Sierra, not helping at all. 'Perhaps they've decided to sell up and he's going to retire early to the Caribbean.'

'No way,' I said, 'he wouldn't leave the girls. He's stayed in Dorset even though it means he has to travel ridiculous distances for work in London. I don't think he would move away.'

'New wifey it is, then,' said Sierra.

Help.

Tuesday 19 June

Minutes spent imagining Ian's new wife – 34,901 (roughly). Pounds in my bank account – more than when I started the day.

*

I'm putting make-up on in the mirror in the hall, ready to go out and meet Ian.

'This isn't anything weird, is it?' asked Flo, looking suspicious.

'What do you mean, weird?' I asked.

'I'm not sure,' said Flo, 'only you're putting lipstick on and wearing that fancy top you wore at New Year.'

'If I remember rightly,' I said, 'you told me I looked like a supply teacher in it, so I'd hardly wear it to impress anyone, would I? And no, it's nothing weird, I just don't go out as much as you, so sometimes it's nice to put on a bit of lippy.'

Flo shuddered. 'Don't ever say the word "lippy" again,' she said. 'It sounds awful. Like something a supply teacher would say to try to make the class think she was cool.'

'Understood,' I said. 'Now be good, get Jess to bed in an hour – and only one more choccy biccy each.' I was being cruel with my abbreviations, but sometimes she deserves it, bossing me about like I'm six years old and she's my primary school teacher.

'Gah, Mum, no!' she shouted at me as I opened the front door. 'Choccy biccy is worse than lippy! Stop it!'

'Bye, darlings!' I shouted back, and shut the door.

On the way to the pub I had a quick scroll of Instagram, just to calm the nerves. I'd wanted a glass of wine before I left but Ian would have known and I wanted to appear cool about the whole second marriage thing.

I had a look to see what @simple_dorset_life had been up to. She'd been making Kefir Colada – I really must tell Lou about her.

'*Did you know that your gut is like a second brain?*' the caption said. '*Feed it the right things and you create a balance and harmony that's reflected in your thoughts. The name Kefir comes from the Turkish word keyif, which means "feeling good" after eating, and it contains more probiotics than natural yogurt. Many studies have shown the influence of probiotics on mental health, so if you want to reduce anxiety you could do a lot worse than to whip up this tasty treat. #feelinggood #kefirlove #simplelife*'.

I definitely did want to reduce anxiety, but suspected the Boat and Anchor might not sell a lot of Kefir. I considered a regular pina colada, but I thought a mini umbrella and a pineapple chunk might look a little out of place as part of a Serious Talk.

I was spared the decision anyway, because when I arrived, Ian was already there and had bought me a large glass of white wine. Probably for the best.

'Hello,' he said, standing up as I approached the table. 'You look nice for a school night.'

'Flo says this top makes me look like a supply teacher,' I confessed, 'but what do fourteen-year-olds even know, anyway?'

We sat down and I took what could probably be called a swig of wine.

'I hope I didn't worry you,' Ian said, 'saying I wanted to meet like this.'

'No, not at all,' I said, lying, 'I've barely thought about it. I'm happy for you, honestly I am.'

'Happy for me?' He looked puzzled.

'For the wedding,' I said, and then remembered that he hadn't told me yet. 'I mean, I just kind of figured that was what you wanted to talk about, that you'd met someone else.'

He laughed. 'You've barely thought about it but you have me married off already?'

'OK,' I confessed, 'so perhaps I've thought about it a bit. Lou thought you might be moving away, but I said I didn't think you'd do that, so Sierra was sure you must have met someone else.' I had another swig.

'So what's she like?' he asked.

'Who?'

'My new bride?'

'Oh, you know: beautiful obviously, but very smart too, and very *together*. She probably has an investment portfolio, but also she volunteers at a children's home when she isn't working as a professional photographer and part-time model.'

'She sounds intense,' said Ian. 'When would she even have time to see me?'

'Oh, she's *very* well organised,' I said. 'She probably has a personal assistant who arranges all your dinners.'

'I see,' said Ian. 'Well, she sounds like a catch. I feel almost disappointed now not to be marrying her.'

'Who *are* you marrying then?' I asked. I took swig number three and noticed the glass was nearly empty.

'I'm not marrying anyone! That's not what I wanted to talk to you about.'

'It isn't?' I asked.

'It isn't,' he said.

Talk about making a fool of yourself. I drained the glass. Ian watched. 'Would you like another drink?'

'Yes,' I said, 'but I'll get them.'

While I was at the bar I messaged WIB. 'Ian is not getting married. *Repeat*. No marriage. Will keep you posted.'

I came back from the bar with our drinks and sat down. 'I wanted to talk to you about my London flat,' he said.

Ian has this flat in London that he inherited when his dad died suddenly of a massive heart attack when Ian was eighteen. He's lived in it, on and off, and sometimes rented it out. It's not one of those 'bought for £10,000 now worth three million' London flats, but any kind of London flat is a nice flat to have.

When we divorced I didn't want to have to split it – it's a piece of his dad, after all – which is how I ended up with the house in Barnmouth.

'I've sold it,' he said.

'What? When? You didn't say anything. I thought you wanted to keep it because of your dad?'

'I did,' he said, 'but my priorities have changed. What I really want is to own somewhere down here that can be a proper home for the girls. Something secure. You know I hate renting. Plus, I wanted a bit of cash to invest in the business and it just felt like the right time.'

'Wow, well, I'm pleased if you're pleased,' I said, 'and I'm sure the girls will be too. Thanks for telling me.'

'There's something else,' he said. 'I got a decent amount for it, so after buying somewhere here and taking what I need for work, I have some left over. I'm putting some of it into savings for the kids, but I want to give you some, too.'

'Oh gosh, no, I don't want any money,' I said.

'I thought you might say that,' he said, 'but it wouldn't really be for you. I don't imagine you'll spend it on hair extensions or anything. Think of it as a maintenance bonus. It was never really a fair split in the divorce, which I know was guilt on your side, and I want to balance things out a bit.'

'I really don't think I'd feel comfortable,' I protested.

'Like I said, it's not really about you. It's something I really want to do, plus it's not millions – six thousand. Maybe you could take the girls over to France to visit your mum and dad? I know they'd love that.'

That was true. I'd been promising Mum and Dad a visit since the separation and they would love to see Jess and Flo. I argued with him for a little while, but quite honestly, I could really do with the money and he genuinely seemed to want to give it to me, so I wasn't about to be too principled about it. You can buy a lot of Sylvanian squirrels and Jaffa Cakes with six thousand pounds.

Wednesday 20 June

Emergency glasses of wine needed to consider work dilemma – 3 (small). Slices of Maggie's chocolate

brownie eaten at work for stress – 3 (large.) Number of
bacon sandwiches I ate during the period in my twenties
when I told everyone I was vegetarian – at least 20.

I showed round a new volunteer at work. She's called
Charlotte and I really liked her until about ninety
seconds into the conversation when she revealed that
she doesn't own a television. What is it with people who
don't own televisions? Why do they feel the need to tell
you as soon as possible after meeting you?

It's the same with vegans.

'Oh, hello! My name's Sarah and I haven't eaten
animal products for eight and a half years!' Good for you,
Sarah. I ate half a packet of ham standing at the fridge
last night while I thought about what to cook for tea.

The TV thing especially gets on my nerves when it
turns out that they *do* watch Netflix for hours every
night in bed – on a tablet.

'Oh, but I don't watch any *live* TV, none of those
awful reality shows.'

Just because you don't watch *Love Island* doesn't make
you a better person than me. Netflix still counts, guys.

Steve has scheduled my 'emergency meeting' for
Friday. He wants me to bring details of all current
funding applications so we can evaluate them as a team.

'Can't you just leave?' asked Sierra when I messaged
WIB about it later from bed.

'I can't exactly just quit,' I said, taking a big glug
of wine (bed wine = best kind of wine), 'I don't have
anything else to go to.'

213

'But you could find something,' said Lou, 'and you were going to have to take a bit of time off over the summer holidays, anyway, weren't you? It could be perfect timing.'

'But what would I do in the meantime?' I said. 'How would I live?'

'You've got the money from Ian!' said Sierra. 'It's perfect! You wouldn't have to use all of it, just enough to cover bills and stuff for a couple of months over the summer while you find another job.'

'Oh yes!' said Lou. 'It's karma, isn't it? No, not karma. The other one that's about coincidences. Synchronicity, that's it. It's synchronicity. The universe is telling you to quit, Frankie. You can't ignore the universe.'

Obviously I don't want to ignore the universe but *could* I quit? I have to admit that I felt pretty excited about the possibility. But how would Ian feel about me using his money to leave work? That didn't seem very fair. I had finished my second glass of wine by this point so I decided to text him, lay out the scenario, and see what he thought.

'I think it's a great idea!' he said. 'It's your money, Frankie, not mine. Plus, if you feel bad because you think it means you're getting an easy time of it over the summer holidays, then remember it *is* the summer holidays – it's not exactly a spa break, is it?'

Oh God, he's right. Do I really want to have six weeks off with the girls? Obviously I love them etc., etc., but still. Summer holidays ... Am I cut out for it? And are there many part-time, flexible jobs in Barnmouth for English lit graduates with a patchy, admin-based work history?

Had some more bed wine and gave it some thought.

Nothing from Cam. No messages, no calls, no 'how's my daughter that I hadn't seen for ten years?' What is the actual matter with him?

Friday 22 June

My emergency meeting with the board was at eleven o'clock, but I could hardly contain myself, watching Steve swagger about, smirking at me.

Every time he walked past me, which was frequently, he would peer over my shoulder or make some comment about hoping I was 'ready to put my best game face on'. I never really understand people like Steve, or what they think they're going to achieve by bullying people. What's the point of making other people feel bad about themselves? Is it really just to make yourself feel superior?

By 10.50 I'd had four cups of coffee and could barely sit still.

At 10.55 the chair of the trustees arrived – Alan – and he and Steve went off into the meeting room.

At eleven o'clock exactly, Steve called me in.

'Thanks so much for coming, Frankie,' he said. 'I know the last few months have been difficult for you, and we appreciate your willingness to address the issues you've been having with workload.'

Fuck off, Steve.

'As I've explained to Alan,' continued Steve, 'the additional responsibilities do seem to have been a little too much for you, especially on top of your family commitments.' He smiled. 'This meeting is an opportunity for you to put forward suggestions you have for changes we could make and for Alan and I to offer support. Do you have anything you'd like to say first, Frankie?'

'Yes,' I said, 'I do. I have a great suggestion in fact.' I handed Alan the envelope I had brought into the room with me. 'Alan, this is my letter of resignation. I've always tried to do my best for the museum but I made it clear when Angela left that the additional work I was being asked to take on wasn't feasible within my hours, nor was I suitably qualified to undertake it. I have received very little in the way of support at a managerial level,' here I paused and looked at Steve, 'and I have come to the conclusion that the only option for me is to move on to a new challenge.'

Steve's jaw had dropped. Alan was reading the letter.

'What's the matter, Steve?' I said. 'Are you not going to offer your support?'

While the adrenalin was still pumping, I decided to call Cam. It rang a couple of times then went to answerphone, which I suspect means that he saw it was me and decided not to answer. I left a message asking him to call me back as soon as he could.

Saturday 23 June

I had a long chat with Mum tonight about Ian giving me the money and then quitting work. I could tell she was anxious about the job situation – she kept passing on snippets of our conversation to Dad, who was listening in the background, and I could hear the worry in her voice. I tried to reassure her that it was a positive thing, and that the money gave me the opportunity to think more carefully about what I wanted to do.

When we first moved down to Barnmouth two years ago in September, it was really just about finding something that worked around Jess and Flo, and then when Ian and I broke up the trustees at the museum were so good about changing my hours to fit our new week, (even if Steve was less impressed) that I don't feel I've had the chance until now to think about what I actually want to do with the rest of my life. This could be that chance.

Mum didn't sound convinced.

I promised her that once I'd found a new job and had settled in, we'd use some of the money to come and visit, perhaps in the new year. That seemed to cheer her up a bit. I didn't tell her about any of the Cam stuff. There didn't seem much point, really, especially not over the phone.

No call back yet from Cam.

Monday 25 June

Back at work today. I keep smiling sweetly at Steve and offering him cups of tea and he keeps staring back at me like he wishes I was dead. It's all very jolly. I've got a four-week notice period, so I will be leaving the week before the summer holidays start. (Trying not to think about that bit.)

After Jess was asleep I had a chat with Flo about Cam. I explained that I hadn't been able to speak to him since we met up, but that I wanted to let him know how she felt about things and what she wanted to do going forward.

'So how *do* you feel about things?' I asked.

'The same, I guess,' she said. 'I was a bit worried in case when we met I suddenly felt all these feelings for him, or sadness or something, but I didn't. He felt like a stranger, and it's hard to feel really cross with a stranger.'

That made sense.

'So like I said,' she went on, 'I don't mind keeping in touch, but I don't think I could ever really think about him as my dad. I have a dad already – me and Jess have a dad.'

'I totally get it,' I said. 'It must be weird to feel that you *should* be feeling something for someone, because you know that technically you're related, but at the same time you don't even know them, really. I'll try calling again tomorrow and I can tell him all those things for you.'

'Thanks, Mum,' she said. 'I know you wanted him to be a decent guy, and it's not your fault he's a dick.' I gave her a kiss on the head.

Tuesday 26 June

Still no reply from Cam, so I called him. He had the decency to answer this time. I had planned out exactly what I was going to say, about how difficult it must be for Flo, and how, although we appreciated having seen him, we weren't sure it was going to turn into a parent/child type of relationship, but I didn't get the chance. I got as far as asking him how he was, when he launched into a sob story about having lost his job with the camping website and needing to leave Barnmouth.

'What's the job got to do with leaving Barnmouth?' I asked. 'I thought you said the whole thing with the job was that you could do it anywhere?'

'Oh,' he said, 'well yes, I mean *technically* I could.'

'Technically?' I said.

'Yes,' he said, 'only I actually got the gig in the first place through an, err, friend, whose dad owns the business, and she happens to live in Barnmouth.'

'This *friend* doesn't happen to be blonde and in her mid-twenties, does she?' I asked.

'What?' said Cam.

'Forget it,' I said. 'So, are you saying you were only ever here in the first place for this friend? That it was sheer coincidence?'

'Well, not coincidence,' he said, 'fate, maybe? Only things haven't worked out with her, and it's made things a bit awkward for work, so I'm having to move on. You understand, don't you, Franny?'

'Oh yes,' I said, 'I understand better than I ever think I really have before.'

And that was that. It was history repeating itself, only this time around I didn't feel heartbroken and bereft, just pissed off. None of this had really been about Flo at all. But it's OK, because Flo's OK, and that's all that matters.

Saturday 30 June

Gender-neutral gifts offered to Jess as options for Macy's party – 14, gender-neutral gift ideas thrown back at me in disgust – 14.

I was Macy's party today. We stopped at Asda on the way for a gift – Jess chose a pink, plastic wand that played a selection of magical tunes and offered up inspiring phrases like 'You can be beautiful too!' and 'Sparkle like the princess you are!'

It was pretty moving stuff.

There was a purple minivan parked outside Macy's house when we arrived. 'Nina's Mobile Nail Salon!' it said on the side, in a glittery comic sans. 'Get Your Glam On Wherever You Are! We Come To You! Manis And Pedis In The Comfort Of Your Own Home!'

Covering the driver's door was a large, sparkly unicorn, rearing up on its back legs to show off a pair of manicured (pedicured?) front hooves.

There were so many capital letters and exclamation points that I felt tired just looking at it. I ushered Jess towards the front door before I accidentally said something derogatory that Jess would then undoubtedly repeat at a quiet moment during the party tea when everyone had their mouths full of pink wafer biscuits.

Macy's mum answered the door. I couldn't remember her name, so had to go with a plain old 'hello!'

She looked disappointed.

'We have come at the right time, haven't we?' I asked, looking past her and into a kitchen adorned with pink streamers and helium balloons.

'Oh yes, of course,' she said, fiddling with her hair sadly. 'Sorry, it's just that I was expecting Ian. He said it was his weekend with Jess?'

'It is, normally,' I said. 'We had to swap for a work thing, so just me, I'm afraid!' She looked genuinely sad about this, although tried not to. Did as-yet-unnamed mum have a crush? Was she single? 'What time do you want me to pick Jess up?'

'Are you not staying?' she said. 'I have some elderflower pressé in the kitchen?'

Was I meant to stay? When Flo was little, birthday party invitations were an opportunity to do fun things, like hang out in Sainsbury's for an hour and a half. Today I intended to take a book to the beach and sit in the sunshine, possibly holding the book in a well-intentioned way while having a little snooze.

'I'd really love to,' I said, 'but I have to get back and help my older daughter build a scale model of a strand of DNA.' Bit of a specific lie, but I was quite pleased with it.

Messaged Ian from the car. 'I think someone has a little crush on you!' I wrote, then panicked. 'Not me,' I wrote hastily, then felt even more stupid. 'Macy's mum – the birthday party? She was very disappointed to see me when she opened the door. I think she might have had her hair done especially.' No reply, but then I remembered he was in New York, which was why I was at the party in the first place.

Spent an hour this evening trying to wash the glitter out of Jess's hair and then cleaning the bath.

Monday 2 July

Had a browse through Tinder tonight, but I'm really not feeling it at the moment. I kept scrolling through pictures of men who just looked so *sad*, and I can't imagine how on earth you could date them and not want to kill yourself. I don't even mean sad in a 'moody and mysterious way', just actually *sad* about life.

I think I might take a break from it over the summer holidays. It's going to be hard enough maintaining my own sanity, let alone someone else's.

Wednesday 4 July

Worrying thoughts about having to give the garden cat mouth to mouth following some kind of bee reaction –
4. Times during the afternoon I wished I hadn't googled 'cat eaten a bee' – numerous.

At lunchtime I went and sat in the museum garden. There was a ginger-and-white cat there, enjoying the sunshine. I watched him watching a bee. The bee was going from flower to flower of the buddleia that's growing out of the wall and the cat was following it with his eyes. I felt a wave of contentment, sitting in the sunshine, watching the cat watching a bee. Everything felt like it fitted just right.

'You know what life is all about don't you, cat?' I said.

He looked at me over his shoulder, turned back to the buddleia, made a little leap and ate the bee.

Are cats meant to eat live bees?

Thursday 5 July

Busy Beavers kicked off big style today when Cassie and her Mean Girls crew caught Jess drinking a Fruit Shoot.

I few months ago I got sucked into a Mumsnet thread about Fruit Shoots and honestly, the vitriol was astonishing. I ended up searching the whole forum just to see – 'Fruit Shoot' came back with over five hundred results. I refined it to 'Fruit Shoot Evil' and it came back with sixty-five conversation streams.

The threads were full of horror stories of poor husbands innocently buying them for their children, (*despite being told not to! When will these Mumsnet men ever learn to do as they are told?*), and of otherwise charming, cultured toddlers throwing down their copies of *Opera Now* magazine and turning into savage beasts at the mere sniff of a bottle.

Jess's Fruit Shoot was spotted by Yvonne, Cassie's lapdog, who looked like she might climax on the spot at the opportunity to grass me up to Cassie. I spotted them muttering and nodding in my direction, and then they got up and came over.

'Frankie,' said Cassie, doing a good line in Fruit Shoot artificial sweetness, 'I couldn't help but notice that Jess has a Fruit Shoot. I just thought I should *flag* that quite a lot of the parents at Busy Beavers are keen *not* to have their children exposed to Fruit Shoots. Some of us prefer to keep our little ones free of nasties!'

Seriously, now, ladies, can we get a little perspective here? It's a fruit squash, not nuclear waste. Sure, it's a bit sickly and probably water would be better, but it's not like you're giving your kids a plastic bottle of meths to swig on.

I don't know what came over me, but I just sort of snapped. I stood up and picked up the offending Fruit Shoot. 'You're so right, Cassie,' I said, 'I don't know what I was thinking, subjecting my poor child to such cruelty.'

She looked momentarily triumphant, but I wasn't done. 'Next time I'll get her a milkshake with her Happy Meal,' I said, and with that I looped the Fruit Shoot up in the air over her head and into the bin like a shorter, chubbier Michael Jordan.

Sierra whooped and high-fived Louise. Cassie just stared, open-mouthed.

'Let's go, ladies,' I said, slinging my bag over my shoulder, 'I've got prosecco and Jaffa Cakes at my house.' I gave a sharp whistle and Jess, in an act of obedience she's unlikely to ever repeat, ran to my side. As we walked out, Jess looked back over her shoulder and called 'Sashay, away.'

Saturday 7 July

Our local primary school had their summer fete this afternoon and as I'm guessing it might be where Jess will go next September (probably should look into that),

I thought we'd all three go along and check it out. Flo might be fourteen, but she still loves a tombola.

We dodged past the 'World Cup football challenge' and 'guess how many severely manhandled sweets are in the jar' competition and headed straight for the tombola, which was being run by a group of excited-looking small boys, all squabbling over who got to hold the bucket of tickets.

It's one of those unspoken summer fete rules that whether you go, there are always the same prizes.

Classic tombola checklist:

- Token bottle of cheap prosecco to keep the parents interested
- Dubious-looking soft toy that might be a dog or might be a bear
- Orange Matchmakers
- Jar of pickled onions
- Wooden sign hung on a piece of wire saying 'Dance between the raindrops' in swirly writing
- Vanilla-scented candle (Poundland)
- Easter egg (suspicious in July)
- Single Orange and Passion Fruit J2O
- Avon lavender bubble bath that looks like it has been in someone's bathroom cabinet since 1982
- Two-litre bottle of Happy Shopper cherryade (is Happy Shopper still even a thing?)
- Ditto limeade (is limeade still a thing?)
- Family Circle biscuit selection
- Can of Lynx Africa

- Bath sponge in the shape of a duck
- Four blackcurrant Fruit Shoots split up from a multipack to make individual prizes (desperate times)

I don't know why primary schools don't just think of their target audience – tired, flustered parents – double the price and make all of the prizes wine. They'd have enough money for that new set of steel drums in no time.

Jess was desperate to win the Brut gift set for Ian but after we'd spent more than it would have cost me to just go into a shop and *buy* it she settled for winning a Kellogg's shower gel. Kellogg's as in cornflakes. Don't ask me, because I didn't understand it either. I can only assume they have taken two things that happen at a similar time of day, and thought it it would work to combine them into one product. Like Gordon's Gin putting their name to a collection of children's bedtime stories. (Not actually a bad idea.)

I won a pack of six Jaffa Cake mini rolls. Best Day Ever.

After the excitement of the tombola we sat on the grass eating Soleros and watched the talent show. I use talent in the loosest possible sense of the word.

It was mainly small girls singing songs with inappropriate lyrics about love and relationships – 'just let me love you for tonight' – but I did enjoy Aaron the Amazing and his Marvellous Magic Show. Aaron looked to be about six, but he had the confidence of a thirty-two-year-old man after two pints of lager on a sunny day.

I mean sure, you could see the handkerchiefs sticking out of his sleeve throughout his whole act, and the rabbit that appeared 'as if by magic' from under his hat had to be carried on by his mum, but somehow that didn't seem to matter.

Hearty applause all round for Aaron.

'Thanks for a great day, Mum,' said Flo when we got home. I tried not to look startled.

Monday 9 July

Had a browse through the job section of the *Dorset Echo*. Slight panic about handing in notice.

Wednesday 11 July

Scandalous moments in Aldi – 1, but massive, *so probably counts as at least 6.*

An amazing thing happened to me today. Ian picked the girls up, as usual, from school, so after work I went to Aldi. I like looking at the special offers without Jess taking all the men's thermal long johns out of their packets or demanding that I buy her a set of three barbecue tools.

I was contemplating a spiraliser and how switching carbs for courgettes would definitely make me a much better person, when I spotted a familiar face. She was wearing sunglasses and her usually coiffed hair was under a Disneyland Paris cap, but it was definitely Cassie.

I once overheard her at toddler group saying that she only ever shopped at Waitrose because she couldn't bear to make a risotto without their truffle oil, so I was a bit surprised to see her looking with such interest at an £8.99 ladies summer blouse. I was even more surprised when I looked in her basket and saw a packet of wafer-thin ham and two family bags of cheese puffs.

I ducked behind the own-brand gin display and watched her make her way to the checkout, stopping on the way for Aldi's *own-brand Fruit Shoots*.

I was beside myself!

I'd already taken my phone out to take a picture of her very presence in Aldi, so I was ready as she reached for the Fruit Shoot substitutes. The photo shows her glancing out cautiously from under her cap. It's like the front cover of *Now* magazine – 'playgroup stalwart falls out of nightclub at 3 a.m. with no underwear'.

I sent it to WIB.

'What the *fuck*?' said Sierra. 'That's incredible. This could blow Busy Beavers *wide open*. We should send this to the BB group.'

'But they'd know it was us,' said Lou. 'I don't want to be the troublemaker.'

'Nah, we just get a burner phone,' said Sierra, 'like drug smugglers do in films. Then it will be an anonymous number and no one will be able to trace us.'

'I think one of us would have to add the burner phone number to the group, though,' I pointed out. 'Anyway, we don't need to expose her, we're better than that. I'm just happy *knowing* about the photo.'

'You are far too nice, Frankie,' said Sierra.

Thursday 12 July

We chickened out of Busy Beavers today and hung out at my house instead. Sierra had wanted to go in and confront Cassie, but I would rather not. There are some people who are oblivious to logical arguments – whatever you say to them, they are never going to be in the wrong so it's just not worth it.

'You know there's only one session left next week, anyway?' pointed out Lou. 'And then it's closed for the summer holidays.'

'Seriously?' I said. 'Aren't the summer holidays prime time for needing to hang out with other parents?'

'You'd think so, wouldn't you?' said Sierra. 'Maybe we should invite everyone here instead, every Thursday? The nice ones anyway.'

'Or,' I said, glancing around at the piles of laundry and empty wine bottles, 'we could not?'

'Why don't we do something at Chapter One?' suggested Lou. 'That upstairs room is lovely – would Dylan let us leave some toys there and meet up once a week, do you reckon?'

'Amazing idea!' said Sierra. 'You ask him, Frankie, he's your boyfriend.'

'He is not my boyfriend!' I protested. 'I've only been there a few times. He's a nice guy, that's all, friendly.'

'Sure, sure,' said Sierra, 'so ask him, then, if he's so friendly.'

So I did. He was well up for it, especially when I said we'd be sure to let people know about the newly refurbished kids' corner. We agreed we'd go to Busy Beavers for the last session next week and invite our favourite parents to our summer holiday club.

*

Spent a long time in bed wondering about Dylan. I hadn't really thought about him like that, but he is quite cute in a slightly less attractive and more dishevelled 'Hugh Grant in *Notting Hill*' kind of way. Plus, he does own a bookshop – that's got to be a big tick. But then there's the whole 'recently dead wife' thing, which he's clearly still coming to terms with. No one wants to try to fill the shoes of a much-loved dead wife, do they? Still, maybe one to file away.

Saturday 14 July

Jess insisted on dressing herself this morning in tights and a wool dress, even though the forecast said twenty-four degrees. At 10 a.m. she came into the kitchen where I was washing the breakfast dishes, complaining about being too hot.

'Why don't we change you into something a bit cooler?' I suggested, quite sensibly I thought.

'No,' she said, folding her arms across her chest and looking cross.

'Well, maybe just take your tights off?' I said. She glared at me and went off into the living room.

Five minutes later I looked up from the dishes to see her in the front garden, completely naked, squatting next to my tub of mint.

'Jess,' I shouted, scooping her up and bringing her back in, 'you know you shouldn't be out the front, plus you can't just go running around outside naked!'

'It's OK, Mummy,' she said, 'I was walking.'

Monday 16 July

Ian came over for tea tonight so we could have a brainstorm about the holidays. We've already agreed that he is going to have the girls for a week near the end of August so he can take them to see his mum for a bit.

Jess is very excited about this as Ian's mum has a dog. She's convinced that she is going to be allowed to take the dog out for walks by herself and that they will have adventures together in a haunted forest and catch ghosts and smugglers – this is what happens when you read impressionable children *Famous Five* books. Ian's mum, Jacqui, lives in Hull, so I'm not sure there will be a huge amount of haunted forest action going on.

Flo is less excited as it means she has to share a bedroom with Flo for a week, plus Jacqui believes in switching the Wi-Fi off at 6 p.m. in case it gets 'too expensive'.

So that's one week taken care of. It's just the other *five* that are starting to worry me a little. Ian is going to do his usual weekends and Wednesdays, but we agreed that with me not working I would take on the rest of the time as work is really busy for him at the moment.

Although I'm delighted to not ever have to see Steve again, the small issue of not having a job means I can't really justify paying for nursery over the summer, which means I am likely to be sectioned around, say, mid-August? I'm genuinely terrified.

We do have a bit extra money now, thanks to Ian, but I need to save most of that to cover living expenses until

I find a new job. Finances aside, though, the difficulty lies in finding activities that appeal to both a teenager and an almost four-year-old. They both like Burger King, but that isn't really a six-week plan.

We sat down around the table, I sliced up the pizza, and discussions began. I had a corkboard (Poundland) that I'd procured especially.

I have to say I was pretty impressed by Flo's focused negotiation skills – 'I'll do zoos, that's fine,' she started with, eyeing the corkboard suspiciously.

'How about activities at the castle?' said Ian.

'No, absolutely not. Nothing that involves role play for me or actors. It's degrading.'

'The cinema?' I said.

'The cinema would be OK,' she conceded, 'as long as the film is a *minimum* PG certificate and I get a popcorn combo.'

'Indoor trampolining centre?' asked Ian.

Flo shrugged. 'Sounds a *bit* lame.'

'What about the Exeter Children's Festival?' I suggested, thinking that the word 'festival' might give it an edge of cool.

'Really?' she sighed. 'But that's for kids!'

'OK, how about this nature trail?' I asked, the picture of innocence, proffering a leaflet I picked up at the museum. This was a strategic move to make the kids' festival seem relatively appealing.

'NO!' She looked visibly horrified. 'All right, I'll do the kids festival and trampolining, so long as I definitely don't have to do any form of outdoor crafts.'

'Deal.'

You might think this seems a little one-sided and that we should have consulted Jess a bit more, but, quite honestly, it makes no odds where you take her as long as she has at least three ponies with her and they sell ice cream.

I added the cinema, trampolining and the kids' festival to the corkboard. It still looked pretty sparse.

'I mean, obviously we can fill in a lot of these spaces by going out for nice walks and things like that,' I said, unconvincingly. 'And maybe playing games at home?'

Flo snorted.

'What about one of those activity camps, Flo?' suggested Ian. 'You know, where you get to go away for a week and learn survival skills or something?'

'Seriously?' said Flo. 'You want to pack me off to some damp, failing country house in the middle of nowhere so I can spend my time cracking codes made out of twigs with a load of nerds?'

'I would be fun!' I said. 'How cool would it be to abseil down a cliff?'

'Really? Not fun at all,' said Flo.

'It's honestly not like that nowadays,' said Ian, offering Flo his phone, 'have a look at this one – six days of water sports in the Mediterranean – that could be fun.'

Flo sat up a little bit, her interest piqued by the word 'Mediterranean'. To be honest, *my* interest was piqued. When I was at school I went on a couple of residential camps but they were both in Somerset, in exactly the kind of crumbly country house Flo was imagining.

One was a four-day drama course where we wrote and staged our own play (I think it was about Take That, which was probably my idea), and the second was a whole week of Shakespeare. I loved it, but I think I could also have got on board with snorkelling off the Languedoc coast.

I had a look at the website.

'Ian, it's £779!' I said. You can get a lot of wine for that.

'But what an amazing experience,' he argued. 'I have some of the flat money put aside for the girls, this could be something we could spend it on if Flo was keen?'

She looked surprisingly keen. I took the phone to look again at the website. The main photo was of a tall-looking boy in a wetsuit, holding a surfboard, his curly, blond hair blowing seductively in the wind. Flo took the phone back.

'This does look more fun than Viking brass rubbings at the castle – or whatever it was you wanted me to go on,' she said.

'You could always ask Sasha if she fancied going with you?' suggested Ian.

'Maybe, Dad,' she said, still looking at the picture of the boy with the surfboard, 'although it might be better actually not to have anyone I know there, to force me to make new friends?'

There were only spaces left on the first week of the summer holidays, so we booked it. She's off to the South of France in ten days. I feel really proud of Flo. Going off to a different country with a group of strangers feels like a very brave thing to do.

I'm going to try not to look too much at the empty spaces on the corkboard.

Tuesday 17 July

Final swimming session of the term, so I dressed sparingly and took a seat poolside, ready to be impressed with all the progress Jess has made.

As far as I could see she has made *none*. I wasn't expecting her to be doing lengths of butterfly or anything, but I thought she might at least be able to make it halfway across the width of the pool without stopping to swallow mouthfuls of water/wave at me.

It was disheartening to say the least. Perhaps swimming is one of those things that just suddenly clicks? Perhaps she will look as if she is drowning for months and months and then one day it will just *happen* and she'll throw the woggle to one side and front crawl gracefully to the side.

I stopped after the class to have a word with the teacher, a bouncy young man called Gregg who looked as though he was barely old enough to buy a lottery ticket.

'Oh, we're so pleased with her!' he said. 'She's making such good progress!'

Is she, Gregg? *Is she?*

I may give it a break after the summer.

Thursday 19 July

When I got to Busy Beavers this afternoon there was a group of parents gathered around the noticeboard. I spotted Sierra and Lou sitting over in the far corner, so I went over.

'What's going on?' I asked. 'Has Cassie published a ranking of her favourite mums or something?'

'Not quite,' said Sierra, avoiding eye contact. I looked at Lou. She looked shifty.

'Why don't you go and have a look?' said Lou. They were both acting very mysteriously. I walked over to the noticeboard, just as I saw Cassie coming in through the main door. A mum near the back of the group spotted her too and nudged the women in front of her. A hush fell and the parents parted as Cassie walked towards the noticeboard.

We both looked at it at the same time. Pinned across the top of the parish council notices and toilet cleaning rota was an A2 printout of a photo, showing a woman in a Disneyland Paris cap taking a four-pack of Aldi Fruit Shoot down from a shelf. The photo was a bit blurry, having been blown up so big, but it was clearly Cassie.

I looked at Cassie. She looked at the photo.

It was like watching Regina George get hit by the bus at the end of *Mean Girls*.

Friday 20 July

Last day of work today. I collected all of the snacks I have secreted in various cupboards and drawers around the office and set my emails to redirect to Steve. (Ha ha!) Cecilia came in with a card and Maggie brought me a tray of my favourite chocolate and orange brownies.

After lunch Steve announced that he had a meeting in Honiton for the rest of the afternoon and just walked out. Just like that! Not even a 'good luck for the future' or 'thanks for all your hard work'. What an absolute dick! It was only me left, then, so I spent a happy hour in Steve's office rearranging things in a subtle but annoying way, turning books upside down on the shelves, adjusting the height of his office chair, that sort of thing, and then I went home.

Saturday 21 July

I went into Dorchester today to go to a few recruitment agencies and look around for shops that might be looking for staff. All of the main car parks were full so I ended up finding a two-hour space on a side street with a parking meter. I was feeling pretty pleased with myself until I realised that all I had in the handy change compartment of the car was twenty-seven pence in sticky coppers, a fistful of sweet wrappers, and a lip balm that had melted in the sun and not made it as far as the bin.

'No cash?' asked a sign on the side of the machine. 'No problem! Just call our payment line to pay by card.'

I called the number.

'To park your blue Seat, registration number WR05 SKO at location number 2179, press one,' said the robot. This threw me for starters, as I've never owned a Seat. I waited for more options.

'To park the same vehicle at a different location, press two.'

'To park a different vehicle, press three.'

I pressed three.

'To park your silver Skoda, registration KY64 KRR, press one,' the robot instructed me. I think that was a hire car Ian and I had a couple of years ago to go to a wedding in Scotland.

'To register a new vehicle, press two.' I pressed two.

'To register a new vehicle, please say the registration now.'

'TV05,' I said in my loudest, clearest voice, 'YVU.'

'Please say the vehicle make now.'

'Renault,' I said.

'In one word, please say the colour of your vehicle,' said the robot.

'Grey,' I said, wondering if it wasn't perhaps more of a silver but keeping quiet so as not to confuse things.

'This may take a moment,' said the robot. *Why?*

'Please confirm that the registration of the vehicle you wish to park is T ... P ... 0 ... 5 ... Y ... V ... N ... If this is correct, say yes.'

'*No!*' I shouted at the robot. The P for a V I could kind of the understand, but since when has a U sounded like an N?

'There seems to have been a problem,' said the robot, 'please press one to return to the main menu.'

Talk about a modern parable. That's the story of my life *right there*.

Job-hunting was a washout. All of the retail jobs are full of students back for the summer and, according to the recruitment agencies, the summer holidays are not really the ideal time to look for a new job. Had I thought of postponing the move until later in the year, they asked? Bit late for that now. Most of the vacancies seemed to be either in call centres or driving HGVs.

(Question: I wonder if you could earn double the money by answering calls remotely on a headset while driving a lorry?)

Wednesday 25 July

Last day of term today and I feel a weird kind of tiredness.

On the one hand I'm looking forward to not having to make packed lunches and rush around in the morning getting everyone ready. The last few weeks have been like a three-legged race where the person you've got your ankle tied to has sort of given up, and you're having to do most of the work, dragging them over the finish line.

But then, at the same time, I feel exhausted in anticipation of six weeks of summer holidays. Six weeks of trying to balance the needs of two children who seem insistent on sleeping at completely opposite times of the day. Six weeks of 'I'm bored' and 'I'm hot' and 'I don't want to go to bed'.

In town at lunchtime I saw not just one but *two* open-top buses full of Year Sixes from a local primary school. The top decks were each full of ten- and eleven-year-olds, shouting and waving at people in the street. Each group had a couple of terrified-looking teachers standing in the middle.

Now, I don't want to be a Scrooge about it, because I know that finishing primary school is a big deal when you're young, but it's hardly winning the World Cup, is it? When I left primary school we just had a big assembly where the head looked over his glasses and gave us a lecture about doing our best. Even when Flo left a few years ago it wasn't that much of a *thing*. One of the teaching assistants brought in a job lot of Calipos, and they each got a class photo, rolled up like a scroll. Then everyone said goodbye and went home.

As much as I want my kids to feel like they're special, they're not *that* special.

Tonight was meant to be child-free for me, but *Mamma Mia 2* has just come out and Ian said he was going to take the girls to see it. Jess has never been to the cinema before and so, when he asked if I wanted to come along as well, I came over all nostalgic and agreed. It didn't start until 6.15 so he gave them tea at home and then came to pick me up.

I was sitting on the front step, waiting for them, but Ian came up the path carrying a large cardboard box.

'The girls are in the car,' he said, 'but I just wanted to drop this off for you.'

'What is it?' I asked, unlocking the door so that he could put it down in the hallway.

'It's just something for the summer holidays,' he said, 'to help keep you entertained.'

'It's not anything too messy, is it?' I asked, imagining a box full of glitter and glue sticks. 'You know I'm not great with crafts.'

'It's not messy, I promise,' he said. 'It's no big deal, you can look later.' He shut the front door before I had chance to protest and we walked to the car.

Ian has always been the sensible one, so obviously he had come to the cinema prepared. 'No, no, no!' he choroused as the girls requested popcorn, pick-and-mix and overpriced drinks. 'We're covered,' he said, patting his backpack.

Inside Screen 3, Jess's voice took on a new echoey quality as she settled on her booster seat.

'Daddy, why is it dark?'

'Mummy, has the film started yet?'

'Daddy, why have you got all those sweets in your bag?'

'Mummy, why are you shushing me?'

Snacks were distributed. Ian and I were sitting at opposite ends, the girls sandwiched between us. He reached around the back of their seats and handed me a can. I peered at it in the semi-darkness – it was 200ml of sparkling pinot grigio.

Who knew you could get wine in a can? This could be a game changer. Sent a picture to WIB.

Ian dropped me home after the film. (I may have cried a teeny bit. At the film, not at being dropped home.) When I got inside I saw the holiday cardboard box. I wasn't sure I could quite face a job lot of coloured cardboard and lollipop sticks, but then I *do* like opening parcels. I sat down on the floor in the hallway and pulled off the Sellotape.

Inside was a layer of scrunched-up tissue paper with an envelope on the top. Inside was a card – one of those awful ones with a cartoon picture of a glass and a naff slogan – 'My head says go to the gym,' it said, 'but my heart says drink more prosecco!' Ian knows I hate those. I bet he thought he was being hilarious.

He'd written inside.

'I've thought a lot about everything that has happened to us over the last couple of years and I know that neither of us were as happy as we could be – you were right to make us face up to it, even if I didn't especially want to see it. What makes me saddest now is feeling like I've lost my best friend. I hope that one day we can go back to how we once were. No matter what happens I will always think that you're an amazing mum. I know you think that it doesn't come as naturally to you as it should, but that's exactly why you're so good at it – you think about it and you want to be the best mum you can be.'

I may have had another little cry at this point. Probably just *Mamma Mia 2* playing on my mind.

'That said,' he continued, *'I know the summer holidays are tough, especially this year. I'm so proud of you for making the change and I know you're going to make it work. For now, though, here's a little something to help you get through the next six weeks. Xxx'*

I pulled off the tissue paper. Underneath were six bottles of prosecco, six double packs of Jaffa Cakes and a six-pack of Wotsits.

I read the card again and then held it, sitting on the floor in the hallway, until it got dark around me.

Thursday 26 July – summer holidays

Flo has to be at Exeter bus station by 8 a.m. tomorrow so today was mainly taken up by packing. I got it into my head that I had to label *everything*, which is ridiculous as we've managed fourteen years so far and I don't think I've ever labelled anything.

We have lost of *lot* of PE kits, though. Perhaps it's finally starting to sink in.

Message on Tinder this evening from Stefan, a thirty-nine-year-old landscape gardener who wanted to know if I would be interested in meeting him *and his wife* in a hotel one afternoon to 'explore possibilities'. He was actually very nice about it, almost apologetic, so I did send a polite no thank you. Then I deleted the app. Maybe just for the summer holidays. I don't think I have the mental space for dating alongside the holiday corkboard.

Friday 27 July

We dropped Flo off at the bus station this morning. Ian came too, to say goodbye.

I could tell she was nervous because she was looking a bit cross and aloof. She shrugged me off when I tried to put my arm around her shoulders as we waited for the coach, but she stood close to me and kept glancing down at Jess, who was making her ponies do a death walk along the edge of the kerb.

Other teenagers were gathering around us and, to be honest, they looked like exactly the kind of kids who would relish a twig-based code-breaking challenge.

I hoped Flo wouldn't notice.

'Ian,' I said, after we'd packed Flo off and waved at the coach until it was out of sight, 'I wanted to say thank you for the box you left me. It was so kind of you.'

'Not a bit cheesy?' he asked.

'Well, the Wotsits, maybe,' I said, 'but apart from that. It was such a lovely thing to do, and lovely things to say. I feel just the same. I really want us to be able to be friends again one day. Properly, like we used to, without it feeling weird.'

He smiled and pulled me in for a hug. 'We will, Frankie,' he said, and I believed him.

Saturday 28 July

This is all totally fine. Summer holidays going very smoothly.

Sunday 29 July

Is it over yet?

Monday 30 July

I was woken up at 5.47 this morning by Jess getting into bed next to me with the iPad to tell me she was going to watch programmes and would I like to watch with her? I said no thank you, it was a little early for me. I tried to go back to sleep but the relentless enthusiasm of Captain Barnacles was too much.

I scrolled through Instagram and found a quote that someone had published about how we only have eighteen amazing summers with our children and how we should cherish every moment.

I can't say that it was great timing for me as I lay there, trying to think about how on earth we were going to fill the time between meals for an entire week.

As a response to the ridiculous person who posted the quote, I thought I would compile a detailed report of my day.

5.47: Arrival in bed of Jess and Captain Barnacles.

6.03: Many cries of 'Watch it with me, Mummy!' Assure Jess that I definitely am enjoying the underwater adventures of Captain Barnacles and his lively crew. Scroll through Instagram with phone hidden behind thigh.

6.05: 'Mummy, you're not watching! Put your phone away!'

6.07: Repeat two previous steps until I can take it no more and decide to get up.

6.24: Make breakfast. Forced to eat Weetos as I foolishly poured milk into the bowl I made for Jess when she had clearly stated she wanted her cereal dry in a measuring jug so that she can carry it around. Milk requested separately in the red beaker. Emotions run high when I cannot locate the red beaker but we negotiate and settle on blue with the red lid.

6.42: Start thinking about lunch.

6.51: Go in the shower while Jess 'organises' my underwear drawer.

7.13: Put pants back into underwear drawer. Take out ponies and Weetos.

7.25: Get Jess dressed. Try to interest her in the Boden summer dress I bought in the NCT new-to-you sale for £2. Jess keener on thick leggings, woollen jumper and Thomas the Tank Engine wellies. I show her the weather forecast and explain what thirty degrees means but she refuses to acknowledge potential heat stroke. Jess wins. I secrete dress and sandals in handbag.

7.43: Wonder how early is *too* early to go to the park.

7.45: Leave for park.

7.50: Return home for ponies.

7.53: Leave again for park.

7.58: Go back because Jess needs a poo.

8.25: Arrive at park. Four other parents already there. Understanding smiles as they spot the wellies. Three of them have had the forethought to brings reusable cups of coffee from home as the park café doesn't open until 9. Very jealous having to make do with slurps of Jess's milk.

(Note to Park Life Café – you are missing a desperate and captive audience.)

8.35: Jess very pink of cheek but in denial.

8.45: Jess runs over looking angry. 'I saw you drinking my milk!' Deny everything. Top beaker up from the water fountain when she isn't looking.

8.53: Jess relents and changes into summer dress and sandals. Winter outfit does not fit back in handbag. Didn't think that through.

9: First in queue to buy coffee. Order latte but then, like *every single time I come to the park*, I see the 'cash only' sign and realise I only have £1.83 of the required £2.50. Tired-looking mum behind me chips in the remaining 67p. Lovely sense of wartime camaraderie.

9.07: Jess engrossed in sandpit-based activity involving ponies. Start listening to a very funny podcast about periods. Jess senses my happiness, despite having her back to me, and immediately insists I push her on the swings.

9.23: I am allowed ten minutes to drink tepid coffee and listen to podcast while Jess befriends some ants.

Etc., etc., until the sweet release of death.

Tuesday 31 July

See yesterday.

Wednesday 1 August

The house is full of the smell of warm bin. No matter how many times I empty it, it still smells like someone has put a ten-day-old pile of potato peelings in the microwave.

I went to take out the food waste and recycling and the outside food waste bin was full of maggots. They seemed to be coming from inside one of the bags, so I wasn't sure what to do with them.

Options:

1. Put maggot bag into main bin so I can clean food waste bin – but then maggots have been *spread*. I may as well just bring them inside and offer them tea.
2. Put maggot bag somewhere else, (on the *path*?), while I clean out food waste bin, but then I have to put the maggots *back* in the food waste, thus rendering the operation pointless other than to give the maggots a nice change of scene for ten minutes.
3. Pick my least favourite neighbour and put the maggots in *their* bin.

In the end I went for just shutting the box again and pretending not to have noticed.

Thursday 2 August

I took Jess to the library this morning.

I'd suggested it to Flo before she went as something we could do together next week, hoping to rekindle those glory days when she was still interested in life and I could get her to do the summer reading challenge.

She'd laughed, though in a cynical way. I'd pictured her as a fifty-three-year-old New York businessman planning the takeover of a small family bagel business. Someone has suggested keeping on Margaret, the seventy-two-year-old bookkeeper who can't really see any more but everyone loves.

(Summer holidays clearly pushing me to insanity already.)

The children's area in the library in Barnmouth is very different from the library I used to take Flo to back in London ten years ago. Then it was just a corner of the main library with rows of shelves of young adult fiction and a couple of those boxes in the shape of trains, full of tatty picture books.

Here it's more like a soft play centre. They have those huge foam blocks for toddlers to toss around, a wigwam, some ride-on toys, a couple of chairs for the grown-ups – it's all going on. I assume they are trying to lure in families who find the concept of reading a little dull on its own but I can't help feeling it distracts a little bit from the *actual books*.

There were two boys there when we arrived who looked about four and six years old. A man – presumably dad – was sitting in the corner on his phone.

Clearly not aware of the whole 'quiet in the library' thing, the boys were having a great time with the toys.

'Reuben!' yelled the smaller one. 'Reuben! *Look at me!*' He proceeded to throw himself off a ride-on tractor and on to the scratchy library carpet. Reuben seemed unimpressed.

'Louis!' he yelled back 'I'm the big boss man! Look at me!' He put on a deep voice. 'Hello there, I'm the boss and I hate myself!' Not sure where that came from. Perhaps the dad is having some issues at work.

Jess gave them a stern look as we passed them. 'We're here to look at the books, aren't we, Mummy?' she said pointedly.

I did my best to ignore Reuben and Louis dashing in and out of the wigwam and driving the tractor into the shelves but I can't say I was sorry when the dad finished his game of phone darts or whatever it was that he was doing with such concentration, and decided it was time to go. I noticed they didn't actually take any books with them.

(Question: why *are* library carpets so scratchy?)

In the afternoon we went to Chapter One for our breakaway summer holiday Busy Beaver group. Possibly need to organise my corkboard a bit better to avoid library/bookshop clashes.

I'd half expected it to be just me, Lou and Sierra but twelve families turned up, making it a bit of a squeeze, if anything. Rather than have toys in the middle and chairs around the outside, like they do a Busy Beavers, I'd put all the toy and books at one end of the room and arranged seats in a cluster at the other end, near the tea and coffee. It meant that all the kids were out of the way and that when new people came in they could actually sit and talk to other parents. I've always found that whole 'around the edge of the room' thing weird at playgroups. So isolating.

Lou and I made drinks and handed around biscuits and Sierra did a brilliant job of welcoming people when they arrived and, if they were on their own, introducing them to people.

About half an hour in a nervous-looking woman with a very neat bob came and sat down next to me. 'I can't thank you enough for putting this on,' she said, looking around conspiratorially, as though she was about to confess to being on the run for stealing Jaffa Cakes from the Co-op, 'I only moved here a few months ago and I was getting a bit panicky about what I was going to do over the summer holidays. It's just me and Billy,' she said, nodding towards a rather sappy-looking small boy in dungarees, 'and to tell the truth I find it pretty lonely. I wanted this to be a fresh start, but I've found it harder than I thought to make friends. That sounds a bit pathetic, I know. I'm Sonia, by the way.'

'I totally get that,' I said. 'I've been here over a year now and it's only in the last few months that I've felt brave enough to really make an effort to get to know people. It's tough, putting yourself out there, so don't beat yourself up about it.'

'I did try the toddler music classes in the Scout hut,' she said, 'but it was just awful. Billy wouldn't join in at all and I felt as though all the other parents were judging me. I ended up sitting by myself in the ring, banging a tambourine and singing 'The Music Man' while Billy sat in his pushchair looking at a book. It was pretty humiliating. I couldn't bring myself to go back again. Busy Beavers isn't too bad, but I've not found people to be hugely friendly – it seems a bit cliquey?'

'There are definitely some established groups,' I agreed, 'and it's always hard to break in to existing friendships.'

'I was there the other week, though, when you stood up to Cassie over the Fruit Shoot scandal,' she said. 'It was incredible! I would never have dared to do something like that.'

I laughed, remembering the Fruit Shoot slam dunk. 'To be honest I don't think I would have dared if I had stopped to think about it,' I said. 'I certainly wouldn't have done it six months ago. I don't know if it's age, or making friends, but there is definitely a feeling creeping up on me of starting to care less about what other people think. It's pretty nice.'

Lou walked past then with the plate of biscuits. I stopped her and took a second chocolate digestive.

I was just finishing packing everything away when Dylan came up the stairs.

'That was amazing!' he said. 'Loads of the mums came and said hello as they left and told me how much they loved the shop, including a couple who'd never been in before. One woman asked about using the room for her mindfulness classes *and* I took £43.92! This was such a great idea, Frankie, thank you.'

I was very relieved. I'd been a bit worried in case the noise of more than a dozen small children squabbling over a box of Duplo would put off customers.

'We had loads more people than I expected,' I said. 'It turns out parents really do get desperate in the summer holidays.'

Friday 3 August

Flo came home today. I went with Ian and Jess to meet her from the bus station. I was really nervous in case she'd had a terrible time and the trip was referred back to, out of context, for years to come. I could picture it now – 'You remember when you sent me all the way to the South of France, Mum, to do *beach games* because you couldn't be bothered to look after me?'

It would be like that *one time*, when she was four, that she went to bed in her school uniform and kept it on for school the next day. I was on my own with her, not long after Cam had left for good, and had the worst stomach bug I have ever had. I picked her up from school just before it set in and then spent the next twelve hours in the bathroom. I had to sit on the toilet and be sick in the bath at the same time as *things* happened at the other end. In between times I lay on the floor, drifting in and out of sleep and crying quietly to myself.

We've gone over it so many times, but in Flo's head I think I was just flipping through a magazine or something, too lazy to get her into her pyjamas.

We watched the bus pull into the depot and as soon as I saw her coming down the steps I knew it wasn't going to be a school uniform scenario. She was beaming. Her hair had blonde flecks from the sea and the sunshine and she was covered in freckles. She bounded down the steps and ran over and hugged us all.

'How was it?' I asked.

'Amazing!' she said. 'I need to go and get my bags and say goodbye to everyone and then I'll be back.'

We watched as she hugged a succession of girls and boys, all of whom looked as full of life as she did, and then she bounced back, dragging her suitcase and with her sleeping bag under one arm. Ian packed everything into the boot and took her and Jess with him. I watched them drive off and waved until I couldn't see them any more, before getting into my car and driving home.

Drank a tumbler of well-earned summer holiday prosecco and watched *First Dates*. I think I must be a bit of a closet romantic, as I swear I just smile the whole way through. Sometimes I cry at the end when they say how much they like each other and agree to go on a second date.

Saturday 4 August

Lay in bed this morning doing a fantasy clothes shop for if I ever win the lottery. What is this current obsession with jumpsuits? I like the theory – minimal thought and effort, no concern over clashing top/bottom – but I'm not sure my bladder is strong enough for getting to the toilet and then remembering you have to basically undress yourself entirely before you can sit down.

Checked, and @simple_dorset_life had been busy making her own croissants. *'Pastry isn't quick to make for croissants,'* said the caption, *'but there's something very soothing about the process of rolling and folding and creating something from scratch. I try to feel every sensation – the softness of the dough, the cold, slippery butter. It roots* me and connects me to myself in a purposeful way. And of course there's the croissant at the end! They're a special treat, served with fresh berries, organic natural yogurt and an invigorating mug of nettle tea.'

I felt so inspired that I went to the Co-op, bought the papers and a four-pack of pain au chocolat and took them back to bed with an 'invigorating mug of cheap instant coffee'. Ate all four pain au chocolat. Spent quite a long time trying to brush flaky pastry off the sheets.

Sunday 5 August

Girls back at four, so spent the time until then doing all the jobs I was too exhausted to do last week, like putting away the sea of clean washing on my bedroom floor, chiselling old toothpaste off the sink, washing my own hair, etc.

Sunday 12 August

This last week in summary (approx.):

- Number of times I've said 'you might want to think about getting up now, Flo, it *is* the afternoon' – 39
- Half-full abandoned cups and beakers collected from around the house and emptied into sink – 18
- Hours spent at the park – 9
- Hours spent at the park wishing I was somewhere else – 8.5 (Had a nice half hour on Tuesday when Jess got engrossed in the sandpit and I had a coffee with no interruptions)

- Unnecessary FaceTime conversations with Mum and Dad because Jess was insistent she wanted to show them 'something important' and then ran off after two minutes – 5
- Raisins picked up off the floor – 291
- Episodes of *Peppa Pig* drawn into watching when I was meant to be using the time to do Useful Things Around The House – 8 (That show is hypnotic)
- Bottles of summer holiday prosecco drunk – 1. OK 1.5. Oh, all right, 2
- Jaffa Cakes – 19 (Best not to think about it)
- Soft play sessions – 0
- Soft play sessions considered and discounted in favour of maintaining own sanity – *many*
- Number of times Jess has said 'Mummy, watch me! Are you watching? Watch me, Mummy!' – Christ, I don't even know

The highlight was bookshop group on Thursday – fourteen families this week. If this carries on, we may have to put a cap on numbers or get people to book or something.

Tuesday 14 August

Because it has been so sunny I have finally caught up with all the washing and *every single thing* in the house is clean. It will only last for today, obviously, because then the things we're wearing now will need washing, but it was a triumphant moment nonetheless.

I thought it would mean that I could finally pair up Jess's socks, so I got her keen on the idea of playing a sorting game. We got everything out of the sock drawer and spread them out on the floor, then we took turns finding pairs and rolling them into balls.

I think the fact that I was genuinely excited about this shows how low my threshold for summer holiday fun is already, and it's only 14 August.

At the end of the game we had *seventeen* random odd socks left. How is this even possible? Where were the other seventeen? I know people make a thing about odd socks, but I kind of assumed that was just to do with getting your laundry organised and that I'd just never in my life before been that *on it* sock-wise, I didn't realise socks *actually* disappeared.

Wednesday 15 August

Finally got Jess to sleep tonight after what felt like weeks of toing and froing, fetching drinks, straightening sheets, rearranging ponies and generally trying not to scream, '*Please just go to sleep before I smother you with this pillow!*' I love the summer but God, it doesn't half screw around with bedtimes. I do feel for Jess. How exactly *is* it fair that you have to go to bed when it's still broad daylight and you can hear other children playing out in their gardens in paddling pools?

On the other hand, how is it fair that I have my drinking time cut into when I can clearly hear other parents outside in *their* gardens opening bottles of beer and enjoying themselves?

Flo was in her room, FaceTiming someone loudly. I tapped on her door and asked her to keep it down a little bit. I was tempted to stand and listen for a while – she probably thinks that's something I'd do – but honestly, have you listened to teenagers talk to each other lately? It's *boring*. Plus I only understand every third word or so. It's all memes and people being savage and getting wrecked, only not in the good old-fashioned way, with a litre of cheap cider in a park – the new way seems to just mean being the victim of a particularly savage meme or something.

Anyway, it's dull, and I'd rather be downstairs on my own, drinking wine and eating chocolate raisins like they are a health food.

(Question: why, during the day, will Jess go out of her way to avoid letting a drop of water pass her lips but as soon as it's bedtime she's dying of a raving thirst and I absolutely must fetch her a drink immediately?)

Thursday 16 August

Things I like about our splinter Busy Beavers group compared to regular scary Busy Beavers:

- The room is actually nice and welcoming and doesn't make you feel like you've just turned up somewhere to give blood
- We have blackcurrant squash for the kids and don't pretend that we only ever give our children water or milk

- No one looks at you in a judgemental way when you have a third chocolate digestive
- We talk about things that really matter, like relationships, pelvic floors, *Love Island*, etc., etc., rather than stupid things like should we be moving into the catchment area for a good college for our toddlers *now*, just to be prepared, or how difficult it is to find a decent violin teacher
- Cassie isn't there (Although wondering if Cassie will be able to show her face again at BB in September after the Aldi papping incident)
- After we've cleaned up, Dylan makes me a coffee and lets me hang around downstairs with the books while he tells me all the insider gossip from the world of bookselling

Who am I kidding? Of *course* Cassie will be at Busy Beavers. She is going to dine out on the outrage for *months*.

Sunday 19 August

Instagram post today that made me feel *most* inadequate: New Zealand's Minister for Women cycled to hospital this afternoon to give birth. Apparently, it was 'mostly downhill' but still, that's a bit hardcore, isn't it? Bike seats aren't kind on the lady bits at the best of times, but if your cervix is partly dilated I can't imagine that's exactly going to *help* matters. Would the baby's head get bumped? Would the bike seat *fall in*? (Probably should have done more research on how labour works before having two children.)

Messaged WIB.

'Have you seen the New Zealand woman who's just cycled to the hospital to give birth?' I asked. 'The only way Ian could get me to even *walk* to the car was by telling me there was a bacon sandwich in the front seat.'

I thought about it and followed it up.

'I had a lot of pork cravings,' I said, 'don't judge me.'

'I read about it,' said Sierra, 'but she was on her way to be induced, so it's not like she was pedalling through contractions or anything.'

Oh well. In that case, sign me up! Christ.

Tuesday 21 August

Flo came into the kitchen today as Jess and I were making cakes.

'When are we going to throw that bowl away?' she asked, nodding at the plastic mixing bowl I was using to cream the butter and sugar.

'What do you mean, throw it away?' I asked. 'This bowl is really useful.'

'It's a bit gross, though, that it's the bowl we are sick in but then you use it for cakes,' she said. 'I'm not sure that's normal.'

'I wash it out in between,' I pointed out. 'It's not like I just tip away the puke and immediately crack in a couple of eggs.'

'Still,' said Flo, 'it's a bit rank.'

I tried to remember how long we'd had the cake/ sick bowl. At least ten years. Maybe I'd had it before Flo was born? Somehow it had become the designated sick bowl, but also it *was* a useful size for baking. *Was* it rank? Maybe. But also it feels like a part of our family heritage. Like other people have family photos or war medals, only we have a cake/sick bowl. I bet @simple_ dorset_life doesn't have a cake/sick bowl. She probably has a cupboard full of charming, mismatched vintage mixing bowls that she's collected from flea markets in small French villages.

'You don't have to eat the cake,' I pointed out.

'I'll eat the cake,' said Flo. 'I'm just saying it's rank.'

(Dilemma: I really want to ask WIB about the cake/ sick bowl to check that it *is* something other families do, but what if it's not?)

Friday 24 August

Ian picked the girls up this morning to take them to his mum's for a week. I spent the rest of the day lying on the sofa in a kind of semi-coma, eating Jaffa Cakes, drinking tea and watching *Homes Under The Hammer*.

Really must start job-hunting.

Saturday 25 August

Felt slightly more human this morning. Found three potential jobs to apply for. One working from home for twenty hours a week doing some admin for a local disability charity, one doing marketing for a dog rescue centre, and one as an editorial assistant at the *Dorset Echo*. Not sure what editorial assistants do exactly, but working for a paper sounds like it could be quite exciting.

The dog rescue application asked me to 'give an example of a time when you have experienced conflict in the workplace and how you managed it.'

I was tempted to tell them about Steve and how I once told him that I 'tolerated him at best' while imagining hitting him with his own stapler but I figured that probably wasn't the relaxed, compassionate sort of vibe that the dogs would appreciate.

Sent off all three. Very pleased with myself.

Sunday 26 August

Distinctly bored by teatime when the girls normally come home from Ian's. Tried FaceTiming them, but no answer. I went for a walk down to the beach, thinking I might treat myself to a gelato from the nice place by the pier, but then remembered it was half past seven on a Sunday.

Made do with a Double Decker from the Co-op.

Monday 29 August

Redownloaded Tinder this afternoon, anticipating a fresh batch of potential suitors from over the summer. There were quite a few new men, many of whom had clearly been busy on fishing trips, climbing mountains, etc., during August, and were showing off their achievements accordingly.

I did have a message that was a couple of weeks old, from a guy called Dom. He's forty-one and a doctor. He used my actual name rather than just starting the message with 'Hey, gorgeous' and made a reference to something I'd said in my profile about the Brontë sisters, so clearly he has been reading the same 'how to write a good first Tinder message' articles as I did earlier in the year.

I replied.

Less than ten minutes later he replied again.

Very promising.

We chatted for a while about books and TV shows we liked and controversial issues like whether the cream or jam goes first on a scone. (Cream first, obviously.) I nearly confided in him about the family cake/sick bowl but thought better of it.

I sent a picture to WIB.

'Wow!' said Lou. 'He looks dishy!' Sometimes I feel like Lou was born in the wrong era.

'Is he really a doctor?' asked Sierra. 'Or has he just posted that picture of himself with a stethoscope round his neck to make himself look more fuckable?'

'Well, he *says* he's a doctor,' I said.

'Of course he *says* he is,' replied Sierra, 'but if he's got kids he could just have picked out something from the Fisher-Price medical kit.'

Tuesday 28 August

Applied for four more jobs this morning, all part-time and badly paid. Is this the choice you have to make? If you don't want, or aren't able, to be at someone's beck and call five days a week, are you destined to work forever for £10.25 an hour?

Message from Dom: 'This might be a bit forward,' he said, 'but are you free on Thursday night?'

I felt a little flutter of excitement. Clearly, he was keen. The girls aren't back until Friday afternoon, so I was free. I left it a while to reply though so I didn't seem desperate.

Seven minutes later I replied.

'Yes, I could be,' I said. So *cool*.

'Great!' he said. 'Here's my address, do you want to come over about 8 p.m.?' I said I thought it might be better to meet somewhere neutral for a first date – safety first and all that.

'Oh, you have to come here,' he said, 'otherwise it won't work.'

'What won't work?' I asked.

'I want you to fuck my housemate,' he said.

I looked at the screen for a bit and scratched my head. As in 'so that he could watch', maybe? Out of pity? Either way it wasn't exactly my dream first-date scenario.

'Um, *what*?' I said. 'You want me to fuck your housemate? Is that a joke I don't get?'

'No,' he wrote back, 'he wants to break up with his girlfriend and we thought if she walked in on him shagging you, that would be a good way to give her the message.'

This was just so awful on so many levels that I didn't know where to start.

'Can he not just *text* her?' I said, possibly missing the point.

'Nah, she's really clingy and annoying,' he replied. 'It needs to be something conclusive.'

I had another look at the stethoscope. Perhaps there *was* a touch of Fisher-Price about it.

No job offers. (Other than fucking housemates, obviously, but I don't imagine I was even going to get paid for that.)

Wednesday 29 August

Rejection email from the disability charity on the grounds of me 'not having the necessary experience'. That's a joke. The job description was all answering the phone and opening the post and I've been managing to do that perfectly well for myself for nearly forty years.

A second rejection from one of the jobs I only applied for yesterday, as a doctor's receptionist. I was relieved about that one, to be honest. All that sniffing – it drives me mad when it's just Jess, so I'm not sure I could cope with a whole room full of it every day.

Thursday 30 August

The girls are still at Ian's mum's but I went along to Chapter One parent group this afternoon. Lots of people were asking whether or not we are going to carry on after the holidays. The general consensus was that people would rather come to our group than to Busy Beavers – friendlier atmosphere and better choice of biscuits being the key reasons given.

I went downstairs to see how Dylan felt about us making it a permanent event. He said he was more than happy to have us. I offered to pay him from the money we collect for coffee and biscuits, but he said that so far he'd got at least one sale out of it every week and that was good enough for him.

All the parents seemed very pleased.

Friday 31 August

Three more job rejections but … drum roll please … two interviews!

Hooray!

One is a marketing job at the dog rescue centre, which I actually think I'd be pretty good at as it's very similar to a lot of what I was doing at the museum. I wonder if I could somehow turn Cecilia's cocker spaniel and its bowel condition into 'experience of working with dogs'? It did sit under my desk a couple of times when Cecilia came in to stuff envelopes.

The second interview is in one of the really lovely interiors shops in town as a 'retail store colleague'. (I.e., to work in the shop.) I don't especially want to work in retail, but Lou wants the staff discount, so I said I might as well try.

Girls home at teatime. They seemed pleased to see me for about five minutes.

Dog interview is on Tuesday, 'retail store colleague' is Wednesday.

Saturday 1 September

Other people with similar ideas on how to spend the last weekend of the summer holidays – 1,923,827. Time from me buying Jess an ice cream to it ending up on the pavement – 12 seconds. (New PB.)

The sun was shining when we woke up this morning. I say 'when we woke up' – when I *first* woke up it was with a naked Barbie shoved in my face at 5.37 a.m., so it was dark, but I quickly quashed 'Barbies' as a concept for that time in the morning and just let Jess get into bed next to me.

When I woke up the second time, *then* the sun was shining, so I decided we'd have a wholesome family day out. It's the last weekend of the summer holidays, after all.

I sent Jess to wake Flo to see what she fancied doing and I went downstairs to make sandwiches. It was an hour before they emerged from Flo's bedroom, by which time I was feeling incredibly pleased with myself as I'd gone as far as boiling eggs.

'We want to do minigolf,' said Flo, coming into the kitchen and grabbing the box of Weetos down off the shelf, 'but only if we can get dark chocolate sorbet from the gelato place.' She took a handful of Weetos straight from the box with her hand and shoved them in her mouth.

'Minigolf it is, then,' I said, passing her a bowl.

'I'm good, thanks, Mum,' she said, wandering off into the lounge with the box. 'I'll just have breakfast and then I'll get dressed.'

'Shall I help *you* get dressed, Jess?' I asked.

'I'm good thanks, Mum,' she said, mimicking Flo with a toss of her hair. 'I'm going to choose my own clothes and look pretty like a pony.'

Most of Jess's ponies are naked save for oversized hair clips and large plastic shoes, so I was intrigued to see what she came up with. I made a cup of tea and took it out into the garden with my phone.

There was a new post from @simple_dorset_life. It was only from last night but it has 325 likes already. I can't imagine I will ever do anything in my entire life that 325 individual people will like. This photo was of a beautiful cup of coffee on a rustic wooden table top. Next to the cup was a vintage silver spoon and in one corner was the merest hint of a succulent.

'I treat myself to one coffee a day,' said the caption, *'so I make sure it counts! I love the ritual of preparing the coffee machine, grinding the beans and steaming the milk before*

sitting down to enjoy each and every sip while my husband spends some time with the twins. It's the tranquillity of the moment as much as the caffeine that gives me fuel for the day ahead. #blessed #coffeeart #simplepleasures # mindfulness'.

An hour later and we were walking down towards the beach, me with a carrier bag of sandwiches, crisps and hard-boiled eggs, Jess wearing a bikini top, tutu and an elaborate hat. She was wearing the hat at an angle and, in fairness, it did have an edge of Applejack about it.

Minigolf was a little on the frustrating side as one or two (million) other families had had the same idea. At each hole we had to wait for about ten minutes for the family in front of us to finish their round. They had a little boy with them who looked about two and was pretty much the same size as the golf club. I'm pretty sure there is a minigolf rule about taking a maximum number of attempts at a hole, but these guys were keen for their children to get the full experience.

Jess got very twitchy and snapped one of the feathers off a plastic parrot, but I hid it behind a fake treasure chest before anyone noticed.

After golf we walked up to the park for our picnic lunch. It was hot and there were small children everywhere running around with no clothes on, splashing in and out of the fountains. Jess immediately took off her tutu and pants and ran off without so much as a sniff of my cheese and tomato sandwiches.

I lay back on the grass. Flo was chatting to me about a girl in her school who had got a tattoo without her parents knowing. She sounded very disapproving.

'Er, Mum,' she said, 'you might want to look at what Jess is doing.'

I turned my head to the side and brought my hand up to shield my eyes from the sun. I could see her crouched in the fountain. At first I thought she might be just examining something in the water but then I looked at her face and recognised the pink cheeks and look of concentrate.

'Oh shit,' I said, jumping up.

Literally.

As I ran towards her I realised things were already past the point of no return. She was about to shit in the fountain, a fountain full of dozens of other unsuspecting children, and I wasn't going to be able to stop her.

I panicked.

I reached the fountain and Jess. She didn't even notice me, so involved was she in her task. I imagined the furore that would follow a poo floating around in the water and I instinctively cupped my hands.

'Mum!' shouted Flo in horror. She'd caught up with me and was staring down at us, Jess squatting just above the water, me with my hands cupped beneath her.

And then there I was, in a public park, with a large poo in my hands.

'Oh my God,' said Flo, laughing now, 'that's hilarious, Stay there!' I realised she was getting her phone out of her back pocket.

'Nooooo!' I wailed. 'Don't film me! *Help* me!'

She was laughing too much, though, the camera pointing at me as I crouched there with the turd, ankle deep in fountain water. Jess, having finished, had stood up and turned around to look at me.

'Where did that come from Mummy?' she asked innocently, looking at my hands.

'From your *bum*,' I said, starting to laugh myself.

She looked unsure.

'Really?' she said.

'Really!'

'Oh,' she said. 'Well, you should wash your hands, Mummy, because that's disgusting.'

'I know!' I said. Flo was mildly hysterical by this point, but still filming. Other parents had started to notice a commotion and were looking over, so I closed my hands (carefully) and tried to look casual as I walked back to our picnic area.

'Quick, Flo,' I said, nodding at the sandwich bag, 'tip the eggs out and hold it open for me.'

'Ergh!' she said. 'You can't put it in there!'

'What do you expect me to do, *carry it home*? Jesus Christ, just open the bag before this thing starts to dissolve or something.'

Once we'd bagged the offending item I left Flo in charge and cleaned myself up in the park toilets. Poo safely disposed of and hands scrubbed, I went back to the girls but couldn't quite bring myself to peel and eat an egg.

We stopped for the promised ice creams on the way home and Jess instantly dropped hers on the floor, obviously.

I sent WIB the link to Flo's video, which she had kindly uploaded to YouTube already. It had only had seven views, which I felt kind of disappointed about. If I'm going to have to catch a shit in my hands in a public park, then the least it could do is go viral.

Had a message on Tinder from a guy called Kier. Didn't tell him about our wholesome family day out.

Sunday 2 September

Classic last day of summer holiday activities completed today:

- Go to Asda to buy skort for Flo for PE kit as cannot find hers. Flo doesn't like the shade of blue and refuses to buy it
- Go to Sainsbury's for skort. No skorts
- Small meltdown (Flo) in Sainsbury's car park. Do I want her to look a fool and have no friends? No, but also doubtful that the shade of blue of her skort will be as influential as wearing no skort at all
- Go back to Asda to buy skort
- Go home for lunch and very small medicinal glass of wine (It's the weekend)
- Flo cleans out school bag and discovers lunch box from July, complete with uneaten sandwiches and what might once have been a satsuma. Both too scared to open it so throw the entire lunchbox in the bin
- Drive back to Asda to buy new lunchbox
- Woman on the front desk at Asda says, 'Hello again!'

- Home again for more whining/wining (Wining = to fill self with wine in times of emergency)

(Question: what actually is the point of a skort? Why can't they just wear shorts? Why the requirement to create the illusion of wearing a skirt for PE?)

Monday 3 September – back to school

First day of Year 10 for Flo. She has been outwardly calm about it, but I know she has been getting nervous over the last couple of weeks so I got up extra early and made her good-luck pancakes for breakfast with smiley faces made out of strawberries.

'Mum, you're so lame,' she said when she came downstairs and into the kitchen, but she was smiling. I don't mind being lame in *that* way.

Jess is back to her usual routine at nursery. We need to keep her place open for when I land my dream job (ha!) and we have her vouchers, anyway. They said they could be flexible if we need to change hours. I applied for a job at Dorset County Council that's part-time and term time only, so there should only be about another *one million* other women applying for that one.

Had a nice little Tinder chat with Kier. He works half his week as a drama teacher and the other half as a therapist. I've always thought that I could probably do with some therapy, so perhaps this way I could get it at the same time as having someone buy me dinner?

Tuesday 4 September

I arrived at the dog rescue centre twenty minutes early and sat in the car eating a Mars Bar (for interview energy). I scrolled through Instagram for inspirational dog accounts. Got distracted by @simple_dorset_life making a late-summer salad with courgetini and nasturtium flowers.

Caption read: '*The convenience of a supermarket is great, but why would you choose to spend hours in the aisles when we have nature's bounty on our doorstep? Nasturtiums don't even charge delivery! #flowersasfood #rawdiet #insideandout*'.

Christ.

I was caught slightly off guard when I went into the interview room and noticed a dog sitting in the corner of the room. It wasn't in a basket or a bed or anything, it was literally just standing there, watching ... like it might have come down from head office to oversee the interview process and feed back to senior management.

I wasn't sure what to do – should I pet it? It was a bit funny-looking. I didn't want to seem unprofessional by cooing over a dog when I was meant to be answering questions about membership databases and social media marketing, so I concentrated on the human members of the interview panel.

I thought it went well – I gave a great little talk about the use of dog-related hashtags and one of the panel seemed to especially like my use of the phrase 'crowd-sourced content' (i.e., getting people to send you pictures of their own dogs to save you work).

They called at teatime to let me know I didn't get it. Lesson: always pet the dog.

Wednesday 5 September

Totally misjudged the tone at the interior shop interview. When the owner asked me about appraisals and what I would expect from her as my manager in terms of support I said, 'Jaffa Cakes?'

It was only meant to be a joke.

They phoned me half an hour after I left. No staff discount for Lou.

Thursday 6 September

Did some job-hunting online this morning. About 93 per cent of the available jobs on the site I looked at seemed to be for cleaners or support workers, neither of which I feel able to do as I am 1) rubbish at cleaning 2) not terribly supportive. I sent an email to a local wedding venue who are looking for a Wedding and Events Coordinator and applied to be the 'Social Media and Marketing Recruitment Officer' at the local NHS trust. I think I was being a bit over-ambitious with that one, plus it's full-time, but I'm getting a bit desperate now. I quite fancied being a Laboratory Assistant, but that's only because I imagined myself in a white coat, examining evidence for Sherlock. It only pays £7.50 an hour, so probably much less glam than it sounds in my head.

I was intrigued by the ad for a 'Loving Dog Sitter' but I think we know my success rate when it comes to dog-based roles.

I picked up three pairs of Flo's dirty socks from around the house this morning. One on the sofa, one in the bathroom and one by the front door. (Why?) What is it about teenagers and socks? I put socks on in the morning and take them off at night. Teenagers seem to randomly shed theirs at intervals, wherever they happen to be, like a snake skin. The front door pair were particularly baffling – surely this would be exactly the place you'd want to put socks *on*?

I've noticed, too, that Flo has been spending a lot of time on her phone this week and smiling to herself. Not that I think smiling in itself is a suspicious behaviour, but when you're fourteen it stands out sometimes. Maybe she has a boyfriend? God!

Friday 7 September – Jess's birthday

Jess had wanted the following at her birthday party:

- Bouncy castle
- Dog that could balance things on its nose
- Party rings
- Cheese sandwiches cut into shapes of different Sylvanian Family animals
- Unicorn
- All of the children from nursery *and* our new bookshop parent group

Jess actually got:

- Me, Ian and Flo
- Pizza and Wotsits
- Trip to the cinema to see *Incredibles 2*
- The promise of a trip to the fair tomorrow

I got:

- Two cans of wine and a grab bag of Twirl Bites

Very satisfactory.

I asked Kier what his favourite biscuit was this evening.

'I do love a good Jaffa Cake,' he said, 'although are they strictly a biscuit?'

I told him about the whole botched interview thing and he said that if *he* owned an interiors shop he would definitely take me on me as his retail store colleague.

Saturday 8 September

I had my favourite kind of period pains today – a pressure in my lower back, as though I'm trying to hold one of those kilogram weights from the old school science labs inside my rectum. It's a rather disconcerting sensation as you essentially spend the whole day feeling like you might be about to poo your pants at any moment – and what successful woman about town doesn't want that?

Of course, what you really need when you're feeling like your insides are being scraped out with a wonky spatula is to go to a fairground. I find the whole 'cup and saucer' experience really adds to the vibe.

God.

The posters for the 'fun fair' – oxymoron right there – had been strategically slapped up around town at child-eye level, in the all the places most likely to engage small children/piss off parents – e.g., outside primary schools, in the car park at nursery, on the noticeboard near the crisps at Micro Soft – and to stop Jess banging on about it every single time she saw it I had promised that we would go for her birthday. It was about three weeks away at the time, far enough in the future for it to seem like a less-pressing issue than 'would Jess go to sleep and leave me enough time to fit in two episodes of *Gilmore Girls* and at least one large glass of wine?'

Thankfully, Flo understands the joy of periods now, so I was able to bribe her to go on all the rides with Jess on the promise of three sets of false eyelashes.

On reflection, Jess could probably have done without the candyfloss, especially as there was a bit of a breeze getting up at that point, but I improvised a hairband with one of my socks and, as long as you didn't look at me below the ankle, I think we got away with it.

We were on our way out, having successfully diverted Jess's gaze from the Hook a Duck (*three pounds!*), and I was starting to relax. Big mistake. The balloon man sensed my weakness and pounced.

'Bumper balloons!' he yelled in my face (it felt like). 'Hours of fun!'

For whom, exactly, I wondered?

'Can I have a bumper balloon, Mummy?' asked Jess, jiggling about excitedly.

'No,' I said, 'we've spent enough money and we don't have room for such a big balloon.' It was one of those giant round ones with an elastic handle that you can punch backwards and forwards.

'We can keep it in my room,' she said, 'there's space for it there.' She was bouncing up and down now. The sock fell out of her hair and I scooped it up. The balloon man looked at it, then down at my feet.

'Only £4,' said the balloon man helpfully.

'Only £4, Mummy!' said Jess, with no concept of the fact that I could buy an entire bottle of wine in Aldi for £4.

'Oh, what a shame!' I said, 'I only have £2 left, never mind.' I took her hand, ready to walk away.

'Ah well,' said the balloon man, 'it's nearly the end of the day, I can let you have it for two.' And he pulled the biggest balloon out of the bunch in his hand, gave it to Jess and smiled at me.

What an utter bastard.

Sunday 9 September

Spent most of the day trying to stop Jess hitting her giant balloon around the house with a plastic golf club. Man, those things really ricochet, don't they?

Whenever I tried to take away either the golf club or the balloon and suggest that she might like to do something different for a while, like perhaps some Peppa Pig colouring sheets or lying down quietly thinking about life, she started screeching and hitting the balloon even more ferociously than she already was. My choices seemed to be a) listen to Jess howling or b) accept the fact that everything I own would soon be smashed into a million pieces.

To be honest, I wasn't feeling either as a relaxing Sunday vibe. Before I had children I imagined my Sundays more like this:

10 a.m.: Small child climbs sleepily into my king-sized bed, rubbing her eyes and looking up at me adorably. 'Mummy, you're so pretty!' she says, like she can hardly believe it. Colin Firth offers to get up and make me coffee and bring me the papers.

10.30: I read about world events (in the fantasy I *care* about world events and am very knowledgeable about politics) while Colin Firth passes me small, freshly baked pastries at intervals. Small child quietly reads *Anne of Green Gables*.

You get the idea.

(Question: why does Colin Firth only sound sexy if you call him 'Colin Firth', as though that's his first name? When we are married, I will have to use his full name at all times. 'Oh, this is my husband, Colin Firth.' 'Colin Firth, darling, would you mind passing my prosecco?', etc, etc.)

Had a 'no' from the wedding venue. 'Loving Dog Sitter' job looking increasingly tempting.

Tuesday 11 September

Flo is still glued to her phone. I tried, casually, to get a look over her shoulder this evening as I came into the living room. Just in the name of internet safety, you understand, nothing creepy. Internet safety is important you know. At least, that's what I told myself when I spent all that time researching apps and trying to set up parental controls on all of our various devices. I don't know what it is about getting old that makes technology seem so much more complicated, but I felt as though I didn't even know what half the words *meant* when I was doing that. I almost called Jess in to help, but I thought that would rather defeat the point – like getting a toddler to unscrew a childproof bottle of Calpol for you.

'What are you doing, Mum?' said Flo, clutching her phone to her chest. Apparently I hadn't been as stealthy as I thought.

'Oh, nothing,' I said, *super* casually. 'I was about to make a cup of tea and just wondered if you wanted one?'

'And you thought you'd find out by trying to look at my phone?' she said.

'It caught my eye, that's all,' I said sitting down on the sofa and switching on the television. Flo stared at me.

'I thought you were making a cup of tea?' she asked. Damn. Caught out.

Wednesday 12 September

The editor of the *Dorset Echo*, Leon, called me this morning about the Editorial Assistant job, which I had actually forgotten about. (Hopefully that didn't come across in our chat.) He asked me, theoretically, how soon I'd be able to start. Apparently, they had someone leave very unexpectedly and are in a rush to fill the role. This could be perfect for me – a desperate employer is exactly what I need. I said I could start as soon as they wanted.

I'm going for an interview tomorrow afternoon.

Thursday 13 September

The first question Leon asked me when I arrived for my interview at the *Echo* today was 'did you write your CV yourself?' This seemed a bit of an odd question to me – who else would have written it? Was he implying that perhaps it looked more like Jess had done it?

'Yes,' I said. 'is there a problem with it?'

'Not at all,' said Leon, 'it's just very nicely laid out, so I wondered if you'd had it professionally done.'

An excellent start. Clearly the bar here is set very low. Leon asked me a few questions about previous jobs and told me a bit about the role.

'It's three days a week,' he said, 'Monday to Wednesday. The paper comes out on Thursday, so our deadline is midday on Wednesday.' He explained that my role would be supporting the editorial team – typing things up, getting content on to the website, that sort of thing.

It didn't sound exactly thrilling but beggars and choosers and all that. Plus, surely working in a newsroom would be exciting, wouldn't it? Even if you weren't doing the reporting?

After the interview I was left on my own to do a short test. I had to read through a mocked-up newspaper article and pick out all the spelling and grammar mistakes. They were all pretty obvious there/their type errors, so I'd feel pretty ashamed, given my English degree, if I didn't get full marks on that one.

They're going to give me a call tomorrow. I've arranged to have dinner with Kier next Wednesday to celebrate/ commiserate the job accordingly.

When I put Jess to bed tonight I could hear Flo in her room, talking to someone on FaceTime. New boyfriend, maybe? Not sure how best to approach it. I don't want to just ignore it because I want her to know I care, but also want to respect her privacy and not jump to conclusions. Decided to ask WIB for advice.

'I think Flo might have a boyfriend,' I wrote.

'Ooh, really?' replied Sierra. 'Has she started reading poetry and listening to Joni Mitchell?'

'I'm not sure that's what modern teenagers do when they get boyfriends,' I said. 'I think it's all about eyeliner and Snapchat filters, nowadays. They spend hours agonising over being "left on read" and who liked whose pictures.'

'What's left on read?' asked Lou.

'I'm not sure,' I said, 'but I heard it in a song, so it's definitely a thing.'

Friday 14 September

I got the job!

I start on Monday. It's really soon but it will at least minimise the amount of time I spend worrying about what to wear and whether or not I'm going to make a fool of myself by not knowing anything about politics.

I've managed to reorganise hours at nursery to that Jess does a full day on Tuesday and up to 3 p.m. on Monday. Sierra is going to pick her up and give her tea on a Monday and Ian will be in charge of Wednesdays as usual, so it should all work out OK. It means Flo has to let herself in after school two days a week and be by herself for a couple of hours, but as long as I leave the remote controls somewhere visible I doubt she'll even realise I'm not there.

Jess refused her dinner tonight. She said the cucumber was 'too spicy'.

Saturday 15 September

I'm totally done with Jess's fussy eating. I can barely get her to eat anything at the moment, let alone anything with a fake semblance of nutrition. I don't understand how she actually stays alive, sometimes. How does she not keel over with exhaustion?

I made myself feel worse by googling some sample menus for three-year-olds. Something like this is apparently what I should be aiming for:

Breakfast: One slice wholegrain toast with sliced egg and tomatoes. Glass of semi-skimmed milk.

Snack: Half a cup of blueberries and a plain yogurt plus water.

Lunch: Bean and rice soup and a small wholemeal roll. Carrot and celery sticks plus a tablespoon of hummus for dipping. Glass of semi-skimmed milk.

Snack: Apple slices, thinly spread with nut butter.

Dinner: Wholewheat pasta with olive oil, fresh tomatoes, mozzarella and basil plus steamed green beans.

Snack: Cottage cheese with fresh pineapple.

There is just so much to talk about in this menu that I don't even *know* where to start. Firstly – soup? Who gives a three-year-old *soup*? Jess can barely eat a cheese sandwich without dropping it or getting it in her hair. Soup takes some serious spoon skills, surely?

Steamed green beans?

Cottage cheese? Can you even imagine?

I decided to keep a food diary for Jess tomorrow so I can compare.

Sunday 16 September

Food diary, Jess:

Breakfast: Toast and Marmite – inside circle of the toast only, so that when you put the four pieces together there is just a round section missing from the middle. Yogurt – half in mouth, half on floor.

Snack: Mini box of raisins. (I also gave her a banana but she sat on most of it.)

Lunch: Roast chicken, one roast potato, about twenty peas, six bits of carrot. (Had to be rinsed and re-plated as I stupidly poured gravy on everything.) Strawberries and cream.

Snack: Cup of dry cereal while she played ponies. Much of it fed to ponies. Two Jaffa Cakes. (Her mother's daughter.)

Tea: Half a cheese and cucumber sandwich, initially rejected because it was in squares and not triangles.

Snack: Apple – carried around for about an hour and nibbled extensively but essentially the same size at the end as when it started.

Monday 17 September

First day at work!

Because the previous Editorial Assistant had left suddenly, I don't get the luxury of any kind of handover this week – no useful bits of information in polypockets or handy Post-it notes left in key places. Instead, I got shown where the kettle was and asked to make five coffees, one white no sugar, one white two sugars, one white with soy milk and two black no sugar. I felt that I might as well have got a job in Costa.

Not exactly the best start, but when I was left alone in the kitchen I did discover a packet of Hobnobs, so I ate two while I waited for the kettle to boil.

Having distributed the drinks, I was handed a stack of paper by Leon. 'These are all the sports and funeral reports from the end of last week and over the weekend,' he said. 'Here's a copy of last week's paper,' he said, adding that to the pile, 'so you can see how they are laid out. If you could get all these typed up this morning that would be a great start. Just Word docs in the relevant folders on the shared drive is perfect. And your desk is that one in the corner.' He pointed to a table stacked high with yellowing editions of local papers.

I took my armful of papers and went and sat down. There was a note on my keyboard with my username and password. I logged in, opened Word and looked at the top sheet on the pile. It was results from the Wednesday night skittle league.

'Match Results for Wednesday 12 September,' it began. The handwriting was barely readable, as though they'd picked the oldest member of the team, cornered him at the end of the evening after eight pints of cider, and given him an ancient biro that someone had found on the bar behind the four-year-old jar of pickled eggs.

'Division A,' it continued, 'Vikings 383 (Stuart Bird 52) Bird in Hand 431 (John Hockey 60), Ring O Bells 392, (Graham Trump 58) Bell Ends 372 (Nigel Wadham 55).'

It carried on like this for literally pages. There were about twenty teams in each division and five divisions in total.

Between 9 and 1, when I went for lunch, the only time anyone spoke was to either to say things like 'Is anyone putting the kettle on?' or to answer the phone to people who had accidentally come through to the newsroom when they wanted the advertising department.

It definitely was *not* the hotbed of intrigue that I'd imagined it might be.

I can't take the stress of Flo's imaginary boyfriend on top of a new job, so I decided to just ask her straight out.

'Do I have a boyfriend?' she said, looking aghast. 'Mum, have you *seen* the boys in my school?' I had, but I thought perhaps that greasy hair and skinny legs was the thing. 'Honestly, they are all gross.'

'You've just seemed to be on your phone quite a bit,' I said, 'and you've been laughing.'

She laughed at that. It did sound a bit pathetic when I said it out loud. 'It's the memes, Mum,' she said. 'Everyone loves a GCSE meme.'

'Do they?' I said doubtfully. 'But what about the other night when you were on FaceTime in your room?'

'That was Grandma and Grandad!' she said. 'They wanted to know what I wanted for my birthday. Honestly, Mum, if I had a boyfriend I'd tell you.' Wow, really? She'd tell me? This seemed like a bit of a parenting win. Open communication, trust etc.

'I'd ask for your advice so I'd know what not to do,' she added. 'No offence, Mum.' Oh. Still, though, she'd tell me. That's the important thing. And really, I am being very useful by experiencing life in all its forms so that she can learn from my mistakes.

Tuesday 18 September

Today I had the absolute thrill of writing captions for the property pages. How many ways actually *are* there to describe a standard three-bedroom semi? Phrases I have severely overused today:

- 'Well-proportioned reception room' – i.e., quite small
- 'Low-maintenance garden' – i.e., quite small
- 'Third bedroom ideal as a nursery or study' – i.e., quite small

I hate to say it, but I almost found myself longing for the challenge of a fundraising application.

Jess had a tantrum on the kitchen floor at teatime because I wouldn't let her eat her pizza frozen. I think she's finding the change in nursery hours a bit tiring. One of my neighbours came to the door mid-tantrum to say that he was having a few people round on Saturday night – just an 'intimate gathering' – and to let me know that it might be a little bit noisy.

I raised my eyebrows and cocked my head towards the kitchen. Jess's screams of 'I hate you! You're a poo!' were clearly audible. He listened for a few seconds and I could almost hear him mentally crossing me off the invite list.

Who am I kidding? I was never *on* the invite list.

I went back into the kitchen and consoled Jess by filling a Sylvanian Families wheelbarrow with frozen peas.

(I wonder if other people hear 'intimate gathering' and think 'pubic lice'?)

Wednesday 19 September

Date night tonight with Kier. I'd been pretty excited about it as the WhatsApping had been going really well and we seemed to have a lot in common – two children, love of Jaffa Cakes, etc. I had a slight red-flag moment when he'd suggested we have dinner at Pizza Express. No offence, Pizza Express, I like a standard pizza chain as much as the next mum of a toddler, but if I'm driving all the way into Dorchester to eat on my own with another grown-up then I want to go somewhere that *doesn't* offer colouring sheets and babyccinos.

His second suggestion was Prezzo, but I chose to brush over the weird Italian chain restaurant obsession and instead offered up Eat Japan, a little sushi restaurant in the town centre whose name someone had clearly spent a *lot* of time over. I thought sushi would be a good test for a first date. After cheese-sandwich Danny I need to filter out the fussy eaters right away.

I was waiting outside at five to seven, pretending to do doing something very important on my phone so as not to look sad and lonely, when I spotted Kier waving at me in the distance.

At least I *thought* it was in the distance.

But then there he was in front of me. All 5' 3" of him. OK, so that's a guess, but I'm 5' 6" and he was a significant chunk smaller than me. I tried to look as if I'd not even noticed, but then I did an awkward crouch to kiss him hello and it felt like it had when I used to bend down to say goodbye to Flo at the primary school gates.

We went inside and up the stairs to the restaurant, me walking behind him and trying to keep at least a stair behind at all times to even things out. All I could think about was what a good job it was that I'd gone for flats.

Once we were sitting down it was fine – from the waist up he was obviously a regular height and he didn't have tiny hands like a child or anything like that. In fact, after the one glass of wine I was allowing myself because of the driving, I was warming up nicely to him. He even did this very sexy thing with the ordering where he asked if he could order for both of us. What he lacked in height he definitely made up for in confidence.

There was a bit of a sticky moment at one point where he seemed to want to address the elephant (small) in the room.

'You looked a little surprised when you first saw me,' he said. 'Was I not what you were expecting?'

This was my chance to be the bigger woman (already a given) and confess that the fact that he was a little shorter than me had just caught me off guard. I mean, it can't be like he doesn't *know* he's short, right? Instead I took the coward's way out and totally blocked him.

'I was just a bit nervous,' I said. 'I don't go on many dates and it's always a bit scary meeting someone new.'

'That's good,' he said, 'and that's totally understandable. I hope you don't feel nervous any more?'

'Definitely not,' I reassured him, 'you're very easy to talk to.' And it was true, he was. If anything he was too easy to talk to. You know how sometimes you meet someone and within an hour or so you're telling each other your whole life histories? It was like that. I never think that's a great sign, though, with a potential partner as it clearly means you don't give a toss about what they think of you already.

After we'd gone our separate ways and I was at home in bed, I lay awake for quite a long time, thinking about the evening. As much as I want to be open-minded about dating and find someone to love for who they are inside, I'd felt uncomfortable about him being shorter than me. Did that make me a bad person? We'd got on well, but there hadn't been that spark – had I simply switched off from him when I'd seen how tall he was? Or was it just that we didn't have a connection?

More importantly, what was I meant to do now? Should I tell him I didn't want to see him again and, more importantly, should I tell him *why*?

Thursday 20 September

Message from Kier this morning.

'Hi, Frankie,' it said, 'thanks so much for meeting up with me last night, I had a lovely evening and found you very easy to chat to. Unfortunately, I don't see it going any further – I think you're probably a bit too old for me and generally I prefer women who are a little more styled? Best of luck with your search for love! X'

Well, that told me didn't it?

Saturday 22 September

That is the last time I try to do something with *nature*.

Jess slept until 8.30 this morning, which I'm not sure has ever happened before, so I woke up all full of energy and enthusiasm for life, otherwise known as 'normal' by people without small children. In my delirious state I decided it would be good fun to go for a walk up on the hills with a picnic. I've heard of other families who do go for walks, for fun.

Flo was about as excited as she was when she had to get the human papilloma virus vaccination (actually googled that, which is ridiculous, because who am I trying to impress? *Myself?*), but I promised that we could stop and get a Frappuccino on the way home and she relented. Jess was very keen indeed.

'Can I bring home a pet?' she asked.

'A pet?' I said. 'No, we're going for a walk, not to get a pet.'

'But Maddie went out with her Mummy last week and they got a pet,' she said.

'Well, that doesn't mean we are getting one,' I said. 'There won't be any pets where we're going. We're going to go for a walk on the hills and into the woods.'

'Will there be birds?' she asked.

'Probably,' I said, and then quickly, realising where this was going, 'but you aren't allowed to catch wild birds and keep them as pets.'

'How about an ant?' she asked.

'No.'

'A goose?'

'Definitely not.'

'What kind of pet then?'

'*No kind.*'

I packed up a picnic, including a mini bottle of white wine, just for emergencies, because it's the weekend, and off we went. It was actually pretty nice. A bit blowy, but Flo paid Jess a lot of attention once she realised she couldn't get a phone signal and there was even a game of hide-and-seek. I'd just spread the towel out for lunch (my best attempt at a picnic blanket), when I noticed Jess wriggling.

'Do you need a wee?' I asked.

'No,' she said, sitting down. 'Can I have a muffin?'

She was squirming on the towel. 'Not before your sandwich,' I said. 'Are you sure you don't need a wee?'

'I'm sure,' she said. She took one bite of a ham sandwich. 'Can I have a muffin now?'

'Eat some more sandwich,' I said.

'I can't,' she said, 'I need a wee.'

Leaving Flo in charge of the picnic towel I took Jess behind the nearest tree and helped her take off her pants. I gathered her skirt up around her waist.

'I'm going to hold you up,' I said, 'so you don't get it on your shoes.' We assumed the position and Jess began her wee. Two seconds in and there was a loud screech from some kind of bird overhead. Startled, Jess twisted around to look behind her at where the noise had come from. The wee twisted with her.

'Jess!' I shouted, making it worse as she then twisted back towards me, showering me all over again. I looked down at my now decidedly pissy Matalan 'could almost be Saltwater Sandals if you squint a bit' sandals. My ankles were wet, too, and my trousers had splashes up to mid shin.

First the shit in the hand and now this?

Flo found it highly amusing, obviously, although not so funny when I took the picnic towel out from under her to dry my legs.

Sunday 23 September

Spent an entire day playing Topsy and Tim.

As far as Jess's made-up games go it was pretty low key – basically she called me Tim instead of Mummy and I had to remember to call her Topsy. Things went smoothly as long as I remembered, less smoothly when I didn't.

'Come and put your shoes on, Jess,' I'd say.

Silence.

'Shoes, please!'

Nothing.

'Come *on*, Jess!'

'*I'm not called Jess! I am Topsy!*'

'Sorry, Topsy, please can you get your shoes on?'

Like that. But about 200 times.

Monday 24 September

Flo asked if I could help her with her geography homework this evening. It was about weather. She had a map of rainfall in the UK and had to explain why some areas of the country get more rain than others.

I *felt* that this should be something I knew straightaway, in the same way that I know facts like mammals give birth to live young, but all I could think was that everyone knows it's a bit rainier 'up north', which I don't think was helpful. (And also not true, it turns out.)

I thought back to my geography GCSE, but the only thing I have ever been able to remember from that is how oxbow lakes are formed. I'm sure we learned other things, and yet somehow that is all that stuck.

I pretended I needed to go to the toilet and quickly googled 'UK rainfall patterns' in the bathroom. I have to say it didn't help me a great deal. It seemed to be a lot to do with prevailing winds, which is an expression I've heard a lot but never really understood.

I went back downstairs, none the wiser, and suggested instead that one of the most effective ways to learn something was to explain it to other people and that she should try that.

'You don't know, do you?' she said, raising her eyebrows in a sceptical way that I didn't feel showed a great deal of respect.

I told her that of course I did, I was just trying to help her establish her own level of knowledge first.

Authority undermined slightly by my phone pinging with a message from Lou saying, 'Is it something to do with prevailing winds?'

Flo rolled her eyes and closed her book with a flourish, saying that it didn't matter anyway as someone could 'DM her the mark scheme'.

Tuesday 25 September

Typed up seven obituaries at work today. By the end of the day I almost wished it was *my* funeral.

Friday 28 September

I have decided that if I'm ever going to have sex with a man again, which *could* happen, then I need to do something to get back in touch with myself. (Pun intended.)

I just don't feel *sexy* nowadays. I spend all day being a mum, and by the time I get into bed the thought of anything sexual is just exhausting. The last couple of times I've tried having a bit of me time I've literally fallen asleep. If I don't even find *myself* arousing enough to stay awake, then I'm not exactly going to ooze sex appeal to a potential new boyfriend, am I?

To make a start, I thought I'd experiment with a bit of erotic fiction. I know, the whole genre is meant to be shit, but also millions of people love it, so it can't be that bad, can it? At the weekend I bought a book on Amazon called *Sweet Sensation* – I felt bad for not supporting Chapter One, but I could hardly go in and buy it from Dylan, could I? 'Oh yeah, hi Dylan, just popped in for a bit of soft porn! How are the kids?'

It arrived on Tuesday but I've kept it in the cardboard packaging in case Jess found it and took it to nursery show and tell or something.

At about 7 p.m. I poured a glass of wine and took it upstairs with the book, feeling a bit shifty. I needed a wee, which is not a sexy start, so I went into the bedroom first to chuck the book on the bed but threw the glass of wine instead. Honestly, I just threw the whole thing, glass and all.

What the hell is the matter with me?

I had to strip the bed and turn the mattress, which is no mean feat on your own. I found a clean sheet and put the wet bedding on to wash. The duvet had a huge wet patch on, so I took the duvet off Flo's bed and hung mine over the bannisters to dry out. Fortunately the pillow escaped, but the whole room stank like a Wetherspoons on a hot day. It certainly wasn't the saucy atmosphere I'd been hoping to create. Goddammit, why am I such a goon?

Hid *Sweet Sensation* under the mattress (avoiding the wet patch).

Saturday 29 September

Second attempt at *Sweet Sensation* tonight.

The cover showed a close-up of melted chocolate being dripped on to a stocking-clad thigh. (When I ordered it, there *was* a part of me that was drawn to it purely for the chocolate.) I made myself comfy and prepared to be eroticised (is that a word?) but honestly, the writing was so bad that there was no way I could 'lose myself in the seduction' as the blurb had promised me.

I did have fun sending my favourite lines to WIB though.

'I taste him and he's sweet, like a cheap banana split bought at a chain pub near a motorway roundabout.'

What about that does not scream sexy? I can't go into a lower-end chain pub without feeling aroused.

'He walks towards me, slinging the reusable shopping bag casually yet seductively over his shoulder. My insides dance like a stripper with an overdue electricity bill.'

'Oh, hang on,' replied Sierra, 'I think I just climaxed.'

'Who doesn't like a man who cares about plastic bag waste?' asked Lou.

Ian has asked me if I want to go on holiday with him and the girls during October half-term. They've been planning it since the summer and have a villa booked in Portugal. He says he doesn't want to put me under any pressure, but just thought it might be nice to spend some time together as a family, to help us get back to being friends. He says the villa has loads of space, so I don't need to decide now.

Sunday 30 September

Today, on our child-free Sundays, Lou and I went to goat yoga.

She'd roped me into it a few months ago when I'd had a couple of glasses of wine and was complaining about my lone weekends being boring, but at the time I'd not really thought about it much. I figured maybe the goats were on leads. Or perhaps baby goats were brought in at intervals and placed strategically on your back, like a sort of massage.

Goat yoga is not like that.

What actually happens is that you place your old beach towel out on the floor of a grubby barn and a yoga teacher attempts to talk you through a regular yoga class while at the same time half a dozen goats run around trying to bite you and pissing on your feet. (Very much like a day out with Jess, really.)

I don't mind yoga, but I'd always thought the whole point was to leave feeling serene and relaxed, not to spend an hour on guard because of animals trying to eat your hair.

Also, I was slightly distracted throughout by the man (if you can call him that – he looked about twenty-four), who seemed to be there in the role of goat herder. He stood at the back throughout the session, presumably ready to jump in if any of the goats went too off-piste. There was something about him that made it very hard for me to concentrate 100 per cent on saluting the sun.

I might have been imagining it, but I was sure I could feel him watching me. I tried to sneak a look during downward dog but it's a bit hard to tell upside down, especially with a goat between your legs.

We'd finished the yoga and were doing a bit of a goat meet-and-greet when goat man came and stood next to me by the pen. Lou was off in the farm toilets, applying copious amounts of hand sanitiser.

'Have you done much yoga before?' he asked, shuffling about a bit and looking adorable. 'You looked like you really knew what you were doing.'

'Not really,' I said, turning my back on the goats. 'I guess I'm just naturally bendy.'

Honestly, I don't know what came over me. Maybe it was all the deep breathing. I swear I saw him blush.

'Well, your husband is a very lucky man then,' he said with a wink, suddenly not seeming as shy. It was my turn to blush. I told him I wasn't married, that it was just me.

'Oh!' he said, taking off his cap and fiddling about with it. 'Well, in that case, maybe I could get your number and take you out sometime? If that isn't too unprofessional of me? I mean, I know you came to see the goats, really, not pick up farmers, but if you wanted...?'

Was he flustered? I leant back with my elbows on the edge of the pen in what I hoped was a casual pose that also showed my boobs at their best.

'Why don't you give me yours?' I said, handing him my phone for him to type in his number. He typed his name – Dustin – (a bit Disney Channel but we can brush over that), added his phone number and handed it back to me.

I smiled, gathered up my stuff and sashayed away to meet Lou. 'Nice to meet you, Dustin!' I called over my shoulder. Who *is* this woman with all the sass?

When I got home I realised I should have got Lou to take some pictures of me for Instagram – @simple_dorset_life might have seen and decided she wanted to be my best friend. I checked her account but she hasn't posted anything for weeks – not since the coffee cup. Very strange. Perhaps she is on some sort of fermented foods retreat.

Monday 1 October

I waited until 7.32 p.m. to message Dustin because it seemed like a casual, spontaneous kind of time for a Monday, like I might have got home from work, had something to eat, and then found myself at a bit of a loose end. He wasn't to know that I was sitting on the floor in Jess's room with the blackout blinds closed, trying to convince her that she was tired.

'Hey,' I typed, (breezy), 'I'm feeling a bit stiff after yesterday. Perhaps I'm not as bendy as I thought!'

One grey tick turned to two.

'Mummy,' whined Jess from her bed, 'I'm really honestly not tired. Can I get up and play Sylvanians, just for a little bit?'

I told her no, it was definitely bedtime.

'But I'm bored,' she said. 'I need something to play with.'

I fumbled around on the floor by the light of my phone and found two members of the raccoon family.

'Play with these,' I said, throwing them towards the bed.

'Ow!' said Jess. 'They hit me on the arm!'

I shushed her and went back to staring at my phone.

Two grey ticks turned to blue. I took a deep breath in and held it. 'Dustin is typing …' my phone told me. Then he wasn't. Then he was again. Then a reply.

'I was a bit stiff after watching you do that downward dog,' he wrote. He followed it up with a little monkey face with his hands over his mouth.

Outrageous. But also very exciting.

'Sorry,' he wrote, 'but every time I close my eyes I keep seeing your bum. It's amazing!'

'Really?' I wrote back, 'I'd always thought I was more a "waist up" kind of girl.'

'Honestly! It's the best bum I've ever seen!'

We chatted for about an hour, until I realised that Jess had given up complaining and had fallen asleep and that my highly desirable bum had gone numb on the floor. We talked about work and books and travel and all the places we'd like to visit. It was exciting.

Later I floated the 'me coming on holiday idea' to Flo and she seemed really keen. I'd thought she might want it just to be her and Jess and Ian, and would feel that I was intruding, but she said she thought it would be really good.

'You and Dad are funny together,' she said, 'like Ant and Dec.'

(Question: which one does she see me as? Hopefully not the one with the drink problem.)

Tuesday 2 October

Message from Dustin at 2 p.m.: 'How has your day been?'

I told him I have been entrusted with downloading the paper's weekly crossword from an online crossword site and about the late-morning scandal concerning a particular street in Barnmouth that has been missed off the recycling collection route for two weeks running.

'Wow, it sounds cutting edge,' he said, clearly impressed. 'I'm so swamped by work at the moment, I could really do with a break.' Oh, I see. The old 'swamped by work' line. I knew immediately where it was going, but I wasn't going to make it easy for him.

'What are you busiest with at the moment?' I asked instead.

'Oh, you know,' he replied quickly, clearly wanting to get it over with, 'the usual farm stuff. It's a bit relentless, to be honest. I hardly ever seem to get time off.'

God, Dustin, spit it out. I did my best to make things more awkward deliberately. He brought this upon himself, after all.

'Well, that's great,' I said, 'being busy is such a positive sign!' I almost laughed to myself, imagining him squirming.

'Yeah, true,' he wrote, 'only I'm not sure it's going to leave me a lot of time for dating, if I'm honest. You're really lovely, but I think perhaps I need to focus on work right now.'

Bastard.

'No worries at all!' I typed.

Seriously? WTF? What was the point of last night?

'Thanks for being so understanding!' he said.

I didn't reply, imagining that to be the end of what was possibly the shortest relationship in history, but then I saw that he was typing again.

'So, what does the rest of the week have in store for you?' he wrote. 'Any fun plans?' I told him not really.

Again with the typing. 'Do you reckon you'll be getting into yoga now? You were a natural!'

I didn't quite understand what was happening. Had I just imagined the dumping? I thought the whole point of telling someone that you didn't have time to date them was that you *didn't* want to talk to them any more. Why was he still messaging me like nothing had happened?

I told him maybe I'd consider yoga if I could find the time. We went backwards and forwards for a while, with him asking questions and me giving one-word answers before I decided I needed to step in. I'd dragged out the initial dumping, I should let him off the hook with this bit.

'It's OK, you know,' I wrote, 'you're allowed not to talk to me any more, it's really fine.'

He seemed surprised. 'Oh,' he wrote, 'but I like chatting to you!'

'Um …' I replied, 'but isn't it a bit pointless if you don't have the time to meet in person? Not that I'm not interested in you as a human being and all that, but I don't need a pen pal.'

'I guess maybe it's a bit weird,' he conceded.

Yes, it's a bit weird, Dustin.

Wednesday 3 October

I thought a lot about Goat Man last night.

Honestly, I don't mind that it was possibly the quickest ever dumping in the whole of history. I don't mind that he turned out to be a bit hopeless, because I feel somehow *reignited*. For a start, it's nice to know that perhaps my bum isn't the disaster zone I imagined it to be. Maybe I could actually meet someone new at some point and feel desirable and sexy.

Also, though, I feel really positive about my reaction to it. I didn't feel especially upset or angry, because I hadn't run away in my mind with fantasies about us travelling the world with our herd of goats, so I felt very relaxed and positive about it.

I like that, as I get older, I feel more in control with relationship stuff because I was pretty intense when I was younger. When I was in secondary school I would get these all-consuming crushes on boys that would last for months and, while I had them, I couldn't think about anything else – I'd spend hours at home, gazing out of my bedroom window, imagining that I could catch a glimpse of my crush staring back up at me, too shy to come to the door but obviously completely in love with me.

I remember when I was maybe twelve or thirteen, there was a boy in school I liked called Mason. I knew that he lived in a flat, which was glamorous enough as I didn't know anyone who lived in a flat, and he used to cycle to school every day from the other side of town. I imagined a romantic but tragic backstory for him – why didn't he go to the school closer to him? Why was he so impoverished that he had to ride a bike? I found out his address, I can't remember how, and I sent him a letter.

I say letter…

I copied out all of the words to that classic 60s hit 'If You Could Read My Mind' by Gordon Lightfoot – I must have felt the song described the passion and desperation of my feelings for him – and sent it to him anonymously. The lyrics included stuff about fortresses, chains and ghosts.

Mason must have been terrified.

I imagined that he would read it and just *know* that it was me, and we'd embrace in the maths cupboard and swear our undying love.

Like I say, intense.

Saturday 6 October – Flo's birthday

Flo has plans with some friends tomorrow for a birthday trip to the cinema and then to Starbucks to see how long they can make Frappuccinos last, so today she decided that she wanted to go into Exeter and spend her birthday money on clothes.

We started off in Topshop.

In case you've never been into Topshop as a chubby thirty-eight-year-old with a Bambi-like fifteen-year-old girl before, let me set the scene.

For a start, everything in Topshop is *tiny*. I don't just mean as in they don't do larger sizes – which they don't – but just genuinely *small*. You pick something off a rail thinking, 'Oh that's quite a nice blouse' and then you realise it has a belt and is actually a dress. T-shirts are just scraps of fabric, more J-cloth than T-shirt. Most lack key components like sleeves or shoulders or mid-sections.

If you make it as far as the underwear section, then be prepared to fall into a pit of despair.

'Mummy, why do you look so sad?' asked Jess as I fingered a lace bralette.

'I'm not sad!' I said cheerily, crying a bit inside. Even when I actually was fifteen there was no way my boobs could have been in anyway supported by the underwear in Topshop. I have always longed to be a lacy bralette type of woman.

I imagined myself briefly in another life, long-limbed, lying on a large double bed, propped up on my pointy elbows, flicking through *Vogue*. A tall, dark, Parisian man brings me a tiny cup of coffee and I sit up, folding myself casually into a cross-legged position. I am wearing his shirt over my lacy bralette, done up with just one button.

'Mummy!' squawks Jess, shattering the fantasy, 'are these pants my size?' She is holding up a scrap of silk that I feel I'd be hard pressed to get around one thigh.

Just when I thought I might have to have a little lie down under the cropped hoodies (*Why*? The point of a hoodie surely is to keep you warm), Flo came over with an armful of clothes. 'I'm ready to try these on,' she said.

Oh joy!

The changing rooms are the very worst bit of Topshop. Changing rooms generally aren't exactly fun. If I were listening to one of those relaxation tapes that asks you to picture your 'happy place', it definitely wouldn't be a changing room.

Topshop as a mum is pretty bad, though. You're forced to sit on one of those plastic stools in a corner, where you can't help but slouch and look sad. Every few minutes a size six teenager will emerge from one of the changing rooms and look at herself in the full-length mirror disapprovingly.

'My thighs look way too big in this,' she'll call out to a friend in another changing room, and all of the mums will look at her with tears in their eyes. You can't help but look creepy because you find yourself gazing longingly at these waif-like teenagers, so beautiful and yet so full of self-loathing. It's not the girls, though, that you are yearning for, it's your youth.

You imagine yourself at fifteen, obsessed with your weight and the single spot on your forehead that's barely visible, and you long to travel back in time to give yourself a good shake. 'You're beautiful!' you want to yell to your teenage self. 'Please just notice it now before it's too late!'

Flo looked stunning in everything she tried on. Fortunately, she doesn't seem to hate herself with the quite the passion of some girls her age, so she was pretty happy with her purchases.

Yo Sushi for lunch – Flo's favourite – where I spent about fifty pounds on seventeen teeny-tiny plates of food.

Sunday 7 October

Fantasies about having the hallway of dreams – 3.
Aspirational interiors catalogues found on pile of unopened
post – 0. (Unless Screwfix counts, which it does not.)

Decided to tackle 'the area' this evening.

'The area' is that place in the house where things just sort of get left while you are having a little think about what to do with them. I'm pretty sure everyone has an 'area' – it's just that rich people can afford a house big enough to disguise it as a utility room.

My area is the top of the sideboard in the hallway, which is extra bad as it's the first thing anyone sees when they come into the house and it really isn't the first impression I am striving for. Ideally, I see the sideboard as home to a tastefully arranged bunch of seasonal flowers, an artisanal, locally made bowl for keys, and a casually arranged pile of post, preferably including a couple of high-end catalogues from interiors companies. The addition of the post would show that yes, I am stylish, but I am also approachable and down to earth because I've not got around to opening my post yet.

(At this point in the fantasy I toss my head back and laugh about how I'm so busy I've not even had chance to browse the latest rug trends. In the fantasy, my hair is also much thicker than in real life.)

I would allow a reed diffuser at a push.

My area currently has none of these things, so I poured myself a smallish gin and tonic – for stamina – and set to work.

Items found in the area and rehomed:

- Two overdue library books (unread)
- Missing baby Sylvanian beaver (won't mention to nursery that it was here all along)
- Packet of cucumber seeds
- Half a bag of Wotsits
- Screwfix catalogue (not really living the catalogue dream)
- Two nail varnishes
- Three Calpol dispensers (useful)
- Loaf tin (?)
- Week-old letter from preschool informing me that 8 October is 'World Cook a Sweet Potato Day' and could Jess please bring a sweet potato to nursery with her

Arse!

Messaged WIB in desperation, thinking a sweet potato would be exactly the sort of thing Louise would have knocking about, but apparently she'd just used her last one to make a rustic farmhouse risotto.

Monday 8 October

Emergency early morning supermarket visits – 2. Number of recipes created by Instagram chefs for 'potato brownies' – I'm guessing none. Glasses of wine drunk to take the taste of potato brownie away – 2. (Legitimate.)

Left early for preschool to track down a sweet potato.

Tesco Express distinctly lacking on the sweet potato front. Risked the five-minute drive in the opposite direction to try the Co-op, as they always seem like the most wholesome of the supermarkets, but there was just an empty green plastic crate where the sweet potatoes were meant to be.

Time was not on my side, so I was forced to instigate Plan B – I bought a regular potato and then, using a sticky biro I found in the glove box, I drew a very smiley, kind-looking face on it. One sweet potato.

I presented it to Jess nervously. I watched her face tensely, looking for signs of mistrust.

'Are you sure this is right, Mummy?' she asked.

'It's not *quite* right, I said, 'but it's the best I can do.' I explained the joke, and luckily she thought it was very funny and clever of me.

Work gets worse and worse. My working day is only meant to be seven and a half hours, but I swear it's actually about three and a half weeks. The newsroom is so quiet it makes you want to scream just to hear a human noise. The only person who really speaks is one particularly arrogant newly qualified reporter who walks with a swagger that implies he's just doing his time at the local paper until he gets the call to become editor of *The Sun*, where he'll work for twenty years before retiring to Jersey with his inappropriately aged wife and his alcoholism.

What can I do, though? I need to stick it out for a few months at least – it's not going to look great at interviews to have only been in a job for a month, is it? I need to just hang on in for a while, to show I've given it a good go, and then I can start looking for something else.

Spaghetti and pesto for tea, followed by potato (non-sweet) and cinnamon brownies. (Grim, but I tried.) Seriously considering the family villa holiday.

Tuesday 9 October

Please God, don't make me have to write another obituary.

Wednesday 10 October

Went into Chapter One at lunchtime to see Dylan to stop me attempting to take my own life through a series of tiny paper cuts administered with report sheets from local football matches. Dylan made me a cup of coffee, which was also a nice break from work, and I admired his new autumn window display. He'd made a big tree out of large twigs and sticks and had hung books from the branches and scattered them around the base like fallen leaves. He'd chosen books with covers in autumnal colours. It looked pretty ace.

Dylan suggested that, to try to make work less tedious, I think about other things I could do with the rest of my time to balance it out. 'You love books,' he said, 'so how about joining a reading group.'

'I've tried the Barnmouth Literary Association,' I said, 'but as you can imagine from the name they're terribly earnest. They *only* talk about books and they just drink tea, even though it's in the evening. The week I went one of the women had prepared a short essay on the book, which she read aloud to the group.'

'Ah,' said Dylan, 'I can see that might not be your thing. Especially the tea.'

'How about if we start one here?' I suggested. 'We could hold it upstairs, or even down here, depending on how many people there were to start with, and you could have a little display in the shop every month and everyone could buy the book from you?'

'It sounds like a great idea,' said Dylan, 'but I'm not sure I can really spare another evening away from the girls.'

'I'd run it!' I said, starting to get excited. 'We can ask the mums from upstairs and Flo would do us some posters, I bet. It would be fun!'

We agreed to give it a go.

We talked a lot about book choices but decided we'd make it more of a group-led decision. For the first meeting we are going to ask people to choose one book they really love and would like to recommend. We're going to have the first meeting in November, after half-term.

Thursday 11 October

I sparked controversy at Chapter One parent group today when I casually mentioned that I thought rich tea biscuits were definitely the best for dunking. The clue is in the name, right? Rich *tea* – they're made for *tea*.

Sierra was aghast. 'No way,' she said. 'If you're going to be as monstrous as to dunk a biscuit in a cup of tea in the first place, then you need something that you can rely on, something sturdy. Like a gingernut.'

'A gingernut?' I said. 'Are you *mad*? The fun of dunking is the element of risk. Where is the excitement and the tension with a gingernut?'

'Personally, I prefer a piece of fruit mid-morning,' said Louise.

'Bollocks,' said Sierra. 'No you don't. You love a Hobnob as much as the rest of us – you just don't want anyone to know about it.'

Lou looked shifty.

A fourth voice piped up from behind us. It was Ricki, Alfie's mum. Ricki is usually pretty quiet, so clearly this was a subject she felt passionate about.

'I'm actually an advocate of a party ring,' said Ricki. I gasped. 'Hear me out,' she said, turning around in her chair to face us. 'Think about it. A party ring is designed to be tossed about at kids' birthdays, isn't it? It's robust.' We nodded, conceding the point.

'Absorbency is low, so it's not as risky as a rich tea, but it's not up there with the gingernut – there's always an element of surprise. And then there's the icing – it's sweet, but not sickly, and the tea dissolves it in a fun way, giving it an edge. A party ring has a lot going on.'

At that moment Alfie fell into a box of Meccano and the debate was cut short. She'd given us a lot to think about, though.

Friday 12 October

Spent some time this evening lying down, studying myself from different angles, in anticipation of, at some point, getting a new boyfriend and having to be seen *naked*. The very thought of it fills me with horror, but I felt it was probably best to *know*, at least.

Fully clothed was not too awful, although I must remember never to let a man look at me from below when I have my hair tied back as basically I look like a fat, bald man with three chins. If any man should ever find himself lying on top of me with his chin nestled in my cleavage, trying to gaze up into my eyes, he's probably not going to be doing it again soon.

Ideally, I want someone to be looking down the length of my body from above my head, while I wear a push-up bra, so that my boobs look passable and my legs are far enough away to have a semblance of slimness about them.

Potentially, a difficult situation to engineer at all times, but not impossible.

Then I decided to try the naked version and almost immediately wanted to start using my full name and actually become a nun. 'Sister Frances, welcome to the blessed church of St Mary, here is your body-length sack. May no person ever set eyes on your puckered, saggy body again.'

(Question: is this why nuns become nuns, so that they can just let it all go and never have to worry about that bit of fat that insists on hanging out over the top of your pants? I feel like it's probably a bit more faith-based, but this must be a perk.)

Honestly, I can barely even bring myself to write about it. I *know* I am meant to love my body – Oprah (or maybe Trisha?) once told me that stretch marks were just 'scars of motherhood' and that we should love them just like we do our children – but it's hard, especially sometimes when you're single. Ian always used to tell me how much he loved my body and, regardless of how sceptical I was about it, it does help to have someone reassuring you, someone who you know genuinely does love seeing you naked, no matter how hairy your legs.

Lying naked, on my back, I had to keep my arms pressed against my sides to stop my boobs disappearing into my armpits. I don't feel like that is going to make for a liberating new sexual encounter, is it? Without the arm barriers, the right one in particular doesn't stand a chance. Since I stopped breastfeeding Jess, it's like the last lot of milk went and they couldn't be bothered to refill themselves.

You know how sometimes, when you do the washing, one sock gets inside another one and when you hang it on the line you notice a lump in the end? Well, imagine two socks like that, hung on the line.

That is my breasts.

Now imagine those breasts attached to me while I am on all fours.

I may never have sex again.

Sunday 14 October

I don't want to go to work tomorrow. Don't make me. *Gah.*

Monday 15 October

Made twenty-five cups of coffee, wrote up three obituaries, collated scores for nineteen skittles matches, uploaded seven stories to *Dorset Echo* website, including one about a 'galloping granny' reunited with her beloved horse.

It seems to me that the only training you really need to be a reporter at a local paper is the ability to find an adjective that begins with the same letter as the subject of your headline.

Most exciting story of the day was that of a Dorset woman who has had dead fish dumped on her doorstep as part of a 'ongoing vendetta', which I feel probably makes it sound a bit more *Godfather* than it actually is.

Come back, Steve, all is forgiven.

Tuesday 16 October

Couldn't take any more at work today so this afternoon I mentioned to Leon, casually, that I noticed my annual leave for next week hadn't been added to the diary and should I pop it in?

He looked puzzled.

'What annual leave?' he said.

I tried to look worried and shocked, like we had only been speaking about it yesterday and how could he have forgotten.

'My family holiday to Portugal?' I said. 'I told you about it at my interview and you said it wouldn't be a problem. You must remember because we chatted about your holiday last year to the same area?'

This was a total lie, but I'd heard him talking to one of the girls from advertising a couple of weeks ago about having been to the Lisbon for his honeymoon. He need never know we were going to the Algarve.

He really *was* confused then. Clearly, he couldn't remember it at all, because it never happened, but my fact about his honeymoon had added gravitas and I was doing my best to make the same expression that Flo does when she 'honestly swears' she *did* tell me she needed £19 and a double packed lunch for a school trip to the Natural History Museum.

Holiday is in the diary. I feel a bit bad about it, but honestly, no one is going to die or anything, are they? Someone else might have to write up the local football match results – not exactly the end of the world.

Interesting conversation on Tinder this evening with a thirty-two-year-old who claims to have spent eight years in 'one of the world's most notorious gangs' but now he's apparently looking into becoming a writer so that he can write about the story of his life, including how he was 'framed' for burning down a secure mental health unit. He did say, 'I guess I'd have to change names and stuff', so good to see he has thought it through.

Obviously I was terrified, but also interested to see exactly how many gang secrets he'd be prepared to offer up to a stranger on the internet.

He wasn't prepared to let on who might have framed him for the fire, but he did think it might have had something to do with him setting fire to the base of a notorious motorcycle gang. Then he teased me by hinting at an 'incident in the Portrait Gallery' and referred to himself as 'Yorkshire's most prolific squatter', which is certainly a claim to fame.

'I shouldn't be giving away my best stories on Tinder, though,' he wrote at one point, 'they're meant to be for getting laid!'

I know I save the all of my best squatting/arson anecdotes for when I really want to seduce someone.

When he started telling me about all the books he'd read recently in prison, I chickened out and unmatched me before he found out where I lived and set fire to my house.

Thursday 18 October

I told Sierra and Lou at Chapter One parent group today that I wouldn't be able to make next week's session as I was going on a villa holiday to Portugal with my ex-husband.

'Oh my God,' said Sierra, 'are you *rekindling*?'

'Oh, how romantic!' said Lou, 'I'm so pleased! That whole thing with the summer holiday box of treats was adorable. All I got from David over the summer holidays was a carrier bag full of the boys' clothes that he had got wet in the sea and not bothered to wash.'

I told them, much to Lou's disappointment, that I wasn't planning any kind of rekindling, (although the summer holiday box really was lovely), but that we were just hoping to get a bit of closure on the separation and hopefully go back to being friends.

'It's ever so brave,' said Lou.

'Is the villa near a bus stop in case it all goes tits up?' asked Sierra.

Friday 19 October

I got caught putting Jess's latest batch of paintings from nursery in the recycling this morning. She was beside herself with grief, of course, those particular paintings being her most special paintings ever, painted just for me etc., etc.

I took them out and told her that I was very sorry and that I would make sure to put them instead into the special box of memories that I keep all of her paintings in. Jess asked if she could look at the box, but I said no, it was in the attic to keep it extra safe and that she was too small to go up there. Then I gave her some chocolate buttons to distract her while I went and put the paintings into the main recycling bin outside.

I do actually have a box under my bed, but it probably doesn't have the things in that Jess would want me to keep. I have the Babygros they both came home from hospital in, and a little silver pot full of Flo's baby teeth which, on reflection, might be a bit gruesome. Not sure if other parents keep those? I have a lot hand and foot prints from them both on various birthdays, the first of which I did for each of them a few days after they were born, and I've saved quite a lot of the notes that Flo has written me over the years too, where she tells me how pleased she is that I am her mummy and how I smell nicer than roses and toasted cheese sandwiches. Sometimes I get the box out and read them all.

Saturday 20 October – Villa Holiday Week

Ian is going to be here in a minute to pick us up. I've decided not to take my diary, just in case – not that I think for a minute that Ian would read it even if he found it, but it hardly ever leaves the house and I think I'd just feel safer.

I hope this holiday is the right thing. Is it ridiculous to go on a family holiday with your ex-husband? I don't *want* it to be. I miss so much having him to talk to, and it would be amazing if we could get back even half of what we had.

Saturday 27 October

It's 3 a.m. and we are finally home after a hideous airport delay but I can't sleep and I wanted to write some things down while they were fresh in my mind.

Basically, it's *all good*. Things started off a bit awkwardly, as you might expect, and there was a lot of 'no, honestly, you take the window seat, I really don't mind,' and weird shuffling around each other because we were scared to make physical contact. Fortunately, Jess made enough fuss on the plane to mean we wouldn't have had time to speak directly to each other, even if we had wanted to, so that was a good icebreaker. She sat in the middle seat between us, and Flo sat across the aisle, opposite Ian.

(She did not make a fuss at all, obviously – she had her phone, *Heat* magazine and a family-size bag of Wispa bites.)

We arrived, got our bags, stood about in the airport for a bit, looking lost – all the usual tourist things – and then Ian found the car-hire desk and we set off. There was one 'why is that lady so fat, Mummy?' moment in the airport, but I hoped that the language barrier might save us from at least some of the embarrassing situations Jess was likely to put us in.

I'm not going to bore myself with a day-by-day account of the holiday, I just wanted to write a little bit about our first evening. Ian had gone out to a supermarket after he'd dropped us off at the villa, and brought back holiday supplies – chiefly pasta, nectarines and wine. (What is it about being abroad that makes you eat nectarines?) He also brought me a packet of European lemon-and-lime flavour Jaffa Cakes. When you're in your late thirties and have two children, that's the kind of rock-and-roll level you reach with holiday experimentation.

I made dinner for us all and then Ian did bedtimes while I took my wine out on to the terrace and tried to make the villa Wi-Fi work. I'm not saying I *can't* go for a week without looking at Instagram, but, well, I don't want to, and I'm a grown-up, so I get to choose.

Once Jess was asleep and Flo was in her room reading, Ian brought the rest of the wine outside and sat down on the lounger next to me. He'd put on a jumper and handed me a blanket that he'd brought from his bedroom.

We sat for a while, lit by fairy lights, listening to the night-time noises.

Eventually, Ian sat up in his lounger and turned to face me. 'I'm really pleased you agreed to come,' he said.

'Well, I'm pleased you asked me,' I said, not sitting up, but turning over on my side towards him, pulling the blanket up under my chin. 'You should have seen my boss's face, though – he looked genuinely concerned, like he must be having memory blackouts.'

'I know some people are going to think it's a bit weird,' he went on, 'but we've always been such good friends, so comfortable picking up where we left off, even when we've not seen each other for a long time. I thought maybe we could try to pretend it was just like that? Like we've both been away and now we're back, and we can go back to how we were before?'

'I'd like that,' I said.

He lay back in the lounger and I rolled back to gaze at the sky.

When we went to bed later that night, (separately, diary, don't get any ideas), I fell asleep almost instantly and had wonderful dreams about opening an ice-cream parlour in the south of France.

*

The main scandal of the holiday was the second night. We'd had a repeat of the 'dinner, kids in bed, wine on the terrace' thing and Ian said he had something he wanted to talk to me about. I felt suddenly very awkward – what if in Ian's mind this holiday *was* a rekindling? The first night had been so nice, and I was just starting to feel so relaxed about everything, I really didn't want him making any declarations.

Turned out I needn't have worried – he had wanted to tell me that he was dating! I know, right? And, get this, it's all thanks to me! Apparently, after I sent him that message when he was in New York about Macy's mum having a crush, he started making an effort to chat to her more at nursery pick-up on Wednesdays and then, before Jess stopped for the summer holidays, Ian asked her out! Macy's mum, who it turns out is called Denise, said yes, and Bob's your uncle.

He says it's very early days and they are only seeing each other once a week or so, when Macy and her brother go to their dad and Ian is free, but honestly, he seemed really happy when he was talking about her. What's even better (selfishly), is that I actually felt really happy about it, too. I definitely don't think I would have done six months ago – but I don't know; there was something about his face and the way his eyes lit up when he was telling me about her, and I couldn't help but be pleased for him.

I did ask how Denise felt about me coming on holiday with them, but he said they had talked about it before he asked me and that she was totally fine with it, that she was really pleased for the girls' sakes that Ian and I wanted to get things back on track and be amicable about everything.

So a bit of a landmark week, really. Ian is moving on and I surprised myself by feeling OK about it. For all the dates I've been on this year, I think it has taken me until now to really feel like I could do it seriously. Not that I've been messing anyone around, just that I guess I've always felt a bit like I'm holding something back?

Monday 29 October – back to school

Back to work. Don't want to talk about it.

Wednesday 31 October

Jess wanted me to go trick-or-treating with her, so Ian fed the girls at his house and then brought them home again when I was back from work. I was totally on board with this as it meant Jess arrived already kitted out in her spooky witch costume, complete with plastic pumpkin basket for collecting treats.

When I opened the door to them I screamed and covered my face with my hands. 'No!' I wailed. 'Please no! Don't hurt me!'

Jess laughed. 'Mummy it's *me*!' She took off her crooked witch nose to prove it.

'Oh my goodness,' I said, 'so it is! You scared me!' She looked pleased with herself. 'It's a great costume!'

'Asda,' whispered Ian behind his hand. I nodded approvingly.

Flo, on the other hand, looked like she was ready for a shift at a strip club. She had on a black mini dress and ripped black fishnets and her hair was backcombed at peculiar angles.

'Wow,' I said, not really sure what else I *could* say.

'Oh, don't worry, Mum,' she said, pushing past me to go upstairs, 'it's not finished yet.' I was relieved. Perhaps she was going to put on a nice pair of tracksuit bottoms or something? 'I haven't done my make-up yet – I forgot to take my false eyelashes to Dad's.'

And this, apparently, is modern Halloween.

When I was small, Halloween consisted of cutting three holes in a bin bag – one for your head and two for your arms. If I was lucky I got to paint a few stars and a moon shape on the bin liner with white poster paint or Tippex. My mum would put a few apples in a washing-up bowl for me to bob and then, with my fringe still wet I'd knock on the neighbour's door and they'd give me a packet of Chewits. I had a perfectly nice time. No one spent any money and no one had to dress up as a prostitute.

I'm not sure supermarkets even sold clothes back then. There certainly wasn't an aisle dedicated to seasonal dressing up. Christmas was just the same. If you were given the role of shepherd in the nativity, you wore a tea towel on your head, tied in place with the cord from your dad's dressing gown. If you were a king then you might have a cape made of an old piece of crushed velvet from the back of your nan's sofa.

We FaceTimed Mum and Dad for Jess to show them her outfit and I reminded Mum about the shepherd in one of my school nativities who had worn a souvenir Corfu tea towel.

'Ooh yes,' said Mum, 'that was Scott Howard, wasn't it? His mum thought she was really something special with all those fancy holidays they went on. As if a shepherd would have been to Corfu.'

Flo went off to meet her friends, most likely on a street corner, and Ian and I took Jess a couple of streets away where they go in for Halloween in a big way. Pretty much every other house had some kind of corpse dangling outside the front door and one had a talking tombstone that worked on a sensor. Jess had a bit of a lip wobble when one man answered the door dressed as Dracula and asked to suck her blood, but even I was a little taken aback, so I can't say I blamed her for that.

It wasn't long before her pumpkin basket was full of mini bags of Haribo and we were allowed to go home. (Points to Ian for choosing a particularly small pumpkin.) Once they'd left and I was on my own I poured a glass of red wine (to look like blood) and got myself comfy with the remote control.

Only one lot of trick or treaters caught me out before I remembered to switch off all the lights at the front of the house. I was totally unprepared, of course, so I gave them each an apple. I fully expect the house to be egged and floured by the time I wake up.

(Question: is egg and flour a *thing* any more or do children nowadays prefer cyberbullying? I can see the appeal – cheaper, quicker, don't have to bother to go to the Spar, etc.)

Thursday 1 November

I told all the mums at Chapter One parent group about my new book group this afternoon. Quite a few of them said they would come along, especially when I told them that they didn't actually need to read anything before the first meeting. One mum, Sadie, admitted that all she's read since her daughter was born two years ago is tweets, Mumsnet threads and the occasional copy of *Woman's Own* magazine.

Lou brought some home-made oatmeal and raisin cookies. (I wonder if this is why the new group is so popular?) They were *amazing*, even without any chocolate chips in.

'You should be on Instagram, Lou,' I told her. 'You could take gorgeous pictures of all of these things and become an internet sensation. You could be the Zoella of healthy snacks.' Lou looked doubtful. 'Honestly,' I said, 'you could be like @simple_dorset_life. Have you heard of her? You should follow her – she's my go-to when I need some aspirational content to envy. Only she doesn't seem to have posted anything recently...'

'I'm not sure I really have the time for Instagram,' said Lou, looking over her shoulder. 'I think Edward needs me anyway, so ...' and she scuttled off before I could tell her more about my other social media obsessions. Edward seemed to be playing happily, so that was a bit weird.

Sunday 4 November

Jess refused to walk to Tesco Express today, even though it's only fifteen minutes away. I could have driven, but when I checked the step-counter on my phone this morning it said I'd done 1,392 steps *altogether* in the last two days, which seemed a tad on the low side. Plus we only needed things for packed lunches tomorrow, so I couldn't justify it on the grounds of 'things I needed to carry' either.

Instead, I dug around in the boot of the car under all the carrier bags that I always forget to actually take into the supermarket with me and found the buggy, which we haven't used in ages and I've half been meaning to take to a charity shop. I thought she'd think it was a treat, which she did for about the first five minutes, but then she decided that what she really wanted was to definitely not be in the buggy at all.

'Can we go home now?' she asked

'Not yet,' I said, 'we're going to the shops first.'

'But I want to go home,' she whined. 'I don't like it in the buggy, it's too scratchy.'

'Well, get out and walk instead then,' I said, 'and we'll put the shopping in the buggy.'

This apparently was a terrible idea. She started to cry and arch her back, pushing herself against the buggy straps. I told her there was really no need to do that; if she didn't like the buggy she could just get out. She was not impressed with my logic. As she screeched, she kept tucking her feet underneath, so they dragged along the ground and caught the wheels. I tipped the front wheels in the air to make it like pushing a wheelbarrow but she somehow managed to get her legs behind the footrest, so her whole body was stiff and it looked like her knees might snap backwards, all the while still screaming. I don't know what the matter was with her – she's not had a tantrum like that in a long time.

I carried on pushing, ignoring the disapproving looks of the three elderly ladies outside Smiths. Every so often she stopped crying and then looked around, surprised, as though she was trying to figure out why it had gone quiet. Then she remembered and would start again.

We were an absolute picture of a happy family Sunday afternoon by the time we got to Tesco Express. I dashed around for ham and crisps and apples, trying not to jam Jess's legs against anyone or knock anything breakable off the shelves. Walked home again, the sobs gradually subsiding.

Got home and realised I'd forgotten bread. Left Jess watching *Friends* with Flo and drove back to Tesco Express on my own.

Monday 5 November

Unfortunate Mooncup-related incident in the queue at the Post Office at lunchtime. Generally, I have been getting on really well with it, and it does seem to have reduced my cramps.

The air in the Post Office was really dry, though, and I kept coughing and coughing. The more I coughed the more I felt things *shift*. By the time I reached the front of the queue I could feel the end of the trimmed stem nudging its way out.

I was clearly looking uncomfortable because the woman behind the counter looked concerned. 'Are you OK, love?' she asked.

'Oh yeah,' I said, shuffling awkwardly from side to side, 'I just have a bit of a cough.'

She looked me up and down sceptically.

'Honestly,' I said, 'I'm fine, just a cough.' I cleared my throat to make my point, dislodging things even further.

I paid for the postage on my parcel as quickly as I could. 'Do you have a bathroom?' I asked as she handed me my change. 'For the cough.'

'We don't,' she said, 'but the café next door does.'

I made a sharp exit.

I walked confidently through the café to the toilets at the back (as confidently as I could with a Mooncup half out of my body), to make it look like I was definitely going to be heading back to the counter to buy a mocha. (I wasn't).

Safely in the toilets, I wasn't sure what to do for the best. Take it out, start again and risk the mess or just try to shove it back up where it was meant to be?

I went for shoving.

Tuesday 6 November

Jess came home from nursery today, very excited indeed.

'Mummy, Mummy!' she shrieked as she ran across the painted hopscotch to where I was huddled for a feeble amount of warmth under the oak tree in the corner of the mini-playground, 'will you adopt me!'

Jess arrived at my legs with a bump and looked up at me expectantly.

'I can't adopt you,' I explained, 'I'm already your Mummy!'

'But what about the children with no mummies and daddies who need our help?' she asked.

'Well, I definitely can't adopt them!' I said. 'I've got my hands full as it is.'

Her chin was starting to wobble.

'You have to adopt me, Mummy, or they won't have anywhere to live!' Her eyes were welling up, but I was at a loss. I wasn't about to promise to open up an orphanage just to avoid a tantrum. (Although I was tempted.)

I noticed she was holding a sheet of paper and I bent down to take it from her.

'*Sponsorship form*' it said. '*We're doing a sponsored sing to raise money to help build an orphanage in India!*'

'You mean will I sponsor you,' I said. 'Of course I will.'

'That's what I *said*, Mummy.' She took my hand – hers slightly sticky and warm – and smiled at me. 'You *are* silly sometimes, Mummy.'

Friday 9 November

Scenes caused in the Co-op – 1. Glasses of wine at home to recover myself – 3.

Stopped in the Co-op on the way home for wine and Oreos (branching out a bit from Jaffa Cakes), and had a really annoying conversation with a woman in the queue behind me.

'Quiet night in with the hubby?' she asked, nodding at the wine.

The word 'hubby' got my back up right away. I told her that no, I was having a quiet night by myself as my children were away for the weekend with their dad – my *ex*-hubby.

'I do envy you,' she said. 'It's like the best of both worlds, isn't it? You get to spend time with your children but then you regularly get the whole weekend to yourself! What a luxury! I bet you have great fun, don't you? Spa weekends, popping into London to see a show – bliss!'

I was so shocked by how tenuous her connection with the real world seemed to be that for a minute I didn't know how to reply. Is that really how she imagined I live? 'Oh yes, fabulous, another weekend without the children, let me give Bunty a call and we can get out the soft-top and take a trip into Mayfair. Let me just finish with this manicure and have my stylist dress me and we can be off!'

And yes, I do appreciate the time I get to myself – I know plenty of married mothers who struggle to get their husbands to even let them lie in until 8 a.m. once a month – but it's not really the *easy option*, is it? I'm not bloody Hannah Montana, living my best mum life all week and then slipping on a glittery wig come Friday night for a weekend of frivolous fun.

Eventually, I found my voice.

'If only it *were* all city mini breaks and hot stone massages!' I said, doing a fake laugh – har har har! 'I actually find it very difficult making ends meet as a single mother of two, so my spare weekends are normally taken up giving blow jobs behind the Co-op for cash so that I can buy school uniform and pay the gas bill.'

Her jaw dropped.

'Sometimes, if I'm lucky, I get an all-nighter and with the extra money I treat myself to an anal bleaching,' I added, 'which has the extra perk of being a work expense, so tax deductible!'

I smiled sweetly, maintaining eye contact until she felt so uncomfortable that she dropped her basket, muttered something about having left the iron on and left the shop. Behind me in the queue there was the sound of clapping. I turned around to see two women with six children between them of various ages.

'Oh God,' I said, looking at the small faces staring up at me, 'I'm so sorry about that.'

'Are you kidding?' said the woman with a toddler on her hip. 'That was incredible! I wanted to laugh so badly I did a tiny wee!'

'Best thing I've heard in ages,' agreed her friend, 'I wish I could be there when she goes home and tells her husband about it.'

Saturday 10 November

Woke up to a washing machine full of pink school shirts. This is what happens when you do laundry drunk.

Generally, I am a fan of housework after a glass of wine or two. It feels like it shouldn't work because drinking is a fun thing and housework is definitely *not fun*, but that's the genius of it. If you can time it just at that moment where the world suddenly feels full of promise, then you can take a fair bit of joy from a shiny floor. Things seem to stretch out a little bit – the washing-up becomes a part of you, you're in the moment … it's basically meditation, and everyone knows how good *that* is for you.

I did once get a little bit over enthusiastic 'organising' my filing after a couple of gins, but I managed to get all of the bills out of the recycling box before the rubbish lorry arrived the next morning.

Monday 12 November

Flo came into the kitchen this evening as I was cooking tea. 'Mum,' she said, 'when are we going to get my prom dress?'

I put down the potato I was peeling.

'Your prom dress?' I asked. 'I didn't think prom was until you left school?'

'It isn't,' said Flo, 'but all the best dresses get taken really early.'

'It is a year and a half away, though,' I said, quite reasonably I thought.

'And then there's transport,' she said.

'Transport? Can I not just give you a lift?'

'Um, no? Last year Tabitha Green arrived in a helicopter, I don't really think I'm going to impress anyone turning up in a ten-year-old Renault full of empty coffee cups and crisp packets.'

'I could clean it up a bit,' I said, 'or Dad could take you. He has a nicer car than me.'

'No way,' said Flo. 'I'm not having either of you anywhere near it. I'll need to have a limo or something. Daniel's dad is a farmer, so he's coming on a JCB.'

When I left school we just signed each other's shirts and then got drunk in the bandstand in the park on a bottle of Cinzano we'd persuaded an old man to buy us from the off-licence.

Tuesday 13 November

Times hopes raised at work – 1. Number of times dashed again on the rock that is my job – 1.

Leon beckoned me over to his desk this morning, looking pleased with himself. He had a press release in his hand.

'How do you fancy having a go at something more challenging?' he asked.

'I would love that,' I said, relief in my voice. Perhaps these last two months have been some sort of elaborate initiation ceremony? Maybe all of the reporters have been chuckling fondly about it over lunch, wondering how many times they can get me to write 'conveniently located for commuters' (i.e., you can hear the motorway from the bedroom) before I crack?

'I've got a press release here from the Arts Centre,' he said, 'about their latest exhibition from a local group of amateur artists. It's about 350 words at the moment, but we need it cut down to 250 to fit a space on page twelve. Are you up for the challenge?'

I said that I was and took the press release. Quite honestly, what else could I do?

I lay awake for quite a long time tonight, wondering what I've done with my working life.

Wednesday 14 November

We had six people for book group tonight, including me, which I was really pleased with for our first session.

Three were parents from the Thursday group but two were people who had seen the poster in the shop – one woman called Hannah, who seemed lovely, and a guy called Sean who had an amazing beard and a rather intense stare.

We drank wine and chatted about recent reads and then I asked everyone to take a few minutes to talk about their favourite-ever books. It was really interesting to hear everyone's choices and why they loved them. Books can have such a profound effect on lives.

When everyone had had a turn we put all the choices in a mug and pulled them out, giving us a book list for the next six months.

We're going to be reading:

- *Tuesdays with Morrie* by Mitch Albom
- *Captain Corelli's Mandolin* by Louis de Bernières
- *The Social Animal* by David Brooks
- *Cat's Eye* by Margaret Atwood
- *1984* by George Orwell
- *Us* by David Nicholls

We set our next meeting for 12 December and I messaged Dylan to tell him how well it had gone and he replied, saying, 'You're a star, Frankie!' with *a love-heart emoji*. Slightly disconcerted by the love heart. Is he trying to tell me something?

Sent WIB a copy of the message. 'What does *this* mean?' I said.

'Ahhh,' said Sierra, 'the classic casual heart emoji.'

'What's the classic casual heart emoji?' I wrote back.

'I don't know,' said Sierra, 'I made it up.'

'Maybe he really loves the book choices?' said Lou. Definitely a possibility.

'Maybe he really loves *you*?' said Sierra. Less helpful.

Thursday 15 November

I think Jess has an imaginary friend. I went up to the bathroom about ten minutes after I'd put her to bed this evening and I heard her whispering in her room.

'Is that comfy, Barney?' she was saying. She doesn't have any ponies named Barney as far as I know. There was a pause, presumably while Barney replied to her. 'Tomorrow I will see if Mummy can find you a snack, but it's bedtime now, so we have to go to sleep otherwise Mummy will shout.'

Bit harsh.

'Don't run off, Barney!' she said. 'You have to stay in here.'

Intriguing.

I was slightly concerned that an imaginary friend might be a sign of parental neglect, but Google reassured me.

'Compared to those who don't create them,' said the internet, 'children with imaginary companions tend to be less shy, engage in more laughing and smiling with peers, and do better at tasks involving imagining how someone else might think.'

Apparently, children who don't watch much television are more likely to create an imaginary friend. Ha ha!

Friday 16 November

Jess asked today if she could have some cornflakes for Barney. I said she could and put a few into a plastic bowl and gave her a teaspoon. She gave the spoon back.

'Don't be silly, Mummy,' she said, laughing, 'Barney can't use a spoon!'

Clearly the boundary between fantasy and reality is a blurry one.

Tuesday 20 November

Panicky message from Lou to WIB at teatime: 'Emergency!' she wrote. 'Help!' She used the little red siren emoji so clearly it was serious.

'What's the matter?' I asked. 'Are you hurt?'

There was a pause, during which I imagined one of the twins impaled on one of those spiky railings. WhatsApp probably wouldn't be Lou's first thought in *that* scenario, but sometimes my imagination runs away with me.

'I was just making dinner,' she wrote, 'and something terrible happened!'

'What were you making?' asked Sierra.

'Oh, it was this new vegan recipe I found online for pizza,' said Lou, 'which uses cauliflower as a pizza base. It looks really good – quite a few people in the comments have said it tastes as good as regular pizza.'

I really hoped one of the twins *wasn't* on a railing.

'The terrible thing that happened, though?' I prompted.

'Oh yes,' wrote Lou. 'So, I was cooking dinner – the cauliflower pizza thing – and I sneezed. Fine. Then I sneezed again – and a little bit of wee came out!'

'How much wee?' asked Sierra.

'I don't know,' wrote Lou, 'I didn't exactly have a measuring jug ready. Not enough to make a puddle on the floor or anything, but enough to mean I had to go and change my pants.'

'Gross,' said Sierra, not very supportively.

'It's not gross, Lou,' I reassured her, 'it's totally normal after having babies to get leaks sometimes. It happens to me all the time. And you've had twins, so, you know…'

'Yeah,' wrote Sierra, 'it's probably like the Bat Cave up there.'

'The Bat Cave?' said Lou. 'I don't want my vagina to look like the *Bat Cave*?'

'The secret is the strategic leg-cross,' I said. 'The first sneeze is manageable, but if you feel a second one coming on, just brace yourself and cross your legs. Sort of like a curtsey?'

'Seriously? I have to cross my legs on every second sneeze for the rest of my *life*? This is why David left me, isn't it? I bet Sandra doesn't piss her pants in the kitchen.'

'Given that he cited "chips" in the break-up, the cauliflower-based pizza would probably be more of a turn-off than the piss,' wrote Sierra. 'He seems like a man who appreciates carbs.'

'But it's so unfair,' said Lou. 'I did all those Kegels! I do yoga! I eat sauerkraut, for God's sake. And for what?'

'I didn't know sauerkraut was good for your pelvic floor?' I said.

'It's not,' said Lou, 'but it's the principle of the thing. I am a *Good Person*. I care about my gut health. I use coconut oil. I shouldn't be pissing myself on the kitchen floor.'

It did seem unfair. Out of the three of us, and without intimate knowledge, I would definitely have rated Lou's vagina as the tightest. Not that anyone would likely have asked me. But in a quiz or something. Sierra always seems like she might be a bit anarchistic about being told to do pelvic floor exercises and I haven't been on a trampoline since 2007.

Thursday 22 November

Glasses of wine while cooking – 2. (Doesn't count when drunk during food prep?) Internal crisis brought on by thoughts about how many times I have made bolognese in my entire life and how much of it I have thrown away uneaten – 1. (Big.)

Chapter One parents' group busy again today. Dylan came up to see me as I was packing up and shuffled about for a bit, looking as though he had something he wanted to say. In the light of the love-heart emoji, it was a little bit unsettling. I really like Dylan, but I think he needs more time to get over Caitlin and I don't want to be some kind of difficult rebound relationship. Plus, it would make using his upstairs room all the time a bit awkward, wouldn't it?

He asked about the group and how the new job was going, and then looked like he had changed his mind about whatever it was he *really* wanted to say, so he went downstairs. Very odd.

I made pasta bolognese for tea tonight – Jess's favourite. I say 'pasta' as a bit of a cover-all – it was meant to be spaghetti, but I didn't realise the packet was open already and when I took it down from the cupboard it all fell out on to the kitchen floor in a rather dramatic, depressing version of pick-up sticks. I would have just picked it all up again – it gets *boiled*, for Christ's sake – but Jess got into rather a flap about the 'germs'.

She must get it from Ian as I've been known to drop a piece of toast, butter-side down, and just pick off any obvious bits of fluff or old sweetcorn before adding the jam. Fortunately I had about ninety-six bags of pasta in the cupboard, all with about half an inch in the bottom, so I mixed them all up together.

(Question: does someone plant these bags? I honestly can't imagine myself making pasta and thinking, 'Hmmm, I don't want to overdo it on the carbs, I probably shouldn't chuck in those last ten shells.' Why would I deliberately leave an amount of pasta that wasn't even enough on its own for one small person? Weird.)

Flo set the table while I dished up and Jess sang a song about a poo in a loo. We all sat down, the pasta bolognese in front of us on the table.

'What's this?' asked Jess, prodding it with her fork.

'Bolognese,' I said. 'You like bolognese,' I added, more confidently than I felt. You just never really know from one minute to the next with a four-year-old.

'Where is the pissgetty?' she asked.

'There isn't any spaghetti,' I said, 'so we are having it a fun way today with lots of different-shaped pasta. It all tastes the same, though, it's just more exciting like this. Like a treasure hunt.'

OK, not really much like a treasure hunt, but sometimes children just need to believe the words.

She looks sceptical.

'Where's the treasure?' she asked.

'Well, if I told you that then it wouldn't be a treasure hunt, would it?' I said.

She filled her fork and got it almost to her mouth.

'It's too hot,' she said, and put it down again.

'Blow on it,' I suggested. 'It will soon cool down.'

She lifted the fork back to her mouth and blew hard. Little pieces of tomatoey mince showered down on the table around her plate. I took a deep but quiet breath.

'It's still too hot,' she said.

'Why not try it?' I said. 'It should have cooled down after that lovely big blow.'

'No, it's too hot.' She put her fork back down and a piece of fusilli fell off her plate and on to the floor. I ate a few mouthfuls, trying to will my shoulders into a normal, relaxed position. She tried again, but a shell fell into her lap. She made a show of picking it up and it burning her fingers.

I refilled my wine glass and took a large gulp. Flo gave me a supportive, sideways glance.

'This is lovely,' she said, 'and just the right temperature. You should eat yours quick, Jess, or I'll have it.'

We played a game of I Spy while Jess waited for her bolognese to cool down, which no one got because Jess was trying to make us guess P for 'pissgetty'.

'Eat your tea now,' I said.

She took a spoonful.

'It's too cold,' she said.

Sunday 25 November

Jess asked me today why I was called Mummy.

'Isn't it confusing,' she asked, not unreasonably, 'that all the mummies have the same name?'

'Well,' I said, 'I have another name too – Frankie – but you and Flo get to call me Mummy because I *am* your mummy.' I didn't feel like I'd done a great job of explaining it, to be honest. Neither did Jess.

'But why *are* you my mummy?' she asked.

'Because I made you in my tummy,' I said.

'And tummy rhymes with mummy?'

'Well, sort of.'

'Tamsin at nursery doesn't have a mummy,' said Jess.

'That's sad for her,' I said, not sure I was ready for a conversation about death.

'Oh, she *has* a mummy,' she said, 'she just doesn't call her mummy so I'm not sure if it's the same thing.'

'Oh, right,' I said. 'What does she call her?'

'Non-Daddy,' said Jess.

'That's unusual,' I said.

'I like you best as Mummy,' said Jess.

'Thanks, Non-Flo,' I said, giving her a hug.

Monday 26 November

Barney is not an imaginary friend. Barney is a *mouse*. Discovered Jess with him this afternoon in a box in her room trying to encourage him on to a Sylvanian double bed with a cheese triangle.

Much distress over the release of Barney into the wild.

Tuesday 27 November

Awkward moments where I wonder if my chat with the smear test nurse counts as flirting – 2. Jaffa Cakes (for smear test recovery) – 6.

I had a smear test during my lunch break today, an event that is surely the highlight of any woman's calendar?

I always feel a bit weird about going for a smear test. It's almost a fourth date kind of scenario, isn't it? Before I left for the surgery I went into the toilets at work to brush my hair, put a bit of make-up on and have a freshen up with an 'intimate wipe' that I'd bought especially for the occasion.

'You look nice!' said the nurse as I walked into the room and she ominously locked the door behind me.

'Thanks,' I replied, 'I like to make an effort for this kind of thing.'

Minutes later I was lying semi-naked on a bed, legs apart, without even having been bought a drink. Before

I had children, I used to get horribly embarrassed by having a smear test, but when you've been through labour a couple of times, one nurse having a quick rummage around doesn't seem like such a big deal.

'Have you got any children?' the nurse asked, as she pulled on her latex gloves.

'Yes, I've got two,' I said. 'Can't you tell?' It was half a joke but also partly a genuine question – I had always thought the view downstairs post-birth would be quite a different one.

Politely ignoring my question, she demonstrated her equipment and got to work. I realise that the speculum tour is meant to be reassuring, so that you know what to expect, but I always feel like I could do without the reminder.

'Hmm …' she said, peering carefully into the darkness, 'you're very *tall*, aren't you? I can't seem to find your cervix.'

'I do have one,' I assured her helpfully.

'Stay there,' she said, 'I just need to get a longer speculum.'

I lay for a while behind the curtain, trying to will my cervix into view. She reappeared. 'I'm just going to have a go with this,' she said, flashing me her new, longer tool. I could almost feel my cervix scurry further up inside me at the sight of it.

She still wasn't having any luck. The expression 'needle in a haystack' sprang to mind, and I pictured her having to put on a head torch and go all the way in.

'I'm really sorry,' she said, starting to look a bit panicky, 'but I still can't find it. I'm going to have a feel with my fingers. I'm ever so sorry.'

'Don't worry about me,' I said, 'you're the one at the dodgy end.'

The hands-on approach paid off, and the elusive cervix was eventually located. She managed to reach it with the speculum and reassured me she now had a 'very good view and everything looked lovely', a great Tinder opening line if ever I heard one.

'Call me!' I wanted to say as I left, but I managed to restrain myself. Probably best.

Wednesday 28 November

Super fun day at work, she writes, sarcastically. I am sad for Ethel Bainbridge and her relatives, of course I am, but why do there have to be so bloody many of them? Her obituary took me an age to write up.

I wonder how many people would come to my funeral? Would it be more if I died tragically young? I feel that people like to make more of an effort when you're young. Also, most of your friends and family are still alive, so that probably boosts the numbers.

What would people say about me? They couldn't exactly talk about my sparkling career, could they? Maybe they'd show a montage of all of my inspirational Instagram images. I *am* up to four pictures now – I've added one beach sunset and one of a random cat I saw in the street.

Thursday 29 November

I arrived at Chapter One just after lunch, ready to set up for the parent group at two. I got there a bit early as I wanted to talk to Dylan about a thought I'd had for our next book group. I launched into telling him all about my idea, which involved books with food themes, and cooking a dish from the story, when he interrupted me.

'I actually had an idea, too,' he said.

'Oh cool,' I said. 'Well, I'm happy to take book suggestions – you're the expert, after all.'

'It's not about the book group,' he said. He looked serious. My heart leapt. Was this about heart emoji-gate? He wasn't going to ask me out, was he? I do really like him, I'm just not sure I'm ready to replace the dead wife. I decided to go with desperate babbling to change the subject.

'It's not about upstairs, is it?' I said. 'Are you sick of us storing our toys in your spare room? Because I'd understand, you can tell me.'

'No,' he said, 'the toys are fine.'

'Oh no,' I said, 'is it me? Am I coming in and bothering you too much? Honestly, Dylan, just tell me to butt out—'

'Frankie, be quiet!' he said. Bit bossy. 'It's not about book group, it's not about toys.' I stood still, mouth closed. 'It is about you, though.'

Oh cripes, I thought.

'I want to offer you a job,' he said.

'A job?' I said. 'What sort of job?'

'In the shop,' he said, 'a sort of shop manager? I haven't thought it completely through yet, I wanted to see what you thought first. I've been thinking for ages about taking someone on, but I wanted it to be the right person – someone who genuinely loves books and loves the shop. At the risk of sounding like Willy Wonka, I think that person is you, Frankie.'

'Oh my God,' I said, 'are you serious?'

'I don't want someone who just comes in and works the till and goes again,' he said. 'I want someone who can help me improve and come up with new ideas. I've been getting by, but I don't want to end up spending all of Caitlin's insurance money just keeping things afloat – I want to invest in turning the shop into something modern and exciting and profitable. Plus, I quite want someone who I can trust to work some Saturdays to give me some time off. I thought that might suit you?' He was looking a bit awkward now. 'Is it a terrible idea?'

'Oh my God, no! It's a *brilliant* idea! Oh Dylan, thank you!'

'I'm guessing you'll have to give notice where you are,' he said, 'so I was thinking we could start in January? It would give us time to think about responsibilities and salary and hours and things like that.'

I didn't know what to say, so I just gave him a huge hug. It felt a long way from the awkward half embrace over the Harry Potter book we'd had when we first met.

I am just so pleased I won't ever have to write another obituary! Well, I will for a few more weeks, but there will be a light at the end of the tunnel! A bit like the light at the end of Ethel Bambridge tunnel yesterday. RIP, Ethel.

Saturday 1 December

Today I took Jess to see the worst Father Christmas – *ever*.

All three of us had gone into Dorchester to do some Christmas shopping. Flo wants clothes and obviously I can't just pick things for her as there is about a 0.4 per cent chance I'd get it right, so I thought we'd have an outing and she could try some things on. Also, I had seen on Twitter that there was a Christmas market selling mulled wine, but that was just a lucky coincidence and definitely not related to my decision to go on the bus.

Once the horror of Topshop was over and I'd spent an obscene amount of money that equated to around £7 per square inch of fabric, I steered everyone towards the Christmas market for a well-earned mulled wine. Just opposite (cleverly positioned), was a log cabin, festooned with plastic holly, advertising visits with Santa Claus. A large plastic Santa face was lit up, just to ram the message home for preschoolers.

'Mummy!' said Jess, tugging at my arm and nearly making me spill my wine. 'Can I see Father Christmas? I've been good!'

Well, that was sneaky. How do you say no to that without implying that you disagree?

'I'm not sure if we have time,' I said, trying to look sad, 'we do have a particular bus to catch and I'm sure Father Christmas is really busy at this time of the year.' We all looked at the empty space where the queue should have been and just saw a lone elf, checking his phone.

'It doesn't *look* busy,' said Jess.

'Maybe Santa is on a break?' I said hopefully, 'and that's why there are no children waiting?'

The elf looked up from his phone and sensing weakness called out 'Come and meet Father Christmas! Only four pounds! Gift every time!'

Jeez.

'Please, please, please, Mummy!' begged Jess. 'I really, really want to see Father Christmas!'

Flo looked dubious. 'It looks a bit lame, Mum,' she said, 'not gonna lie.'

'Ergh, it does, doesn't it?' I said. 'But then, Jess is only four; perhaps it's magical when you're four?'

'Maybe,' said Flo doubtfully, 'it doesn't look that magical to me, though. Definitely more grotty than grotto. I'm going to HMV instead.'

So Flo buggered off and I took Jess over to where the elf was shoving his phone into his back pocket and picking up a decidedly unfestive metal cash box. 'Only four pounds, gift every time,' he said flatly as we approached.

'I know,' I said, 'you already said that.' I gave him four pound coins and he locked them away in his box and hid it behind a plastic log before showing us into Santa's lair.

The inside of the cabin had been covered with green tarpaulin and sprayed liberally with snow in a can. Tinny Christmas music was playing from a cheap-looking CD player, not very well hidden behind a bin liner full of what I hoped were gifts rather than actual rubbish.

Santa himself was sitting in the middle of the cabin on a tatty armchair that looked like it could well have come out of a skip. There *was* a rather atmospheric mist in the cabin, but also a bit of a vanilla smell, so I think it might just have been Santa vaping.

'Ho ho ho,' said Santa in a London accent, 'Merry Christmas, innit?'

I let Jess sit on his lap, briefly, while he asked what she wanted for Christmas and she reeled off a list of her preferred pets. After a minute or two he interrupted her to give her a gift from the bin liner and we were ushered back into the street.

Outside Jess was keen to unwrap her first present of the year.

'What is it, Mummy?' she asked, turning it over in her hands. I looked. It was a phone case for a Samsung Galaxy J3.

Monday 3 December

Meeting with Leon this morning to hand in my notice. He looked genuinely disappointed, and not just in a 'now I'll have to find someone else and it's been less than three months' way.'

'I totally understand,' he said. 'You're way too good for this job and, to be honest, if we hadn't really needed you, I would have probably told you that from the start. I wish you all the best for the book shop, that sounds right up your street.'

All much more civilised than when I left the museum.

He did add that, in light of how long I'd been there, he hoped I wouldn't be offended if they didn't do a collection for a gift, which seemed fair enough.

I uploaded a story to the website this afternoon about a Santa's Grotto in Dorchester that has been closed down for laundering stolen goods. Apparently, the authorities were called when management at the shopping centre in Dorchester received multiple complaints about a Father Christmas in a cabin outside the centre handing out suspicious gifts from a bin liner.

Tuesday 4 December

Drunken stories shared with teenage daughter from my past – 1. Drunken stories I wish I'd kept to myself – also 1.

*

Flo asked me this evening what it felt like to be drunk. I was holding a glass of wine at the time, which felt a bit awkward, although I was also quite pleased as by her age I definitely knew already.

I watched a Mumsnet Live about teenage drinking a while ago and, apparently, teenagers nowadays aren't drinking cider in parks and throwing up in each other's bathrooms like they used to. It's a good thing, I guess, but also I feel a bit sad for them that they'll never know the thrill of successfully sneaking three bottles of Diamond White out of the house without them clinking in your bag and giving you away.

I tried to be honest, as advised by Mumsnet experts, and say that it can be fun and make you feel more relaxed and confident if you only drink a little bit, but can make you do and say stupid things if you're not careful. I told her about the time I had to leave an important work dinner to be sick in the street because of a hangover from the night before (classy), and how drinking too much can cripple you with self-loathing and shame the next day. (Don't remember that bit on Mumsnet, but I was kind of running with it by that stage.)

She looked at me with a mixture of what looked like pity and disgust. I put my glass down.

Thursday 6 December

Discussions at Chapter One parent group today about having a Christmas party. I'd been thinking about it for a few weeks already, and had come up with the following:

For: I really do love Christmas, excuse to eat Elizabeth Shaw mints for breakfast, etc.

Against: Playgroup Christmas parties notoriously hellish to arrange: there is always one child afraid of Father Christmas who has to be taken outside for some 'fresh air'; squabbles between children over gifts.

'Hang on,' said Sierra, after I'd laid out my pros and cons, 'who said it has to be about the kids? I mean, let's be serious, we don't come to Chapter One to provide *them* with intellectual stimulation, do we? We come so that we can shove them in a corner and drink tea with other adults.'

'That's true,' said Lou. 'I didn't come to Busy Beavers that first time to entertain the boys, I came because I wanted a grown-up to talk to me. And you did! And here we are. We should be celebrating.'

So we decided that we *will* have a Christmas party, but that we won't have a Father Christmas or gifts for the children or party bags or anything complicated like that. Each parent will bring a plate/bowl/bag of food – supermarket cakes positively encouraged – and Sierra, Lou and I are going to chip in and buy a few bottles of prosecco.

We're also going to do grown-up presents. Everyone is going to bring something small, we'll stick them in a sack, and then it will be a lucky dip. The children will have just as much fun as they would at any party because of the popping of corks, general excitement etc., but no one will have to dress up as Santa or break up any fights over who got the best pack of Pokémon cards.

Hooray for Christmas!

Tried to do some @simple_dorset_life stalking when I went to bed as I was sure she would be prepping some delicious Christmas treats using courgettes and coconut flour but the account has gone!! I am in shock. Who am I meant to compare myself to now?

Read some of *Tuesdays With Morrie* instead. I'd forgotten how much I love reading.

Friday 7 December

We have to do Jess's primary school application by mid-January, so today Ian and I went to look at a couple of options. I say that like there are loads – there are only really two. One is only about a ten-minute walk away from us, so would be our first choice. The second we'd need to drive to, but I wanted to go and visit two just so that we had a comparison and felt like we'd done our research.

School number two – the further away one – was fine, although we were shown around by the one of the women from the school office rather than the headteacher and, according to my Mumsnet research, this is a Bad Sign. She was perfectly lovely and answered all of our questions, but she seemed a bit hesitant to let us go into all of the classrooms, which made us wonder about the teaching methods.

School number one – thank God – was amazing. The headteacher showed us around herself and was one of those women who manages to be friendly yet professional at the same time, so you immediately want to entrust her with important tasks like researching life insurance for you. She was very forthcoming about the school's bullying policy, before we had even asked the question, and I liked that they still do hot dinners as the whole building smelt of gravy and reminded me of being eight years old and getting lunch dished up in plastic trays with separate compartments for your faggots, potatoes and peas.

Jess said she liked the smell, too, and she liked that the pegs had pictures next to them.

'Would I be able to choose my own picture?' she asked the headteacher.

'You might be able to,' she said. 'You would have to check with your teacher.'

'If we can then I want mine to be RuPaul,' she said. Really *must* stop her watching *RuPaul's Drag Race*.

I messaged a match on Tinder today, called Marcus.

'Hey, Marcus,' I wrote, 'thanks for swiping! What's a fun fact about you that not many people know? My starter for ten is that I once passed out mid-air … Frankie.'

(True fact.)

I had a swift reply.

'Passed out mid-air?' wrote Marcus. 'Well, that is gonna need a bit more back story. Here is something iv not told any1 yet. Iv been writing a play in my head at work for the last couple of weeks. Just to lazy to put it on paper'.

Word for word.

I replied, suggesting that if he wanted to write a play he *might* need to improve his spelling.

Another speedy response:

'Yeah I can't spell never been able to,' he wrote, 'so I don't even try any more. The play is a bit melo dramaish/ silly slapstick so it wouldn't really mater about gramer n shit'.

Oh yes, of course, you're totally right, Marcus. If you're writing comedy then the *rules of English* don't apply. It's not *sexy*, is it? If he can't even be bothered to write 'anyone', I don't imagine Marcus is the sort of man to bring you a cup of tea in bed without asking.

I really think Tinder should introduce an option to unmatch on the basis of poor spelling and grammar. It might encourage people to up their game a little bit.

Marcus was the final proof I needed though that Tinder is *not* going to be the way for me to meet the man of my dreams. It's been 'interesting' giving it a go, but I think I'm more of a face-to-face kind of person. Talking to someone in real life is so much easier than messaging them, plus you don't get distracted by spelling mistakes. So, I've booked a speed-dating night! It's not until mid-January, but I thought that would give me a bit of time to work myself up to it. This year has been about dipping my toe, next year … who knows?

Monday 10 December

'Have you had an invite to Cassie's New Year's Eve party?' Sierra asked WIB this evening.

'No!' I said, outraged. 'Have you?'

'Ha ha! No. Someone from the Busy Beavers WhatsApp group just messaged me to ask. I think word might have got out that it was me who put up that poster of her in Aldi.'

'Also, didn't you guys go last year,' asked Lou, 'and drink all of her husband's best Scotch playing that boasty parent bingo game?'

'Oh yeah,' I said, 'there was that too.'

I started to feel a bit sorry for myself, but then remembered last New Year and how rubbish I'd felt about it, and how Flo had told me I looked like a supply teacher. Perhaps it might not be so bad *not* to have to do that again.

'Let's have our own party,' wrote Sierra. 'We can have it at my house. You know, the party house of dreams. We could invite Chapter One group people, and your book group, Frankie? So long as both of you promise not to throw up in my copper pans.'

'But I've got the girls that weekend,' I said, 'and David is taking Sandra off to a cabaret event at a B & B in Blackpool or something awful, isn't he?'

'God,' said Lou, 'don't remind me. To think that could have been me!'

'We'll make it kids too,' said Sierra. 'We've got loads of space. People can stay over if they want to, but to make it easier we could celebrate New Year early – pretend we're somewhere else in the world that's ahead of us, so we get the champagne without having to stay up until midnight?'

There was a pause while we were all clearly googling time zones.

'How about Omsk?' I wrote.

'Where the frig is Omsk?' wrote Sierra.

'Isn't it Russia?' wrote Lou.

'I think so,' I said. 'It's six hours ahead so we can sing Auld Lang Syne at 6 p.m. and be happily home in bed by ten.'

Tuesday 11 December

Jess is already ridiculously excited about Christmas and there are still two weeks to go. Every ten minutes or so she asks me how many sleeps it is, and should she get the carrot out ready for Rudolph. I keep telling her that Rudolph is definitely not going to want a eat a carrot that's been hanging around in her room for a fortnight.

Chopped the end off a potato and suggested she go and give it to her ponies as practice. I could hear her upstairs role-playing Christmas morning.

'Oh, Rainbow Dash, look what Father Christmas bought me! It's a My Little Pony costume so I can dress up and look just like you! And two puppies! Aren't they sweet?'

I feel like real Christmas morning is probably going to be a disappointment for her.

Wednesday 12 December

Book group tonight to talk about *Tuesdays with Morrie*, which was actually my choice. I wouldn't say it's my favourite ever book of all time, but I find it so difficult to have favourites as different books speak to me in different ways and at different times.

I first read *Tuesdays With Morrie* about fifteen years ago. I remember loving it then and have wanted to reread it for a long time. I felt quite nervous as the meeting started, because I wanted everyone to love it as much as I did and I felt that if they didn't then I'd be responsible.

Fortunately it went down well, particularly with Sean, who I actually thought might cry at one point.

'It was so simple,' he said, 'but so powerful. Which I guess echoes the whole theme of the book and the idea of happiness coming from very simple things.'

'I loved it too,' said Hannah, helping herself to another Fondant Fancy. 'That whole idea of acknowledging emotions and then letting them go, that really spoke to me. I've started practising that and it's amazing.'

'I'd hate to have someone have to wipe my bum,' said Marjorie, one of the upstairs playgroup mums, kind of missing the point.

I think Hannah might be my favourite so far. She was a way of saying 'sandwiches' very precisely, with a lot of emphasis on the D, that I really love.

Message from Sierra when I got home.

'I think we might have a bit of a *Mean Girls*-style issue,' she wrote. 'Word has got out about our New Year's Eve party and a few people have been messaging me, hinting at being asked. One of them even said she wanted to come to us rather than to Cassie's party because last year she accidentally broke a glass at Cassie's and Cassie made her replace it.'

'Blimey,' I replied, 'that's a bit much, isn't it?'

'It was a wedding present or something,' wrote Sierra. 'Anyway, the point is – do we invite all these extras and steal Cassie's guests?'

'You know what we *should* do, don't you?' said Lou. 'We should invite *Cassie*.'

There was a silence.

'Could we?' I asked.

'Bloody hell,' said Sierra, 'I'm going to do it. Ha!'

Thursday 13 December

Different scams I would definitely fall for as a pensioner – at least 12. Chunks of Toblerone eaten without really noticing every time I went into the kitchen – 9. But basically Christmas, so totally acceptable.

A man in very unflattering orange overalls came to the door this morning. He said he was replacing the gas pipes in our street and could he have a look at my gas meter. I moved all the wellington boots and half rolls of wallpaper and carpet offcuts and empty lightbulb boxes out of the way and he connected some cables and looked at some readings.

It was only after he'd gone that it occurred to me that I hadn't asked for any proof that he was who he said he was, I just let him into my home, a complete stranger.

I'm going to be one of those single pensioners who gets their drive tarmacked without realising it, aren't I? Flo will come and visit me and my living room will be full of badly drawn countryside scenes that I've exchanged on the doorstep for my life savings.

(Note to future self: always ask for ID before you let a man root around in your understairs cupboard.)

Friday 14 December

Fish finger sandwiches and beans for tea. Flo raised her eyebrows at me when I put the plates on the table.

'If you went to that new café on the seafront you'd pay £8.95 for a fish finger sandwich,' I pointed out.

She looked around the kitchen. 'I'm not really getting the "hipster café" vibe' she said, 'especially not with that pile of your pants on the table.'

Fair point about the pants, so I moved those to the stairs for later. I put the cactus from the windowsill in the middle of the table, rinsed out the empty bean tin, and filled it with cutlery.

'Alexa,' I said, 'play some alternative folk music.'

'It's beautiful, Mummy!' said Jess, leaning over to get a fork and putting her elbow in her beans.

'Do we have any organic, small-batch ketchup?' asked Flo.

Saturday 16 December

Crumbs in the bed – at least one million *(feels like)*. *Genius ideas for ways to make extra money from soft play* – 1. *Actual glasses of wine drunk in secret from a Fruit Shoot bottle* – 0 *(disappointing)*.

Jess woke me up at 5 a.m. saying she was hungry and was it Christmas yet.

No, it was 5 a.m. As in basically still the goddamn night. I fobbed her off with my phone and a couple of Hobnobs from the stash I keep in my bedside table. She looked suspicious.

'Why have you got biscuits in your bedroom, Mummy?' she asked. '*I'm* not allowed biscuits in bed.'

'I don't know, Jess,' I lied, 'they must have fallen in there when I unpacked the shopping.' Fortunately, she was playing *Cooking Mama* already and didn't question me further.

'Mummy, do you want to do some chopping?' she said, poking the phone into my face and showering me with crumbs. I looked at the clock. 5.07 a.m.

'It's a little bit too early for me to be chopping,' I said, 'why don't you lie down for a bit?' She tried to, but her hands were full, and she ended up leaning on the Hobnob hand and crunching the biscuit into bits on the sheet. About sixteen million pieces of toasted oats immediately lodged themselves underneath me, making it impossible to get comfortable.

I closed my eyes anyway.

'Mummy, do you want to see the dinner I made?' The phone was in my face again, right up next to my eyes, the blur of *Cooking Mama* burning my retinas.

I sighed. The Hobnob crumbs shifted menacingly. 5.14 a.m.

'Shall we get up?' I said, giving in.

'I'm quite tired,' says Jess. 'Maybe you could bring me breakfast in bed?'

Or maybe you could go back to your own bed and leave me to sleep until there is light in the sky, like a normal human being? I thought.

'How about some Weetos?' I said out loud.

By 9, Jess had watched two hours of television already and I'd had four pieces of toast, neither of which would be *Supernanny* recommendations, I'm sure.

The rain was coming down like a crack addict after a weekend binge, Flo was unlikely to wake up for another, ooh, three days or so, and even Sainsbury's wasn't due to open for another hour. It was in pure desperation then that I found myself at Micro Soft at 9.27 on a Sunday morning, sitting in the car waiting for it to open.

There was one other woman waiting to go in. She had two boys with her who charged ahead as soon as the magnetic gate opened for them. The buzz of that gate always makes me want to empty my pockets, like I've just arrived at prison visiting time. (I've never visited anyone in prison, but I imagine you might have to empty your pockets, in case you're smuggling in a key in a Mars Bar or something.)

The mum was definitely well prepped. She'd brought her own pair of socks, which she put on before heading up the foam steps to go down the slide. When she came out, she used hand sanitiser.

I admired her optimism but given Lou's 'fact' about ball pit bacteria, hand sanitiser in a soft play area feels a bit like getting a J-cloth out to clean up after a tsunami.

I watched her go in again and down the slide. She seemed to be laughing, like she was genuinely enjoying herself. Strange. I set up camp in the café.

I have a love/hate relationship when it comes to the café at Micro Soft. I use café in the loosest sense as I don't exactly feel as if I'm on a Parisian pavement, sipping cappuccino or anything; it's really just an area of chairs nearer the tills than some other chairs. The coffee is rank and comes in those mugs with handles that are too small to get even one finger in, rendering them pointless in the extreme.

They do, however, sell Jaffa Cakes. This, in my mind, is marketing genius. There is nowhere I can think that I need a Jaffa Cake *more* than at soft play. This is the love part.

The hate part is that they are the four Jaffa Cake snack packs and they charge an entire pound for them. A whole pound! Full-size packs are quite often on offer in Tesco for 50p, so this is just outrageous. I'm weak, though: I NEED them, and if you are at the point in the day/week/your life that soft play is your only option, are you in any fit state to be planning ahead and bringing your own? It's so damn clever.

I've spent quite a bit of time thinking about other things that I think soft play centres could make a killing on. Here are my top three:

Alcohol in Fruit Shoot bottles.

This would be a special grown-up section of the café fridge – probably top shelf – where Fruit Shoot bottles have been repurposed to contain wine in various colours and, possibly just in the school holidays or Inset days, gin. (I considered prosecco but I think there would be a potential mess/stickiness issue with the fizziness and the pop-up Fruit Shoot lid.)

Obviously, you'd have to be very careful not to get the bottles muddled with the regular Fruit Shoots. The ball pit really would get messy then.

VIP soundproof viewing area.

I picture this room adjacent to the soft play, with a connecting wall replaced with floor-to-ceiling soundproof glass. You'd be able to keep an eye on your children, if you're into that sort of thing, and they could see you smile and wave from time to time, but it would be *silent* save for the contented sighs of other parents scrolling through Instagram and sipping their Fruit Shoots.

Soft-play therapy sessions.

It feels crazy to me that parents go to soft play to escape the tedium and loneliness of home, just to sit at our own solitary table in the middle of a large warehouse, feeling equally despondent. Soft-play group therapy would bring together mums, dads, grandparents and carers in small groups so that we could share our woes. You might have to pay a little bit extra on top of the regular entry price, but all participants would get a snack pack of Jaffa Cakes.

You're welcome, Micro Soft.

(Question: whatever happened to *Supernanny*? Perhaps she had children and realised that not everything in life can be solved with a firm yet fair set of house rules and a sheet of smiley-face stickers.)

Monday 17 December

I caught Flo watching a YouTube video about how to descale a kettle. Are we at a point now where she will literally watch anything?

'Why don't you watch something that might be useful for your actual life,' I suggested, 'like a video about *Macbeth* or simultaneous equations?'

'This is interesting,' she said, not looking up.

I wouldn't mind if she actually descaled the kettle. Come to think of it, I don't think I've *ever* descaled the kettle. Perhaps I need to watch the video.

Thursday 20 December

Instagram illusions shattered – 1, badly. Daytime glasses of prosecco – 3. (But in paper cups so barely count.)

Chapter One parent group Christmas party day!

The grown-up Christmas theme went down extremely well and we had more people than we've ever had before, including a couple of dads, who caused quite the stir. (One of them, Oliver, is single, and, as Lou described him, 'a bit of a dish'.) We all crammed in and ate Wotsits and Matchmakers and pre-cooked cocktail sausages out of the plastic box. We drank prosecco out of paper cups and I made Dylan come upstairs so we could raise a toast and say thank you for letting us invade his bookshop.

'It's your bookshop now too, Frankie, don't forget,' he said, smiling and raising his paper cup.

A few of the mums looked puzzled and Dylan told everyone about the new job and how pleased he was that I was going to be there from the New Year and everyone clapped and raised their cups again.

It felt like a long way from the Busy Beavers Christmas party I went to last year where I sat on my own in a corner with a mini gluten-free mince pie while Cassie made the children line up in alphabetical order to be given 'gender-neutral' gifts by what I think was her husband, forced unwillingly into a Santa costume.

Everyone was talking about Sierra's New Year's Eve party. Apparently, someone messaged the Busy Beaver's WhatsApp group about it and loads of people have said they are going to come. Cassie hasn't replied to Sierra's invite.

Over a second paper cup of prosecco I complained to Sierra and Lou about @simple_dorset_life doing a disappearing act.

'Ah,' said Lou, 'I may have a bit of a confession.'

It turns out that Lou WAS @simple_dorset_life! It makes total sense now, of course, all that buckwheat and yoga, plus the picture that looked suspiciously like Sierra's garden after we'd been at her house, I don't know why I didn't think of it before.

'But hang on,' I said, 'you were always talking about how marvellously happy you were with your perfect family and perfect husband – what was all that about?'

Lou sighed. 'I guess I just wanted it to be true,' she said. 'Or at least I thought I did. But this year, the more I've hung out with you guys, the more I've realised that my life is actually pretty OK how it is, without the Instagram filter.'

Sierra raised her paper cup. 'I'll cheers to that.'

Friday 21 December – last day of term

Thank God. Everyone is exhausted.

I've decided I'm going to shut my diary for a week over Christmas and just eat Toblerone and play games and not be so bloody introspective the whole time. Ian is coming here on Christmas Eve so we can do Jess and Flo's stockings in the morning, and then he's staying through until Boxing Day.

For now, though, I'm going to open the Harveys Bristol Cream and a box of mince pies and spend the evening watching crappy TV while I go through the Christmas *Radio Times* with a highlighter. I don't even care that I always forget to look at what I've highlighted.

Saturday 29 December

Christmas week in numbers (approximately):

Glasses of prosecco: 8
Glasses of prosecco disguised as Buck's Fizz
(so basically fruit juice): 14

Elizabeth Shaw mints: 281
Mince pies: 23
Hours watching Christmas TV: 31
Fucks given about the above: Big Fat *Zero*

Monday 31 December

Amazing new best friends – 2. Regrets about 2018 – 0. High hopes for 2019 – many.

New Year's Eve Party Day!

I had a brief moment this morning when I wondered if I'd really be able to stomach a load of booze and Christmas snacks at Sierra's. I forced myself to have a cup of tea and a chunk of Toblerone, though, and felt much perkier. That's the thing with Christmas – it's when you feel *most* like you might actually be sick if you eat any more that you need to power on through and eat a turkey sandwich. A bit like life, I guess.

We FaceTimed Mum and Dad before we went out to wish them Happy New Year in advance. They'd been in two minds about coming over this Christmas, but Dad isn't such a big fan of travelling any more, plus they have friends in the town who own a restaurant and they put on a big Christmas dinner for all the expats and are doing a New Year's Eve party, too. We've made plans to go over in February half-term, which we're all really excited about. Parents' box double-ticked for the year.

*

We arrived at Sierra's at about 4 p.m. A tall, dark man wearing a Rudolph jumper opened the door. He was dashingly handsome. I had a bit of a 'Bridget and Mark Darcy at the turkey curry buffet' moment and spluttered a bit before he helpfully stepped in.

'I'm Clyde,' he said, smiling and holding out his hand. 'You must be Frankie? Sierra has told me all about you.' On cue, Sierra appeared behind him.

'Frankie!' she said, waving a bottle of prosecco in one hand and what looked like a mini quiche in the other. 'Off you go, Clyde – get the woman a drink!' She smiled up at him and he positively glowed in her presence. She stood on her tiptoes and gave him a kiss before ushering him into the kitchen. We stood in the hallway while I hung up our coats.

'Well, Clyde is a bit gorgeous, isn't he?' I said, once he was in the kitchen, out of earshot.

'Isn't he?' said Lou, who had appeared behind Sierra. 'She's kept him well hidden.'

'He *is* gorgeous,' said Sierra through a mouthful of quiche, 'although he does a pretty good job of keeping *himself* hidden normally. If he's away as much next year I may have to open a B & B just for the adult company.'

Sierra was just closing the door when the bell rang. It was Cassie. She was on her own. All three of us stared at her. She looked kind of awkward.

'Hello,' she said eventually, 'I hope you don't mind me coming? Everyone else at home has Christmas flu so I had to cancel *our* party. Not that many people were coming,' she added, looking a bit sad. 'So, well. Here I am.' She held up a bottle she was carrying. 'I have Aldi gin?'

The gin broke the tension and Sierra held out her hand, pulling Cassie in for a hug. 'Get yourself in here,' she said. 'Talk to the handsome man just through there in the Rudolph jumper – he'll get you a drink.'

We went through into the living room and I spotted Oliver, the single dad who came to the Christmas party, chatting to some of the Chapter One mums. He was wearing a Father Christmas hat.

'What's he doing here?' I asked Sierra. 'He's only been to one group!' Sierra and Lou exchanged glances.

'We just thought he seemed nice,' said Lou, not at all innocently, 'and he mentioned that he didn't have any New Year plans.'

'Oh, I see,' I said, 'I see what's going on here.' They laughed. 'Bit of casual Christmas matchmaking, is it?'

'Well, you did sneak him a few glances at Chapter One,' said Sierra, 'and you never know – magic of Christmas and all that. Perhaps he could be your "midnight Omsk time" kiss?' I made a mental note to position myself strategically later on.

At about 5.30, half an hour *before* midnight Omsk time, Sierra, Lou and I were in Sierra's kitchen, about to taste test the two batches of Christmas brownies that Lou had brought with her.

'Seriously,' said Lou, 'I bet you a round of gin and tonics that you can't tell which of these is the full-fat, full-sugar version, and which is made with Medjool dates and grated courgettes.'

We both eyed them suspiciously. They *looked* the same, but no one really wants the first thing they eat in a brand new year to be a mouthful of fake vegetable brownie, do they? Flo came into the kitchen. She was wearing a party hat, carefully so as not to mess up her hair. 'What are you doing?' she asked.

'We're about to try and spot which of these brownies is made with courgettes,' I told her.

'Let's do one each,' said Sierra, 'that way at least one of us gets a decent one.'

It seemed fair. In lieu of a coin we tossed the cap of a tonic water bottle.

'Heads!' I shouted. We all looked at it. 'Oh,' I said, 'it doesn't have a head does it? Ah sod it, I'm having this one,' and I reached into the Tupperware nearest Lou for the brownie that looked like it had the most calories. Sierra took one from the other box.

'Sorry, Frankie,' said Sierra, spraying me with brownie crumbs, 'I reckon you've got the courgette one because this is *amazing*. I can practically *feel* the butter smearing itself into a warm layer on my thighs.'

'Hang on, though,' I said, 'this one's ace too. Lou, can courgettes and dates honestly taste this good?'

'Nah,' said Lou, 'who am I kidding?' She reached for her glass of prosecco. 'I used butter and sugar in both of them.'

Jess came in carrying my phone, which was a bit worrying as I didn't know she'd taken it. 'Can I take a picture, Mummy?' she asked, taking one before I'd had chance to say yes. I took the phone from her and looked at the photo. Sierra had her mouth half-open, full of chocolate brownie. Flo was laughing, pointing at her. Lou had her glass raised and her arm round my shoulder. I looked happier than I remembered seeing myself look in a long time.

'Well, that's definitely one for Instagram,' I said.

I wrote the caption:

Sod the courgettes. #blessed #fullfatbrownies #passtheprosecco

Acknowledgements

Firstly a massive thank you to everyone who has ever read my blog. Without you I would never have been able to grow my blog into something that would one day lead to my editor at Ebury, Gillian Green, emailing out of the blue to ask 'Have you ever thought about writing fiction?' Thank you to Gillian for deciding to take a punt on me, even though I responded to that question by telling her that I had once written 15,000 words of a murder mystery but had had to stop because 'I didn't know who did it and I didn't have any clues.' Thanks too to the whole team at Ebury for their help and support turning my words into a real-life book.

Thank you to my family WhatsApp group, my daughters, my mum and my sister Annabel, for their constant encouragement – 'how's the book coming along?' – and to my three cats, Endeavour, Humphrey and Camille, for hanging out on the bed with me while I worked through edits. Thank you to Tinder for providing me with a seemingly endless stream of sad-looking men holding giant fish – invaluable for research purposes – and to my writing dream team, Debbie, Gemma, Lou and Sophia, for midnight sausage sandwiches and ongoing moral support – 'Have you finished the Arvon wine yet? That might help.'

Jo Middleton

Thank you to Lucy for offering thoughtful insight and inspiration – 'Just write about all the shit we did when our girls were little?' – and to Kathie for sharing the real-life story that inspired poo-in-the-fountain-gate. Thank you to the tutors on my Arvon writing retreat – to Chris Manby for helping me to give the book some much-needed structure and to Mike Gayle for noticing that Frankie wasn't initially terribly nice to her ex-husband – 'Is this why I am single in real life, Mike?'

And thanks for buying my book! I hope you enjoy reading it as much (ideally more) as I enjoyed writing it.